"Tybalt is coming. He has found me. I shall be free. . . ."

I was happy. Had I ever known such exaltation? Only when one is about to lose it does one realize how sweet life is.

The lantern was flickering. Never mind. They are coming. The door is moving.

Soon now.

Then I was no longer alone. I was caught up.

"Judith . . ."

It was Tybalt, as I had known it would be. He was holding me in his arms and I thought: I did not die of fear, but I shall die of bliss.

"My love," he said. "Judith, my love."

"It's all right, Tybalt," I said, comforting him. "It's all right . . . now. . . ."

By Victoria Holt
Published by Fawcett Books:

MISTRESS OF MELLYN
KIRKLAND REVELS
BRIDE OF PENDORRIC
MENFREYA IN THE MORNING
THE KING OF THE CASTLE
THE QUEEN'S CONFESSION
THE SHIVERING SANDS
THE SECRET WOMAN
THE SHADOW OF THE LYNX
ON THE NIGHT OF THE SEVENTH MOON
THE CURSE OF THE KINGS
THE HOUSE OF A THOUSAND LANTERNS
THE LEGEND OF THE SEVENTH VIRGIN
THE PRIDE OF THE PEACOCK
THE DEVIL ON HORSEBACK
MY ENEMY THE QUEEN
THE SPRING OF THE TIGER
THE MASK OF THE ENCHANTRESS
LORD OF THE FAR ISLAND
THE DEMON LOVER
THE JUDAS KISS
THE TIME OF THE HUNTER'S MOON
THE ROAD TO PARADISE ISLAND
THE LANDOWER LEGACY
SECRET FOR A NIGHTINGALE
THE SILK VENDETTA
THE INDIA FAN
THE CAPTIVE
SNARE OF SERPENTS
DAUGHTER OF DECEIT
SEVEN FOR A SECRET
THE BLACK OPAL

ℐ ℐ ℐ Victoria Holt

THE CURSE
of
THE KINGS

FAWCETT CREST • NEW YORK

A Fawcett Crest Book
Published by Ballantine Books
Copyright © 1973 by Victoria Holt

http://www.randomhouse.com

ISBN 0-449-20951-2

This edition published by arrangement with Doubleday & Company, Inc.

Alternate Selection of the Literary Guild, after June 1973
Selection of the Doubleday Book Club, March 1974
Selection of the Reader's Digest Condensed Books

Printed in Canada

First Fawcett Crest Edition: August 1974
First Ballantine Books Edition: July 1982

Contents

I The Curse

When Sir Edward Travers died suddenly and mysteriously, there was consternation and speculation, not only in the neighborhood of his home, but throughout the country.

Headlines in the newspapers ran: DEATH OF EMINENT ARCHAEOLOGIST. WAS SIR EDWARD TRAVERS A VICTIM OF THE CURSE?

A paragraph in our local paper stated:

With the death of Sir Edward Travers, who recently left this country to carry out excavations among the tombs of the Pharaohs, it is being asked: Is there any truth in the ancient belief that he who meddles with the resting places of the dead invites their enmity? Sir Edward's swift and sudden death has brought the expedition to an abrupt end.

Sir Ralph Bodrean, our local squire and Sir Edward's closest friend, had given financial aid to the expedition and when, a few days after the announcement of Sir Edward's death, Sir Ralph had a stroke, there was further speculation. He had, however, suffered a similar affliction some years before, and although he recovered from this second as he had from the first, his health was considerably impaired. It was, as might be expected, hinted that these misfortunes were the result of the Curse.

Sir Edward's body was brought back and buried in our churchyard, and Tybalt, Sir Edward's only son and himself a brilliant man who had already attained some distinction in the same profession as his father, was, of course, chief mourner.

The funeral was one of the grandest our little twelfth-century church had ever seen. There were people present from the academic world as well as friends of the family, and, of course, the press.

I was at the time companion to Lady Bodrean, wife of Sir Ralph, a post which did not suit my nature but which my financial needs had forced me to take.

I accompanied Lady Bodrean to the church for the funeral service and there I could not take my eyes from Tybalt.

I had loved him, foolishly because hopelessly, from the time I had first seen him, for what chance had a humble companion with such a distinguished man? He seemed to me to possess all the masculine virtues. He was by no means handsome by conventional standards, but he was distinguished looking—very tall, lean and neither fair nor dark; he had the brow of a scholar yet there was a touch of sensuality about his mouth; his nose was large and a trifle arrogant, and his grey eyes deep set and veiled. One would never be quite certain what he was thinking. He was aloof and mysterious. I often said to myself: "It would take a lifetime to understand him." And what a stimulating voyage of discovery that would be!

Immediately after the funeral I returned to Keverall Court with Lady Bodrean. She was exhausted she said, and was indeed more complaining and fretful than usual. Her temper did not improve when she learned that reporters had been to the court to discover the state of Sir Ralph's health.

"They are like vultures!" she declared. "They are hoping

for the worst because a double death would fit in so well with this foolish story of the Curse."

A few days after the funeral I took Lady Bodrean's dogs for their daily walk and my footsteps led me out of habit to Giza House, the home of the Traverses. I stood at the wrought-iron gate, where I had stood so many times, looking along the path to the house. Now that the funeral was over and the blinds had been drawn up it no longer looked melancholy. It had regained that air of mystery with which I had always associated it, for it was a house which had always fascinated me, even before the Traverses came to live there.

To my embarrassment Tybalt came out of the house and it was too late for me to turn away because he had seen me.

"Good afternoon, Judith," he said.

I quickly invented a reason for being there. "Lady Bodrean was anxious to know how you were getting on," I said.

"Oh, well enough," he answered. "But you must come in."

He smiled at me which made me feel ridiculously happy. It was absurd. Practical, sensible, proud Judith Osmond to feel so intensely about another human being! Judith Osmond in love! How had I ever fallen into such a state and so hopelessly too?

He led me up the path through somewhat overgrown shrubs and pushed open the door with the knocker which Sir Edward had brought from some foreign country. It was cunningly wrought into the shape of a face . . . a rather evil one. I wondered whether Sir Edward had put it there to discourage visitors.

The carpets were thick at Giza House so that footsteps were noiseless. Tybalt took me into the drawing room where the heavy midnight blue velvet curtains were fringed with gold and the carpet was deep blue with a velvety pile. Sir Edward had found noise distracting, I had heard. There was evidence of his vocation in that room. I knew some of the weird figures were casts of his more spec-tacular finds. This was the Chinese room, but the grand piano which dominated it brought with it the flavor of Victorian England.

Tybalt signed to me to sit down and did the same.

"We're planning another expedition to the place where my father died," he said.

"Oh!" I had said I did not believe in this story of the Curse yet the thought of his going back there alarmed me. "You think that wise?" I asked.

"Surely you don't believe these rumors about my father's death, do you, Judith?"

"Of course not."

"He was a healthy man, it was true. And suddenly he was struck down. I believe he was on the verge of a great discovery. It was something he said to me the day before he died. He said: 'I believe shortly I am going to prove to everyone that this expedition was very much worth while.' He would say no more than that. How I wish he had."

"There was an autopsy."

"Yes, here in England. But they were unable to find the cause. It was very mysterious. And now Sir Ralph's stroke."

"You don't think there is a connection?"

He shook his head. "I think my father's old friend was shocked by his sudden death. Sir Ralph has always been somewhat apoplectic and had a mild stroke once before. I know that doctors have been warning him for years to show a little moderation. No, Sir Ralph's illness has nothing to do with what was happening in Egypt. Well, I am going back and I shall attempt to find out what it was my father was on the point of discovering and . . . if this had anything to do with his death."

"Take care," I said before I could stop myself.

He smiled. "I believe it is what my father would have wished."

"When will you leave?"

"It will take us three months to get ready."

The door opened and Tabitha Grey came in. Like everyone at Giza House she interested me. She was beautiful in an unobtrusive way. It was only after one had seen her many times that one realized the charm of those features and the fascination of that air of resignation, a kind of acceptance of life. I had never been quite sure of her position at Giza House; she was a sort of specially privileged housekeeper.

"Judith has called with Lady Bodrean's good wishes."

"Would you like some tea, Judith?" asked Tabitha.

I declined with thanks, explaining that I should be going back without delay, or I should be missed. Tabitha smiled sympathetically implying that she understood Lady Bodrean was no easy taskmistress.

Tybalt said he would walk back with me and this he did. He talked all the time about the expedition. I was fascinated by it.

"I believe you wish you were going with us," he said.

"With all my heart."

"Would you be prepared to face the Curse of the Pharaohs, Miss Osmond?" he asked ironically.

"Yes, I certainly should."

He smiled at me.

"I wish," he said earnestly, "that you *could* join our expedition."

I went back to Keverall Court bemused. I scarcely heard Lady Bodrean's complaints. I was in a dream. He *wished* that I could join them. Only by a miracle could I do that.

Then Sir Ralph died and there was more talk of the Curse. The man who had led the expedition and the man who had helped to finance it—and both dead! There must be some significance in this.

And then . . . my miracle happened. It was incredible; it was wonderful; it was like something from a dream. It was as fantastic as the fairy story. Cinderella was to go— not to the ball—but with the expedition to Egypt.

I could only marvel at the wonder of it; and I thought constantly of everything that had led up to this.

It really began on my fourteenth birthday when I found the piece of bronze in Josiah Polgrey's grave.

II   The Bronze Shield

My fourteenth birthday was one of the most eventful days of my life because on it not only did I find the bronze shield but I learned some truths about myself.

The shield came first. I found it during the hot July afternoon. The house was quiet for neither Dorcas, Alison, nor the cook and the two maids were anywhere to be seen. I suspected that the maids were exchanging confidences about their sweethearts in their attic bedroom; that cook was drowsing in the kitchen; that Dorcas was in her garden; that Alison was mending, or embroidering; and that the Reverend James Osmond was in his study pretending to prepare next Sunday's sermon and in fact dozing in his chair—now and then being awakened by a sudden jerk of the head or his own genteel snore and murmuring: "Bless my soul!" and pretending to himself—as there was no one else to pretend to—that he had been working on his sermon all the time.

I was wrong, at least about Dorcas and Alison; they were most certainly in one of their bedrooms discussing how best they could tell the child—myself—for now that she was fourteen years old they believed she should no longer be kept in the dark.

I was in the graveyard watching Pegger, the sexton, dig a grave. I was fascinated by the churchyard. Sometimes I would wake in the night and think of it. Often I would get out of bed, kneel on the window seat and look down at it. In the mist it would seem very ghostly indeed and the grey tombstones were like figures risen from the dead; in the bright moonlight they were clearly gravestones but they lost none of their eeriness for that. Sometimes it was pitch dark, and the rain might be teeming down, the wind howling through the branches of the oaks and buffeting the ancient yews; then I would imagine that the dead had left their graves and were prowling round the churchyard just below my window.

It was years ago that I had begun to feel this morbid interest. It probably started when Dorcas first took me to put flowers on Lavinia's grave. We did that every Sunday. Now we had planted a rosemary bush within the marble curb.

"That's for remembrance," said Dorcas. "It will be green all the year round."

On this hot July afternoon Pegger paused in his digging to mop his forehead with a red bandanna handkerchief and regarded me in the stern way he regarded everybody.

"You've a taste for graveyards, Miss Judith," he said. "You'm like me, I reckon. As I stand here, turning over the earth, I think of the one who'll be laid to rest in this deep dark grave. Like as not I've known 'un all me life— for that's how it be in a parish like St. Erno's."

Pegger spoke in a sepulchral voice. I suppose this was due to his connection with the church. He had been sexton all his life and his father before him. He looked like one of the prophets from the Old Testament with his mane of white hair and beard, and his righteous indignation against the sinners of the world into which category all but himself and a very chosen few seemed to fall. Even his conversation had a biblical flavor.

"This be the last resting place of Josiah Polgrey. He's

lived his threescore year and ten and now he's to face his Maker." Pegger shook his head gravely as though he did not think highly of Josiah's chances in the next world.

I said: "God may not be as stern as you, Mr. Pegger."

"You come near to blasphemy, Miss Judith," he said. "You should guard well your tongue."

"Well, what would be the use of that, Mr. Pegger? The recording angel would know what was in my mind whether I said it or not—so even to think it might be just as bad, and how can you help what you think?"

Mr. Pegger raised his eyes to the sky as though he thought I might have invited the wrath of God to descend on me.

"Never mind," I soothed him. "Why you haven't had your lunch yet. It must be two o'clock."

On the next grave lay another red bandanna handkerchief similar to that with which Mr. Pegger had mopped his brow, but this one, I knew, was tied about a bottle containing cold tea and a pasty which Mrs. Pegger would have made on the previous night so that it would be ready for her husband to bring with him.

He stepped out of the grave and seating himself on the curb round the next grave untied the knot in the handkerchief and took out his food.

"How many graves have you dug in your whole lifetime?" I asked.

He shook his head. "More than I can say, Miss Judith," he replied.

"And Matthew will dig them after you. Just think of that." Matthew was not his eldest son who should have inherited the doubtful privilege of digging graves of those who had lived and died in the village of St. Erno's. Luke, the eldest, had run away to sea, a fact which would never be forgiven him.

"If it be the Lord's will I'll dig a few more yet," he answered.

"You must dig all sorts and sizes," I mused. "Well, you wouldn't need the same size for little Mrs. Edney and Sir Ralph Bodrean, would you?"

This was a plot of mine to bring Sir Ralph into the

conversation. The sins of his neighbors was, I think, Mr. Pegger's favorite subject, and since everything about Sir Ralph was bigger than that belonging to anyone else, so were his sins.

I found Sir Ralph, our Squire, fascinating. I was excited when he passed on the road either in his carriage or on one of his thoroughbreds. I would bob a little curtsy—as taught by Dorcas—and he would nod and raise a hand in a quick imperious kind of gesture and for a moment those heavy lidded eyes would be on me. Some had said of him—as long ago someone had said of Julius Caesar—"Hide your daughters when he passes by." Well, he was the Caesar of our village. He owned most of it; the outlying farmlands were on his estate; to those who worked with him he was said to be a good master, and as long as the men touched their forelocks with due respect and remembered he *was* the master and the girls did not deny him those favors which he desired, he was a good master, which meant that men were assured of work and a roof over their heads and any results which might ensue from his dallying with the maidens were taken care of. There were plenty of "results" in the village now and they were always granted the extra privileges over those who had been sired elsewhere.

But to Mr. Pegger the Squire was Sin personified.

Out of respect for my youth he could not talk of our Squire's major qualifications for hell fire, so he gave himself the pleasure of touching on his smaller ones—all of which, in Mr. Pegger's opinion, would have ensured his entry.

There were houseparties at Keverall Court almost every weekend; in the various seasons the guests came to hunt foxes, otters, and stags, or to shoot pheasants which were bred on the Keverall estate for this purpose, or merely to make merry in the baronial hall. They were rich, elegant—often noisy—people from Plymouth and sometimes as far as London. I always enjoyed seeing them. They brightened the countryside, but in Mr. Pegger's estimation they desecrated it.

I considered myself very lucky to visit Keverall Court

every day except Saturday and Sunday. This had been a
special concession because the Squire's daughter and
nephew had a governess and were also taught by Oliver
Shrimpton, our curate. The rather impecunious rector
could not afford a governess for me, and Sir Ralph had
graciously given his consent—or perhaps had raised no
objection to the proposal—that I should join his daughter
and nephew in their schoolroom and profit from the in-
struction given there. This meant that every day—except
Saturdays and Sundays—I passed under the old portcullis into the courtyard, gave an ecstatic sniff at the stables,
touched the mounting block for luck, entered the great hall
with its minstrels' gallery, mounted the wide staircase as
though I were one of the lady visitors from London, with
a flowing train and diamonds glittering on my fingers,
passed along the gallery where all the dead—and some
living—Bodreans looked down on me with varying expressions of scorn, amusement, or indifference and into
the schoolroom where Theodosia and Hadrian would be
already seated and Miss Graham the governess would be
busy at her books.

Life had certainly become more interesting since it had
been decided that I share lessons with the Bodreans.

On this July afternoon I was interested to learn that the
Squire's current sin was, as Mr. Pegger said, "putting in
his nose where God hadn't intended it should go."

"And where is that, Mr. Pegger?"

"In Carter's Meadow, that's where. He wants to set up
digging there. Disturbing God's earth. It's all along of
these people who've been coming here. Filling the place
with heathen ideas."

"What are they going to dig for, Mr. Pegger?" I asked.

"For worms I'd reckon." That was meant to be a
joke for Mr. Pegger's face creased into what did service
for a smile.

"So they're all coming down to dig, are they?" I pictured them—ladies in silks and velvets, gentlemen in white
cravats and velvet smoking jackets all with their little
spades in Carter's Meadow.

Mr. Pegger brushed the pasty crumbs from his coat

and tied the bottle back into the red handkerchief.

"It's digging up the past, they'm saying. They reckon they'm going to find bits and pieces left behind by them as lived here years and years ago."

"What *here*, Mr. Pegger?"

"Here in St. Erno's. A lot of heathens they were, so why any God-fearing gentleman should bother himself with them is past my understanding."

"Perhaps *they're* not God-fearing, Mr. Pegger; but it's all very respectable. It's called archaeology."

"What it's called makes no difference. If God had intended 'em to find these things He wouldn't have covered 'em up with his good earth."

"Perhaps it wasn't God who covered them up."

"Then who?"

"Time," I said portentously.

He shook his head and started to dig again, throwing the soil up onto the bank he had made.

"Squire were always one for taking up with these fancies. I don't like this one. Let the dead bury their dead, I say."

"I believe someone else said that some time ago, Mr. Pegger. Well, *I* think it would be interesting if we found something very important here in St. Erno's. Roman remains perhaps. We'd be famous."

"We weren't meant to be famous, Miss Judith. We were meant to be . . ."

"God-fearing," I supplied for him. "So the Squire and his friends are looking for Roman remains close by. And it's not a sudden fancy of his. He's always been interested. Famous archaeologists often come to stay at Keverall Court. Perhaps that's why his nephew is named Hadrian."

"Hadrian!" thundered Mr. Pegger. "It's a heathen name. And the young lady too."

"Hadrian and Theodosia."

"They'm not good Christian names."

"Not like your Matthew Mark Luke John Isaac Reuben . . . and the rest. Judith is in the Bible. So I'm all right."

I fell to thinking of names. "Dorcas! Alison!" I said. "Did you know, Mr. Pegger, that Theodosia means divinely given? So you see it *is* a Christian name. As for Hadrian, he's named after a wall and a Roman Emperor."

"They're not good Christian names," he repeated.

"Lavinia," I said. "I wonder what that means."

"Ah. Miss Lavinia," said Mr. Pegger.

"It was very sad, wasn't it, to die so young?"

"With all her sins upon her."

"I don't think she had many. Alison and Dorcas speak of her as though they loved her dearly."

There was a picture of Lavinia hanging in the rectory on the landing just at the top of the first flight of stairs. I used to be afraid to pass it after dark because I imagined that at night Lavinia stepped out of it and walked about the house. I used to think that one day I would pass it and find the frame empty because she had failed to get back into it in time.

I was such a fanciful child, said Dorcas, who was very practical herself and could not understand my strange imaginings.

"Every mortal man has sins," declared Mr. Pegger. "As for women they can have ten times as many."

"Not Lavinia," I said.

He leaned on his spade and scratched his white mane of hair. "Lavinia! She were the prettiest of the rectory girls."

Well, I thought, that might not have meant a great deal if I were not so familiar with Lavinia's picture, for neither Alison nor Dorcas were exactly beauties. They always wore somber-colored skirts and jackets, and thick strong boots —so sensible for the country. Yet in the picture Lavinia had a velvet jacket and a hat with a curling feather.

"It was a pity she was ever on that train."

"In one moment she had no idea what was about to happen and the next . . . she was facing her Maker."

"Do you think it's as quick as that, Mr. Pegger? After all she would have to get there . . ."

"Taken in sin, you might say, with no time for repentance."

"No one would be hard on Lavinia."

Pegger was not so sure. He shook his head. "She could have her flighty ways."

"Dorcas and Alison loved her, and so did the reverend. I can tell by the way they look when they say her name."

Mr. Pegger had put down his spade to mop his brow once more. "This be one of the hottest days the Lord have sent us this year." He stepped out of the hole and sat down on the curb of the next grave so that he and I were facing each other over the yawning hole. I stood up and peered down into it. Poor Josiah Polgrey who beat his wife and had his children out working on the farm at five years old. On impulse I jumped down into the hole.

"What be doing, Miss Judith?" demanded Mr. Pegger.

"I just want to see what it feels like to be down here," I said.

I reached up for his spade and started to dig.

"It smells damp," I said.

"A fine muss you'll be getting yourself in."

"I'm already in it," I cried, as my shoes slipped down into the loose earth. It was a horrible feeling of being shut in with the walls of the trench so close to me. "It must be terrible, Mr. Pegger, to be buried alive."

"Now you come out of there."

"I'll dig just a bit while I'm here," I said, "to see what it feels like to be a gravedigger."

I dug the spade into the earth and threw out what it had picked up as I had seen Mr. Pegger do. I repeated the operation several times before my spade struck something hard.

"There's something here," I called.

"You come out of there, Miss Judith."

I ignored him and went on probing. Then I had it. "I've found something, Mr. Pegger," I cried. I stooped and picked up the object. "What is it, do you know?"

Mr. Pegger stood up and took it from me. "Piece of old metal," he said. I gave him my hand and he pulled me out of Josiah Polgrey's grave.

"I don't know," I said. "There's something about it."

"Dirty old thing," said Mr. Pegger.

"But look at it, Mr. Pegger. Just what is it? There's a sort of engraving on it."

"I'd throw that away . . . sharp about it," said Mr. Pegger.

But *I* would do no such thing, I decided. I would take it back with me and clean it. I rather liked it.

Mr. Pegger took up his spade and continued to dig while I tried to wipe the earth from my shoes and noticed with dismay that the hem of my skirt was decidedly grubby.

I talked for a while with Mr. Pegger, then I went back to the rectory carrying the piece of what appeared to be bronze with me. It was oval shaped and about six inches in diameter. I wondered what it would be like when it was cleaned and what I would use it for. I didn't give much thought to it, because talking about Lavinia had made me think about her and what a sad house it must have been when the news was brought that Lavinia, beloved daughter of the Reverend James Osmond and sister of Alison and Dorcas, had been killed in the train which was traveling from Plymouth to London.

"She was killed outright," Dorcas had told me as we stood at her grave while she pruned the roses growing there. "It was a mercy in a way for she would have been an invalid for the rest of her life had she lived. She was twenty-one years old. It was a great tragedy."

"Why was she going to live in London, Dorcas?" I had asked.

"She was going to take up a post."

"What sort of post?"

"Oh . . . governess, I think."

"You *think!* Weren't you sure?"

"She had been staying with a distant cousin."

"What cousin was that?"

"Oh dear, what a probing child you are! She was a very *distant* cousin. We never hear of her now. Lavinia had been staying with her so she took the train from Plymouth and then . . . there was this terrible accident. Many people were killed. It was one of the worst accidents in living memory. We were heartbroken."

"That was when you decided to take me in and bring me up to take Lavinia's place."

"Nobody could take Lavinia's place, dear. You have a place of your own."

"But it's not Lavinia's. I'm not a bit like her, am I?"

"Not in the least."

"She was quiet, I suppose, and gentle; and she didn't talk too much, probe or be impulsive or try to order people about . . . all the things that I do."

"No, she was not like you, Judith. But she could be very firm on occasions, although she was so gentle."

"So then because she was dead and I was an orphan you decided to take me in. I was related to you."

"A sort of cousin."

"A distant one, I suppose. All your cousins seem to be so distant."

"Well, we knew that you were an orphan and we were so distressed. We thought it would help us all . . . and you too of course."

"So I came here and it was all because of Lavinia."

So considering all this I felt that Lavinia had had a marked effect on my life; and I fell to wondering what would have happened to me if Lavinia had not decided to take that particular train to London.

It was cool in the stone hall of the old rectory, cool and dark. On the hall table stood a great bowl of buddleia, lavender, and roses. Some of the rose petals had already fallen onto the stone flags of the hall floor. The rectory was an old house, almost as old as Keverall Court. Built in the early days of Elizabeth's reign it had been the residence of rectors over the last three hundred years. Their names were inscribed on a tablet in the church. The rooms were large and some beautifully paneled but dark because of the small windows with their leaded panes. There was an air of great quietness brooding over the house and it was particularly noticeable on this hot day.

I went up the staircase to my room; and the first thing I did was wash the soil from the ornament. I had poured water from the ewer into the basin and was dabbing it with cotton wool when there was a knock on the door.

"Come in," I called. Dorcas and Alison were standing there. They looked so solemn that I completely forgot the ornament and cried out: "Is anything wrong?"

"We heard you come in," said Alison.

"Oh dear, did I make a lot of noise?"

They looked at each other and exchanged smiles.

"We were listening for you," said Dorcas.

There was silence. This was unusual. "Something *is* wrong," I insisted.

"No, dear, nothing has changed. We have been making up our minds to speak to you for some time; and as it is your birthday and fourteen is a sort of milestone . . . we thought the time had come."

"It is all rather mysterious," I said.

Alison drew a deep breath and said: "Well, Judith . . ." Dorcas nodded to her to proceed. "Well, Judith, you have always been under the impression that you were the daughter of a cousin of ours."

"Yes, a distant one," I said.

"This is not the case."

I looked from one to the other. "Then who am I?"

"You're our adopted daughter."

"Yes, I know that, but if my parents are not the distant cousins, who are they?"

Neither of them spoke, and I cried out impatiently: "You said you came to tell me."

Alison cleared her throat. "You were on the train . . . the same train as Lavinia."

"In the accident?"

"Yes, you were in the accident . . . a child of one year or so."

"My parents were killed then."

"It seems so."

"Who were they?"

Alison and Dorcas exchanged glances. Dorcas nodded slightly to Alison which meant: Tell her all.

"*You* were unharmed."

"And my parents killed?"

Alison nodded.

"But *who* were they?"

"They . . . they must have been killed outright. No one came forward to say who you were."

"Then I might be anybody!" I cried.

"So," went on Dorcas, "as we had lost a sister we adopted you."

"What would have happened to me if you hadn't?"

"Someone else would have done so, perhaps."

I looked from one to the other and thought of all the kindness I had had from them and how I had plagued them—talking too much and too loudly, bringing mud into the house, breaking their prized crockery; and I ran to them and put my arms about them so that the three of us were in a huddle.

"Judith! Judith!" said Dorcas smiling, and the tears—which always came rather readily to her—glistened in her eyes.

Alison said: "You were a comfort to us. We needed comfort when Lavinia was gone."

"Well," I said, "it's nothing to cry about, is it? Perhaps I'm the long-lost heiress to a great estate. My parents have been searching high and low for me . . ."

Alison and Dorcas were smiling again. I had further food for my flights of fancy. "It's better than being a distant cousin anyway," I said. "But I do wonder *who* I was."

"It is clear that your parents were killed outright. It was such a . . . violent disaster that we heard many people were unrecognizable. Papa went and identified poor Lavinia. He came back so upset."

"Why did you tell me that I came from distant cousins?"

"We thought it better, Judith. We thought you'd be happier believing yourself related to us."

"You're thinking I was unclaimed . . . unwanted, and that might have upset me and thrown a shadow over my childhood."

"There could have been so many explanations. Perhaps you only had your parents and no other relations. We thought that very likely."

"An orphan born of two orphans."

"That seems possible."

"Or perhaps your parents had just come to England."

"A foreigner. Perhaps I'm French, or Spanish. I am rather dark. My hair looks quite black by candlelight. My eyes are much lighter though, just ordinary brown. I do look rather like a Spaniard. But then lots of Cornish people do. That's because the Spaniards were wrecked along our coasts when we destroyed the Armada."

"Well, all ended well. You came to be as our very own and I can never tell you what a joy that has been for us."

"I don't know why you're looking so glum. It's rather exciting I think, not to know who you are. Just think what you might discover! I might have a sister or brother somewhere. Or grandparents. Perhaps they'll come and claim me and take me back to Spain. Señorita Judith. It sounds rather good. Mademoiselle Judith de . . . de Something. Just imagine going to see my long-lost family in their wonderful old château."

"Oh Judith, you romance about everything," said Dorcas.

"I'm glad she's taken it like this," added Alison.

"What other way should I take it? I never did like those distant cousins anyway."

"So you don't feel that you were . . . deserted . . . unwanted . . . unclaimed?"

"Of course not. They didn't know that my parents had been killed. Nobody told them and as they were in a foreign country they weren't missed. They just thought they had slipped out of their lives. As for the little baby, *me*, well they often dream of me. 'I wonder what the child is like,' they say. 'She will be fourteen today. Dear little Judith.' But I suppose *you* named me that."

"You were christened by Papa soon after we brought you to the rectory."

"Well," I said, "it's all very exciting. A nice birthday surprise. Look at this. I found it. I think when it's cleaned up it will be rather unusual."

"What is it?"

"I've no idea. What would you say, Dorcas? There are scratchings on it. Look."

"Where did you find it?"

"In Josiah Polgrey's grave. Mr. Pegger was digging it and I had a go, and lo and behold my spade struck this. I shall clean it up and then see what I shall use it for. It's a sort of birthday present from Josiah Polgrey."

"What an idea! I've seen something like this before," continued Alison. "I think it may have some significance."

"What do you mean, Alison? *Significance?*"

"Sir Ralph would know."

Dorcas and Alison exchanged looks. Alison said, speaking rather slowly: "I think, Judith, that you should take it along to Keverall Court and ask if you may show it to Sir Ralph."

"Whatever for?"

"Because he's interested in this sort of thing."

"Things that are dug up you mean?"

"Certain things. Of course this may be just nothing . . . but there *is* something about it. I think it may be very old indeed and you have stumbled on something important."

I was excited. It was true there was talk of digging up Carter's Meadow. How interesting if I had been the first to find something!

"I'll take it right away," I said.

"I should wash first, change your dress and comb your hair."

I smiled at them. I loved them very much; they were so normal. It was my birthday; they had just told me that I had been unclaimed, my parents had been killed and I might be just anybody; I may have stumbled on something important from centuries ago and they were worried about my changing my dress and making myself presentable to see Sir Ralph!

Under the portcullis, into the courtyard, sniffing the stables and touching the mounting block for luck; and then into the great baronial hall. The heavy iron-studded door creaked as I pushed it open. How silent it seemed! I stood there for a second or so looking at the two suits of armor on either side of the wide staircase and the weapons on the walls; on the refectory table were pewter utensils, and there was a great bowl of flowers too.

I wondered what Hadrian and Theodosia were doing and what fun I would have tomorrow when I told them what I had found. I had already magnified it into something priceless. The greatest archaeologists in the world were shaking me by the hand. "We are so grateful to you, Judith. We have been digging for years and never have we found anything quite so wonderful as this."

I heard the scraping of a chair behind me. I had not noticed Derwent, the footman, dozing in a chair.

"Oh, it's you," he said.

"I want to see Sir Ralph immediately. It is a matter of the utmost importance."

He looked at me superciliously. "Now, Miss. This is another of your tricks, I know."

"It's no trick. I have found something which is of great value. My aunts"—I called Dorcas and Alison aunts; it simplified the relationship—"said I was to bring it to Sir Ralph without delay and woe betide anyone who tries to keep this from him."

I hugged the piece of metal against me and faced him squarely.

"He's taking tea with her ladyship."

"Go and tell him I am here," I said imperiously.

Because there had been some talk about Carter's Meadow, and Sir Ralph's interest in what could be dug out of the earth was well known, I eventually prevailed on Derwent to go and tell Sir Ralph that I had found something which my aunts thought might be of interest. Consequently within five minutes I was in the library, that fascinating room full of Sir Ralph's collection of exotic pieces.

I laid the metal on the table, and from that moment I knew that I had made an impression.

"Good God," said Sir Ralph; he used oaths of which, I reflected, Dorcas, Alison, and the Reverend James would not have approved, "where did you find this?"

I told him that it was in Josiah Polgrey's grave.

His bushy eyebrows were lifted. "What were you doing there?"

"Helping to dig it."

He had two kinds of laughter—one a wild sort of roar and the other inward when his chin shook and I think that was when he was most amused. He was amused in that way now and pleased. He spoke jerkily always as though he were in too much of a hurry to complete his sentences.

"H'm," he said. "Graveyard, eh?"

"Yes. It's important, isn't it?"

"Bronze," he said. "Looks prehistoric to me."

"That's very interesting I believe."

"Good girl!" he said. "If you find anything more, bring it to me."

He nodded in a way which I realized meant dismissal, but I had no intention of being dismissed like that.

I said: "You want me to leave you my er . . . bronze?"

He narrowed his eyes and his jaw wagged slightly. "Yours!" he bellowed. "It's not yours."

"I found it."

"Findings—keepings, eh? No, not with this sort of thing, my girl. This belongs to the nation."

"That's very strange."

"Number of things you'll find strange before you're much older."

"Is it of interest to archaeologists?"

"What do you know of archaeologists?"

"I know they dig and find things. They find all sorts of wonderful things. Roman baths and lovely tiles and things like that."

"You don't fancy yourself as an archaeologist because you found this, do you?"

"It's doing the same as they do."

"And that's what you'd like to do, is it?"

"Yes, I would. I know I'd be good at it. I'd find wonderful things that people didn't know were there in the earth."

He laughed then—the wild roar. "You fancy archaeologists are constantly finding jewels and Roman villas. You've got a lot to learn. Greater part of the time is spent digging looking for things of little value—things like this—the

sort of things that have been found times out of number.
That's what the majority of them do."

"I wouldn't," I said confidently. "I'd find beautiful
things, significant things."

He laid a hand on my shoulder and led me to the door.

"You'd like to know what this is you've found, wouldn't
you?"

"Yes. After all *I* found it."

"I'll let you know when I get the verdict on it. And
meanwhile, if you find anything else, you'll know what
to do with it, won't you?"

"Bring it to you, Sir Ralph."

He nodded and shut the door on me. I went slowly
down through the hall and out into the courtyard. I
had lost my piece of bronze but it was pleasant to remind
myself that I had contributed to the knowledge of the
world.

Although my find was identified as part of a shield,
possibly of the Bronze Age, and it appeared that many
of its kind had been found before, it brought about several
changes which were important.

In the first place it sent up my prestige in the schoolroom. When I arrived for lessons both Hadrian and Theodosia were far more respectful than they had been before.
I had always thought Theodosia rather a silly little thing—
although she was about a year older than I—and Hadrian
was slightly older still. They were both fair, Theodosia
rather fragile looking with innocent blue eyes and a chin
that receded a little. I was taller than she and, in reality,
almost as tall as Hadrian. I never felt the difference in
our ages, and in spite of the fact that they lived in this
mansion and I came from the rectory I was a kind of
leader and was constantly telling them what they ought
to do.

They had been informed by their father that I had
found something of some importance and had had the good
sense to bring it along to him. He would like to see
them show as much interest as I had.

I spent the morning on and off explaining how I had

dug Josiah Polgrey's grave and how I had found the object, and I drove poor Miss Graham to despair. I drew the object for them. It had become enormous in my mind; it shone like gold. It had belonged to some king, who had buried it in the earth so that I should find it.

I whispered to them that we should all get spades and dig in Carter's Meadow because that was where they thought there was a lot of treasure. That afternoon we found spades in the gardeners' sheds and set to work. We were discovered and reprimanded; but the result was that Sir Ralph decided that we might learn something about archaeology and ordered the long-suffering Miss Graham to give us lessons. Poor Miss Graham was obliged to read up on the subject and she did her best in a difficult situation. I was fascinated—far more than the others. Sir Ralph discovered this and his interest in me, which began when I discovered the bronze shield, seemed to grow.

Then Sir Edward Travers and his family came to the old Dower House. The Traverses were already friends of the Bodreans; they had visited Keverall Court many times and Sir Edward was behind the plans for Carter's Meadow. My find had increased that interest and was probably the reason why, since he was looking for a country house, Sir Edward decided on the Dower House.

Sir Edward was connected with Oxford University in some way but was constantly engaged on expeditions. His name was often in the papers and he was very well known in academic circles, but Sir Edward needed a country residence where he could be quiet to compile his finds and set it all out in book form after he returned from one of his trips, usually in far-off places.

There was a great deal of excitement when we heard they were coming. Hadrian told me that his uncle was delighted and that now nothing could stop them digging up Carter's Meadow—parson or no parson.

I was sure he was right for the poor Reverend James was not the man to go into battle. His objections were entirely due to the prodding of his more forceful parishioners. All he wanted was to be able to lead a quiet life and the chief duty of Dorcas and Alison was to keep from him anything that might disturb him. I believe he was delighted by the coming of Sir Edward, for even the most militant of his flock would not dare raise issue with such an important gentleman.

So the Traverses arrived and the Dower House became Giza House.

"Named after the Pyramids, I believe," said Dorcas, and we confirmed this by looking it up in the encyclopedia.

The dark old Dower House with the overgrown garden which had stood empty for so long was now inhabited. I could no longer so easily scare Theodosia with stories that it was haunted and dare her and Hadrian to run up the path and look through the windows. It lost none of its strangeness though. "Once a house is haunted," I told the nervous Theodosia, "it's haunted forever."

And sure enough it was not long before we began to hear strange rumors of the house which was full of treasures from all over the world. Some of them were very odd indeed, so that the servants didn't feel at home with them; and because of these strange things the place was "creepy." If it had not been for the fact that Sir Edward was such an important man whose name was often in the papers, they would not have stayed there.

So there was digging in Carter's Meadow and important tenants at Giza House. We learned that although Sir Edward was a widower he had two children—a son, Tybalt, who was grown up and at the university—and a daughter, Sabina, who was about the same age as Theodosia and myself and was therefore to share our lessons.

It was some time before I saw Tybalt but I decided to dislike him before I set eyes on him, largely because Sabina spoke of him with awe and reverence. She did not so much love as adore him. He was omniscient and omnipotent according to her. He was handsome, in fact godlike.

"I don't believe anyone is as good as that," I said scornfully, glaring at Hadrian, forcing him to agree with me. Theodosia could think what she liked; her opinion was unimportant.

Hadrian looked from me to Sabina and came down on my side. "No," he declared, "nobody is."

"Nobody but Tybalt," insisted Sabina.

Sabina talked constantly and never minded whether anyone was listening or not. I told Hadrian this was because she lived in that strange house with her absent-minded father and those servants, two of whom were very strange indeed, for they were Egyptians named Mustapha and Absalam and wore long white robes and sandals. I had heard from our rectory cook that they gave the other servants the "creeps" and with all the peculiar things that were in that house and those two gliding about so that you never knew whether they were spying on you and you not seeing them—it was a queer household.

Sabina was pretty; she had fair curls, and big grey eyes with long golden lashes and a little heart-shaped face. Theodosia, who was quite plain, very soon adored her. I quickly saw that their friendship strengthened the alliance between Hadrian and myself. Sometimes I used to think it had been better before the Traverses came because then the three of us made a pleasant little trio. I admit that I bullied them a little. Dorcas was always telling me that I must stop trying to organize everyone and believing that what I wanted for them was the best from every point of view. It was a fact that although Hadrian and Theodosia were the children of the big house and I came from the impecunious rectory and had been allowed to have lessons in their schoolroom as a favor, I did behave rather as though I were the daughter of Keverall Court and the others were the outsiders. I had explained to Dorcas that it was just because Hadrian could never make up his mind and Theodosia was too silly to have any ideas about anything.

Then there was Sabina, good-natured, her lovely hair always falling into place in a manner most becoming, while my thick straight dark locks were always escaping in disorder from anything with which I tried to bind them. Her grey eyes would sparkle with gaiety when she spoke of frivolous things or shine with fervor when she talked of Tybalt. She was a charming girl, whose presence had changed the entire atmosphere of our schoolroom.

Through her we learned of life in Giza House. How her father was shut in his room for days and silent-footed Mustapha or Absalam took his meals to him on trays. Sabina had luncheon in a small dining room just off the schoolroom at Keverall as I did each day except Saturdays and Sundays, but in Giza House when her father was working she often had meals alone or with her companion-housekeeper, Tabitha Grey, who gave her lessons at the piano. She always referred to her as Tabby and I christened her the Grey Tabby which amused them all. I pictured her as a middle-aged woman, with greying dusty-looking hair, grey skirts, and dull muddy-colored blouses. I was very surprised eventually to meet a striking-looking youngish woman.

I told Sabina that she was no good at describing anything. She had made Grey Tabby sound like a dowdy old woman and I was sure that that wonder hero Tybalt would turn out to be a pale-faced youth with eyes ruined by looking at too much crabbed writing on ancient manuscripts—which he must have done, mustn't he, since he was so clever—round-shouldered and knowing absolutely nothing about anything but long dead people and what weapons they had used to battle.

"One day you may be able to see for yourself," said Sabina laughing.

We could hardly wait. She had so played on our imaginations—particularly mine which Alison had once said worked overtime—that this miraculous brother of hers was never far from my thoughts. I was longing to see him. I had so built up this picture of the stooping bespectacled scholar that I believed it to be true and had forced Hadrian to do the same. Theodosia took Sabina's version. "After all," she said, "Sabina's seen him. You haven't."

"People get bemused," I said. "She sees him through rose-colored spectacles."

We could hardly wait when the time came for him to come down from Oxford. Sabina was exalted. "Now you will see for yourselves." One morning she came in in tears because Tybalt was not coming, after all. He was going up to Northumberland on a dig and he would no doubt spend the entire vacation up there. Sir Edward was going to join him.

Instead of Tybalt we had Evan Callum, who was a friend of Tybalt. Wishing to earn a little money, he was going to spend the period before he went back to the university grounding us in the rudiments of archaeology, a subject in which he was quite proficient.

I forgot my disappointment about Tybalt and threw myself with fervor into my new studies. I was much more interested in the subject than the others. Sometimes in the afternoons I would go down to Carter's Meadow with Evan Callum and he would show me something of the practical work which had to be done.

Once I saw Sir Ralph there. He came over to speak to me.

"Interested, eh?" he said.

I replied that I was.

"Found any more bronze shields?"

"No. I haven't found anything."

He gave me a little push. "Finds don't come often. You started off with yours." His jaw wagged in the amused way, and I had a notion that he was rather pleased to see me there.

One of the workers who had come down with the party showed me how to piece a broken pot together. "First aid," he called it, until it could be treated properly and perhaps find its way into a museum. He showed me how to pack a piece of pottery which had been put together in this "first-aid" manner and which was to be sent away to the experts who would restore it and place it in its period where it might or might not betray some little detail of how life was lived four thousand years before.

I had dreamed of finding something in Carter's Meadow; golden ornaments, things that I had heard had been found in tombs. This was very different. I was disappointed for a while and then I began to develop a burning enthusiasm for the task itself. I could think of little else than the wonder of uncovering the record of the rocks.

Our lessons with Evan Callum were taken in the after-

noons, because the mornings were spent with Miss Graham
or Oliver Shrimpton learning what were called the three
Rs. Reading, Writing, and Arithmetic. In addition, Theodosia, Sabina, and I had to do needlework with Miss
Graham and three mornings a week we worked for an
hour on our samplers. The alphabet had to be worked, a
proverb, our names, and the date. Naturally we chose
the shortest proverb we could find but even so the task
was laborious. Horrible little cross stitches on a piece of
cotton and if one stitch was too large or too small it had
to be unpicked and put right. I was in revolt against such
time wasting and I was so frustrated that my sampler
suffered through it. There was music and we strummed
on the piano under Miss Graham's supervision, but now
we had Grey Tabby it was decided that she should give
the music lessons. So with our periodic lessons in archaeology our education was running on quite unconventional
lines. We had our teachers from three sources—Miss
Graham from Keverall Court, Grey Tabby and Evan
Callum through Giza House, and from the rectory Oliver
Shrimpton. Dorcas was delighted. It was an excellent way,
she said, of three families pooling their educational re-
sources and providing an excellent education for the
young people involved. She doubted that anywhere in
the country a girl was getting such a well-grounded train-
ing. She hoped, she added, that I was making full use of it.

What did intrigue me were the sessions with Evan
Callum. I told him that when I was grown up I should
go with expeditions to the far places of the world. He
replied that he thought that as a female I might find
this difficult unless I married an archaeologist; but all
the same he encouraged me. It was gratifying to have such
an apt pupil. We were all interested but my natural enthusiasm was perhaps more intense and more obvious.

I became particularly fascinated by the Egyptian scene.
There was so much to be discovered there. I loved hearing about that old civilization; the gods that were worshiped, the dynasties, the temples that had been discovered;
I caught my enthusiasm from Evan. "There's a treasure
store in the hills of the desert, Judith," he used to say.

Of course I pictured myself there, making fantastic discoveries, receiving the congratulations of people like Sir Edward Travers.

I had imagined myself having long conversations with him but he, I must say, was a disappointment. He never seemed to see any of us. He had a strange far-away look in his eyes as though he were looking far back into the past.

"I expect that awful old Tybalt is just like him," I said to Hadrian.

Tybalt had become a new word which I had introduced into our vocabulary. It meant "mean, despicable." Hadrian and I used to tease Sabina with it.

"I don't care," she said, "nothing *you* say can change Tybalt."

I was fascinated by Giza House though and although I was a hopeless musician I used to look forward to going there. As soon as I entered the house I would become excited. There was something peculiar about it. "Sinister," I told Hadrian who agreed as he usually did with me.

In the first place it was dark. The bushes which surrounded the house might have been responsible for that, but in the house there were so many rich velvet curtains —not only at windows but over doors and alcoves in which were often strange images. It was so thickly carpeted that you rarely heard people come and go and I always had the sensation in that house that I was being watched.

There was a strange old woman who lived at the top of this house in what appeared to be an apartment of her own. Sabina referred to her as Old Nanny Tester.

"Who is she?" I demanded.

"She was my mother's Nanny and Tybalt's and mine."

"What's she doing up there?"

"She just lives up there."

"But you don't want a nanny now surely."

"We don't turn old servants out when they have served us many years," said Sabina haughtily.

"*I* believe she's a witch."

"Believe what you like, Judith Osmond. She's old Nanny Tester."

"She spies on us. She's always peering out of the window and dodging back when we look up."

"Oh don't take any notice of her," said Sabina.

Every time I went to the place I looked up to the top window for Nanny Tester. I had convinced myself that it was a strange house in which anything could happen.

The drawing room was the most normal room, but even that had an Oriental look. There were several Chinese vases and images which Sir Edward had picked up in China. There were some beautiful pictures on the walls— delicate and in pastel shades; there was a big cabinet in which were Chinese figures—there were dragons and fat Buddhas with sly sleepy looks and thin ones sitting with apparent comfort in a position which I had tried unsuccessfully to copy; there were ladies with inscrutable faces and mandarins with cruel ones. But the grand piano gave the place an air of normality and it was on this that we strummed out our lessons under the tuition of Grey Tabby who was as enigmatical as one of the Chinese ladies in the cabinet.

Whenever I had an opportunity I would peep into other rooms forcing Hadrian to look with me. He was reluctant but he was afraid not to do as I wished because he knew that I would call him a coward if he refused.

We had been studying with Evan Callum some of the lore of old Egypt and I was greatly fascinated. He gave us an account of some recent discoveries there in which Sir Edward Travers had been involved; and then he went on to give us a little insight into the history of that country.

When I listened to Evan Callum I would be transported out of the schoolroom into the temples of the gods. I listened avidly to the story of the self-begotten god Ra— often known as Amen Ra; and his son Osiris who with Isis begot the great god Horus. He showed us pictures of the masks which priests wore during religious ceremonies and told us that each god was represented by one of the masks.

"The idea being," he explained, "that the great gods

of the Egyptians possessed all the strengths and virtues of men, but in addition they had one attribute of an animal; and this animal was their particular sign. Horus was the hawk because his eyes saw all and quickly." I pored over the pictures he showed us. I was an apt pupil.

But I think what interested me most were the accounts of burials when the bodies of the important dead were embalmed and put in their tombs and there left to rest for thousands of years. With them would often be buried their servants who might have been killed merely that they might accompany them and remain their servants in the new life as in the old. Treasure was stored in their tombs that they might not suffer poverty in the future.

"This custom, of course," Evan explained to us, "has led to many of the tombs being robbed. Throughout the centuries daring men have plundered them . . . daring indeed for it is said that the Curse of the Pharaohs descends on those who disturb their eternal rest."

I was very interested to hear how it was possible to keep a person's body for centuries. "The embalming process," Evan explained, "is one which was perfected three thousand years before the birth of Christ. It was a secret and no one has ever really discovered how the ancient Egyptians did it so expertly."

It was absorbing. There were books with pictures. I was never tired of talking of this fascinating subject; I wanted to ignore other lessons for the sake of going on with Evan.

Sabina said she had seen a mummy. They had had one at Giza once.

Evan talked to her about it and I was a little envious that Sabina who had not taken particular note of it should have had the opportunity which I should have made such use of.

"It was in a sort of coffin," said Sabina.

"A sarcophagus," supplied Evan.

"We've still got it, I believe," said Sabina. "But the mummy has gone." She shuddered. "I'm glad. I didn't like it. It was horrible."

"It was interesting," I cried. "Just imagine. It was

somebody who had actually lived thousands of years ago!"

I couldn't get the thought of it out of my mind and a few days later when we went for our music lesson I decided that I was going to see it. Theodosia was at the piano. She was better than the rest of us and Tabby gave us extra tuition.

I said: "Now is the time." And Sabina led us to that strange room. This was the one, of course, which I had heard about, the room which gave the servants "the creeps" and which they wouldn't enter alone.

I saw the sarcophagus at once. It stood in a corner of the room; it was like a stone trough. Along the top of it were rows of hieroglyphs.

I knelt down and examined them.

"My father is trying to decipher them," explained Sabina. "That's why it's here. Later it will go to the museum."

I touched it wonderingly. "Just imagine . . . thousands of years ago people made these signs and someone was embalmed and laid inside there. Don't you think that's wonderful? Oh, how I wish they'd left the mummy!"

"You can see them in the British Museum. It's just like someone done up with a lot of bandages."

I stood up and looked about the room. The walls of one side were lined with books. I looked at their bindings. Many were in languages I could not understand.

I said: "There's a strange feeling in this room. Are you aware of it?"

"No," said Sabina. "You're trying to frighten us."

"It's because it's dark," said Hadrian. "It's the tree outside the window."

"Listen," I said.

"It's the wind," said Sabina scornfully. "And come on. We mustn't be found in here."

She was relieved when she shut the door behind us. But I couldn't forget that room.

For the next few days I looked up everything I could find about ancient burials. The others were impatient with me because when I had an idea I was obsessed by it and would talk of nothing else. Sabina was very impatient and Theodosia had begun to agree with everything Sabina said.

She declared she was tired of all this talk about mummies. They were nothing but dead people anyway. She had heard that if they were exposed to the air and the wrappings removed they all crumpled to dust. Why get excited about a lot of dust?

"But they were real people once. Let's go and look at the sarcophagus again."

"No," wailed Sabina. "And this is *my* house, so if you go without me you're trespassing."

"I believe you're afraid of that room," I declared.

She indignantly denied this.

I became more and more obsessed and wanted to know exactly what it felt like to be embalmed and laid to rest in a sarcophagus. I forced Hadrian to join me and together we found some old sheets and one of these we cut into strips, and when we all went to Giza House for our music lesson Hadrian and I contrived to have ours first and then we went into the garden where we had hidden our sheets and bandages in an old summerhouse. We retrieved them and together we went into the room in which was the sarcophagus. I put the sheet over my head—having cut holes in it for my eyes—and made Hadrian bind me up with the bandages. I scrambled into the sarcophagus and lay there.

My only excuse is that I was young and thoughtless. It just seemed a tremendous joke—and an exciting one too. I thought I was very brave and bold to lie in that sarcophagus alone in the room for I had twinges of doubt and felt that my boldness might arouse at any moment the wrath of the gods.

It seemed a long time before the door opened. Sabina said: "Oh, why do you want to keep looking at it . . ." And I knew Hadrian had brought them in as we had arranged.

Then they saw me. There was a bloodcurdling scream. I tried to scramble out of the trough-like receptacle which smelled peculiar and was so cold. It was the worst thing that I could have done for Theodosia, seeing this thing rising from the dead, as she believed, began to scream.

I heard Hadrian shout: "It's only Judith."

I saw Sabina was as white as the sheet which was wrapped round me; and then Theodosia slid to the floor in a faint.

"It's all right, Theodosia," I cried. "It's Judith. It's not a real mummy."

"I believe she's dead," said Sabina. "You've killed her."

"Theodosia!" I wailed. "You're not dead. People can't die like that."

Then I saw the stranger standing in the doorway. He was tall, and so different from anyone I had ever seen before that for the moment I thought he was one of the gods come for vengeance. He looked angry enough.

He stared at me. What a sight I must have looked—my bandages hanging about me, the sheet still over my head.

From me he looked to Theodosia. "Good God," he said and picked her up.

"Judith dressed up as a mummy," squealed Sabina. "It's frightened Theodosia."

"How utterly stupid!" he said, giving me such a look of contempt that I was glad of the sheet to cover my shame.

"Is she dead, Tybalt?" went on Sabina.

He did not answer; he walked out of the room with Theodosia in his arms.

I scrambled out of the bandages and sheet and rolled them into a bundle.

Sabina came running back into the room.

"They're all fussing round Theodosia," she informed us, and added rather gleefully: "They're all angry with you two."

"It was my idea," I said, "wasn't it, Hadrian?"

Hadrian agreed that it was.

"It's nothing to be proud of," said Sabina severely. "You might have killed her."

"She's all right?" I said anxiously.

"She's sitting up now, but she looks pale and she's gasping."

"She was only a bit frightened," I said.

"People can die of fright."

"Well, she isn't going to."

Tybalt came into the room. He still looked angry.

"What on earth did you think you two were doing?"

I looked at Hadrian who waited as usual for me to speak. "I was only being a mummy," I said.

"Aren't you a little old for such tricks?"

I felt small and bitterly humiliated.

"You didn't think, I suppose, of the effect this might have on those who were not in the joke?"

"No," I said, "I didn't think."

"It's quite a good habit. I should try it sometime."

If anyone else had said that to me I should have been ready with a pert answer. But he was different . . . right from the beginning I knew it.

He had turned to Hadrian. "And what have you to say?"

"Only the same as Judith. We didn't mean to hurt her."

"You've behaved very stupidly," he said; and turned and left us.

"So that's the great Tybalt!" said Hadrian waiting until he was out of earshot.

"Yes," I said, "the great Tybalt!"

"You said he stooped and wore glasses."

"Well, I was wrong. He doesn't. We'd better go now."

I heard Tybalt's voice as we went down the stairs.

"Who is that insolent girl?"

He was referring to me of course.

Sabina joined us in the hall. "Theodosia is to go back in the carriage," she said. "You two are to walk back. There's going to be trouble."

She seemed rather pleased about it.

There *was* trouble. Miss Graham was waiting for us in the schoolroom.

She looked worried—but then she often did. She was constantly afraid, I realized later, that she would be blamed and dismissed.

"Young Mr. Travers came over in the carriage, with Theodosia," she said. "He has told Sir Ralph all about your wickedness. You are both going to be severely punished. Theodosia has gone to bed. Her ladyship is most anxious and has sent for the doctor. Theodosia is not very strong."

I couldn't help feeling that Theodosia was making the most of the occasion. After all what was she worried about? She knew now that I had been the mummy.

We went into the library, that room where three of the walls were lined with books and the other was almost all window—large, mullion, window-seated, and with heavy dark green curtains. It was a somewhat oppressive room because so many objects seemed to be huddled together under the enormous glass chandelier. There were carved wooden tables from India and figures with similar carving. Chinese vases and an ornate Louis Quinze table supported by gilded cherubs. Sir Ralph had had this assortment of treasures brought to him from all parts of the world and had gathered them together here irrespective of their suitability. All this I noticed later. At this time I was aware only of the two men in the room. Sir Ralph and Tybalt.

"What is all this, eh?" demanded Sir Ralph.

Hadrian always seemed to be struck dumb in the presence of his uncle so it was up to me to speak. I tried to explain.

"No right to be in that room! No right to play such silly tricks. You're going to be punished for this. And you won't like it."

I did not want Tybalt to see that I was afraid. I was thinking of the worst punishment that could befall me. No more lessons with Evan Callum.

"Have you nothing to say for yourself?" Sir Ralph was glaring at Hadrian.

"We only . . . pretended."

"Speak up!"

"It was my idea," I said.

"Let the boy speak for himself, if he can."

"We . . . we thought it would be a good idea for Judith to dress up . . ."

Sir Ralph made an impatient noise. Then he turned to

me. "So you were the ring leader, eh?"

I nodded and I was suddenly relieved because I was sure I saw his chin move.

"All right," he said. "You'll see what happens to people who play such tricks. You go back to the rectory now and you'll see what's in store for you." Then to Hadrian, "And you, sir. You go to your room. You're going to have the whipping of your life because I'm going to administer it myself. Get out."

Poor Hadrian! It was so humiliating—and in front of Tybalt too!

Hadrian was severely beaten which at sixteen was hard to endure.

When I arrived back at the rectory it was to find Dorcas and Alison very disturbed, as they had been already informed of my sinful folly.

"Why Judith, what if Sir Ralph had refused to have you at Keverall Court again?"

"Has he?" I asked anxiously.

"No, but orders are that you are to be punished and we daren't go against that."

The Reverend James had retired to his study muttering something about pressure of work. This was trouble and he was going to be out of it.

"Well," I demanded, "what are they going to do to me?"

"You are to go to your room and read a book which Mr. Callum has sent for you. You are to write an essay on its contents and to have nothing but bread and water until the task is completed. You are to do this if you stay in your room for a week."

It was no real punishment for me. Dear Evan! The book he chose for me was *The Dynasties of Ancient Egypt* which fascinated me; and our cook at the rectory in the safety of her kitchen declared that she was not taking orders from Keverall Court; nor was she having me on bread and water. The next thing, she prophesied, would be Dr. Gunwen's brougham at the door and nobody was going to make her starve little children. I was amused that I who had often been called a limb of Satan should have suddenly become a little child. However during that period some of my favorite foods were smuggled in to me. There was a hot steamy pasty I remember, and one of her special miniature squab pies.

I had quite a pleasant two days for my task was finished in record time; and I learned later from Evan that Sir Ralph, far from expressing his disapproval of my exploit, was rather pleased about it.

We were growing up and changes came, but so gradually that one scarcely noticed them.

Tybalt was frequently at Giza House. One of my favorite dreams at that time was that I made a great discovery. This varied. Sometimes I dug up an object of inestimable value; at others I found some tremendous significance in the hieroglyphs about the sarcophagus at Giza House, and this discovery of mine so shook the archaeological world that Tybalt was overcome with admiration. He asked me to marry him and we went off to Egypt together where for the rest of our lives we lived happily ever after piling up discovery after discovery, so that we became famous. "I owe it all to you," said Tybalt, at the end of the dream.

The truth was that he scarcely noticed me, and I believed that if ever he thought of me it was as the silly girl who had dressed up as a mummy and frightened Theodosia.

It was different with Theodosia. Instead of despising her for fainting he seemed to like her for it. She had opportunities for knowing him which were denied me. After lessons were over I went back to the rectory while she, now that she was growing up, joined the family at dinner and the guests were often Tybalt and his father.

Hadrian went off to the university to study archaeology, which was his uncle's choice rather than his. Hadrian had confided to me that he was dependent on his uncle, for his parents were in meager circumstances. His father— Sir Ralph's brother—had married without the family's consent. As Hadrian was the eldest of four brothers and Sir Ralph, having no son of his own had offered to take him and educate him—so Sir Ralph had to be placated.

"You're lucky," I said. "Wouldn't I like to go and study archaeology."

"You were always mad about it."

"It's something to be mad about."

I missed having Hadrian to order around. He was so meek; he had always done what I wanted.

Then Evan Callum ceased to come to teach because he had graduated and had taken a post in one of the universities. Miss Graham and Oliver Shrimpton continued to teach us and we still had music lessons with Tabitha Grey; but the changes were setting in.

Dorcas tried to teach me a few of what she called "home crafts" which meant trying to impart a light touch with pastry and showing me how to make bread and preserves. I was not really very good at that.

"You'll need it one day," she said, "when you have a home of your own. Do you realize you're nearly eighteen, Judith. Why some girls are married at that age."

When she said that there was a little frown on her brow. I believed that she and Alison worried a little about my future. I knew that they hoped I would marry—and I knew whom.

We all liked Oliver Shrimpton. He was pleasant, not exactly ambitious but he had an enthusiasm for his work. He was an asset in the parish and for the last two or three years since the Reverend James seemed to get more and more easily tired he had—as Dorcas and Alison admitted—practically carried the parish on his own shoulders. He got on well with the old ladies and the not-so-old ones liked him very much. There were several spinsters who couldn't do enough in church activities and I guessed their enthusiasm had something to do with Oliver.

He and I had always been good friends. I had not shone at the subjects he had taught but living under the same roof with him for so long I regarded him as a kind of brother. I sometimes wondered though if I had never seen Tybalt I might have been reconciled to the idea of marrying him and going on in the rectory which had been my home all my life—for it was a foregone conclusion that when the Reverend James retired or died, Oliver would come into the living.

I could not talk to anyone of my feelings for Tybalt. They were absurd anyway, for surely it was ridiculous to feel this intense passion for someone who was hardly aware of one's existence.

But our relationship did undergo a change and he began to be a little aware of me. Tabitha Grey was very kindly and she noticed how despondent I was when Evan Callum ceased to teach us. As I grew older she seemed to grow younger. I suppose at fourteen anyone of twenty-four seems very old; but when one is nearly eighteen, twenty-eight seemed younger than twenty-four did at fourteen. Tabitha was Mrs. Grey so she had been married. Ever to have called her Grey Tabby was incongruous. She was tall with rippling dark hair and large light brown eyes; when she played the piano her expression changed, something ethereal touched it and she was then undoubtedly beautiful. She was gentle-natured, by no means communicative; sometimes I thought there was a haunting sadness in her face.

I had tried to find out from Sabina what exactly her position was in the household.

"Oh, she just manages everything," said Sabina. "She's there for me when my father and Tybalt are away; and she looks after the servants—and Nanny Tester too, though Nanny won't admit it. She knows quite a lot about Father's work. He talks to her about it—so does Tybalt."

I was more interested than ever and that gave us something in common. I had one or two talks with her after our music lesson. She became quite animated discussing Sir Edward's work. She told me that on one occasion she had been a member of his party when they had gone down to Kent working on some Roman excavation.

"When Sabina is married I shall go again," she said. "It's a pity that you're a girl. If you had been a boy you might have taken archaeology up as a profession."

"I don't think we have the money for that at the rectory. I was lucky they tell me to get the sort of education

I have. I shall have to earn some money. What I shall do, I don't know . . . except that I shall probably have to be a governess."

"You never know what's waiting for you," she said. Then she lent me some books. "There's no reason why you shouldn't go on reading and learning all you can."

It was when I went to Giza House one late afternoon to return some books that I heard music. I guessed Tabitha was playing and glancing through the window into the drawing room I saw her seated at the piano and Tybalt was with her; they were playing a duet. As I watched the duet ended; they turned to each other and smiled. I thought then: How I wish he would smile at me like that.

As people do they seemed to guess that they were being watched and both of them looked simultaneously towards the window and saw me.

I felt rather ashamed for being caught looking in but Tabitha waved that aside.

"Come in, Judith," she said. "Oh, you've brought the books back. I've been lending these to Judith, Tybalt. She's very interested."

Tybalt looked at the books and his eyes lit up quite warmly.

"What did you think of them?"

"I was fascinated."

"We must find some more for her, Tabitha."

"That was what I was going to do."

We went into the drawing room and we talked . . . how we talked! I had not felt so *alive* since Evan Callum had left.

Tybalt walked back to the rectory with me, carrying the books; and he went on talking too, telling me of the adventures he had had; and how excited he had been when he had found certain things.

I listened avidly.

At the door of the rectory he said: "You really are very interested, aren't you?"

"Yes," I answered earnestly.

"Of course I always knew that you were interested in mummies."

We laughed. He said goodbye and that we must have another chat. "In the meantime," he said, "go on reading. I'm going to tell Tabitha what books to give you."

"Oh, thank you!" I said earnestly.

Dorcas must have seen us from one of the windows. "Wasn't that Tybalt Travers?" she said as I started to ascend the stairs.

I said it was; and because she waited for some explanation I went on: "I took some books back to Giza and he walked back with me."

"Oh!" was all she said.

The very next day she mentioned him again. "I've heard that they're expecting a match between Tybalt Travers and Theodosia."

I felt sick. I hope I didn't show it.

"Well," went on Dorcas cautiously, "it's to be expected. The Traverses and the Bodreans have been friends for years. I'm sure Sir Ralph would like to see the families united."

No, I thought. Never. Silly little Theodosia! It wasn't possible.

But of course I knew that it was highly probable.

Oliver Shrimpton had an opportunity of a living in Dorset. Dorcas and Alison were very upset.

"What we shall do without you, Oliver, I can't imagine," said Alison.

"You've been wonderful," Dorcas told him.

He went to see the Bishop, and I have never seen Dorcas and Alison quite so happy as they were when he came back.

I was in my room reading when they came in. "He's refused it," they said.

I said, "Who?"

"Oliver."

"But what has he refused?"

"I don't believe you're listening."

"It takes a little time to tear oneself away from

ancient Egypt to the rectory of St. Erno's."

"You get too deep into those books. I don't think it's good for you. But Oliver has been to see the Bishop and refused the living. He has explained that he wishes to stay here, and the understanding is that when Father retires he will become rector here."

"That's wonderful news," I said. "Now we shan't have to worry about losing him."

"He must be very fond of us," said Dorcas, "to do so much for us."

"Fond of some of us," said Alison significantly.

Evan Callum came down to stay at Giza House with the Traverses. I believe he was invited quite often to Keverall Court.

He called at the rectory to see me and we had a very interesting talk. He told me I had been his most promising pupil and it was a great shame that I had not been able to take up the subject in earnest.

Miss Graham found another post and left; and then lessons were over. It was quite clear that I was never going to be a musician; but I didn't need that excuse now to go to Giza House. I could go into the library there and select books and if they were not some of Sir Edward's precious ones, I could take them home.

I saw very little of Theodosia now. There were many parties at Keverall Court to which naturally I was not invited; and there was entertaining at Giza too which was quite different—although Tybalt and his father often went to Keverall and Sir Ralph and Lady Bodrean visited Giza—but I gathered from Tabitha that there were dinner parties when the conversation sparkled and of course it centered round the work of those guests—this fascinating absorption with the past.

Life was quite changed for me. I did some of the parish visiting with Dorcas and Alison. I took flowers from the garden to the sick; I read to those whose eyesight was failing; I took food to the bedridden and went off to the town to shop for them in the little trap we called the jingle—a two-wheeled vehicle drawn by our own Jorrocks, who was something between a horse and a pony.

I was settling down to becoming the typical rectory daughter. That Christmas Oliver and I brought in the yule log and I made the Christmas bush with Alison and Dorcas. This consisted of two wooden hoops fastened one into the other at right angles and we decorated this framework with evergreens—an old Cornish custom which we continued to follow rather than have the Christmas tree which, said some of the old folk, was a foreign invention. I went carol singing and when we called at Keverall Court we were invited in for hot pasties and saffron cake and a sip from the great wassailing bowl. I saw Theodosia and Hadrian in the great hall and I felt a nostalgia for the old days.

Soon after that Christmas we had a frosty snap—rare with us. The branches of trees were white with hoar frost and the children could even skate on the ponds. The Reverend James caught a cold and this was followed by a heart attack; and although he recovered slightly, within a week he was dead.

Dorcas and Alison were heartbroken. To me he had been remote for a long time. He had spent so much time in his bedroom; and even when he was in a room with us he scarcely spoke so it was like not having him there at all.

Cook said it was a Happy Release, because the poor Reverend Gentleman would never have been himself again.

And so the rectory blinds were drawn down and the day came when bells tolled and we lowered the Reverend James Osmond into the grave which Mr. Pegger had dug for him and then we went back to the rectory to eat cold ham and mourn.

Fear of the future mingled with the grief of Alison and Dorcas; but they were expectant, looking to me and to Oliver to bring about the obvious solution.

I shut myself in my room and thought about it. They wanted me to marry Oliver, who would become the rector in the Reverend James Osmond's place and we could all go on living under this roof as before.

How could I marry Oliver? I couldn't marry anyone but Tybalt. How could I tell Dorcas and Alison that? Moreover it was only in my wild and improbable dreams that that happy state of affairs could come about. I wanted to explain to them: I like Oliver. I know he is a good man. But you don't understand. I only have to say Tybalt's name and my heart beats faster. I know that he is unaware of me . . . in that way. I know that they will think marriage with Theodosia a good match—but I can't help it.

Oliver had changed since he had become rector. He was as kind as ever to us; but of course, as Dorcas said to Alison, unless something was *arranged,* they and I would have to move out.

Quite suddenly something was arranged. Poor Alison! Poor Dorcas!

It was Alison who broached the subject. I think Oliver had been trying to but was too kind to do so for fear it would appear that he was asking them to leave.

Alison said: "Now that we have a new rector it is time for us to go."

He looked very relieved, then he said: "I want to talk to you. I'm thinking of marrying."

Dorcas's eyes shone as though she were the bride-to-be.

"I could not of course ask the lady until I had something to offer her. And now I have . . . and I am indeed fortunate. She has accepted me as her future husband."

Alison was looking at me reproachfully. You might have told us! she was implying—so I couldn't have shown her how startled I was.

Oliver went on: "Miss Sabina Travers has promised to marry me."

We congratulated him—I wholeheartedly, Dorcas and Alison in a bewildered way.

As soon as I went to my room I knew they would come to me. They stood looking at me—dismay and anger on their faces.

"To think that all this time he was deceiving us."

"You are not being fair," I protested. "How has he deceived us?"

"Leading us to think . . ."

"But he did no such thing. Sabina! Well, yes, there was always a sort of rapport between them. She wasn't any better at Latin and Greek than I, but she's very pretty and feminine. And I think she'll do quite well as the rector's wife."

"She's far too frivolous. I don't think she's capable of carrying on a serious conversation."

"She'll be wonderful with the parishioners. She'll never be at a loss for words and she'll be able to listen to all their troubles without really hearing them. Think what an asset that will be."

"Judith, you don't seem to *care!*" cried Alison.

Dorcas said: "There's no need to put on a brave face with us, dear."

I burst out laughing. "Listen to me, both of you. I wouldn't have married Oliver if he'd asked me. He's been too much like my brother. I'm fond of him; I like Sabina. Do believe me when I say I could never have married him, convenient as it would have been."

Then I went to them and hugged them both, the way I used to do when I was younger.

"Dear Dorcas and dear Alison, I'm so sorry. It's the end of the old life. We've got to leave the rectory. But even if I had been willing, Oliver had other plans, hadn't he?"

They were touched as always by my demonstrations of affection.

"Oh, it's not that," said Dorcas. "We were thinking of your happiness."

"And that could not be here," I said. Then I added: "Just think. Oliver and Sabina! Why he'll be Tybalt's brother-in-law!"

They looked at me in surprise as though to say What has that to do with our predicament?

Then Alison said: "Well, what we have to do is to start making plans at once."

So we made our plans.

The Reverend James Osmond had left very little money; there would be the tiniest of incomes for his daughters, but if they could find a reasonable cottage they could just about manage to exist.

As for me, I was dependent on them. They were happy to share everything they had with me but it would be far from an affluent existence.

"But it was always intended that I should be equipped to work if need be," I said.

"Well," admitted Dorcas, "that was one of the reasons why we were so pleased to be able to give you such a good education."

"We might hear of something congenial," suggested Alison.

It was no use sitting down waiting to hear. I promised myself and them that as soon as they were settled in their new home I would go and find a post.

I was uneasy—not at the prospect of working but of leaving St. Erno's. I pictured myself in some household far away from Giza House when I should quickly be forgotten by its inhabitants. And what should I do? Become a governess like Miss Graham? It was the kind of post for which I was most suited. Perhaps as I had had a classical education more advanced than most rectory girls, I might teach in a girls' school. It would be less stultifying than working in some household where I was not considered worthy to mix with the family and yet was that little bit above the servants, which made it impossible for them to accept me. What was there for a young well-educated woman to do in this day and age?

I could not bear to think of the future. I began to say to myself: If I had never found the bronze shield the Traverses might not have come to Giza House. I should never have met Tybalt, and Oliver would never have met Sabina. Oliver and I might in time have recognized what a convenient thing it would have been for us to marry and we might have done so. We might have had a peaceful, mildly happy life together as so many people do;

and I should have been spared the anguish of leaving everything that was important to me.

Sir Ralph came to the rescue. There was a cottage on his estate which was vacant and he would allow the Misses Osmond to have it for a peppercorn rent.

They were delighted. It had solved half the problem.

Sir Ralph was determined to be our benefactor. Lady Bodrean needed a companion—someone who would read to her whenever required to do so, assist her in her charities, give the help she needed when she entertained. In fact a secretary companion. Sir Ralph thought that I might be suitable for the post, and Lady Bodrean was ready to consider me.

Alison and Dorcas were delighted.

"After our disappointment everything is working out so well," they cried. "We have our cottage and it would be wonderful to have you not too far away. Just imagine, we should be able to see you frequently. Oh it would be wonderful . . . if . . . er . . . you could get along with Lady Bodrean."

"Ah, 'there's the rub,' " I quoted lightheartedly. But I felt far from that.

And not without reason. Lady Bodrean, I had always felt, had never really cared for me to join her daughter and nephew in the Keverall Court schoolroom. On the rare occasions when I had seen her I had been met by frosty stares.

She always reminded me of a ship, for with her voluminous petticoats and skirts which rustled as she walked she seemed to sail along without being aware of anyone in her path. I had never tried to ingratiate myself with her, being conscious of a certain antagonism. Now I was in a different position.

She received me in her private sitting room, a small apartment—as rooms went in Keverall Court—but it was about twice the size of the cottage rooms. It was over-crowded with furniture. On the mantelpiece were vases and ornaments very close together; there were cabinets filled with china and silver and a what-not in one corner of the room full of little china pieces. The chairs were covered by tapestry worked by Lady Bodrean herself. There were two firescreens also of tapestry and two stools. The frame with a new piece stood close to her chair and she was working at this when I was shown into her room.

She did not look up for quite a minute implying that she found her work more interesting than the new companion. It might have been disconcerting if I had been the timid sort.

Then: "Oh, it's Miss Osmond. You've come about the post. You may sit down."

I sat, my head high, the color in my cheeks.

"Your duties," she said, "will be to make yourself useful to me in any capacity which arises."

I said: "Yes, Lady Bodrean."

"You will look after my engagements, both social and philanthropic. You will read the papers to me each day. You will care for my two Pomeranians, Orange and Lemon." At the mention of their names the two dogs reclining on cushions on either side of her raised their heads and regarded me with contempt. Orange—or it might have been Lemon—barked; the other one sniffed. "Darlings," said Lady Bodrean with a tender smile, but her expression was immediately frosty when she turned back to me. "You will, of course, be available for anything I may require. Now I should like to hear you read a passage to me."

Opening *The Times* she handed it to me. I started to read of the resignation of Bismarck and the plan to cede Heligoland to Germany.

I was aware of her scrutinizing me as I read. She had a lorgnette attached to a gold chain about her waist and she quizzed me quite openly. The sort of treatment one must expect when one was about to become an employee, I supposed.

"Yes, that will do," she said in the middle of a sentence so that I knew that engaging a companion was of greater moment than the fate of Heligoland.

"I should like you to start . . . immediately. I hope that is convenient."

I said I should need a day or so to settle my affairs, though what affairs I was not sure. All I knew was that I wanted to postpone taking up my new post for I found the prospect depressing.

She graciously conceded that I might have the rest of that day and the next in which to prepare myself. The day after that she would expect me to take up my duties.

On the way back to the cottage—which had the delectable name of Rainbow Cottage although the only reason known for this was that the flowers which used to be grown in the garden were all the colors of the rainbow—I tried to think of the advantages of my new position, and told myself that while I was going to hate being employed by Lady Bodrean I would have opportunities of seeing Tybalt.

III   The Months of Bondage

My room at Keverall Court was close to that of Lady
Bodrean, in case she should want me at any time. It
was a pleasant enough room—all the rooms at Keverall
were gracious, even the smallest—with its paneled walls
and mullioned window. And from the window I could
see the roof of Giza House, by which I was foolishly
comforted.

I had not been in the house long when I came to the
conclusion that Lady Bodrean disliked me. She would
ring her bell quite often after I had retired for the night
and would tell me peevishly that she could not sleep. I
must make tea for her, or read to her until she dozed;
and I would often sit shivering because she liked a cold
bedroom, and she was comfortable enough under her
blankets while I was often in my dressing gown. She
was never satisfied with anything I did. If there was
nothing of which to complain she was silent; if there was
then she would refer to it over and over again.

Her personal maid Jane commiserated with me.

"Her ladyship seems to have it in for you," she admitted. "It's often like that. I've seen it before. A regular servant's got a sort of dignity. There's always housemaids or parlormaids or lady's maid wanted. But companions and such like—well that's up another street."

I suppose some natures could have borne it better than mine, but I had never been one to accept injustice; and in the old days when I had come to this house I had come on equal terms with Theodosia. It was very hard to accept the new position and it was only the alternative of banishment from St. Erno which made me stay on.

I took my meals alone in my room. During them I usually read the books I had borrowed from Giza House. I didn't see Tybalt during this time for he and his father had gone away for a while on some expedition into the Midlands, but Tabitha always had books for me.

She would say: "Tybalt thought this would interest you."

These books, my visits to Tabitha, and the knowledge that Dorcas and Alison were happily settled provided the only brightness in my life at that time.

I saw Theodosia now and then. She would have been quite pleasant to me if her mother would have allowed it. There was nothing malicious or proud about Theodosia. She was negative; she took her color from people about her. She would never be actively unkind, but at the same time she did little to alleviate my position. Perhaps she remembered the past when I had been inclined to bully her.

When I saw Sir Ralph he would ask me how I was getting on and he gave that amused look which I had seen so often. I could not say to him: "I dislike your wife and I would leave her tomorrow if I did not know that however unhappy I am here I should be far more so elsewhere."

I went to Rainbow Cottage to see Dorcas and Alison as often as I could. It was an interesting little place about three hundred years old, I think, and it had been built in the days when any family who could build a cottage in a night could claim the land on which it had been erected

as their own. It was the custom in those days to collect
bricks and tiles and to start building as soon as it was
dark and work through the night. Four walls and a roof
constituted a dwelling and that was done by morning. After
that, the place could be added to. That was what had
happened to Rainbow Cottage. When the Bodreans had
acquired the cottage they had used it for their dependents
and added to it considerably, but some of the old features
remained, such as the old talfat—a sort of ledge high
up on the wall on which children used to sleep and
which was reached by a ladder. Now it boasted a mod-
erately good kitchen with a cloam oven in which Dorcas
used to make the most delicious bread I had ever tasted;
then there was a copper in which they cooked the scalded
milk to make clotted cream. They were really very happy
in Rainbow Cottage with its pleasant little garden; though
of course they missed the spacious rectory.

I used to hate leaving them and going back to Keverall
Court and my onerous duties, and consoled myself by
doing malicious imitations of Lady Bodrean as I paraded
round the cottage sitting room brandishing an imaginary
lorgnette.

"And Sir Ralph," they asked timidly. "Do you see
much of him?"

"Very little. I'm not exactly one of the family, you
know."

"It's a shame," said Dorcas hotly; but Alison silenced
her.

"When you were having lessons there it was so different," complained Dorcas.

"Yes, I never thought then that I wasn't one of them.
But then I hadn't a post, and it was amazing how little
I was aware of Lady Bodrean . . . fortunately."

"It may change," hazarded Alison.

I was optimistic by nature, and even at that dreary time
I had my dreams. The dinner party—one of the guests,
a lady, was unable to come. They could not sit down with
thirteen. Very well, there is the companion. "She's quite
presentable. After all she was educated here." And so I
went down to dine in a gown which Theodosia found for

me—she had looked frightful in it but it was just right for me—and there I was "Next to someone you know," whispered Theodosia. "Oh!" cried Tybalt. "How delightful to see you!" And we talked and everyone was aware of how absorbed he was by his neighbor at the dining table and afterwards he would not leave her side. "How glad I am," he said, "that Lady X . . . Y . . . Z . . ." What did her name matter? "How glad I am that she could not come tonight."

Dreams! Dreams! But what else was there for me during that unsatisfactory period of my life?

I had read until I was hoarse.

"Your voice is not good today, Miss Osmond. Oh dear, how tiresome! One of the chief duties I look for is your reading."

She would sit there and in and out went the needle with its trail of red or blue or violet wool and I was sure she was not listening to what I was reading. If only I could have read from one of the books I brought from Giza House! Sometimes I had the mischievous thought that I would substitute one and see whether she knew the difference.

Sometimes she would lay aside her tapestry and close her eyes. I would go on reading, unsure whether she was awake or not. Sometimes I stopped to see if she had noticed. Often I caught her sleeping; but then she would catch me for she would awake suddenly and demand to know why I was not reading.

I would say meekly: "I thought you were sleeping, Lady Bodrean. I was afraid I should disturb you."

"Nonsense," she would retort. "Pray go on and *I* will say when we shall stop."

She kept me reading on that day until my eyes were tired and my voice weary. I began to think of escaping at any price, but I always came back to the thought of going away and never seeing Tybalt again.

Orange and Lemon turned out to be blessings for they needed daily exercise and this gave me the opportunity to get away from the house and it was easy to slip over to Giza House and have a chat with Tabitha.

One day I called and knew immediately that something exciting had happened. She took me into the drawing room and told me that Sir Edward was planning an expedition to Egypt. It was going to be one of his most ambitious efforts. She hoped to accompany the party. "Now that Sabina is married," she said, "there is no need for me to stay here."

"You will have some job to do?"

"Not an official job, of course, but I can make myself useful. I can housekeep if that should be necessary and I have picked up quite a lot. I can be useful in a fetch-and-carry sort of way as amateurs are."

I looked at her ecstatically. "How I envy you!"

She smiled that gentle sweet smile of hers. "Lady Bodrean can be trying I daresay."

I sighed.

Then she went on to talk about the expedition.

"Will Tybalt be accompanying his father?" I asked.

"Indeed yes. It's going to be one of the most important missions so far. I gather the archaeological world is talking of nothing else. Of course you know that Sir Edward is perhaps one of the greatest men of his profession in the world."

I nodded. "And Tybalt is following in his footsteps."

She looked at me shrewdly and I wondered whether I had betrayed the state of my feelings.

"He is his father all over again," she said. "Men such as they are have one great passion in their lives . . . their work. It's something that those about them must always remember."

I could never resist talking about Tybalt.

"Sir Edward seems so much more remote. He hardly seems to see anyone."

"He does come down from the clouds now and then . . . or should I say up from the soil. One should never expect to know men like them in a few years. They're a lifetime study."

"Yes," I said. "I suppose that's what makes them interesting."

She smiled gently. "Sometimes," she went on, "I have thought that it would be well for such men to live the lives of hermits or monks. Their work should be their families."

"Did you know Lady Travers?"

"At the end of her life, yes."

"And you think Sir Edward is happier as a widower than he was as a husband?"

"Did I give that impression? I came to them as a rather privileged housekeeper. We had known them for some years and when the need arose . . . I took this post as you have taken yours."

"And Lady Travers died after that?"

"Yes."

I wanted to know what Tybalt's mother was like, and as Dorcas and Alison had often told me, I was far from tactful. So I blundered on: "It wasn't a very happy marriage, was it?"

She looked startled. "Well . . . They had little in common and as I said men like Sir Edward perhaps don't make model husbands."

I was certain then that she was warning me.

She said brightly: "You remember Evan Callum."

"Of course."

"He's coming to visit us. I hear that Hadrian will be returning also. They'll be here soon, both of them. They'll be interested to hear about Sir Edward's expedition."

I stayed talking although I knew I shouldn't. I wanted to glean all I could. Tabitha was quite animated.

"It would be wonderful if you could come," she said. "I am sure you would prefer it to looking after that not-very-agreeable lady."

"Oh, if only I could."

"Never mind. Perhaps some day . . ."

I went back to Keverall Court in a daze. I was dreaming again. That was my only comfort. I dreamed that Tabitha was taken ill; she couldn't go. Someone must take her place, said Sir Edward. "I know," cried Tybalt. "What about Miss Osmond? She was always interested."

How ridiculous and how unkind to wish an illness on Tabitha!

"I am surprised, Miss Osmond," said Lady Bodrean. "I have been ringing my bell for half an hour."

"I'm sorry. I forgot the time."

"Forgot the time! You are not here to forget time, Miss Osmond. You are not paid for that, you know."

Oh, why didn't I tell the disagreeable old woman that I would serve her no longer!

Simply because, said my logical self, if you did you would have to do something. You would have to go away and how would you ever see Tybalt if you did?

I had somehow betrayed my inability to accept my position with resignation and this was something Lady Bodrean seemed to have made up her mind to enforce.

She reminded me far more than was necessary that I was a paid servant. She tried to curtail my liberty whenever possible. She would send me on an errand and time me. She would make me walk round the gardens with her carrying her basket while she cut flowers; she would tell me to arrange them—and my efforts in this artistic endeavor had always amused Dorcas and Alison. They used to say, "If anyone can *dis*arrange a bowl of flowers, that is Judith." At the rectory it was a joke; here it was a serious matter. If she could humiliate me, she did; and she was seeking and finding many opportunities.

At least, I said to myself, this has taught me what a happy home Dorcas and Alison gave me and I ought to be forever grateful for that.

I shall never forget the day she told me that there was to be a ball at Keverall Court.

"Of course a young lady in my daughter's position must be brought out formally. I am sure you realize that, Miss Osmond, because although you yourself are not in the same position, you did learn something of gracious living when you were allowed to take lessons here."

"Graciousness is something that I miss nowadays," I retorted.

She misunderstood. "You were very fortunate to be

allowed to glimpse it for a while. *I* always think it is a mistake to educate people beyond their stations."

"Sometimes," I said, "it enables the sons and daughters of erudite churchmen to be of use to their betters."

"I am glad to see you take that view, Miss Osmond. I have to confess you do not always show such becoming humility."

She was an exceedingly stupid woman. I had learned that Sir Ralph had married her for her fortune. Why he should have done so was beyond my understanding when he was a rich man in his own right. But what I could understand was why he had acquired his reputation for seeking consolation elsewhere.

"Now," she went on, "there will be a great deal for you to do. Invitations to be drawn up and sent out. You've no idea, Miss Osmond, what giving a ball like this entails."

"I can hardly be expected to," I replied, "coming from such a stratum of society."

"Dear me no. It will be an education for you to learn. Such experience for one in your position is so useful."

"I shall do my *humble* best," I retorted with irony.

But that, of course, was lost on Lady Bodrean.

Jane, Lady Bodrean's personal maid, winked at me.

"A nice cup of tea?" she said. "I've got it all ready."

She had a little spirit lamp in her room, which she had made very comfortable.

I sat down and she poured out.

"My word, she's got it in for you."

"I gather my company doesn't give her much pleasure. I wonder she doesn't allow herself the treat of being rid of it."

"I know her. She's enjoying herself. She likes tormenting people. She was always like that. I've been with her since before she married. She's got worse."

"It couldn't have been very comfortable for you."

"Oh, I know how to handle her. Sugar, Miss Osmond?"

"Thank you. Yes," I said thoughtfully, "she does seem to dislike me more than is warranted. Mind you, I am ready to admit I don't perform my duties with great efficiency. I can't imagine why she doesn't do what she is always hinting she will. Dismiss me."

"She doesn't want that. Who's she going to torment then?"

"There's a fairly large staff to choose from. Surely from among you all she could find some highly torment-able type."

"Oh you joke about it, Miss Osmond. Sometimes I think you're going to explode though."

"So do I," I said.

"I remember you coming here for your lessons. We used to say, 'My word, that one's got more spirits than all the rest of them put together. Regular little firebrand!' "

"And now you see the metamorphosis of Judith Osmond."

"Eh? I've seen it happen before. The nursery governess before that Miss Graham. Nice spirited sort of girl, she was. But she hadn't been here long when things started to happen. Sir Ralph had his eyes on her and when Lady Bodrean got to work . . . My word, she changed. In the old days Sir Ralph, he were a one. No woman safe from him. He's changed a lot too. He's got quieter. I've seen him have some funny dizzy turns too. Slowed him down a bit. There've been some scandals." She came closer to me and her lively brown eyes were alight with pleasure. "Women," she said. "Couldn't leave a pretty girl alone. The fur used to fly. Many times I've heard . . . being in the next room, you know. Couldn't help but hear even if I tried not to."

I could picture her, ear to keyhole while a younger Don Juan of a Sir Ralph stood accused before his wronged wife.

"After a while she seemed to make up her mind that there was nothing she could do about it. He'd go his way, she'd go hers. He wanted a son, of course. And there wasn't another child after Miss Theodosia. So Mas-ter Hadrian came to live here. But she, her ladyship, seemed to be more of a tartar every day; and once she gets her knife into someone . . . she's going to use it."

I said: "I should get out, I suppose."

Jane moved farther towards me and whispered confidentially. "You could find a better place. I've thought about this. What about Miss Theodosia?"

"What of her?"

"This ball . . . well, it's a sort of coming out. All the fine rich gentlemen of the neighborhood will be invited. Then they'll have balls and such like goings on. You know what it's all leading up to."

"Miss Theodosia is being paraded before them, in all her charms, and by no means the least of these is the nice golden dowry glittering round her neck. 'Young gentleman, show your credentials and make your bid.' "

"You always had your answer, didn't you? I used to say to Miss Graham, 'My goodness, that one's got a bit of lip, she has.' But what I'm getting at is this. Before long they'll find a husband for Miss Theodosia, and then you're her friend . . . so . . ."

"I, her friend. Please don't let Lady Bodrean hear you call me that. I'm sure she would be most indignant."

"Now you're getting bitter. It's all along of once being treated like one of them and now finding yourself here in a paid job. You have to be clever. Now you and Theodosia were together as children. You were the one who used to order *her* about. Theodosia's not like her mother. Suppose you remind her of your friendship."

"Ingratiate myself with the daughter of the house?"

"You could become friends with her again and when she marries . . . you see what I mean? Miss Theodosia wants a companion and who better than her old friend. What do you think of it?"

"Machiavellian!" I said.

"You can laugh. But I wouldn't like to think of spending *my* life looking after an old tartar like that."

"Suppose Theodosia doesn't marry?"

"Theodosia not marry! Of course she will. Why they've got the man for her already. I heard Sir Ralph talking to her ladyship about it. Quite a to do there was. She said: 'You've got an obsession with those people. I think you wanted Hadrian for Sabina.' "

"Oh?" I said faintly.

"I wouldn't mind taking a bet with you, Miss Osmond, that before the year's out the engagement will be announced. After all there's a title. Money, well I'm not so sure of that, but Miss Theodosia will have enough, won't she? When her father dies she'll inherit everything I reckon. Why she'll be one of the richest young ladies in the country. Of course, I wouldn't say they're exactly poor, but money's always useful and they say that *he* has poured a fortune into this work of his. A funny way of squandering your money I must say. When you think of what you can do with it . . . and it all goes in digging up the ground in foreign places. They say some of those places are so hot you can hardly bear it."

I said, although I knew the answer already: "So for Theodosia they've chosen . . . ?"

"The son, of course. Mr. Tybalt Travers. Oh yes, he's the one they've chosen for Theodosia."

I could scarcely bear to sit there and listen to her chatter.

Sir Edward and Tybalt had returned to Giza House and they came to dine at Keverall Court. I contrived to be in the hall when they arrived, pretending to arrange some flowers.

Tybalt said: "It's Miss Osmond, isn't it?" As though he had to look twice to make sure. "How are you?"

"I'm the companion now, you know."

"Yes, I heard. Are you still reading?"

"Avidly. Mrs. Grey is so helpful."

"Good. Father, this is Miss Osmond."

Sir Edward gave me his vague look.

"She's the one who dressed up as the mummy. She wanted to know what it felt like to be embalmed and placed in a sarcophagus. She's read several of your books." Now Sir Edward's attention was on me. His eyes twinkled. I think the mummy adventure amused him. He was more like Tybalt now.

I wished that I could have stayed there talking to them. Lady Bodrean had appeared at the top of the staircase.

I wondered whether she had heard my voice.

"My *dear* Sir Edward . . . and Tybalt!" She swept down the stairs. "I thought I heard you talking to the companion."

I went to my room then and stayed there all the evening. A respite from my tyrant because she was busy with her guests. I pictured them at the dinner table and Theodosia looking pretty in pink satin—gentle, amenable, with an immense fortune which would be so useful in financing expeditions to exotic places.

I don't think I ever felt quite so hopeless as at that moment, and with the recent encounter with Tybalt fresh in my mind—which confirmed everything I had ever thought him—I was more certain than ever that he was the only man for me. I asked myself whether I should offer my resignation without delay.

But, of course, that was not my nature. Until he was married to Theodosia I would continue to dream . . . and hope.

I walked the dogs over to Giza House and as I did so a voice called "Judith."

I turned and there was Evan Callum coming out of Giza House.

"Judith," he cried, his hand outstretched to take mine, "this is a pleasure."

"I heard you were coming," I said. "It is so good to see you."

"And how is everything with you?"

"Changed," I said.

"And not for the better?"

"The rector died. You know that Oliver married Sabina, and I am now companion to Lady Bodrean."

He grimaced.

"Ah," I said with a smile, "I see you have an inkling of what that means."

"I worked in the house once, you remember, as a sort of tutor to you all. Fortunately my work did not come under her jurisdiction. Poor Judith!"

"I tell myself fifty times a day not to be sorry for

myself. So if *I'm* not you must not be."

"But I am. You were the best of my pupils. You had such an enthusiasm; and that is one of the greatest assets in this profession."

"Are you accompanying them on this expedition?"

"Unfortunately, no. I'm not experienced enough for such an honor. There'll be much coming and going between Keverall and Giza, I believe. Sir Ralph is being persuaded to help finance the project."

"He was always vitally interested. I hope they'll succeed in getting what they want."

"Tybalt has no doubt of it." He looked round him: "How this brings back the old days. You, Hadrian, Theodosia, Sabina. Oddly enough the one who was least interested was Sabina. Have they changed?"

"Sabina has become the rector's wife. I see very little of her. My duties do not give me much time. I visit Dorcas and Alison when I can manage it and I come over here to see Mrs. Grey who has been so kind in lending me books."

"On our subject of course."

"Of course."

"Good. I could not bear for *you* to tire. I hear Hadrian will be home at the end of the week."

"I didn't know. I am not told such things."

"Poor Judith. Life's unfair sometimes."

"Perhaps I've had my share of luck. Did you know that I was found on a train?"

"An abandoned child!"

"Not exactly. It was in an accident. My parents were killed and no one claimed me. I might have gone to an orphanage . . . never have met any of you . . . never have found a piece of a Bronze Age shield and never read any of the books from Giza House."

"I always thought you were the rector's distant cousin."

"Many people did. Dorcas and Alison thought it would be kinder to let it be known that I was some sort of distant relation. But I was unknown. And my great piece of luck was that they took me in and life was wonderful until now. Perhaps I have to pay now for that marvelous piece of luck I had in the beginning. Do you think life works out like that?"

"No," he said. "This is just a phase. They come to all of us. But Theodosia's at Keverall, and she's a friend of yours. She would never be unkind, I'm sure."

"No, but I see little of her. I am always kept so busy dancing attendance on her Mamma."

He gave me a compassionate look.

"Poor Judith," he said, "perhaps it will not always be so. I shall hope things change for you. We must meet . . . often."

"Oh, but the social barriers will be set up between us because when you visit Keverall Court you will come as a guest."

"I should soon leap over any barrier they put between us," he assured me.

He said he would walk with me and I was greatly comforted by his return to St. Erno's.

Hadrian arrived at the end of the week. I was in the garden whither I had been sent to gather roses when he saw me and called to me.

"Judith!" He took my hand and we studied each other.

Hadrian had become good-looking—or perhaps he had always been so and I had not particularly noticed before. His thick brown hair grew too low on his forehead—or did I think it was too low because one of Tybalt's most striking features was his high forehead? There was something inherently pleasant in Hadrian and however bitter he became the twinkle was never far from his blue-grey eyes. He was of medium height and broad-shouldered; and when he greeted me, his eyes always lit up in a manner which I found comforting. I felt that Hadrian was one of the people on whom I could rely.

"You've become a scholar, Hadrian," I said.

"You've become a flatterer. And a companion! To my aunt. How could you, Judith!"

"It's very easily explained. If one does not inherit money one needs to earn it. I am doing precisely that."

"But you a companion! Cutting roses . . . I bet you always cut the wrong ones!"

"How right you are! These red ones, I am sure, should have been yellow. But I have the consolation of knowing that had I picked yellow, red would have been the chosen color."

"My aunt's a tyrant! I know. I don't think it's right that you should be doing this. Who suggested it?"

"Your uncle. And we have to be truly grateful to him for had he not arranged that I should come here, I should be cutting roses or performing some such duty for some other tyrant possibly miles from here—so I shouldn't be chatting with you, nor have seen Evan and er . . ."

"It's a shame," said Hadrian hotly. "And you of all people. You were always such a bully."

"I know. It's just retribution. The bully now bullied. Hoist with her own petard. Still, it's pleasant to know that some members of the household don't regard me as a pariah now that I have to perform the humiliating task of earning a living."

Theodosia came into the garden. She was in white muslin with pale blue dots and she wore a white straw hat with blue ribbons. She's grown quite pretty, I realized.

"I was thinking that it's like old times now we're all together," said Hadrian. "Evan and Tybalt . . ." I noticed that Theodosia blushed slightly, and I thought of Jane's words. It was true then. No, it couldn't be! Not Tybalt and Theodosia. It was incongruous. But she was almost pretty; she was suitable; and she was an heiress. Surely Tybalt would not marry for money. But of course he would. It was the natural order of things. Sabina had not married for money, for Oliver as a rector would have little of that useful commodity. How we had changed, all of us. Frivolous Sabina becoming the rector's wife; plain Theodosia to marry my wonderful Tybalt; and myself, the proud one, the one who had taken charge of the school room, to be the companion whose daily bread was service and humiliation.

"Evan, Tybalt, myself, you, Judith, and Sabina and Oliver in their rectory," Hadrian was saying.

"Yes," said Theodosia. She looked at me rather shyly apologetic because she had seen so little of me since I had come to Keverall Court. "It's . . . it's nice to have Judith here."

"Is it?" I said.

"But of course. You were always one of us, weren't you?"

"But now I am the companion merely."

"Oh, you've been listening to Mamma."

"I have to. It's part of the job."

"Mamma can be difficult."

"You don't have to be with her all the time," comforted Hadrian.

"There seems very little time when I'm not."

"We'll have to change that, won't we, Theodosia?"

Theodosia nodded and smiled.

These encounters lifted my spirits. It was to some extent a return to the old ways.

There was a great deal of talk about the coming ball.

"This will be the biggest we've had for years," Jane told me. "Miss Theodosia's coming out." She gave me her wink. "Timed, you see, when all these people are here. Lady B. is hoping there'll be an announcement before they go off to Egypt."

"Do you think that Mr. Travers would take his bride with him?"

"There won't be time for that by all accounts. There'll have to be the sort of wedding that takes months to prepare for, I reckon. Her ladyship wouldn't stand for anything else. No quiet little wedding like Sabina and the new rector had. Lady B. wouldn't let her only daughter go like that."

"Well," I said, "we haven't got them betrothed yet, have we?"

"Any day now, mark my words."

I began to believe she was right when I talked to Theodosia, who since the return of Hadrian was seeing far more of me than she had before. She seemed as though she wanted to make up to me for previously keeping out of my way.

The only time Lady Bodrean was the least bit affable to me was when she talked of Theodosia's coming out ball; I knew at once that she was hoping to make me envious. Theodosia could have had all the balls she wanted if she had left me Tybalt.

"You might go along to the sewing room," Lady Bodrean told me, "and give Sarah Sloper a hand. There are fifty yards of lace to be sewn onto my daughter's ball gown. And in an hour's time I shall be ready for the reading and don't forget before you go, to walk Orange and Lemon."

Sarah Sloper was too good a dressmaker to allow me to put a stitch into her creation. There it was on the table —a froth of soft blue silk chiffon with the fifty yards of pale blue lace.

Theodosia was there for a fitting, so I helped get her into the dress. She was going to look lovely in it, I thought with a pang. I could imagine her floating round the ballroom in the arms of Tybalt.

"Do you like it, Judith?" she asked.

"The color is most becoming."

"I love dancing," she said. She waltzed round and I felt we were back in the schoolroom. I went to her and bowed. "Miss Bodrean, may I have the pleasure of this dance?"

She made a deep curtsy. I seized her and we danced round the room while Sarah Sloper watched us with a grin.

"How delightful you look tonight, Miss Bodrean."

"Thank you, sir."

"How gracious of you to thank me for the gifts nature has bestowed on you."

"Oh Judith you haven't changed a bit. I wish . . ."

Sarah Sloper had jumped to her feet suddenly and was bobbing a curtsy for Sir Ralph was standing in the doorway watching us dance.

Our dance came to an immediate halt. I wondered

what he would say to see the companion dancing so familiarly with his daughter.

He was clearly not annoyed: "Rather graceful, didn't you think, Sarah?" he said.

"Why yes, sir, indeed, sir," stammered Sarah.

"So that's your ball dress, is it?"

"Yes, Father."

"And what about Miss Osmond, eh? Has she a ball dress?"

"I have not," I said.

"And why not?"

"Because a person in my position has no great use for such a garment."

I saw the familiar wag of the chin.

"Oh yes," he said, "you're the companion now. I hear of you from Lady Bodrean."

"Then I doubt you hear anything to my advantage."

I don't know why I was speaking to him in that way. It was an irresistible impulse even though I knew that I was being what would be termed insolent from one in my position and was imperiling my job.

"Very little," he assured me, with a lugubrious shake of the head. "In fact nothing at all."

"I feared so."

"Now do you? That's a change. I always had the impression that you were a somewhat fearless young lady." His bristling brows came together. "I don't see anything of you. Where do you get to?"

"I don't move in your circles, sir," I replied, realizing now that he at least bore me no malice and was rather amused at my pert retorts.

"I begin to think that's rather a pity."

"Father, do you like my gown?" asked Theodosia.

"Very pretty. Blue, is it?"

"Yes, Father."

He turned to me. "If you had one what color would it be?"

"It would be green, Father," said Theodosia. "It was always Judith's favorite color."

"That's said to be unlucky," he replied. "Or it was in

my day. They used to say 'Green on Monday, Black on Friday.' But I'll swear Miss Osmond's not superstitious."

"Not about colors," I said. "I might be about some things."

"Doesn't do to think you're unlucky," he said. "Otherwise you will be."

Then he went out, his chin wagging.

Theodosia looked at me with raised eyebrows. "Now why did Father come in here?"

"You should know more about his habits than I do."

"I believe he's quite excited about my ball. Judith, Mrs. Grey was saying that you were reading books, some of which had been written by Sir Edward Travers. You must know quite a lot now about archaeology."

"Enough to know that I'm very ignorant about it. We both have a smattering, haven't we? We got that from Evan Callum."

"Yes," she said. "I wish I knew more."

She was animated. "I'm going to start reading. You must tell me what books you've had."

I understood of course. She was desperately anxious to be able to talk knowledgeably to Tybalt.

The invitations had been sent out; I had listed the guests and ticked them off when the acceptances came in. I had helped arrange what flowers would be brought from the greenhouses to decorate the ballroom, for it was October and the gardens could scarcely supply what was needed. I had compiled the dance programs and chosen the pink-and-blue pencils and the silken cords which would be attached to them. For the first time Lady Bodrean seemed pleased and I knew it was only because she wanted me to know what care went into the launching into society of a well-bred girl. She may have noticed that I was downcast at times and this put her into a good humor so that I wanted to shout at her: "I care nothing for these grand occasions; Theodosia is welcome to them. My melancholy has nothing to do with that."

I went to Rainbow Cottage when I had an hour or so to spare. Dorcas and Alison always made a great fuss of me; they tried to keep my spirits up with griddle cakes which I used to be rather greedy about as a child.

They wanted to hear all about the ball.

"It's a shame they don't ask you, Judith," said Dorcas.

"Why should they? Employees are not asked to family balls surely."

"It's different in your case. Weren't you in the schoolroom with them?"

"That, as Lady Bodrean would inform you, is something for which to feel gratitude and not an excuse for looking for further favors."

"Oh Judith, is it really unbearable?"

"Well, the truth is that she is so obnoxious that I get a certain delight in doing battle. Also she is really rather stupid so that I am able to get in quite a lot of barbs of which she is unaware."

"If it is too bad, you must leave."

"I may be asked to. I must warn you that I expect dismissal daily."

"Well, dear, don't worry. We can manage here. And you'd find something else very quickly I'm sure."

Sometimes they talked about village affairs. They worked a good deal for the church. Having done so all their lives they were well equipped for the task. Sabina was not really very practical, they whispered, and although she could chatter away to people, a little more than that was expected of a rector's wife. As for Oliver he was quite competent.

I reminded them that they used to say he had carried the parish on his shoulders when their father was alive.

That was true, they agreed grudgingly. I knew they found it hard to forgive poor Oliver for not marrying me and even more difficult to forgive Sabina for being the chosen one.

It was comforting to remember that they were there in the background of my life.

There was a great deal of coming and going between Giza House and Keverall Court. As Sir Ralph was not feeling very well, Tybalt and his father visited him frequently. They were going into the details of the expedition.

I quite shamelessly tried to be where I might catch a glimpse of them. Even Sir Edward knew me now and would give me his absent-minded smile.

Tybalt exchanged a word or two with me—usually asking what I was reading. I longed to hear from him about the expedition but naturally I couldn't ask him about that.

Two days before the ball a most extraordinary thing happened.

When I emerged from Lady Bodrean's apartment and was about to go for my daily walk I found Theodosia in the corridor. I fancied she had been looking for me.

She looked excited.

"Hello, Judith," she said, and there was a little lilt in her voice.

"Were you waiting for me?" I asked.

"Yes, I've something to tell you."

My heartbeats quickened; my spirits sank. This is it, I thought. Tybalt has asked her to marry him. The engagement will be announced at the ball.

She slipped her arm through mine. "Let's go to your room," she said. "You will never guess what it is," she went on.

I thought: I can't bear it. I've imagined it so many times, but I know I can't bear it. I'll have to go away . . . at once. I'll go and tell Dorcas and Alison and then I'll get a post far away and never see any of them again.

I stammered: "I know. You . . . you're engaged."

She stopped short and flushed hotly, so I knew that although this might not be the surprise she had for me now, it was coming soon.

"You always thought you knew everything, didn't you? Well, clever Judith is wrong this time."

Clever Judith was never more delighted to be wrong.

She threw open the door of my room and walked in; I followed shutting the door behind me. She went to my cupboard and opened the door. Hanging there was a green chiffon evening dress.

"What is it!" I cried in astonishment.

"It's your ball dress, Judith."

"Mine! How could it be." I went to it, felt the lovely soft material, took the dress down and held it against me.

"It's absolutely right," declared Theodosia. "Put it on. I long to see you in it."

"First, how did it get there?"

"I put it there."

"But where did it come from?"

"Oh do try it on first and I'll explain."

"No. I must know."

"Oh, you're maddening! I long to see that it fits. Father said you were to have it."

"But . . . why?"

"He said: 'Cinderella must go to the ball.' "

"Meaning the companion?"

"You remember he saw us dancing. That day he said to me, 'That girl Judith Osmond, she's to go to the ball.' I said, 'Mamma would never hear of it,' and he said, 'Then don't tell her.' "

I began to laugh. I saw myself at the ball dancing with Tybalt. "But it's impossible. She will never allow it."

"This is my father's house, you know."

"But I am employed by your mother."

"She won't dare go against him."

"What an unwelcome guest I should be."

"Only by one. The rest of us all want you to go. Myself, Evan, Hadrian, Tybalt . . ."

"Tybalt! . . ."

"Well, of course he doesn't know yet, but I am sure he would if he did. Hadrian knows though. He's very amused, and we're all going to have a lot of fun hiding you from Mamma, if that's possible."

"I don't suppose it is for a moment. I shall be ordered out of the ballroom within an hour."

"Not if you come as my father's guest, which you will do."

I began to laugh.

"I knew you'd enjoy it."

"Tell me what happened."

"Well, Father said you'd always been a lively girl, and he wished I'd shown more of your spirit. He was afraid you didn't have much of a life with Mamma and he wanted you to go to the ball. That's why he wanted to know what color dress. It was secret with Sarah Sloper. I chose the material and Sarah used me as a model. You're a bit taller than I and just a little thinner. We worked on that. And I'm absolutely sure it's a perfect fit. Do put it on now."

I did so. The transformation was miraculous. It was indeed my color. I let down my thick dark hair, and with my eyes shining and color in my cheeks I would have been beautiful I thought but for my nose which was too large. Hadrian always used to laugh at my nose. "It's a forceful one," he said. "It betrays your character. No one who was meek could ever have such a nose. Your powers, dear Judith, are not in your stars but in your nose." I giggled. In such a beautiful gown I could forget that offending feature.

"You look quite Spanish now," said Theodosia. "Your hair ought to be piled high on your head and you should have a Spanish comb. You'd look marvelous then. I wish it were a masked ball. Then it would be so much easier to hide you from Mamma. But she will know it is Father's wish and will say nothing . . . at the ball at least. She wouldn't want a scene there."

"The storm will come later."

I didn't care. I would face that. I was going to the ball. I should have a little dance program with a pink cord and pencil and I would keep it forever, because I was certain that Tybalt's initials would be on it.

I seized Theodosia in my arms and we danced round the bedroom.

The night of the ball had come. Thank Heaven, Lady Bodrean would be too busy to want to be bothered with me. "My goodness," Jane had said, "we're going to have a session. There's her hair to do and I've got to get her into her gown. When it comes to what jewels she's to wear it'll be this and that—and that's no good and what about this. It's a good thing I know how to handle her."

So I was free to dress myself in the close-fitting green

satin sheath over which were yards and yards of flowing silk chiffon. Nothing could have been chosen to suit me better. And when I had come up to dress I found that Theodosia had laid the Spanish comb on my dressing table. Hadrian was there to support me too. I felt that the position had changed since he had come back. I really had friends in the house now.

And on this night of the ball I prepared to enjoy myself.

Sir Ralph and Lady Bodrean stood at the head of the great staircase to receive their guests. Naturally I did not present myself. But what fun it was to mingle with the guests who were so numerous that I was sure I could escape Lady Bodrean's eye. In any case she would hardly recognize me in my finery.

I danced with Hadrian who said it was rather like some of the tricks we used to get up to in our youth.

"We were always the allies," he said, "you and I, Judith."

It was true.

"I'm sorry," said Hadrian, "that it's my aunt you have to work for."

"Not more sorry than I. Yet it gives me a chance to be at Keverall."

"You love the old house, don't you?"

"It seems like part of my life. Don't forget I was here almost every day."

"I feel the same. Theodosia's lucky. It'll be hers one day."

"You sound envious."

"I sound as I feel then. You see I'm a bit of a charity boy myself."

"Oh, no, Hadrian. You're Sir Ralph's nephew, almost a son."

"Not quite."

"Then, I tell you what you should do," I said lightly, "marry Theodosia."

"My cousin!"

"Why not? Cousins marry often. It's a very useful way of keeping the property well within the family."

"You don't think she'd have me, do you? I fancy now

her gaze is fixed in another direction."

"Is that so?"

"Have you noticed her being eagerly intent every time anyone mentions the subject?"

"What subject?"

"Archaeology. She's so excited about this expedition. You'd think she was going on it."

"Trying to impress someone. Perhaps it's you! After all it is your subject."

"Oh no. Nothing of the sort. I'm not the chosen one."

I couldn't bear to talk of Theodosia and Tybalt so I said quickly: "Don't you wish you were going out to Egypt with the party?"

"I'd enjoy it in a way. I hear that Sir Edward is very much a lone wolf. He keeps his team in the dark. It's the way some people work. I was talking to Evan about it. We should have been flattered if we'd been asked to join the party of course. But at our stage it would only be in a minor capacity."

"And Tybalt?"

"Well, he's the great man's son. I daresay he won't be kept entirely in the dark."

"I suppose one day he'll be as great as his father."

"He has the same passionate absorption."

"I saw him dancing with Theodosia but I didn't see Sir Edward."

"He'll probably look in later."

The band had stopped; the dance was over. Hadrian led me to a seat sheltered by pots of palms.

"I feel like a fox in his lair," I said.

"You mean a vixen," corrected Hadrian.

"I admit to a kindred spirit with that creature on certain occasions but at the moment I'm far too mellow."

Evan came up with Theodosia and sat down with us. Theodosia looked at me in my green dress with great pleasure.

"You are enjoying the ball, Judith?" she asked anxiously.

I assured her I was.

Then Tybalt appeared. I thought he had come to claim Theodosia but instead he sat down. He did not seem the least bit surprised to see me.

Evan then said that he believed Theodosia had promised him this dance. They went off and Hadrian said he had a partner to find; that left Tybalt and myself alone.

"Are you enjoying the dance?" I asked.

"It's not much in my line, you know."

"I saw you dancing a little while ago."

"Most ungracefully."

"Adequately," I assured him. "You will be gone very soon," I went on. "How you must be longing to set out."

"It's a most exciting project of course."

"Tell me about it."

"You really *are* interested, aren't you?"

"Enormously."

"We'll go by ship to Port Said and overland to Cairo. We shall stay for a while and then make our way towards the ancient site of Thebes."

I clasped my hands ecstatically.

"Do tell me more about it. You're going to the tombs, aren't you?"

He nodded. "My father has been preparing for this project for some time. He was out there several years ago and he's always had the impression that he was on the verge of some great discovery. It's been in his mind for years. Now he's going to satisfy himself."

"It'll be wonderful," I cried.

"I think it's the most exciting project that I've ever undertaken."

"You have been there before?"

"Yes, with my father. I was very inexperienced then and it was a great concession for me to be there at all My father's party discovered one of the tombs which must have been prepared for a great nobleman. It had been robbed, thousands of years ago. It was very disappointing as you can imagine. All the hard work, the excavating, the probing, the hopes . . . and then to find that the tomb has been so completely cleared that there is nothing left which would help to reconstruct the customs of this fascinating country. I'm getting carried away with my enthusiasm, but it's your fault, Miss Osmond. You seem so interested."

"I am, tremendously so."

"So few people outside our little world understand a thing."

"I don't feel myself to be exactly outside it. I was very fortunate. I took lessons at Keverall Court and as you know Sir Ralph has always been interested in archaeology."

"Fortunately, yes. He is helping us a great deal."

"It was he who engaged Evan Callum to give us lessons. Then, of course, there was what was going on at Carter's Meadow. I sometimes gave a hand there . . . in a very unprofessional way, as you can guess."

"But you caught the fascination, didn't you? I can hear it in your voice and see it in your face. And I remember how excited you were when you came to the house for books. And I do believe, Miss Osmond, that you are not one of those ridiculously romantic people who believe that this is all digging and finding wonderful jewels and the remains of old palaces."

"I know such finds are few."

"It's true. But I am sure you would like to dance. So if you don't mind a little discomfort?"

I laughed and said: "I'll bear it."

And there I was, dancing with Tybalt. It was like a dream come true.

I loved him all the more because he kept putting his feet in the wrong places. He apologized and I wanted to cry: Your treading on my toes is bliss.

I was so happy. Alison and Dorcas had said that I had the gift of shutting out everything but the moment and enjoying it to the full. I was glad of it on that night. I would not go beyond this glorious moment when Tybalt's arms were about me and I was closer to him than I had ever been.

I longed for the music to go on and on but it stopped of course and we returned to our alcove where Theodosia was seated with Evan.

I danced with Evan who said how glad he was to see

me there. I told him about how I had found the dress
in my cupboard and Sir Ralph had wished me to come
to the ball.

We laughed and talked about the old days and later we
went to supper and were joined there by Theodosia, Hadrian, and Tybalt.

How gay I could be on such an occasion. I sparkled
and made sure that the conversation circled about me.
Theodosia was very gentle and did not mind, any more
than she had in the schoolroom, the fact that I drew attention from her.

Tybalt was naturally a little aloof from our frivolous
chatter. He was more mature than the rest of us and I
could not help noticing how insignificant Hadrian and
Evan were in comparison. When Tybalt was talking of
archaeology he glowed with an intense and single-minded
passion which I was sure only a man who could feel
deeply would experience. I believed then that if ever
Tybalt loved a woman it would be with the same un-
swerving devotion which he gave to his profession. Because I wanted to see Tybalt animated, glowing with that
enthusiasm which thrilled and excited me, I introduced
the subject of archaeology and almost immediately he
was the center of a fascinated audience.

When we paused Theodosia said: "Oh, you are all
so clever . . . even Judith! But don't you think this salmon
is delicious?"

Hadrian then told us a story of a fishing expedition he
had enjoyed on the Spey, in the Scottish Highlands, where,
he said, the best salmon in the world was caught. He was
explaining how he had plunged into the river and pulled
in the struggling fish, showing us the size of it at which
we all laughingly expressed disbelief, when Lady Bodrean
walked past our table in the company of several of the
guests.

I was saying: "Of course, you know that all fishermen
double the size of their catch and it wouldn't surprise me
if Hadrian trebled his."

And there she was, her eyebrows raised in astonishment as slowly her outraged feelings were visible in the expression on her face.

There was a silence which seemed to go on for a long time; then she took a step towards our table. The men rose, but she stared incredulously at me. I attempted to put on a calm smile.

One of her guests said: "Oh, it's Mr. Travers, I believe."

Tybalt said yes it was; and then Lady Bodrean recovered herself. She made introductions, leaving me until last and then: "Miss Osmond," she said, almost making my name sound obscene.

Nobody noticed and there were a few moments of polite conversation, and then Lady Bodrean and her party passed on.

"Oh dear!" said Theodosia, very distressed.

"I somehow felt it would happen," I added, trying to pretend that I was not really perturbed.

"Well," said Hadrian, "Sir Ralph has to answer for his guests."

"What's happened?" asked Tybalt.

I turned to him. "I really shouldn't be here."

"Surely not," he said. "Your company has made it such an interesting evening."

That made everything worth while.

"I may well be sent packing tomorrow morning."

Tybalt looked concerned and I felt absurdly happy.

Theodosia started to explain. "You see my father thought Judith should come to the ball and he and I put our heads together. I chose her dress and Sarah Sloper made it . . . but Mamma did not know."

Tybalt laughed and said: "There is always some drama surrounding Miss Osmond. If she is not dressing up as an embalmed body and getting into a sarcophagus she is dressing up in a beautiful gown and coming to a ball. And in neither place it seems is she expected to be."

Hadrian put his hand over mine. "Don't worry, Judith. You'll weather tomorrow's storm."

"Mamma can be very fierce," said Theodosia.

"But," put in Evan, "Judith came as the guest of Sir Ralph. I don't see how Lady Bodrean can object to that."

"You don't know Mamma," said Theodosia.

"I assure you I do and the outlook seems stormy, but since Judith came at Sir Ralph's invitation I can't see that she has done anything wrong."

"In any case," I said, "this storm is for tomorrow. At the moment it's a beautiful night. There's salmon which we hope was caught in the Scottish Highlands and champagne from the appropriate district. The company is invigorating, so what more could we ask?"

Tybalt leaned towards me and said: "You live in the moment."

"It's the only way to live. Tonight I'm a kind of Cinderella. Tomorrow I return to my ashes."

"I'll be Prince Charming," said Hadrian. "The music's starting. Let's dance."

I did not want to leave Tybalt, but there was nothing else I could do.

"Congratulations," said Hadrian as we danced. "You were the calmest of the lot. You put up a good show. I suppose you're really quaking in your glass slippers."

"I'm resigned," I said. "I have a feeling that very soon I shall be back in Rainbow Cottage writing humble letters to prospective employers."

"Poor Judith. It's hateful being poor."

"What do you know about that?"

"Plenty. I have my troubles. I have to crave my uncle's benevolence. My creditors are yapping at my heels. I must speak to him tomorrow. So you see, like you tonight I want to eat drink and be merry."

"Oh, Hadrian. Are you really in debt?"

"Up to the eyes. What wouldn't I do to be in Theodosia's shoes."

"I don't suppose she gets as big an allowance as you."

"But think of the credit! Did you know that my uncle is fabulously rich? Well, dear Theodosia will inherit all that one day."

"I hate all this talk about money."

"It is depressing. It's one of the reasons why I'd like to be rich. Then you can forget there's such a thing in the world as money."

We laughed, danced, and joked; but both of us were, I suppose, thinking of what the next day would bring. My ability to live in the moment was only with me when Tybalt was there.

I hoped to see him again, but I didn't; and before all the guests had departed I thought it advisable to return to my room.

I was wrong in thinking that the storm would break the next morning. Lady Bodrean had no intention of allowing it to wait as long as that.

I was still in my ball dress when the bell rang vigorously.

I knew what that meant and I was rather glad because the dress gave me confidence.

I went along to Lady Bodrean's room. She was in her ball gown, too—violet-colored velvet with a magnificent train edged with fur that looked like miniver. She was quite regal.

"Well, Miss Osmond, what have you to say for yourself?"

"What do you expect me to say, Lady Bodrean?"

"What I do not expect is insolence. You were at the ball tonight. How dared you intrude and mingle with my guests."

"It is not really very daring to accept an invitation," I replied.

"Invitation? Have you the effrontery to tell me that you sent yourself an invitation?"

"I did not. Sir Ralph gave instructions that I was to go to the ball."

"I do not believe it."

"Perhaps your ladyship would wish me to call him." Before she could reply I had seized the bell rope and pulled it. Jane came running in. "Lady Bodrean wishes you to ask Sir Ralph if he will come here . . . if he has not already retired."

Lady Bodrean was spluttering with rage, but Jane, who, I believe, knew what had been happening, had hurried off to call Sir Ralph.

"How dare you presume to give orders here?" demanded Lady Bodrean.

"I thought I was obeying orders," I said. "I was under the impression that your ladyship wished Sir Ralph to come here to corroborate my story, for clearly you did not believe me."

"I have never in all my life been subjected to such . . . such . . . such . . ."

"Insubordination?" I supplied.

"Insolence," she said.

I was intoxicated with happiness still. I had danced with Tybalt; he had talked to me; I had conveyed to him my interest in his work. He had said, "Your company has made it such an interesting evening." And he had meant that, for I was sure he was not the man to say what he did not mean. So how could I care for this foolish old virago who in a few moments was going to be confronted by her husband who, I knew, would confirm what I had said.

He stood there in the doorway. "What the . . ." he began. Then he saw me and there was that now familiar movement of the jaw.

"What's Miss Osmond doing here?" he asked.

"I sent for her. She had the temerity to mingle with our guests tonight."

"She was one of them," he said shortly.

"I think you have forgotten that she is my companion."

"She was one of your guests tonight. She came to the ball on my invitation. That is enough."

"You mean you invited this young woman without consulting me!"

"You know very well I did."

"This young woman is under the impression that because she was allowed to have a little education and some of it under this roof that entitles her to special treatment. I tell you I will not allow this. She came here as a companion and shall be treated as such."

"Which means," said Sir Ralph, "that you will make her life unbearable. You will be as unpleasant to her as you know how—and my God, that, madam, is a great deal."

"You have foisted this person on me," she said. "I will not endure it."

"She will continue as before."

"I tell you . . . that I will not have you force me to have people . . . like this in my household."

"Madame," said Sir Ralph, "you will do as I say . . ."

He gripped the chair; I saw the blood suffuse his face; he reeled slightly.

I rushed forward and caught his arm. He looked about him and I helped him to a chair. He sat there breathing heavily.

I said: "I think we should call his valet. He is unwell."

I took it upon myself to instruct Jane to do so.

Jane hurried away and shortly came back with Blake, Sir Ralph's personal servant.

Blake knew what to do. He unloosened Sir Ralph's collar and taking a small tablet from a box put it into his employer's mouth. Sir Ralph lay back in the chair, his face, which had been a suffused purple, becoming gradually paler but the veins at his temples standing out like tubes.

"That's better, sir," said Blake. Then he looked at Lady Bodrean. "I'll get him to bed now, my lady."

Sir Ralph rose shakily to his feet and leaned heavily on Blake.

He nodded at me and a shadow of amusement came into his face.

He muttered: "Don't forget what I say. I mean it."

Then Blake led him away.

When the door shut Lady Bodrean turned on me.

"Now," she said, "you can see what you have done."

"Not I," I replied significantly.

"Go back to your room," she said. "I will talk to you later."

I went back. What a night! She would not get rid of me. She dared not. Nor was I sure that she wanted to. If I went she would be deprived of the joy of making my life miserable. I was sure she did not want that.

But I could cope with her and I did not wish to think

of her on such a night. I had so many more memories to brood on.

At the end of that month Sir Edward with his expedition, which included Tybalt, left for Egypt.

Evan went back to the university where he had a temporary post as lecturer in archaeology; Hadrian went to Kent to do some work on a Viking burial ship which had been discovered somewhere along the east coast, and I returned to the monotony of serving Lady Bodrean which was only enlivened by her attempts to humiliate me. But the thought that I had friends in Sir Ralph and Theodosia was comforting. There were no more walks to Giza House because Tabitha had accompanied the party but I walked past it several times. It seemed to have reverted to the old days when we had called it the haunted house. The blinds were drawn, the furniture was under dust covers, and there were only three or four servants there. The two Egyptians, Mustapha and Absalam, had gone with Sir Edward.

I longed for the return of the expedition. And Tybalt.

I called more often at Rainbow Cottage since I couldn't go to Giza; there was always a welcome there. Dorcas and Alison were delighted when I gave them an account of the ball and the beautiful green dress which I had found in the cupboard.

I had been surprised at their attitude right from the beginning when they had been so delighted that I was to go to Keverall Court. I was young—and although my nose prevented me from being beautiful I could look quite attractive at times. I had assessed myself often in the last months comparing myself with Theodosia. I had a vitality which she lacked; and my animation was attractive, I was sure. Although my temper was inclined to flare up, any storm was soon over; I had an ability to laugh at life and that meant laughing at myself. I had my very thick dark hair—not easy to handle because it was almost straight; I had large brown eyes with lashes as thick and black as my hair; and fortunately I had a good healthy set of teeth. I was taller than Theodosia and Sabina and inclined to be thin. I lacked Theodosia's pretty plumpness and Sabina's hourglass figure. Moreover I had youth which was supposed to be a never failing attraction for aging roués. Sir Ralph's reputation was far from good. I had heard the blacksmiths talking to some of the farmers about the old days when Sir Ralph was in his prime as a seducer of young maidens. They were immediately silent when I, at that time in the company of Hadrian and Theodosia, had appeared. And yet Dorcas and Alison had been delighted that I was to have a post at Keverall Court.

I reasoned that they believed that Sir Ralph had given up his wild life. He was far too old to pursue it; and, remembering him on that night when he had come to Lady Bodrean's room, I could well believe it. All the same I did think it rather strange that Dorcas and Alison had so willingly allowed me to go into the lecher's lair.

Now they wanted a detailed account of the ball.

"A dress!" they had cried. "What a charming idea."

A further surprise because I had believed that one of the tenets of society was that young ladies did not accept dresses from a gentleman.

This was different. Theodosia had made it so. I had come to the conclusion that Sir Ralph liked me. I amused him in some way, which Theodosia had failed to do.

I was content to have been to the ball and to have enjoyed it. Had I not been presented with the dress I could never have gone.

It was so much easier to accept the cozy outlook I found at Rainbow Cottage rather than to probe the motives of Sir Ralph. For all his faults he was a kindly man. The servants certainly liked him better than they did his wife. As for myself, I felt fully competent to deal with any situation which might arise. I was fortunate in having Rainbow Cottage so close that I could run straight out of Keverall Court to it, if need be.

So I told them all about the ball. Dorcas was very interested in the food, Alison in the flower arrangements; and both of them much more interested in what had happened to me.

I danced the waltz round the tiny sitting room in Rainbow Cottage, knocking over the what-not which resulted in two casualties—the handle of one of Dorcas's little Goss china cups and a finger chipped on her eighteenth-century flower girl.

They were rueful but happy to see me happier; so they made light of the breakages. The cup handle would stick and the finger wouldn't be noticed. And with whom had I danced?

"Tybalt Travers! He's a strange man. Emily's sister who works there says both he and his father give her the creeps."

"Creeps!" I said. "The servants there are creep mad!"

"It's a queer sort of house and a strange profession, I think," said Dorcas. "Fiddling about with things that people handled years and years ago."

"Oh, Dorcas, you're talking like some country bumpkin."

"I know you're very interested in it. And I must say some of the pictures in those books you used to bring here would have given me nightmares. I used to wonder whether we ought to take them away."

"What pictures!"

"Skulls and bones . . . and I think those mummies are horrible things. And Sir Edward . . ."

"Well, what of Sir Edward?"

"I know he's very well known and very highly thought of but they say he's a bit peculiar."

"Just because he's different from themselves . . . just because he doesn't go around seducing all the village maidens like Sir Ralph did . . . they think that's odd!"

"Really, Judith, where do you learn such things?"

"From life, Alison dear. Life all around me."

"You get so vehement every time these Traverses are mentioned."

"Well, they're doing this wonderful job . . ."

"I do believe you'd like to be out there with them fiddling about with all these dead mummies!"

"I could imagine nothing I should like more. It would be a little different from dancing attendance on the most disagreeable woman in the world."

"Poor Judith, perhaps it won't last forever. Do you know I think we might manage here. There's quite a big garden. We might grow vegetables and sell them."

I grimaced at my hands. "I don't think I have the necessary green fingers."

"Well, who knows, something may turn up. That young man who used to teach you. He was at the ball, wasn't he?"

"You mean Evan Callum."

"I always liked him. There was something gentle about him. You used to talk about him a great deal. You were better at his lessons than any of the others."

I smiled at them benignly. They had made up their minds that marriage would solve my problems. I had failed to bring it off with Oliver Shrimpton so they had chosen Evan Callum as the next candidate.

"I daresay he will be coming down here again. All this interest about the expedition . . ."

"Why doesn't *he* give people the creeps?" I demanded. "His profession is the same as Sir Edward's and Tybalt's."

"He's more . . . normal."

"You're not suggesting that the Traverses are not normal!"

"They're different," said Dorcas. "Oh yes, Mr. Callum will be here again. Sir Ralph, they say, is involved in this Egyptian matter. I heard that he's helping to finance it because his daughter is going to marry Tybalt Travers."

"Where did you hear that?" I asked.

"Through Emily."

"Servants' gossip."

"My dear Judith, who knows more about a family's affairs than the servants?"

They were right of course. The servants would hear scraps of conversation. I pictured Jane with her ear to the keyhole. Some of them pieced together torn-up letters which had been thrown into wastepaper baskets. They had their ears and eyes open for household scandals.

There was no doubt that the general expectation was that Tybalt was destined for Theodosia.

I went back to Keverall Court thoughtfully.

He doesn't love her, I told myself. I should know if he did. He enjoyed dancing with me at the ball far more than with Theodosia. How could a man like Tybalt be in love with Theodosia!

But Theodosia was rich—a great heiress. With a fortune in his hands such as Theodosia could bring him, Tybalt would be able to finance his own expeditions.

To Sir Edward very little mattered but his work and Tybalt was following very close in his footsteps.

This was why the servants in the house had the "creeps."

On the day Tybalt married Theodosia I would go away. I would find a post as far as possible from St. Erno's and I would try to build a new life out of the ruins of my old one. He might be obsessed by his work; I was by him; and I knew, as surely as I knew anything that when I lost him all the savor would go from my life.

Dorcas had said: "When Judith is enthusiastic about something her whole heart's in it. She never does anything by halves."

She was right; and now I was enthusiastic as I had never been in my life before—enthusiastic for one man, one way of life.

Theodosia, as though to make up for her neglect, sought me out a good deal. She liked to talk about the books she was reading and I could see she was making a great effort to perfect herself in the subject of archaeology.

She would invite me to her room and it often seemed as though she were on the verge of confidences. She was a little absent-minded; sometimes she would seem very happy, at others apprehensive. Once when I was in her room she pulled open a drawer and I saw a bundle of letters tied up with blue ribbon. How like Theodosia to tie up her love letters with blue ribbon! I wondered what was in them. Somehow I could not imagine Tybalt's writing love letters—and to Theodosia!

Dearest Theodosia,
    I long for the day when we shall be married. I am

planning several expeditions and these need financial backing. How useful your fortune will be . . .

I laughed at myself. I was trying to convince myself that the only thing he would want from Theodosia was her fortune. And even if he did, as if he would write such a letter!

"How is Mamma behaving these days?" she asked me idly one afternoon when she had invited me to her room.

"Very much as usual."

"I expect she has been even worse since the ball."

"Your expectations are correct."

"Poor Judith!"

"Oh, we all have our problems."

"Yes," she sighed.

"Surely not you, Theodosia?"

She hesitated. Then she said, "Judith, have you ever been in love?"

I felt myself starting to flush uncomfortably but fortunately it was not meant to be a question so much as the preliminary to confidences.

"It's wonderful," she went on, "and yet . . . I'm a little scared."

"Why should you be scared?"

"Well, I'm not very clever, as you know."

"If he's in love with you . . ."

"If! Of course he is. He tells me so every time I see him . . . every time he writes . . ."

I half wanted to make an excuse to escape, half wanted to stay and be tortured.

"I really find archaeology rather boring, Judith. That's the truth, and of course it's his life. I've tried. I've read the books. I love it when they find something wonderful, but it's mostly about tools for digging and kinds of soil and so on and all those boring pots and things."

"If you're not interested perhaps you shouldn't pretend to be."

"I don't think he expects me to be. I shall just look after him. That's all he wants. Oh, it will be wonderful, Judith. But I'm worried about my father."

"Why should you be worried about him?"

"He won't like it."

"Won't like it! But I thought he was anxious for you to marry Tybalt."

"Tybalt! I'm not talking of Tybalt."

This was singing in my ears. It was like listening to some heavenly chorus. I cried: "What! Not Tybalt. You're joking!"

"Tybalt!" she cried. And she repeated his name with a sort of horror. "Tybalt! Why I'd be scared to death of him. I'm sure he thinks I am quite foolish."

"He's serious, of course, which is much more interesting than being stupidly frivolous."

"Evan is not frivolous."

"Evan! So it's Evan!"

"But of course it's Evan. Who else?"

I began to laugh. "And those letters tied up with blue ribbon . . . and all this sighing and blushing. Evan!" I hugged her. "Oh, Theodosia, I'm so happy . . ." I had the presence of mind to add: "for you."

"Whatever's come over you, Judith?"

"Well, I didn't think it was Evan."

"You thought it was Tybalt. That's what people think because that's what Father wants. He'd love to see a match between our families. He's always been a great admirer of Sir Edward and interested in everything he does. And he would have loved me to be like you and able to learn about all this stuff. But I'm not like that, and how could anybody want Tybalt when there's Evan!"

"Some might," I said calmly.

"Then they must be *mad*."

"So mad that they might think you're mad to prefer Evan."

"It's good to talk to you, Judith. We don't like to tell Father, you see. You know what families are. Evan's people were very poor and he's worked his way up. There was some relative who helped him and Evan wants to pay him back every penny he's spent on him. And we're going to do that. *I* think it's to his credit that he's come so far. It's nothing to be ashamed of. Why Tybalt inherited all sorts of advantages, whereas Evan worked for his."

"It's very laudable," I said.

"Judith, you like Evan, don't you?"

"Of course I do; and I think you and he are ideally suited."

"That's wonderful. But what do you think Father will say?"

"There's one way of finding out. Ask him."

"Do you think one could do that?"

"Why ever not."

"But if he refuses."

"We'll stage an elopement. A ladder against the wall, the bride-to-be escaping down it and then off to Gretna Green or as that's rather a long way from Cornwall, perhaps a special license would be better."

"Oh Judith, you're always such *fun*. You make everything seem a sort of joke. I'm so glad I've told you."

"So am I," I said with heartfelt conviction.

"What would *you* do?"

"I should go to your father and say, 'I love Evan Callum. Moreover I am determined to marry him.' "

"And suppose he says no?"

"Then we plan the elopement."

"I wish we could do that now."

"But you must ask your father first. He may be delighted."

"He won't be. He's got this fascination for the Traverses. I believe he would have gone to Egypt if he'd been well enough."

"You'll probably go some time with Evan."

"I'd go anywhere with Evan."

"What does Evan say?"

"He says that we're going to be married whatever happens."

"You may be cut out of your father's will."

"Do you think I care for that? I'd rather have Evan and starve."

"It won't come to that. Why should it? He has a good job at the university, hasn't he? You have nothing to fear.

Even if you don't inherit a vast fortune you will be a professor's wife."

"Of course. I don't care about Father's money."

"Then you're in a strong position. You must fight to marry where you please. And you can't begin too soon."

She hugged me again.

I was so happy. How pleasant it is to work for someone's happiness when doing so contributes to your own!

Theodosia was right when she had said that her father would not be pleased about the wedding.

When she broke the news there was a storm.

Theodosia came to my room in tears.

"He won't have it," she said. "He's furious. He says he'll stop it."

"Well, you have to stand firm if **you really** want to marry."

"You would, wouldn't you, Judith?"

"Do you doubt it?"

"Not for a moment. How I wish I were like you."

"You can be."

"How, Judith, *how?*"

"Stand firm. No one can make you marry if you won't say the appropriate words."

"You'll help me, won't you, Judith?"

"With all my heart," I said.

"I have told Father that he can cut me out, that I don't care. That I love Evan and that I'm going to marry him."

"That's the first step then."

She was greatly comforted and she stayed in my room while we made plans. I told her that the first thing she must do was write to Evan and tell him the state of affairs. We would see what he would say.

"I shall tell him that you know, Judith, and that we can count on you."

I was surprised to receive a summons from Sir Ralph. When I went to his apartments he was in an armchair in a dressing gown and Blake was hovering. He dismissed Blake and said, "Sit down, Miss Osmond."

I obeyed.

"I have the impression that you are interfering in my daughter's affairs."

"I know that she wishes to marry," I said. "I cannot see that I have interfered."

"Indeed! Didn't you tell her to come and deliver her ultimatum to me?"

"I did tell her that if she wished to marry she should tell you so."

"And perhaps ask my permission?"

"Yes."

"And if I did not give it, to defy me?"

"What she will do is entirely a matter for her to decide."

"But you, in her position, would not think of obeying your father?"

"If I decided to marry then I should do so."

"In spite of the fact that you went against your father's wishes?"

"Yes."

"I guessed it," he said. "Propping her up. That's what you've been doing. By God, Miss Osmond, you have a mighty big idea of your importance."

"I don't know what you mean, Sir Ralph."

"At least you admit to some ignorance. I'm glad to see you have a little humility."

I was silent.

He went on: "You know that my daughter Theodosia wishes to marry this penniless fellow."

"I know that she wishes to marry Professor Evan Callum."

"My daughter will be a very rich woman one day . . . providing she obeys my wishes. Do you still think she should marry this man?"

"If she is in love with him."

"Love! I didn't know you were sentimental, Miss Osmond."

Again I was silent. I could not understand why he had sent for me.

"You are advising my daughter to marry this man."

"I? She had already chosen him before I was aware of her intention."

"I had a match arranged for her, a much more suitable one."

"Surely she is the one who should decide its suitability."

"You have modern ideas, Miss Osmond. In my day daughters obeyed their parents. *You* don't think they should."

"In most matters. But in my opinion marriage is something which should be decided on by the partners concerned."

"And my daughter's marriage does not concern me?"

"Not as closely as it does her and her future husband."

"You should have been an advocate. Instead of which I believe you have a fancy for the profession of the man my daughter would marry . . . if I permit it."

"It's true."

I saw the movement in his jaw and my spirits rose because again I was amusing him.

"I believe you know that I wanted another marriage for my daughter."

"There has been a certain amount of speculation."

"No smoke without fire, eh? I'll be frank. I wanted her to marry but to a different bridegroom. You have your ear to the ground, Miss Osmond, I'm sure."

"I heard suggestions."

"And you don't think it's a bad idea that my daughter chose this one? That's it. In fact, Miss Osmond, are you just a little pleased about it?"

"I don't know what you mean."

"Don't you? This is the second time you've admitted ignorance. That's not like you . . . and especially to feign it. You will help my daughter to disobey her father, won't you? You will be pleased to see her become the wife of this young fellow. You're a wily one, Miss Osmond. You have your reasons."

He lay back in his chair, his face suffused with color. I could see that he was laughing. I was overcome by confusion at the insinuation in his words.

He knew that I was delighted that Theodosia was in

love with Evan Callum, because I wanted Tybalt for myself.

He waved a hand. I was glad to escape.

A few days later Sir Ralph declared that he would permit an engagement between his daughter and Evan Callum.

Theodosia was in a state of bliss.

"Who could have believed, Judith, that there would have been such a complete turnabout."

"I think your father is really rather a sentimental man and you're so obviously in love."

"It's strange, Judith, how little one knows of people who have been close to one all one's life."

"I don't think you're the first to have discovered that."

The marriage was to be at Christmas time and Theodosia was plunged into a whirl of preparations.

Lady Bodrean did not approve. I heard her arguing with Sir Ralph about it. I hurried off to my own room but Jane reported afterwards, and I quite unashamedly listened to her account which I suppose was as bad as eavesdropping myself.

"My word," said Jane, "did the fur fly! They seem to think he's not good enough for our heiress. 'Have you taken leave of your senses?' asks Lady B. 'Madam,' says he, 'I will decide on my daughter's future.' 'She happens to be my daughter too.' 'And it is fortunate for her that she has not turned out like you or I'd be sorry for this young man she's going to marry.' 'So you're sorry for yourself,' says she. 'No, madam, I know how to look after myself,' he says. 'You knew how to scatter your bastards all over the countryside.' 'A man must amuse himself somehow,' he said. Oh he's the master all right. If she'd got hold of a meek man, she'd have ruled him. But not our Squire. Then she said, 'You told me that she was to marry Tybalt Travers.' 'Well, I have changed my mind.' 'That's a sudden turnabout.' 'She's in love with this fellow.' 'Love,' she snorted. 'Something you don't believe in, madam, I know, but I say she shall marry this fellow she's chosen.' 'You've changed your mind. How long is it since you said: "I want my daughter to marry

the son of my old friend Edward Travers?" ' 'I've changed
my mind, that's all that's to be said . . .' And on and on
they went throwing insults at each other. My word, we
do see life."

I thought a great deal about Sir Ralph. I was really
quite fond of him.

When Alison and Dorcas heard the news they were
astounded.

"Theodosia to marry Evan Callum! How very strange!
You were so much better at all that work that he's so
keen on than she was."

I could see that they were nonplused. Another attempt
to marry me off had failed.

Evan and Theodosia were married on Christmas Day
with Oliver Shrimpton performing the ceremony. I sat
at the back of the church between Dorcas and Alison;
Sabina was with us.

When the bride came down the aisle on her husband's
arm, Sabina whispered to me: "It'll be your turn next."

I noticed that her eyes went to Hadrian in the front
pew.

Good Heavens! I thought. Is that the way some people
are thinking?

As for myself I had always looked upon Hadrian as
a brother. I laughed to myself to think of what Lady
Bodrean would have to say if she knew that. She would
think it highly presumptuous of the companion to think
of Sir Ralph's nephew as a brother.

The bridal pair were spending the Christmas and Boxing
nights at Keverall Court. After that they were going to a
house in Devon which one of the dons at the university
had lent them for their honeymoon. I was allowed to
spend the day at Rainbow Cottage, returning early next
morning. I wondered at this concession; then it occurred
to me that Lady Bodrean probably thought that Sir Ralph,
who now quite clearly had become a kind of protector to
me, might invite me to the evening's entertainment which
was being given to celebrate both Christmas and the wedding.

I spent a quiet day, and in the evening Alison and Dorcas invited one or two of their friends and we had a pleasant evening playing guessing games.

Two days later the radiant bride left with her husband. I missed her. Everything seemed flat now that the excitement of the wedding was over. Lady Bodrean became peevishly irritable and complained continually.

I had an opportunity to talk with Hadrian who was as usual worried about money.

"There's only one thing I can do," he said, "and that is find an heiress to marry me as Evan has."

"I am sure that did not enter his mind," I said hotly.

Hadrian grinned at me. "With the best intentions in the world, he must have a feeling of relief. Money's money, and a fortune never did any harm to anyone."

"You're obsessed by money!"

"Put it down to my lack of it."

At the end of January he left and it was about that time Lady Bodrean was indisposed for a few days and I had a little freedom.

Sir Ralph sent for me and said that since Lady Bodrean did not require my services I might read the papers to him.

So each morning I sat with him for an hour or so and read *The Times;* but he would never let me get very far. I realized that he wanted to talk.

He told me a little about the expedition.

"I should have gone with them, but my doctor said No." He tapped his heart. "Couldn't have it giving out, you know. I'd have been a nuisance. Heat would have been too much for me."

I was able to reply intelligently because of the little knowledge I had acquired.

"It's a pity we couldn't send you up to the university. You'd have done well, I think. Always had a feeling for it, didn't you? That's what's needed—a *feeling*. I always had it myself, but was never anything but an amateur."

I said that there was a great deal of pleasure to be found in being merely an amateur.

"With Sir Edward it's a passion. I reckon he's one of

the top men in his profession . . . I'd go so far as to say *the* top."

"Yes, I believe he is considered so."

"And Master Tybalt's the same."

He shot a quick glance at me and I felt the telltale color in my cheeks. I remembered his insinuations about us in the past.

"He'll be another like his father. Very difficult man to live with, was Sir Edward. His wasn't a very happy marriage. There are some men who marry a profession rather than a wife. Always up and off somewhere. When at home buried in his books or his work. She didn't see him for days at a stretch when he was at home. And he was nearly always away."

"I suppose she wasn't interested in his work."

"His work came first. With those sort of men it always does."

"Your daughter has married an archaeologist."

"That fellow! I've got his measure. He'll be talking in a classroom all his life, theorizing about this and that. And when his day's work is over he'll go home to his wife and family and forget all about it. There are men like that—but they're rarely the ones who rise to the top of their profession. Would you like to see some reports of what is happening in Egypt?"

"Oh, I should enjoy that."

He regarded me with that familiar shake of the jaw.

I read some of the reports to him and we discussed them. How that hour used to fly!

I had slipped into a new relationship with Sir Ralph which surprised me sometimes but it had all come about so gradually. That interest which he had always shown in me had become the basis of a friendship which I should not have thought possible.

It was in early March that the news came of Sir Edward's mysterious death and the speculations arose about the Curse of the Pharaohs.

IV   Tybalt's Wife

Sir Ralph was deeply shocked and this shock resulted
in another stroke, which impaired his speech. It was
then that rumors circulated about the significance of his
illness. It was the Curse of the Kings, said these rumors,
for it was known that he had backed the expedition
financially. He was unable to attend the funeral but a few
days later he sent for me and when I went to his room I
was surprised to see Tybalt there.

It was pitiful to see the once robust Sir Ralph the
wreck he now was. His efforts to speak were painful
and yet he insisted on attempting to do so because there
was something he wanted to say.

He indicated that he wished us to sit on either side of
him.

"Ju . . . Ju . . ." he began and I realized he was trying
to say my name.

"I'm here, Sir Ralph," I said, and when I laid my
hand on his he took it and would not release it.

His eyes turned towards Tybalt, and his right hand

moved, for it was with his left that he held mine.

Tybalt understood that he wanted his hand so he laid it in that of Sir Ralph. Sir Ralph smiled and drew his hands together. Tybalt then took my hand and Sir Ralph smiled faintly. It was what he had wanted.

I looked into Tybalt's eyes and I felt the slow flush creeping over my face.

Sir Ralph's implication was obvious.

I withdrew my hand but Tybalt continued to look at me. Sir Ralph had closed his eyes. Blake had tiptoed in.

"I think it would be better, sir," he said, "if you and Miss Osmond left now."

When the door shut on us Tybalt said to me: "Will you walk to Giza House with me?"

"I must go to Lady Bodrean," I replied. I was shaken. I could not understand why Sir Ralph should have placed us in this embarrassing position.

"I want to talk to you," said Tybalt. "It's important."

We went out of the house together and when we had walked a little distance from it, Tybalt said: "He's right you know. We should."

"I . . . I don't understand."

"Why, Judith, what has happened to you? You are usually so forthright."

"I . . . I didn't know you knew so much about me."

"I know a great deal about you. It's a good many years since I first met you disguised as a mummy."

"You will never forget that."

"One doesn't forget one's first meeting with one's wife."

"But . . ."

"It's what he meant. He was telling us that we should marry."

"He was wandering in his mind."

"I don't think he was. I think it has been his wish for some time."

"It is becoming clear to me. He thought I was Theodosia. He had hoped that you and Theodosia would marry. You did know that, didn't you?"

"I think it was talked over with my father."

"So . . . you see what happened. He had forgotten that

Theodosia was married. He thought that I was his daughter. Poor Sir Ralph. I'm afraid he is very ill."

"He is going to die, I fear," replied Tybalt. "You have always been interested in my work, haven't you, vitally interested?"

"Why yes."

"You see, we should get on very well. My mother was bored by my father's work. It was a very dismal marriage. It will be different with us."

"I don't understand this. Do you mean that you will marry me because Sir Ralph has implied that he wants you to?"

"That's not the only reason, of course."

"Tell me some others," I said.

"For one, when I leave for Egypt, you could come with me. You would be pleased by that, I'm sure."

"Yet, even that does not seem to me an adequate reason for marrying."

He stopped and faced me. "There are others," he said, and drew me close to him.

I said: "I would not wish to marry because I would be a useful member of an expedition."

"Nevertheless," he replied, "you would be."

Then he kissed me.

"If love came into it . . ." I began.

Then he laughed and held me tightly against him.

"Do you doubt that it does?"

"I am undecided and I should like some sort of declaration."

"First let me have one from you because I'm sure you will do so better than I. You're never at a loss for words. I'm afraid I am . . . often."

"Then perhaps I shall be even more useful to you. Writing your letters, for instance. I shall be a good secretary."

"Is that *your* declaration?"

"I suppose you know that I have been in love with you for years. Sir Ralph knew it, I believe."

"I had no idea I was so fortunate! I wish I had known before."

"What would you have done?"

"Asked myself whether if you knew me better you might have changed your mind, and wondered whether I dared allow that to happen."

"Are you really so modest?"

"No. I shall be the most arrogant man in your life."

"There are no others of any importance . . . and never have been. I shall spend my life if necessary convincing you of that."

"So you agree to share it with me?"

"I would die rather than do anything else."

"My dearest Judith! Did I not say that you had a way with words!"

"I have told you quite frankly that I love you. I should like to hear you say that you love me."

"Have I not made it clear to you that I do?"

"I should love to hear you say it."

"I love you," he said.

"Say it again. Keep saying it. I have so long dreamed of your saying those words. I can't believe this is really true. I am awake now, am I? I'm not going to wake up in a minute to hear Lady Bodrean ringing the bell?"

He took my hand and kissed it fervently. "My dear *dear* Judith," he said. "You put me to shame. I don't deserve you. Don't think too highly of me. I shall disappoint you. You know my obsession with work, I shall bore you with my enthusiasms."

"Never."

"I shall be an inadequate husband. I have not your gaiety, your spontaneity, everything that makes you so attractive. I can be dull, far too serious . . ."

"One can never be too serious about the important things of life."

"I shall be moody, preoccupied. I shall neglect you for my work."

"Which I intend to share with you, including the moods and the preoccupation, so that objection is overruled."

"I am not able to express my feelings easily. I shall forget to tell you how much I love you. You alarm me. You are carried away by your enthusiasm always. You think too highly of me. You hope for perfection."

I laughed as I laid my head against him. "I can't help my feelings," I said. "I have loved you so long. I only want to be with you, to share your life, to make you happy, to make your life smooth and easy and just as you wish it to be."

"Judith," he said, "I will do my best to make you happy."

"If you love me, if you allow me to share your life, I shall be that."

He slipped his arm through mine and gripped my hand tightly.

We walked on and he talked of the future. He saw no reason why our marriage should be delayed; in fact he would like it to take place as soon as possible. We were going to be very busy with our plans. Would I mind if after the ceremony we stayed at Giza House and plunged straight into our arrangements?

Would I mind? I cared for nothing as long as I could be with him. The greatest joy which could come to me was to share his life forevermore.

There was astonishment at Rainbow Cottage when I told Dorcas and Alison my news. They were glad that I was to be married but they were a little dubious about my bridegroom. Oliver Shrimpton would have been so much more eligible in their opinion; and the rumors in St. Erno's were that the Traverses were rather odd people. And now that Sir Edward had died so mysteriously they felt that they would have preferred me not to be connected with such a mysterious affair.

"You'll be Lady Travers," said Alison.

"I hadn't thought of that."

Dorcas shook her head. "You're happy. I can see that."

"Oh Dorcas, Alison, I never thought it possible to be so happy."

"Now, now," said Dorcas, as she used to when I was a child. "You could never do things by halves."

"Surely one should not contemplate marriage 'by halves' as you say."

"No, but you hope for too much. You think everything's going to be perfect."

I laughed at her. "In this marriage," I said, "everything is."

I said nothing at Keverall Court about my engagement. It hardly seemed appropriate with Sir Ralph so ill; and the next day he died.

Keverall Court was in mourning, but I don't think anyone missed Sir Ralph as much as I did. The great joy of my engagement was overshadowed. But at least, I thought, he would have been pleased. He had been my friend, and during the weeks before his death, our friendship had meant a good deal to me, as I believed it had to him. How I wished that I could have sat in his room and told him of my engagement and all that I hoped to do in the future. I thought of him a great deal and remembered incidents from the past—when I had brought the bronze shield to him and he had first become interested in me, how he had given me a ball dress and had defended me afterwards.

Lady Bodrean put on a sorrowing countenance but it was clear that it hid a relief.

She talked to me and to Jane about the virtues of Sir Ralph; but I sensed that the lull in her hostility to me was momentary and she was promising herself that now that I had lost my champion I should be at her mercy. Little did she know the blow I was about to deliver. I was to be married to the man whom she had wanted for her daughter. It was going to be a great shock to her to learn that her poor companion would soon be Lady Travers.

Hadrian came home. I told him the news.

"It's not officially announced yet," I warned him. "I shall wait until after the funeral."

"Tybalt's lucky," he said glumly. "I reckon he's forestalled me."

"Ah, but you wanted a woman with money."

"If you'd had a fortune, Judith, I'd have laid my heart at your feet."

"Biologically impossible," I told him.

"Well, I wish you lucky. And I'm glad you're getting away from my aunt. Your life must have been hellish with her."

"It wasn't so bad. You know that I always enjoyed a fight."

That night I had a strange intimation from Sir Ralph's lawyers. They wanted me to be present at the reading of his will.

When I called at Rainbow Cottage and told Alison and Dorcas of this they behaved rather oddly.

They went out and left me in the sitting room and were gone some time. This was strange because my visit was necessarily a brief one and just as I was about to call them and tell them that I must be going, they came back.

Their faces were flushed and they looked at each other in a most embarrassed fashion, and knowing them so well I realized that each was urging the other to open a subject which they found distasteful or distressing in some way.

"Is anything wrong?" I asked.

"There is something we think you ought to know," said Dorcas.

"Yes, indeed you must be prepared."

"Prepared for what?"

Dorcas bit her lip and looked at Alison; Alison nodded.

"It's about your birth, Judith. You are our niece. Lavinia was your mother."

"Lavinia! Why didn't you tell me?"

"Because we thought it best. It was rather an awkward situation."

"It was a terrible shock to us," went on Dorcas. "Lavinia was the eldest. Father doted on her. She was so pretty. She was just like our mother . . . whereas we were like Father."

"Dear Dorcas!" I said, "do get on and tell me what this is all about."

"It was a terrible shock to us when we heard she was going to have a child."

"Which turned out to be me?"

"Yes. We smuggled Lavinia away to a cousin . . . before it was noticeable you see. We told people in the village that she had taken a situation, a post of governess. And you were born. The cousin was in London and she had several children of her own. Lavinia could look after them and keep her own baby there. It was a good arrangement. She brought you to see us, but of course she couldn't come here. We all met in Plymouth. We had such a pleasant time and then saw her off on that train."

"There was an accident," I said. "She was killed and I survived."

"And what was going to happen to you was a problem. So we said you were a cousin's child and brought you here . . . to adopt you, as it were."

"Well, you are in fact my aunts! Aunt Alison! Aunt Dorcas! But why did you tell me that story about being unclaimed?"

"You were always asking questions about the distant cousins who, you thought, were your close family, so we thought it better for you to have no family at all."

"You always did what you thought best for me, I know. Who was my father? Do you know that?"

They looked at each other for a moment and I burst out: "Can it really be? It explains everything. Sir Ralph!"

Their faces told me that I had guessed correctly.

"He was my father. I'm glad. I was fond of him. He was always good to me." I went to them and hugged them. "At least I know who my parents are now."

"We thought you might be ashamed to have been born . . . out of wedlock."

"Do you know," I said, "I believe he really loved her. She must have been the one love of his life. At least she gave him the great solace he needed married to Lady Bodrean."

"Oh Judith!" they cried indulgently.

"But he has been kind to me." I thought of the way he looked at me; the amused twinkle in his eyes, the shake of his chin. He was saying to himself: This is Lavinia's daughter. How I wished that he was alive so that I could tell him how fond I had grown of him.

"Now Judith," said Dorcas, "you must be prepared. The reason you are expected to be at the reading of the will is because he has left you something. It may well come out that you are his daughter and we wouldn't want it to come as a shock to you."

"I will be prepared," I promised.

They were right. I was mentioned in Sir Ralph's will. He had left a quarter of a million pounds to Archaeological Research to be used depending on certain conditions, in whatever way Sir Edward or Tybalt Travers thought fit; he had left an income for life to his wife; to Hadrian an income of one thousand a year; to Theodosia, his heiress, the house on the death of her mother and one half of the residue of his income; the other half was to go to his natural daughter, Judith Osmond; and in the event of the death of one of his daughters her share of his fortune would revert to the other.

It was astounding.

I, penniless, unclaimed at birth, had acquired parents and from one had come a fortune so great that it bewildered me to contemplate it.

Dramatic events had taken place during the recent weeks. I was to be married to the man I loved; and I should not go to him, as I had thought, a penniless woman. I should bring with me a great fortune.

I thought of Sir Ralph taking my hand and Tybalt's and placing them in each other. I wondered if he had told Tybalt of our relationship and of what he intended to do.

I then felt my first twinge of uneasiness.

The truth of my birth was now known throughout the village. That I was Sir Ralph's daughter surprised few; there was a certain amount of gossip among Oliver's parishioners who recounted how I had been educated with his legitimate daughter and nephew and afterwards taken into Keverall Court, albeit in a humble position. They had guessed, they said, being wise after the event. Alison and Dorcas were alternately pleased and ashamed. Alison said that she was glad her father had not had to face this scandal; their sister, the rector's daughter, the mistress of Sir Ralph who had borne him a child! It *was* rather scandalous. At the same time I, who meant far more to them than their dead sister's reputation, was now a woman of means whose future was secure. I had also so charmed my father that he had shown the world that I was almost as important to him as his legitimate daughter.

The scandal would die down; the benefits remain.

They had been so anxious for me to marry but now I was about to do so they were, I sensed, not so pleased. As a young woman of means I no longer needed the financial support a husband could give me, and it was for this support that they had selected first Oliver and then Evan for me; and now, before I had known of my inheritance I had become engaged to that rather strange man whose father had recently died mysteriously. It was not what they had planned for me.

When I went to them after the reading of the will they looked at me strangely as though I had become a different person.

I laughed at them. "You foolish old aunts," I cried, "for aunts you have turned out to be, the fact that I'm going to be rich doesn't change me at all! And let me tell you, there is going to be no cheeseparing in this house again. You are going to have an income which will enable you to live in the manner to which you have been accustomed."

It was a very emotional moment. Alison's face twitched and Dorcas's was actually wet. I embraced them.

"Just think of it," I said. "You can leave Rainbow Cottage. Sell it if you wish"—for Sir Ralph had left it to them—"and go and live in a lovely house, with a maid or two . . ."

Alison laughed. "Judith, you always did run on. We're

quite happy here and it's our very own now. We shall stay here."

"Well, you shall never worry about making ends meet again."

"You mustn't go spending all the money before you've got it."

That made me laugh. "I believe there's quite a lot of it, and if you think my first thought wouldn't be to look after you, you don't know Judith Osmond."

Dorcas dabbed her eyes and Alison said seriously: "Judith, what about *him.*"

"Him?"

"This er . . . this man you plan to marry."

"Tybalt."

They were both looking at me anxiously.

"Now that er . . ." began Alison. "Now that you have this . . . fortune . . ."

"Good Heavens," I cried, "you don't think—"

"We . . . we wondered whether he knew . . ."

"Knew what?" I demanded.

"That you . . . er . . . were coming into this money."

"Aunts!" I cried sternly. "You are being very wrong. Tybalt and I were meant for each other. I'm passionately interested in his work."

Alison said with a touch of asperity quite alien to her: "I hope he's not passionately interested in your money."

I was angry with them. "This is monstrous. How could he be? Besides . . ."

"Now, Judith, we are only concerned for your good," said Dorcas.

My anger melted. It was true. All their anxiety was for my welfare. I kissed them again. "Listen," I said, "I love Tybalt. Do you understand that? I always have. I always will. And we are going to work together. It's the most ideal match that was ever made. Don't dare say anything else. Don't dare *think* anything else . . ."

"Oh, Judith, you always swept everything along with you. I only hope . . ."

"Hope. Who has to hope when one *knows.*"

"So you really love him?"

"Do you doubt it?"

"No. We were wondering about him."

"Of course," I said, "he doesn't show his feelings as I do. Who does?"

They agreed that few did.

"He may seem aloof, remote, cool—but he's not so."

"It would break our hearts if you weren't happy, Judith."

"There's nothing to be afraid of. Your hearts are going to remain intact."

"You really are happy, Judith," said Alison.

"I'm in love with Tybalt," I said. "And he wants to marry me. And that being so, how could I possibly be anything but happy?"

It was different at the rectory. Sabina welcomed me warmly.

"Oh this is *fun,* Judith," she cried in her inconsequential way. "Here we are, the old gang all happily tied up together. It is interesting, isn't it? The only one left out is poor Hadrian. Of course we were uneven weren't we. Three women and four men. What a lovely proportion—and a rare one. Tybalt wasn't really one of us though. In the schoolroom I mean. And dear old Evan and *darling* Oliver . . . well they were the teachers. I'm so pleased. After all you did bully us, didn't you, Judith, so Tybalt is just right for you. I always say to Oliver you need someone to bully *you.* And now you've got Tybalt. Not that he'll bully in the way you did but he'll keep a firm hand. You can't imagine anyone bullying Tybalt, can you? Oh, Judith, aren't you lucky! And I can't think of anyone I'd rather have for my darling perfect brother."

This was more comforting than the views at Rainbow Cottage.

And she went on. "It was all so exciting. Sir Ralph and all that . . . and the *money!* You'll be able to go everywhere with Tybalt. My father was always having to get people interested, to back his trips you know. Not that he didn't spend a lot on it himself. We'd have been *fabulously* rich, my mother used to say, if it hadn't been for my father's *obsession.*"

So it seemed that whenever my coming marriage was discussed, my recently acquired fortune always seemed to come under consideration.

I couldn't help enjoying my interview with Lady Bodrean.

After the will had been read I presented myself to her. She regarded me as though I were quite distasteful, which I suppose I was.

"So," she said, "you have come to hand in your notice."

"Certainly I have, Lady Bodrean."

"I expected it would not be long before you did. So I am to be inconvenienced."

I replied: "Well, if I was so useful to you, a fact which you very carefully concealed, I would be willing to stay for a week or so until you have replaced me."

"You know by now that you were *forced* on me. I had not employed a companion before you came."

"Then you will have no objection to my leaving immediately."

She had obviously come to the conclusion that the new turn in my fortunes meant that I would no longer be a good object for oppression and she decided I should go at once, but she pretended to consider this.

That I was Sir Ralph's daughter was, I am sure, no surprise to her. In fact I think his behavior towards me had convinced her of our relationship and it was for this reason that she had been particularly unpleasant to me. But that Tybalt should have asked me to marry him was something which puzzled her. She had wanted Tybalt for her own daughter and the fact that Theodosia had married Evan Callum and I had won the prize was galling to her.

"I hear you are shortly to be married," she said, her lip curling.

"You have heard correctly," I told her.

"I must say I was surprised until . . . er . . ."

"Until?" I said.

"I know that Sir Ralph confided a great deal in Sir
Edward. They were close friends. I've no doubt he told
him the position and it was for this reason that er . . ."

"You have always been very frank in the past, Lady
Bodrean," I said. "There is no need to be less direct now
that we meet on an equal footing. You are suggesting that
Sir Tybalt Travers has asked me to marry him because I
am Sir Ralph's daughter?"

"Sir Ralph was eager for a union with that family. Of
course he would have preferred his *true* daughter to
have made the match—instead of which she must go off
with this penniless schoolteacher."

"As I may now presume to correct you, something
which was beyond my range before my true identity was
discovered, I must remind you that Professor Callum is
far from penniless. He holds a good post in one of the
country's foremost universities and the term schoolteacher
is hardly the correct one to apply to a lecturer in archaeology."

"He was not the man Sir Ralph wished his daughter to
marry. She was foolish and flouted us—and it seems to
me that Sir Ralph then decided that since Theodosia had
been so foolish he would offer her chance to you."

"My future husband is not a prize packet on a dish
to be offered round."

"One might say that there was quite a prize to be
offered to him. I am surprised at the manner in which
my husband has left his fortune. I would say it is a victory
for immorality and extravagance."

I would not let her see that she had scored. This suggestion that I was being married for my money was not
a new one.

However, I said goodbye to Lady Bodrean and left
her with the understanding that our association as employer and employee was terminated.

I went back to Rainbow Cottage which would be my
home until my marriage.

We were to be married very soon. Tybalt insisted.
Dorcas and Alison thought it was somewhat unseemly to

have a wedding so soon after a funeral; and I had to remember that that funeral had turned out to be my father's.

When I put this point to Tybalt he said: "What nonsense! You didn't know it was your father until afterwards."

I agreed with him. I was ready to agree with him on anything. When I was with him, I forgot all my misgivings. He was so eager for our wedding, and although he was by no means demonstrative he would look at me in a way which sent me into a state of bliss, for I knew that he was contemplating our future with the utmost pleasure. He took me into his confidence completely about his plans. This bequest of Sir Ralph's was a boon. Such a large sum of money suitably invested would bring in an income which could be entirely devoted to those explorations in which Sir Ralph had always delighted.

He talked a great deal about that other expedition which had ended abruptly and fatally for Sir Edward. He made me see the arid countryside, feel the heat of that blazing sun. I could visualize the excitement when they had found the door in the mountainside and the flight of steps leading down to corridors.

When he talked of ancient Egypt a passion glowed in him. I had never seen him so enthralled by anything as he was by his work, but I used to tell myself that our marriage was going to be the most important thing that ever happened to either of us, even more so than his work. I would see to that.

I was often at Giza House. It seemed different now that it was to be my home. Tabitha welcomed me warmly. She told me at the first opportunity how pleased she was that Tybalt and I were to marry.

"At one time," she whispered, "I greatly feared that it might be Theodosia."

"That seemed to be the general idea."

"There was a great deal of talk about it. I suppose because of the friendship between Sir Ralph and Sir Edward. And they died within a short time of each other." She looked very sad. "I am sure you are the one for Tybalt." She pressed my hand. "I shall never forget how you used to come and borrow the books. Those were not very happy days for you I fear."

I told her that nothing that had gone before was of any more importance. In the last weeks life had given me all that I had ever hoped for.

"And you dreamed your dreams, Judith!" she said.

"I was a great dreamer. Now I am going to live."

"You must understand Tybalt."

"I think I do."

"At times you will feel that he neglects you for the work."

"I shan't because it's going to be my work too. I'm going to join him in everything he does. I'm as excited as he is about all this."

"That's as it should be," she said. "I hope when you become mistress of Giza House you will not wish me to leave."

"How could I? We're friends."

"I have always been a close friend of Tybalt and his father. If I may continue here in my role as housekeeper I should be very happy. On the other hand if you should prefer . . ."

"What nonsense!" I cried. "I want you to be here. You're my friend too."

"Thank you, Judith."

Tybalt said he would show me the house but when he did we didn't get farther than that room in which the sarcophagus had once stood because he would show me books his father had written and plans of sites they had excavated. I didn't mind. I was just so happy to be with him, to listen and be able to make intelligent comments.

It was Tabitha who showed me the house and introduced me to the staff. Emily, Ellen, Jane, and Sarah were the maids, normal girls all four of them and so like others of their kind that it took me some time to know which was which. But there were three strange people in that house.

I had seen the two Egyptian servants, Mustapha and Absalam, strange, alien, and, I had heard, even sinister;

I had listened avidly to the stories I had heard of them in the village.

Tabitha explained that Sir Edward liked them to look after him. They would cook him exotic dishes such as she knew nothing of. He had employed them on digs in Egypt and for some reason had taken a fancy to them; he had kept them with him and brought them to England.

She said they had been desolate but fatalistic about his death. They were certain it had come about because he had incurred the Curse of the Pharaohs.

"They are very concerned because Tybalt plans to carry on where his father left off. I think if it were possible for them to dissuade him they would do so."

When I was presented to them as the future Lady Travers they eyed me with suspicion. They would have seen me some years before racing up the path or round the garden.

I was prepared for them. Janet Tester was another matter. She was the old woman who had been nurse to Tybalt and Sabina, after fulfilling the same role for their mother; but she remained with them after Lady Travers's death. I remembered Sabina's saying that Old Nanny Tester went off into "funny fits," and her chatter about the old woman had been so interspersed with other matters—in Sabina's habitual manner—that I had not really taken a great deal of notice, because there was so much at Giza House to concern me. I had seen Nanny Tester on one or two occasions and had thought her a peculiar old woman, but as there was so much that was strange in Giza House, she did not seem so unusual as she would have elsewhere.

I had heard stories that the house gave the maids "the creeps"; and this I had thought had something to do with the strange objects it contained—the sarcophagus, for instance, and that never-to-be-forgotten mummy. Mustapha and Absalam clearly had something to do with it too—and I began to realize, so had Nanny Tester.

"I must explain Janet Tester to you," said Tabitha, before she took me up to introduce us. "She's a strange woman. She is really quite old now. She came as nurse to Sir Edward's wife, to whom of course she was devoted. She stayed on to look after Tybalt and Sabina; but when Lady Travers died she was almost demented. We have to be a bit careful with her, and treat her gently. Her mind wanders a bit. Sir Edward would have pensioned her off but she didn't want to go. She said she'd always been with the family and wanted to stay. There was the ideal apartment at the top of this house, completely shut off from the house. Janet was struck with it and asked to have it. She keeps to herself, although of course we keep an eye on her."

"What an unusual arrangement."

"You'll find you're marrying into an unusual family. Tybalt is like his father, far from conventional. Sir Edward never wanted to be bothered with everyday things. He brushed them aside and took the easy way out. Tybalt is very like him in that and lots of ways. It was either a matter of having Janet Tester here or sending her to some sort of home. That would have made her really unhappy. Tybalt goes up to see her, when he remembers her existence. Sabina comes in quite often. That keeps her happy. Sabina is her pet. It used to be Tybalt but since he's following in his father's footsteps she's turned to Sabina."

We mounted the stairs. What a silent house it was; our feet sunk into those thick carpets which covered every space of floor.

I commented on them and Tabitha said: "Sir Edward could not endure noise while he was working."

The house was a tall one, and Janet Tester's apartment consisted of several attic-type rooms above the fourth story.

I was unprepared for the white-haired, gentle-looking woman who opened the door when we knocked. She wore a crisply laundered sprigged muslin blouse and a black bombazine skirt.

Tabitha said: "Janet, I've brought Miss Osmond to see you."

She looked at me and her eyes were misty with emotion. "Come in, come in," she said.

It was a charming room with its sloping roof, and it was prettily furnished with handmade rugs on the floor and lots of embroidered cushion covers. There was a fire burning and the kettle on a hob was beginning to sing.

"You'll take some tea with me," she said, and I replied that I should love to.

"You've heard of me then?" I said.

"Why bless you, yes. Tybalt told me and I said to him 'Now you tell me what she's like, Tybalt,' and all he could say was 'She's enthusiastic about the work.' How like him! But I knew. I've seen you often tearing about down in the gardens there. What a one for mischief you were! I'll make the tea."

"Shall I do that," asked Tabitha, "while you and Miss Osmond have a chat?"

The expression in the gentle old face changed startlingly. The eyes were almost venomous, the lips tightened. "I'll do it, thank you," she said. "I'll make my own tea in my own room."

When she was making it Tabitha gave me a glance. I imagined she was preparing me for the strangeness she had mentioned in Janet Tester.

The tea was made. "I always stir it," she told me, "and let it stand five minutes. It's the only way to get the right brew. Warm the pot, I used to say to Miss Ruth . . ."

"That's Lady Travers," explained Tabitha and this remark brought forth another venomous glance.

"And the tea must go into a *dry* pot," went on Janet Tester. "That's very important."

She purred as she poured out the tea.

"Well, I hope you'll be happy, my dear," she said. "Tybalt used to be such a good boy."

"*Used* to be?" I asked.

"When he was a little one he was always with me. He was his mother's boy then. But when he went away to school and started to grow up he turned to his father."

She shook her head sadly.

"Tybalt had a natural bent for archaeology right from the start," explained Tabitha. "This delighted Sir Edward, and naturally Tybalt had so many advantages because of his father."

Janet Tester was stirring the spoon round and round in her cup. I could sense an uneasy atmosphere.

"And now you're going to marry him," she said. "How time flies. It seems only yesterday I was playing peekaboo with him."

The thought of Tybalt's playing peekaboo was so funny that I couldn't help laughing. "He's come a long way since then," I said.

"I hope it's not on the road to ruin," said Janet Tester stirring fiercely.

I looked at Tabitha who had lifted her shoulders. I decided then that Tybalt's and his father's profession was not a happy subject so I asked about his childhood.

That pleased her. "He was a good boy. He didn't get into all that much mischief. Miss Ruth doted on him. He was her boy all right. I've got some pictures."

I reveled in them. Tybalt sitting on a furry rug all but in the nude; Tybalt a wondering two year old; Tybalt and Sabina.

"Isn't she a little pet?" doted Nanny Tester.

I agreed. "Such a little chatterbox. Never stopped."

I remarked that it was a trait which had remained with her.

"Little minx!" said Nanny Tester fondly.

There was a picture of Tybalt, standing beside a rather pretty woman with a lot of fluffy hair who was holding a baby on her lap. "There they are with their mother. Oh, and here's Tybalt at school." He was holding a cricket bat. "He wasn't good at sports," said Nanny Tester in a disappointed voice. "It started to be all study. Not like Sabina. They all said she couldn't concentrate. But of course *he* walked off with all the prizes. And then Sir Edward who'd scarcely noticed the children before, started to prick up his ears."

She conveyed her feelings by so many gestures—the tone of her voice, a contemptuous flick of the hand, a turning down of the lips, a half closing of the eyes. I had been with her a very short time but I had learned that she dis-

liked Tabitha, and Sir Edward; she had adored Miss Ruth
and while Tybalt, the child, had qualified for her devotion
I was not so sure how she regarded the man.

I was interested—greatly so—and I did get the impression that had Tabitha not been with me, I should have
understood so much more about Janet Tester.

I sensed Tabitha's relief when we could politely leave;
Tabitha went on ahead of me and Janet suddenly caught
my hand in hers when we were in the little hall. Her
fingers were dry and strong.

"Come again, Miss Osmond," she said, and whispered:
"Alone."

As we descended the stairs I said: "What a strange
little woman!"

"So you sensed that."

"I thought she was not exactly what she seemed. At
times she was so gentle—at others quite the reverse."

"She has a bit of an obsession."

"I gathered that. Miss Ruth, I suppose."

"You know what these old nurses are like. They are
like mothers to their charges. Far closer to them than
their own mothers. She disliked Sir Edward. I suppose
she was jealous and because her Miss Ruth had no interest
in his work she blamed him for doing it. Very illogical as
you can see. Tybalt's mother wanted him to go into the
Church. Of course he was quite unsuited to that profession
and from an early age had made up his mind to follow
his father. Sir Edward's delight more than made up for
Lady Travers's—and Janet's—disappointment. But they
bore a grudge against Sir Edward for it. I'm afraid Lady
Travers was a rather hysterical woman and I've no doubt
she confided a great deal in Janet who could see no wrong
in her. It was a disastrous marriage in many ways—although Lady Travers brought a big fortune with her when
she married."

"Money again," I said. "It's odd how that subject seems
to crop up continually."

"Well, it's a very useful commodity, you must admit."

"It seems to have a big part to play in certain marriages."

"That's the way of the world," said Tabitha lightly. "It's

good to be out of Janet's rooms. They stifle me."

Later I thought a good deal about that encounter. I understood Janet's dislike of Sir Edward, but I did wonder why she felt so strongly—and her attitude had betrayed to me that she did—about Tabitha.

The weeks before my wedding were flying past. Dorcas and Alison wanted quite a celebration. They seemed so relieved that they no longer had to preserve the secret of my birth that they were almost like children let out of school. Moreover, anxieties for the future had been swept away. The cottage was theirs; I was going to give them an allowance; my future was settled although—in spite of their efforts to hide this—they had misgivings about my bridegroom. Tybalt had little to say to them and their meetings were always uneasy. When I was present I would keep the conversation going but when I went out of the room and returned I would be aware of the awkward pauses when none of them had anything to say. Yet they could chatter away to Oliver naturally about parish affairs and with Evan would talk of the old days and the pranks we used to get up to.

Tybalt was always so relieved when he and I were alone. I was so besottedly in love, always making the affectionate gesture, that his lack of demonstrativeness was not so noticeable as it might have been. Sometimes we would sit close together looking at plans, his arm about me while I nestled close and asked myself whether this was really happening to me; but the conversation was almost always of the work he and his father had been doing.

Once he said: "It's wonderful to have you with me, Judith." And then he added: "You're so absolutely keen. I never knew anyone who was so exuberantly enthusiastic as you."

"You are," I said. "Your father must have been."

"But in a quieter way."

"But very intense," I said.

He kissed me then lightly on the forehead. "But you express yourself so forcefully," he said. "I like it, Judith. In fact I find it wonderful."

I threw my arms about him and gathered him to me as I used to Dorcas and Alison. I hugged him and cried: "I'm so happy."

Then I would tell him about how I had decided to hate him when Sabina had spoken of him in such glowing terms. "I imagined you stooped and wore spectacles and were pale with lank greasy hair. And then you burst upon us, in the mummy room, looking fierce and vengeful like some Egyptian god come to wreak vengeance on one who had desecrated the old sarcophagus."

"Did I really look like that?"

"Exactly—and I adored you from that moment."

"Well, I must remember to look fierce and vengeful sometimes."

"And that you should have chosen me . . . is a miracle."

"Oh Judith, surely you are too modest."

"Far from it! As you know, I used to dream about you . . . how you suddenly discovered my worth."

"Which I did in due course."

"When did you discover it?"

"When I knew that you had come to borrow the books and were so interested. Or perhaps it began when I saw you emerging from those bandages. You looked as though you had suffered a fatal accident rather than embalmment. But it was a good effort."

I took his hand and kissed it.

"Tybalt," I said, "I am going to look after you all the days of your life."

"That's a comforting thought," he said.

"I'm going to make myself so important to you that you will hate every moment you spend away from me."

"I've reached that stage already."

"Is it true? Is it really true?"

He took my hands in his. "Understand, Judith, I lack your powers of expression. Words flow from you expressing your innermost thoughts."

"I know I speak without thinking. I'm sure you never do."

"Be patient with me."

"Tell me one thing. Are you happy?"

"Do you think I'm not?"

"Not completely."

He said slowly: "I have lost someone who was closer to me, until you came, than anyone else in the world. We worked together; we would be thinking along the same lines together often without speaking. He is dead, and he died suddenly. He was there one day and the next he was stricken down . . . mysteriously. I mourn him, Judith. I shall go on mourning him for a long time. That is why you must be patient with me. I can't match your exuberance, your pleasure in life. My dear, dear Judith, I believe that when we are married I shall begin to grow away from this tragedy."

Then I put my head against him and kept my arms tightly about him.

"To make you happy, to give you something to replace what you have lost . . . that shall be my mission in life."

He kissed my head.

"Thank God for you, Judith," he said.

There was a little friction between Tybalt and the aunts over the wedding. This, said Alison firmly, could not take place until a "reasonable" time had elapsed since the deaths of Sir Edward and Sir Ralph.

"Fathers of both bride and groom so recently dead!" said Dorcas. "You should wait at least a year."

I had never seen Tybalt express his feelings so forcibly.

"Impossible!" he cried. "We shall be leaving for Egypt in a matter of months. Judith must come as my wife."

"I can't imagine what people will say," Dorcas put in timidly.

"That," said Tybalt, "does not concern me in the least."

Dorcas and Alison were deflated, but afterwards I heard them saying to each other: "It may not concern him, but it concerns us and we have lived here all our lives and shall do so until the end."

"Tybalt is unconventional," I soothed. "And worrying what people think is really rather unnecessary."

They did not answer, but they shook their heads over me and my affairs. I was besotted; and they were sure that to let a man see before marriage how much you adored him was wrong. Afterwards, yes. Then it was a wife's duty to think as her husband did, to submit to him in all ways—unless of course he turned out to be a *criminal*—but before the marriage one did not "make oneself cheap"; it was the custom for a man to go down on his knees before marriage.

I laughed at them indulgently. "My marriage, as you should know, is going to be like no marriage that ever was. You can't expect me to do what is expected of me."

When they were with me they grew excited sometimes, for after all a wedding in the family was an event. They produced all manner of objects for my bottom drawer; and they talked about the reception and worried because Rainbow Cottage was too small for it and the bride's house was the necessary place for it.

I could laugh at them mockingly but I sensed their uneasiness. They did not wish me to wait a year so much for convention but because they thought it would give me time to see clearly as they called it. The fact was that they had chosen Oliver for my husband; Evan was second choice; but Tybalt did not appeal to them at all.

Dorcas caught a cold—something she invariably did when she was anxious; and her colds had to be nursed because they turned to bronchitis.

Tybalt came hurrying over to Rainbow Cottage. His eyes were glowing with excitement as he took my hands in his. For the moment I thought it was pleasure in seeing me. Then I discovered another reason.

"A most exciting thing has happened, Judith. It's not very far from here. Dorset in fact. A workman digging a trench has unearthed some Roman tiles. It's quite a find. It seems very likely that this is going to lead to a great discovery. I've had an invitation to go along and give an opinion. I am leaving tomorrow. I want you to come with me."

"That's wonderful," I cried. "Tell me all about it."

"I know very little yet. But these discoveries are so

exciting. One can never be sure what we're going to turn up."

We walked about the Rainbow garden talking about it. He did not stay long though for he had to go back to Giza House to make some preparations and I went into Rainbow Cottage to tell the aunts that I was leaving next day.

I was astonished at the opposition.

"My dear Judith!" cried Alison. "What are you thinking of? How can you . . . an unmarried woman, go off with a man?"

"The man I am going to marry."

"But you are not married yet," croaked Dorcas.

"It wouldn't be right," said Alison firmly.

"Dear aunts," I said, "in Tybalt's world these little conventions don't count."

"We are older than you, Judith. Why, many a girl has anticipated her marriage to her own bitter cost. She trusts her fiancé, goes away with him and discovers that there are no wedding bells."

I flared up. "At one moment you are suggesting Tybalt is marrying me for my money and at the next that he plans to seduce me and then discard me. Really, you are being so absurd."

"Why we suggested no such thing," said Alison firmly. "And if those sort of things are in your mind, well, Judith, you really ought to stop and consider. No bride should feel her bridegroom capable of such a thing."

How could I argue with them? I went to my room and started to pack for the next day's trip.

That evening when I was in my room Alison tapped at the door. Her face was strained. "I'm worried about Dorcas. I do think we should have Dr. Gunwen at once."

I said I would go and fetch him, which I did.

When he came he said that Dorcas had bronchitis and Alison and I were up all night with the bronchitis kettle in Dorcas's room.

I knew the next day that I could not go to Dorset and leave Alison to nurse Dorcas alone, so I told Alison that I was going over to Giza House to explain matters to Tybalt.

Before I could speak, he began to tell me that the finds

were even better than had at first been thought. I interrupted him: "I'm not coming, Tybalt."

His expression changed. He stared at me incredulously. "Not coming!"

"My Aunt Dorcas is ill. I can't leave Alison to nurse her. I must stay. She has these turns and it is rather frightening when she does. She is really very ill."

"We could arrange something. One of the servants could go over to take your place."

"Aunt Alison wouldn't have that. It wouldn't be the same. I must be there in case . . ."

He was silent.

"Please understand, Tybalt. I want to come . . . to be with you more than anything, but I just can't leave Rainbow Cottage now."

"Of course," he agreed, but he was very disappointed. I trusted not in me.

Tabitha came out into the front garden where we were standing.

"I've come to explain that I can't go," I said. "My aunt is ill. I must stay here to help."

"But of course you must," said Tabitha.

"Would you come in Judith's place?" asked Tybalt. "I'm sure you'd find it of paramount interest."

Paramount interest. Was that a reproach? Did he feel that I should have found it of *paramount* interest?

Tabitha was saying: "Well, since Judith must stay, I will go in her place. You cannot leave your aunts now, Judith."

Tybalt pressed my arm. "I was so looking forward to showing you this marvelous discovery. But there'll be plenty of time . . . later."

"The whole of our lives," I said.

In a few days, much to our relief Dorcas began to recover.

She was touched that I had stayed behind to help nurse her and comfort Alison.

I heard her say to Alison when she thought I couldn't

hear: "However impulsive Judith is, her *heart's* in the right place."

I knew they talked a great deal about me and my coming marriage. I did so want to reassure them; but they had taken it into their heads that Tybalt had asked me to marry him because he had preknowledge of my inheritance.

I was greatly looking forward to the day when I would leave Rainbow Cottage naturally because I longed to be Tybalt's wife and in addition I wanted to escape this atmosphere of distrust and to prove to them that Tybalt was the most wonderful husband in the world.

Tybalt and Tabitha were away for two weeks and when they returned they were so full of what they had seen that they talked of little else. I was filled with chagrin because I could not join in their conversation as I would have wished.

Tybalt was amused. "Never mind," he said, "when we're married you'll go everywhere with me."

The wedding day was almost at hand. Sabina had said that we might have a discreet reception at the rectory. After all, Dorcas had been ill and Rainbow Cottage was small and the rectory had been my home and she was Tybalt's sister. "I insist on it," she cried. "I can tell you, Judith, you are the most fortunate woman in the world . . . with one exception because even Tybalt could not be as wonderful as Oliver. Tybalt is *too* perfect. I mean he knows everything . . . all about those ancient things, whereas darling Oliver knows about Greek and Latin. Not that Tybalt doesn't too, but you couldn't imagine Tybalt's preaching a sermon or listening to the farmers telling him about the droughts and the mothers about their babies . . . But our mother wanted him to do just that . . . Isn't it *odd*. She would have been pleased I'd married darling Oliver, you know. Old Nanny Tester is. But she was always a bit odd . . . since Mamma died, that is. Bats in the Belfry, they say of people like her. It means that they are a little peculiar in the head. Perhaps that's why she likes churches. . . ."

I said: "Really, Sabina, you do dodge from one thing to another, like a butterfly."

"My father used to say I was like a grasshopper. He didn't really approve of me, I wasn't clever like Tybalt. However grasshoppers are rather nice. I always liked them. Not so pretty as butterflies but hopping around seems to me a rather pleasant way of going on. Better than staying in the same place all the time. . . ."

"What *are* you talking about, Sabina? We're supposed to be discussing my wedding."

"Of course. It's to be here. I insist. Darling Oliver insists. You'll be married in *his* church and we'll have just a few friends as my father . . . and yours . . . what a surprise and fancy your being Sir Ralph's daughter all that time and our not knowing. What was I saying? Oh, you're to have your reception in the old rectory."

It did seem a good idea; and even Dorcas and Alison accepted it, though they insisted that in view of the recent deaths it must just be a quiet family affair.

When I discussed the matter with Tybalt he was rather vague. I could see that it was immaterial to him where we had a reception or whether there was none.

He wanted us to be married, he said. Where and how was unimportant.

He had a surprise for me.

"We'll have a honeymoon. You won't want to go straight back to Giza House."

"That," I said, "is immaterial to *me*. All I ask is that I am with you."

He turned to face me and with an unusually tender gesture took my face in his hands. "Judith," he said, "don't expect too much of me."

I laughed aloud—I was so happy. "Why I expect *everything* of you."

"That's what makes me uneasy. You see, I am rather selfish, not admirable in the least. And I am a man with an obsession."

"I share in that obsession," I told him with a laugh. "And I have another. You."

He held me against him. "You make me afraid," he said.

"You afraid? You are not afraid of anything . . . or anyone."

"I'm certainly afraid of this high opinion you have of me. Where could you possibly have got it?"

"You gave it to me."

"You are too imaginative, Judith. You get an idea and it's usually something you want it to be and then you make everything fit into that."

"It's the way to live. I shall teach you to live that way."

"It's better to see the truth."

"I will make this my truth."

"I can see it is useless to warn you not to think too highly of me."

"It is quite useless."

"Time will have to teach you."

"I said we will grow closer together as the years pass. We shall share everything. I never thought it was possible to be so happy as I am at this moment."

"At least you will have had this moment."

"What a way to talk! This is nothing to what it is going to be like."

"My darling Judith, there is no one like you."

"Of course there isn't! I am myself. Reckless, impulsive, the aunts would tell you. Bossy, Sabina and Theodosia will agree and Hadrian will confirm that. They are the ones who have known me the longest. So *you* must not have too high an opinion of *me*."

"I'm glad there are these little faults. I shall love you for them as I hope you will love me for mine."

I said: "We are going to be so happy."

"I came to tell you about our honeymoon. I'm going to take you to Dorset. They are so excited about this discovery. I long to show it to you."

I said that was wonderful; but it did occur to me that there would no doubt be a great many people there and a honeymoon on our own might have been more appropriate.

But Tybalt would be there—and that was all I asked.

There was so much to do in preparation even for a

"discreet" wedding, including sessions in Sarah Sloper's cottage which seemed to go on for hours. There was I in my white satin wedding gown with Sarah kneeling at my feet, her mouth full of pins, and as soon as she had it free she would talk all the time.

"Well, fancy it coming to this. You, Miss Judith . . . and *him*. He was for Miss Theodosia, you know, and she gets the little professor and you get *him*."

"You make it sound as though it's some sort of lottery, Sarah."

"They do say marriage be a lottery, Miss Judith. And you being Sir Ralph's girl and all. I always guessed that. Why he had a real fancy for you. And Miss Lavinia. Pretty as a picture she were but I'd say you took more after Sir Ralph."

"Thank you, Sarah."

"Oh, I weren't meaning it *that* way, Miss Judith. You'll look pretty enough in your bride's dress. Brides always do. That's why there's nothing I like making better. And is it to be orange blossom? I reckon there's nothing like orange blossom for brides. I had it myself when I married Sloper. That's going back a bit. And I've still got it. Put away in a drawer it be. I look at it now and then and think of the old days. You'll be able to do that, Miss Judith. It's a pleasant thing to do when things don't turn out just as you'd fancied. And don't we all have fancies eh, on our wedding days?"

"I look on it as a beginning of happiness not a climax."

"Oh, you and your talk. Always was one for it. But as I say it's nice to have a wedding day to look back on— as long as it don't make you fretful." She sighed and went on fervently: "I hope you'll be happy, Miss Judith. Well, we can but hope. So let's pray the sun'll shine on your wedding day. They do say 'Happy the bride the sun shines on.' "

I laughed; but this assumption that my marriage would be a perilous adventure was beginning to irritate me.

On a rather misty October day I was married to Tybalt in the church I knew so well. Oddly enough as I came down the aisle on the arm of Dr. Gunwen, who had offered to "give me away," there being no one else to perform this necessary duty, I was thinking of how my knees used to get sore from kneeling on the mats which hung inside the pews for that purpose. An extraordinary thought to have when I was on my way to marriage with Tybalt!

A fellow archaeologist and friend of Tybalt's was his best man. He was named Terence Gelding and was accompanying us to Egypt. On the night before the wedding I had not seen Tybalt. He had gone to the station to meet his friend and bring him back to Giza House where he was spending a few days. Tabitha told me on my wedding morning that they had all stayed up too late talking. I felt that vague tinge of jealousy which I had begun to notice came to me when others shared an intimacy with Tybalt and I was not present. It was foolish of me but I supposed I had dreamed so long of this happening that I could not entirely believe that it was true; there had been covert remarks about my marriage from several directions and it seemed that these insinuations had penetrated even my natural optimism. I could not help feeling a twinge of uneasiness and distrust of this sudden granting by fate of my most cherished desire.

But as I made my vows before Oliver, and Tybalt put the ring on my finger, a wonderful happiness surged over me and I was more completely happy than I had ever been.

It was disappointing that as we came into the porch the rain should begin to pelt down.

"You can't walk out in that," said Dorcas at my elbow.

"It's nothing," I said. "Just a shower and we only have to go over to the rectory."

"We'll have to wait."

She was right, of course. So we stood there, I still holding Tybalt's hand saying nothing, staring out at the rain and thinking: I'm really married . . . to Tybalt!

I heard the whispers behind me.

"What a pity!"

"What bad luck!"

"Not wedding weather by any means."

A gnome-like creature came walking up from the grave-yard. As it approached I saw that it was Mr. Pegger, bent double with a sack, split down one side, over his head to keep him dry. He carried a spade to which the brown earth still clung. So he had been digging somebody's grave, and was, I supposed, coming to the porch for shelter until the downpour was over.

When he saw us he pulled up short; he pushed the sack farther back and his fanatical eyes took in Tybalt and me in our wedding clothes.

He looked straight at me. "No good'ull come of such indecent haste," he said. "It's ungodly."

Then he nodded and walked past the porch with the self-righteous air of one determined to do his duty how-ever unpleasant.

"Who on earth is that old fool?" said Tybalt.

"It's Mr. Pegger, the gravedigger."

"He's impertinent."

"Well, you see he knew me as a child and no doubt thinks I'm still one."

"He objects to your marriage."

I heard Theodosia whisper: "Oh, Evan, how un-pleasant. It's like an . . . *omen.*"

I did not answer. I felt suddenly angry with all these people who for some ridiculous reason had decided that there was something strange about my marriage to Tybalt.

I looked up at the lowering sky and I seemed to hear Sarah Sloper's reedy voice: "Happy be the bride the sun shines on."

After a few minutes the rain stopped and we were able to pick our way across the grass to the vicarage.

There was the familiar drawing room decked out with chrysanthemums of all shades and starry Michaelmas daisies. A table had been set up at one end of the room and on this was a wedding cake and champagne.

I cut the cake with Tybalt's help; everyone applauded and the unpleasant incident in the porch was temporarily forgotten.

Hadrian made a witty speech and Tybalt responded
very briefly. I kept saying to myself: "This is the supreme
moment of my life." Perhaps I said it a little too ve-
hemently. I could not forget Mr. Pegger's eyes peering
at us in that fanatical way from under that absurd sack.
The rain had started again in a heavy downpour which
made itself heard.

Theodosia was beside me. "Oh, Judith," she said,
"I'm so glad we're sisters. Here you are marrying Tybalt
and this is what they wanted for me. So Father got his
wish that his daughter marry Tybalt. Hasn't it turned out
wonderfully?" She was gazing across the room at Evan
who was talking to Tabitha. "I'm so grateful to you . . ."

"Grateful . . . ?"

She floundered a little. Theodosia had never been able
to express her thoughts gracefully and often landed in a
conversational morass from which she found it difficult
to extricate herself.

"Well, for marrying Tybalt and making it all come
right so that I need not have any conscience about not
pleasing Father . . . and all that."

She made it sound as though by marrying Tybalt I
had conferred some blessing on all those who had been
saved from him!

"I'm sure you'll be *very* happy," she said comfortingly.
"You always knew so much about archaeology. It's a
struggle for me to keep up with Evan, but he says don't
worry. He's perfectly satisfied with me as I am."

"You're very happy, Theodosia?"

"Oh . . . blissfully. That's why I'm so . . ." She stopped.

"Grateful to me for marrying Tybalt and making it all
work out smoothly. I can assure you I didn't marry him
for that reason."

Sabina joined us.

"Isn't this *fun*. The three of us together. And now we're
all married. Judith, do you like the flowers? Miss Crewe
arranged them. Most of them came from her garden.
Green fingers, you know. And she always makes such a
success of the decorations in the church. And here we all
are together. Do you remember how we used to talk in

the schoolroom? Of course dramatic things *would* happen to Judith. They always did, didn't they? Or perhaps you made it sound dramatic and then you did turn out to be Sir Ralph's daughter . . . Wrong side of the blanket of course . . . but that makes it more exciting. And now you've got Tybalt. Doesn't he look wonderful? Like a Roman god or something . . . He was always different from everybody else . . . and so are you, Judith . . . in a way. But we're sisters now, Judith. And you're Theodosia's sister. As I say it is wonderful!"

She gazed at Tybalt with that adoration I had seen so many times before.

"Fancy Tybalt's being a bridegroom! We always thought he would never marry! He's married to all that *nonsense,* Nanny Tester says, 'Like your father ought to have been.' I used to point out to her that if Papa had married all that nonsense I wouldn't have been here nor would Tybalt because archaeology, wonderful as Papa and Tybalt seem to find it, does not produce *people,* living ones anyway. Only mummies perhaps. Oh, do you remember the day when you dressed up as a mummy? What a day that was! We thought you'd killed Theodosia."

They were all laughing. I knew that Sabina would restore my spirits.

"And you said Tybalt stooped and wore spectacles and when you saw him you were struck dumb. You *adored* him from that moment. Oh yes you did, you can't deny it."

"I'm making no attempt to," I said.

"And now you're married to him. Your dreams have come true. Isn't that a wonderful *fairy tale* ending?"

"It's not an ending," said Theodosia soberly. "It's really a beginning. Evan is so pleased because he's been invited to join the expedition."

"Has he really?" cried Sabina. "That's a great honor. When he's away you must come and stay."

"I'm going with him," declared Theodosia fiercely. "You don't think I'd let Evan go without me."

"Has Tybalt said you may? Papa never liked wives around. He said they cluttered and distracted, unless they

were workers themselves and quite a lot of them are . . .
but you're not, Theodosia. So Tybalt has said you may!
I daresay that as he's now a married man himself he has
sympathy for others. You'll be company for Judith.
Tabitha's going. Of course she's very knowledgeable.
There she is talking to Tybalt now. I'll bet you anything
you like they're talking about Egypt. Tabitha's beautiful,
don't you think? She always seems to wear the right things.
Elegance I suppose. Different from me. That silver grey
now . . . It's just *right!* You'll have to be careful, Judith,"
she added playfully. "I was surprised that you allowed
Tybalt to go off with her to Dorset. Oh I know that you had
to stay behind, but she's young really. About a year, possibly two years older than Tybalt, that's all. Of course she
is always so quiet, so restrained, but it's the quiet ones you
have to be wary of, so they say. Oh, Judith, what a way
to talk to a bride on her wedding day. You're quite disturbed, I believe. As if I meant it. Tybalt will be the
most *faithful* husband in the world! He's too busy anyway
to be anything else. The wonder is that he married at all.
I'm sure you're going to be wonderfully happy. Your
being interested in his world and all that and quite rich
so there won't be money problems and Sir Ralph leaving
all that money to archaeological research. Wasn't that
wonderful! You've married the most wonderful man in
the world with one exception of course. But even darling
Oliver isn't grand and distinguished like Tybalt . . .
although he's more *comfortable* and I wouldn't change
him for anyone in the world . . ."

"Oh doesn't she run on," I said to Theodosia. "No one
else gets a chance."

"It's revenge for your domineering attitude in the schoolroom and you're only so silent because it's your wedding
day. If you weren't thinking of Tybalt, you would never
have allowed me to have the floor for so long."

"Trust you to make the most of your opportunities.
Look, here's Hadrian."

"Hello," said Hadrian. "A family gathering. I must
join it."

"We were talking about the expedition," said Sabina. "Among other things."

"Who isn't?"

"Did you know Evan and Theodosia are coming?" I asked.

"I had heard there was a possibility. We shall all be together . . . all except you, Sabina, and your Oliver."

"Oliver has the church and parish . . . besides, he's a parson not an archaeologist."

"So you're going too, Hadrian."

"It's a great concession. Gives me a chance to escape my creditors."

"You are always talking about money."

"I've told you before I'm not rich enough to ignore it."

"Nonsense," I said.

"And now, Judith, *you've* joined the band of plutocrats. Well, it will be good experience for us, Tybalt tells me. We'll have to keep together in case this irate god rises from his lair to strike us."

"Do gods have lairs?" asked Sabina. "I thought that was foxes. There's a big red one raiding Brent's Farm. Farmer Brent lies in wait with a shot gun."

"Stop her someone," said Hadrian, "before she flies off at a tangent."

"Yes," I said, "we don't want to hear about foxes. The expedition is of much greater interest. I'm so looking forward to it. It'll soon be time to leave for Egypt."

"Which is the reason for the hasty wedding," said Hadrian. "What did you think of the weird character in the porch?"

"It was only old Pegger."

"Talk about a prophet of doom. He couldn't have appeared at a less appropriate moment . . . or from his point of view I suppose a more appropriate one. He seemed so delighted to be the harbinger of misfortune."

"I wish everyone would stop hinting at misfortune," I complained. "It's most unsuitable."

"Of course it is," agreed Hadrian, "and here comes your reverend husband, Sabina. He'll probably say a blessing or exorcise the evil spirits conjured up by that old ghoul in the porch."

"He'll do no such thing," said Sabina, slipping her arm through Oliver's as he came up.

"Just in time," said Hadrian, "to prevent this inconsequential wife of yours from giving a dissertation on the duties of a parish priest and where that might lead to Heaven—and Sabina—only knows. I'm going to take the bride away from you for a cozy tête-à-tête."

We stood alone in a corner and he looked at me shaking his head. "Well, well, Judith, this is so sudden."

"Not you too," I protested.

"Oh I don't mean it as old Pegger did. I mean coming into a fortune and marrying at the batting of an eyelid or the twinkling of an eye—to keep the metaphors facial."

I laughed at him. Hadrian always restored my spirits.

"Had I known that you had inherited a fortune I would have married you myself."

"What a lost opportunity!" I mocked.

"My life is full of them. Seriously, who would have thought that the old man would have left you half his fortune. My pittance was a bit of a blow."

"Why, Hadrian, it's a pleasant income, and is in addition to what you will earn in your profession."

"Affluence!" he murmured. "Tybalt is a lucky devil. *You* and all that money. And there's what my uncle left to the Cause."

"How I wish I could stop people talking about money for a few moments."

"It's money that makes the world go round . . . or is that love? And lucky Judith to have both!"

"I can see my aunts making frantic signs."

"I suppose it's time for you to depart."

"Why yes, the carriage will be taking us to the station in less than an hour. And I have to change."

Dorcas came hurrying up. "Judith, do you realize what the time is?"

"I was just mentioning it to Hadrian."

"I think it is time you changed."

I slipped away with Dorcas and Alison and we went

to the room which Sabina had set aside for me. There hung my silver grey grosgrain coat and the skirt of the same material and the white blouse with many frills and the little grey velvet bow at the neck.

Silver grey. So elegant. Yes, when worn by a woman like Tabitha.

"You look lovely," cooed Dorcas.

"That's because you see me through the eyes of love," I said.

"There'll be someone else who will be looking at you in the same way," said Alison quickly. There was an almost imperceptible pause before she added: "We hope."

I went out to the porch. The carriage was there and Tybalt was waiting for me.

Everyone crowded round; the horse was whipped up. Tybalt and I had started on our honeymoon.

What shall I say of my honeymoon? That it fell short of my expectations? At first it was wonderful and the wonder lasted for two nights and a day. Then Tybalt was all mine. We were very close during that time. We had broken our journey to Dorset and spent the night, the following day and the next night at a little inn in the heart of the Moor.

"Before we join the Dig," he told me, "I thought we should have this little respite."

"It's a wonderful idea," I told him.

"I thought you were so eager to see this mosaic pavement they've discovered?"

"I'm more eager to be alone with you."

My frank admission of my devotion amused him and at the same time I fancied made him rather uneasy. Again he stressed that he lacked my powers of expression.

"You must not think, Judith," he said, "that because I do not constantly profess my love for you that it isn't there. I find it difficult to speak easily of what I feel most deeply."

That satisfied me.

I shall never forget the inn in the little moorland village. The sign creaking just outside our window——a gabled one, for the inn was three hundred years old; the sound of the waterfall less than half a mile away sending its sparkling water over the craggy boulders and the big feather bed in which we lay together.

There was a fire burning in the grate and as I watched the flickering shadows on the wallpaper—great red roses —and Tybalt's arms were about me, I was completely happy.

Breakfast was served to us in the old inn parlor with the brass and pewter on the shelves and hams hanging from the rafters. Hot coffee, bread fresh from the oven, ham and eggs from the nearby farm, scones and home-made strawberry jam with a basin of Devonshire cream the color of buttercups. And Tybalt sitting opposite me, watching me with that look almost of wonder in his eyes. If ever I was beautiful in my life I was beautiful on that morning.

After breakfast we went out onto the moors and walked for miles over the short spring turf. The innkeeper's wife had packed a little hamper for us and we picnicked by a tiny trickling stream. We saw the wild moorland ponies, too scared to come near us; and the only human beings we encountered on that day were a man driving a cart-load of apples and pears who raised his whip to us and called a greeting, and another on horseback who did the same. A happy idyllic day and then back to the delicious duckling and green peas and afterwards the cozy bed-room and the flickering fire.

The next day we caught the train to Dorset.

Of course I was fascinated by the Roman site, but I wanted only one thing in my life at that time and that was to love and be loved by Tybalt. The hotel at which we stayed was full of people who were with the working party, which made it rather different from our Dartmoor haven. I was proud of the respect with which Tybalt was greeted and, although it was brought home to me that I was an amateur among professionals and I was constantly bewildered by technicalities, I was as eager as ever to learn—a fact which delighted my husband.

The day after we reached the hotel, Terence Gelding,

Tybalt's best man, arrived. He was tall and rather lean with the same serious and dedicated expression I had noticed among so many of Tybalt's associates. Rather aloof, he seemed a little nervous of me, and I imagined he was not altogether pleased about Tybalt's marriage. When I mentioned this to Tybalt he laughed.

"You have such odd fancies, Judith," he said; and I remembered how often Alison and Dorcas had said the same of me. "Terence Gelding is a first-class worker, trustworthy too, reliable. Just the kind of man I like to work with me."

He and Terence Gelding would talk animatedly for long periods, and try as I might to follow their conversation it was not always easy.

When there was a possibility that an amphitheatre may have existed close to the site the excitement was great and a party went out to examine certain finds which might have proved an indication that this was correct. I was not invited to go.

Tybalt was apologetic.

"You see, Judith," he explained, "this is a professional affair. If I took you, others would expect to take people."

I understood and I determined that in a very short time I should have learned so much that I would be considered worthy to join in on such occasions.

Tybalt kissed me tenderly before leaving. "I'll be back in a few hours. What will you do while I'm away?"

"Read a book I've seen here dealing with Roman remains. Very soon I'm going to be as knowledgeable as you are."

That made him laugh.

I spent the day alone. I would have to be prepared for this sort of occasion, I reminded myself. But, interested as I was in this absorbing subject, I was a bride on her honeymoon, and an early Roman floor, even if it was a geometric mosaic, could not really compare with the springs and boulders of Dartmoor.

After that he was often at the site with the workers. Sometimes I went with him. I talked to the more humble members of the party; I studied maps; I even did a little digging as I had in Carter's Meadow. I watched first-aid methods in the restoration of a plaque on which was engraved the head of a Caesar. I was fascinated—but I longed to be alone with Tybalt.

We were two weeks on the Roman site. I believe Tybalt was reluctant to leave. On our last evening he spent several hours closeted with the director of the expedition. I was in bed when he came in. It was just after midnight.

He sat on the bed, his eyes shining.

"It's almost certain that there's an amphitheatre," he said. "What a discovery! I think this is going to be one of the most exciting sites in England. Professor Brownlea can't stop talking of his luck. Do you know they've found a plaque with a head engraved. If they can discover whose, it will be a great find."

"I know," I said, "I've seen it being pieced together."

"Unfortunately there is quite a bit missing. But, of course, the floor mosaics are most exciting. I would place the date of the black and white at round about 74 A.D."

"I'm sure you'd be right, Tybalt."

"Oh, but one can't be sure . . . not unless there is absolute proof. Why are you smiling?"

"Was I?" I held out my arms to him. "Perhaps because I was thinking that there are exciting things in life other than Roman remains."

He came to me at once and for a few moments we embraced. I was laughing softly. "I know what you're thinking. Yes, there are more exciting things. But I imagine the tombs of the Pharaohs win by a head."

"Oh, Judith," he said, "this is wonderful to be together. I want to have you there with me when we leave."

"Of course. It was for that reason you married me."

"That and others," he said.

"Well, we have discussed that . . . now let us consider the others."

I amused him. My frank enjoyment of our love was something which I am sure would have completely shocked Dorcas and Alison. But then so many people would have considered me bold and brazen.

I wondered if Tybalt did. I asked him. "You see," I

explained, "it has always been almost impossible for me to pretend."

He said: "I don't deserve you, Judith."

I laughed, completely happy. "You can always try to be worthy," I suggested.

And I was happy. So was he. As happy as he was on his mosaic pavement or with his broken plaque or ruins of his amphitheatre? Was he? I wondered.

It was foolish of me to have these niggling doubts. I wished that I could forget the Cassandra-like faces of Dorcas and Alison, the hints and innuendos, the fanatical eyes of old Pegger in the porch. I wished that Sir Ralph had not left me a fortune; then I could indeed have been sure that I had been married for myself.

But these matters could be forgotten . . . temporarily. And I promised myself that in time I would banish them altogether.

Then we returned to Giza House.

It was the first week of November when we arrived in the late afternoon, and a dark and gloomy one. The October gales had stripped the trees of most of their leaves; but as the carriage brought us from the station the countryside seemed unusually silent for the wind had then dropped. It was typical Cornish November weather—warm and damp. As we pulled up at the wrought-iron gates of Giza and descended from the carriage, Tabitha came out to greet us.

"Not a very pleasant day," she said. "You must be chilled. Come in quickly and we'll have tea at once."

She was looking at us searchingly, as though she suspected the honeymoon had not been a success. Why did I get the impression that everyone seemed to have come to the conclusion that Tybalt and I were unsuited?

Imagination! I told myself. I looked up at the house. Haunted! I thought; and remembered teasing Theodosia and frightening her by making her run up the path. I thought of Nanny Tester probably peering out from a top window.

"Giza House always intrigued me," I said as I stepped into the hall.

"It's your home now," Tabitha reminded me.

"When we get back from Egypt, Judith may want to make some changes in the house," said Tybalt slipping his arm through mine. He smiled at me. "For the time being we must concentrate on our plans."

Tabitha showed us our room. It was on the first floor next to that room in which I had seen the sarcophagus. Tabitha had had it redecorated while we were away.

"You're very good," said Tybalt.

In the shadows I saw Mustapha and Absalam. I noticed their dark eyes fixed intently on me. They would be re-membering me of course as the rowdy child and after-wards the "companion" from Keverall Court who came to borrow books. Now I was the new mistress. Or did Tabitha retain that title?

How I wished people had not sown these misgivings in my mind with their sly allusions.

Tabitha conducted me first to our room and left me there to freshen up while she returned to the drawing room with Tybalt. One of the maids brought hot water and when I had washed I went to the window and looked out. The garden had always been chock-a-block with shrubs and the trees made it dark. I could see the spiders' webs on the bushes, glistening where the light caught the globules of moisture as so often I had seen them before at this time of year. The curtains were deep blue edged with gold braid in a Greek key pattern. The bed was large, a fourposter canopied and curtained. The carpet was thick. Bookshelves lined one side of the wall. I looked at these. Some of them I had borrowed and read. They all referred to one subject. It occurred to me that this had been Sir Edward's bedroom before he had left for that fatal journey, and it seemed then that the past was enveloping me. I wished that a different room had been chosen for us. Then I remembered that I was the mistress of the house and if I did not like a room I could say so.

I changed my traveling clothes and went down to the drawing room. Tybalt and Tabitha were sitting side by side on the sofa examining some plans.

As soon as I entered Tabitha jumped up. "Tea will arrive immediately," she said. "I daresay you are ready for it. Traveling is so tiring."

Ellen wheeled the tea wagon in and stood by while Tabitha poured.

Tabitha wanted to know how we had enjoyed the honeymoon and then Tybalt began a long explanation of the Roman site.

"You must have had a very interesting time, Tybalt," said Tabitha smiling. "I trust Judith found it equally so."

She looked at me slightly apprehensively and I assured her that I had enjoyed our stay in Dorset very much.

"And now," said Tybalt, "we must begin to work out our plans in earnest. It's astonishing how the time flies when there is so much to do. I want to leave in February."

So we talked of the trip and it was pleasant sitting there in the firelight while the dark afternoon faded into twilight. I could not help thinking of those occasions when I had dreamed of sharing Tybalt's life.

"I'm happy," I assured myself. "I've achieved my dream."

My first night in Giza House! One of the maids had lighted a fire in the bedroom and the flickering flames threw their shadows over the walls. How different from those of the Dartmoor cottage; these seemed like sinister shapes which would assume life at any moment. How silent the house was! There was a door behind a blue velvet curtain. I opened this and saw that it led into the room where the sarcophagus had been.

I had entered in advance of Tybalt; and the room in firelight with only two candles burning in their tall candlesticks on the dressing table seemed alive with shadows.

I started to wonder about Sir Edward and his wife who had never lived in this house, for she had died before they came here. And in the attic apartments of this house was Nanny Tester, who would be aware that Tybalt and I had returned from our honeymoon. I wondered what she was doing now and why Tybalt was so long. Was he talking to Tabitha, telling her things which he did not want me to know? What an idea! I must not be jealous of the time he spent with Tabitha.

It's the house, I said to myself. There's something about this house. Something . . . evil. I felt it right from the first before they came here when I used to frighten Theodosia.

Tybalt came into the room, and the sinister shadows receded; the firelight was comforting; the candlelight, I remembered, was becoming.

"What," he asked, "are you doing in that room?"

"I found this door. It's the room where the sarcophagus was."

He laughed. "You weren't thinking of dressing up as a mummy were you . . . to frighten me?"

"You . . . frightened of a mummy! I know you love them dearly."

"Not," he replied, "as dearly as I love you."

On the rare occasions when Tybalt said things like that, my happiness was complete.

"Do you like the room I had prepared for you?" asked Tabitha next morning. Tybalt had gone to his study; he had a great deal of correspondence to deal with concerning the expedition.

"It's a bit ghostly," I said.

Tabitha laughed. "My dear Judith, what do you mean?"

"I always thought there was something rather haunted about Giza House."

"It's all those trees and shrubs in the garden, I daresay. That room is the best in the house. That's why I had it made ready for you. It used to be Sir Edward's."

"I guessed it. And the room which leads from it is where the sarcophagus used to be."

"He always used that room for whatever he was working on. He often worked late at night when the fancy took him. Would you like to change the room?"

"No, I don't think so."

"Judith, anything you want you must do, you know. You're mistress of the house now."

"I can't get used to being the mistress of anything."

"You will in time. You're happy, aren't you?"

"I have what I've always wanted."

"Not many of us can say that," she replied with a sigh. "And you, Tabitha?"

I wished that she would confide in me. I was sure there were secrets in her life. She was youngish—a widow I supposed. Life was by no means over for her and yet there was about her a resignation, a subtle secrecy which was perhaps one of the reasons why she was so attractive.

She said: "I have had my moments. Perhaps one should not ask for more than that."

Yes, there was something decidedly mysterious about Tabitha.

Christmas was not far off. Sabina said we must celebrate Christmas Day at the rectory, and she would insist on my aunts joining us.

I fancied Dorcas and Alison were a little reproachful. They were so conventional. I think they believed I should have gone to them at Rainbow Cottage or they come to me at Giza House.

I swept all that away by pointing out the convenience of Sabina's suggestion and what fun it would be to be back in the old drawing room where so many of our Christmases had been celebrated.

The days were passing swiftly. There was Christmas to think of and always, of course, the expedition. Tabitha and I decorated the house with holly and mistletoe.

"It was something we never did before," said Tabitha.

The maids were delighted. Ellen told me that it was more like a house since I'd come home. That was a compliment indeed.

They liked me, those maids; they seemed to take a pleasure in addressing me as "my lady." It invariably startled me, and sometimes I had to assure myself: Yes, it's true. You're not dreaming this time. This is the greatest dream of all come true.

It was at the beginning of December when the first uneasy situation occurred.

I had never quite understood Mustapha and Absalam. In fact they made me uncomfortable. I would be in a room and suddenly find them standing close behind me— for they seemed to move about together—having been completely unaware of their approach. I often looked up suddenly to find their dark eyes fixed upon me. Sometimes I would think they were about to speak to me; but then they seemed to change their minds. I was never quite sure which one was which and I believe I often addressed them wrongly. Tabitha could easily tell the difference but then she had known them for a very long time.

It was afternoon—that hour when dusk was beginning to fall. I had gone to our bedroom and on my way saw that the door which led from the corridor into that room which I called the Sarcophagus Room was ajar. I thought perhaps Tybalt was there, so I looked in. Mustapha, or was it Absalam, was standing silhouetted against the window.

I went in and as I did so, the other Egyptian was standing behind me . . . between me and the door.

I felt the goosepimples rise on my skin. I was unsure why.

I said: "Mustapha . . . Absalam, is anything wrong?"

There was a brief silence. The one by the window nodded to the other and said: "Absalam, you say."

I turned and faced Absalam.

"My lady," he said, "we are your most humble slaves."

"You mustn't say that, Absalam. We don't have slaves here."

They bowed their heads.

Mustapha spoke then. "We serve you well, my lady."

"But of course," I replied lightly.

I saw that the door was shut. I looked at that which led into our bedroom. It was half closed. But I knew Tybalt would not be there at this hour of the day.

"We have tried to tell you many times."

"Please tell me now then," I said.

"It must not be," said Mustapha shaking his head gravely.

Absalam began to shake his.

"What?" I asked.

"Stay here, my lady. You tell Sir Tybalt. You tell. He must not go."

I began to grasp their meaning. They were afraid to go back to Egypt, the scene of the tragedy which had overtaken their master.

"I'm afraid that's impossible." I said. "Plans are going ahead. They couldn't be altered now."

"Must be," said Mustapha.

"I am sure Sir Tybalt would not agree with you."

"It is death, there. There is a curse . . ."

Of course, I thought, they would be very superstitious.

I said: "Have you spoken to Sir Tybalt?"

They shook their heads in unison. "No use. No use to speak to his great father. No use. So he die. The Curse comes to him and it will come to others."

"It's a legend," I said, "nothing more. All will be well. Sir Tybalt will make sure of that."

Absalam came to me and stood before me. The palms of his hands were together, his eyes raised. "My lady, must speak. My lady is the new wife. A husband listens to his beloved."

"It would be impossible," I said.

"It is death . . . death."

"It is good of you to be so concerned," I said, "but there is nothing I can do."

They looked at me with great sorrowing eyes and shook their heads mournfully.

I slipped through to the bedroom. Naturally, I told myself again, they would be superstitious.

That night as we lay in bed I said to Tybalt: "The Egyptians spoke to me today. They are very frightened."

"Frightened of what?"

"What they call the Curse. They believe that if we go to Egypt there will be disaster."

"If they feel that they must stay behind."

"They asked me to speak to you. They said a husband loves his beloved and would listen."

He laughed.

"I told them it was futile."

"They are very superstitious."

"Sometimes I'm a little frightened."

"You, Judith?"

I clung to him.

"Only because of you," I assured him. "What if what happened to your father should happen to you?"

"Why should it?"

"What if there is something in this Curse?"

"My dear Judith you don't believe *that*."

"If anyone else was leading this expedition I would laugh the idea to scorn. But this is you."

He laughed in the darkness.

"My *dear* Judith," he said.

And that was all.

I was longing for the days to pass. What dark ones they were before Christmas. There was a great deal of rain and the fir trees glistened and dripped; the soft-scented southwest wind blew through the trees and moaned outside the windows. Whenever I saw the Egyptians their eyes seemed to be fixed on me, half sorrowfully, half hopefully. I saw Nanny Tester but only in the presence of Tabitha for she kept mainly to her own apartments and only rarely emerged.

Theodosia and Evan came to stay at Keverall Court for Christmas, and Tybalt and I and Sabina and Oliver were invited for Christmas Eve. Hadrian was there too; he was going to stay until we left for Egypt.

It had long been a custom to sing carols in the Keverall Court ballroom on Christmas Eve and many of the people from the neighborhood joined the company. Oliver officiated as the Reverend James Osmond used to and it was a very impressive occasion for there was a torchlight procession from the church to Keverall.

After the singing Lady Bodrean's chosen guests went to the hall where we had a supper consisting of the various pies which had been popular for centuries—squab, mutton, beef; and, of course, hot Cornish pasties. These were all eaten with mead and a beverage known as Kev-

erall punch which was made in an enormous pewter bowl
—the recipe, known only to the steward of Keverall, had
been handed down through the last four hundred years.
It was rather potent.

I was amused by Lady Bodrean's attitude towards me.
When she did not think herself observed she regarded
me with a sort of suspicious wonder, but she was all
charm when we stood face to face.

"It is a pleasure to see you, Lady Travers," she said.
I felt myself giggling inwardly as I graciously acknowledged
her greeting.

After we had partaken of the pies and punch we went
to the church for the midnight service and strolled home
in the early hours of Christmas Day. It was all as we had
done it many times before; and I felt it was good that
all the friends of my childhood were gathered together at
such a time.

Christmas Day at the rectory was pleasant too. It was
amusing to see Sabina presiding at the table where once
Alison had sat. There was the turkey with the chestnut
stuffing and brandy butter which I remembered used to
cause Dorcas and Alison such concern. Sabina showed
no such anxiety. She chattered away making us all laugh
as we teased her. The plum pudding was ceremoniously
carried in with its flaming brandy jacket and followed
by mince pies shining with their coating of castor sugar.

Theodosia and Evan with Hadrian were not with us,
of course, they being at Keverall Court; so the conversation for once was not of the coming expedition; for this
I was grateful because I was sure that Dorcas and Alison
would not have enjoyed it.

Afterwards we played charades, miming scenes and
childish guessing games at which I excelled and Tybalt
did not. Dorcas and Alison looked on and applauded my
success, which exasperated while it touched me.

In the early hours of the morning as Tabitha, Tybalt,
and I walked the short distance from the rectory to Giza
House, I found myself wondering whether there would
always be the three of us together. I was fond of Tabitha,
but there were times when the old saying seemed very

apt: Two's company; three's a crowd. Was it because when Tabitha was with us Tybalt's attitude towards me seemed to change? Sometimes he seemed almost formal as though he were afraid to betray to her that affection which more and more he was beginning to show when we were alone.

January was with us. There was a cold snap, and the hoar frost glistening on the shrubbery trees gave them a look of fairyland.

Tybalt at the breakfast table going through the mail, frowned and made an exclamation of disgust.

"These lawyers!" he complained.

"What's happened?"

"Sir Ralph's will is taking a long while to settle. It's a clear example of procrastination. It seems as though it's going to be months before everything is clear."

"Does it matter so much?" I asked.

"You know he has left this trust. We were relying on it. It will make a great deal of difference to the expedition. We shall be less restricted for funds with this additional income. You'll discover, Judith, how money is swallowed up in expeditions like this. We have to employ possibly a hundred workmen. Then of course there are all the other workers. They have to be paid; they have to have living quarters. That's why one cannot begin such an undertaking until all these tiresome financial matters are taken care of. We're almost always frustrated by a question of expense."

"And you can't touch this money or the interest, or whatever it is, until the will is proved?"

"Oh, it will be all right. With such a sum made over to us we shall be able to anticipate. But there will be formalities. I daresay I shall have to go to London. I should have to in any case, but later."

"So it is only a minor irritation."

He smiled at me. "That's true, but minor irritations can mean delays."

He then began to talk to me in the way I loved and he

told me that he believed his father had discovered the way into an unbroken tomb.

"He was so excited. I remember his coming to the house. He had rented a house from one of the most influential men in Egypt who was interested in our operation and allowed us to have his palace, which was a great concession. It's a very grand and beautiful residence with magnificent gardens and a band of servants to look after us. It's called the Chephro Palace. We pay a nominal rent—a concession to independence; but the Pasha is really very interested in what we are doing and eager to help. We shall use this palace again."

"You were telling me of your father?"

"He came in from the hills. It was night. There was a moon and it was almost as light as day. It's impossible, of course, to work in the heat of the afternoon and those moonlit nights were made full use of. He was riding a mule and as he came into the courtyard, I saw him from my window, and I guessed something had happened. He was a man who rarely showed his feelings, but he showed something then. He seemed exuberant. I thought I would wait until he had washed and changed and had had a light meal which Mustapha and Absalam always prepared for him. Then I would go down and wait for him to tell me. I knew I would be the one he would tell first. I said nothing to anyone for it might have been something he wished kept secret. I knew that a few days before we had been in despair. It was several months earlier that we had discovered the door in the rock; we had penetrated through a corridor only to be led to a tomb which had been rifled probably two thousand years earlier. It had seemed then as though we had come to the end of our quest and all the work and expense would lead to nothing. But my father had had this strange feeling. He would not give up. He was certain we had not discovered all. I was of the opinion that only some tremendous discovery could have made him excited on that day."

Tabitha joined us.

"I am telling Judith about my father's death," he said. Tabitha nodded gravely; she sat down at the table and propping her elbows on the table leaned her chin on her hands. Her eyes were misty as Tybalt went on:

"I went down when I thought he would be refreshed and then I found him ill. I did not believe it was serious. He was a man of immense physical as well as mental vitality. He complained of pains and I saw that his limbs trembled. I suggested to Absalam and Mustapha, who were very upset, that we get him to bed. This we did. I thought: In the morning he will tell me. That night he died. Before he did I was sent for. As I knelt by his bed I could see that he was trying to tell me something. His lips moved. I was certain he was saying 'Go on.' That is why I am determined."

"But why did he die at precisely that moment?"

"There was talk of the Curse which was absurd. Why should he be cursed for doing what many had done before him? He had merely been to the site on which we were working. It was not as though he had violated one of the tombs. It was ridiculous."

"But he died."

"The climate is hot; he may have eaten tainted food. That, I can assure you, has happened more than once."

"But to die so suddenly."

"It was the greatest tragedy of my life. But I intend to carry out my father's wishes."

I put out my hand and pressed his. I had forgotten Tabitha. Then I saw that there were tears in her beautiful eyes; and I thought peevishly I must admit, why are there always the three of us!

During the cold spell Nanny Tester caught a chill which turned to bronchitis, as in the case of Dorcas. I was quite useful nursing her, having had experience with Dorcas. The old woman would lie in bed watching me with her bright beady eyes; I think she liked to have me there which was fortunate, for she had what seemed to me an unreasoning dislike for Tabitha. It was really most unfair because Tabitha was considerate in the extreme, but sometimes she would become really restless when Tabitha was in her room.

In February Tybalt went to London to make further arrangements about supplies and to see the lawyers; I had hoped to go with him but he had said that he would have so much to do that he would be able to spend little time with me.

I waved him off at Plymouth station and I couldn't help thinking of Lavinia's going on that same journey with her baby in her arms and Dorcas and Alison seeing her off. And then an hour later she was dead.

To love intensely was a mixed blessing I decided. There are moments of ecstasy but it seems that these have to be paid for with anxiety. One was completely happy only when one had the loved one safe beside one. When he was absent one's imagination seemed to take a malicious delight in presenting all kinds of horrors which could befall him. Now I must visualize the piled-up carriages, the cries of the injured, the silence of the dead.

Foolish! I admonished myself. How many people travel on the railways? Thousands! How many accidents are there? Very few!

I went back and threw myself into the nursing of Nanny Tester.

That evening as I sat with Tabitha I told her of my fears.

She smiled at me gently. "Sometimes it is painful to love too well."

She spoke as though she knew and I wondered afresh what her life had been. I wondered why she never spoke of it. Perhaps she will one day, I thought, when she gets to know me better.

Nanny Tester was recovering.

"But," said Tabitha, "these attacks always leave their mark. After she's been ill she always seems to emerge a little more feeble. Her mind wanders quite a bit."

I had noticed that. I noticed too that my presence seemed to soothe her, so I used to take up her food and sometimes I sat with her. I would take a book and read or do odd bits of needlework. Sabina used to call often. I would hear her chattering away to Nanny Tester and her visits were always a success.

One day I was sitting by her bed when she said: "Watch her. Be careful."

I guessed she was wandering in her mind and said: "There's no one here, Nanny." She had asked me to call her this. "People in the family do," she explained.

"I could tell you some things," she murmured. "I was always one to keep my eyes open."

"Try to rest," I said.

"Rest! When I see what's going on in this house. It's him and it's her. She eggs him on. Housekeeper! Friend of the family! What is she? Tell me that."

I knew then that she was talking about Tabitha, and I had to hear what it was she wanted to tell me.

"Him and her . . . ?" I prompted.

"You don't see. That's how it often is. Those it concerns most don't see what's under their very eyes. It's the one who looks on, who sees."

"What do you see, Nanny?"

"I see the way things are between them. She's sly. We can do without her. There's nothing she does I couldn't do."

That was hardly true but I let it pass.

"I never knew housekeepers like that one. Sitting down to dinner every night with the family; running the house. You'd think she was the mistress. Then he goes away and what happens. She's called away. Oh it's some family affair. Family! What family? She'll be called away now he's away, I can see it coming."

She was wandering obviously. "You watch out, my lady," she murmured. "You're nursing a viper in your bosom."

The term made me smile; and when I thought of all Tabitha did in the house and how charming and helpful she was I was sure that the old woman had got an obsession, probably because she was jealous.

The house seemed different without Tybalt; the bedroom was full of shadows. A fire was lighted every night and I lay in bed watching the shadows. I often fancied I heard noises in the next room and one night got out of bed to see if anyone was there. How ghostly it looked with the light of the crescent moon faintly illuminating it; the books, the table at which Sir Edward had often worked, the spot where the sarcophagus had stood. I half expected Mustapha and Absalam to materialize. I went back to bed and dreamed that I went into the room and the sarcophagus was there and from it rose a mummy from which the wrapping suddenly disintegrated to show Mustapha and Absalam. They kept their dark eyes on me as they advanced pointing to me; I heard their voices distinctly as they echoed through emptiness. "Stop him. A man listens to his beloved. The Curse of the Kings will come upon you."

I awoke shouting something. I sat up in bed. There was no light but that from the crescent moon, for the fire was nothing but a few embers. I got out of bed; I opened the door expecting to see the sarcophagus there, so vivid had the dream been. The room was empty. I shut the door quickly and got back to bed.

I thought: When we come back I will change this house. I will have the dark shrubs taken away; I will plant beautiful flowering shrubs like the hydrangeas which grow so luxuriantly here—lovely blues and pinks and white blooms and red fuchias dripping their bells from the hedges. We will replace the darkness by the brightest of colors.

In that mood I slept.

Every morning I went hopefully to the breakfast table looking for a note from Tybalt to say that he would be back. None came.

Tabitha had a letter in her hand when I went down.

"Oh, Judith. I'll have to go away for a few days."

"Oh?"

"Yes, a . . . a relative of mine is ill. I must go."

"Of course," I said. "I haven't heard you speak before of relatives."

"This one is in Suffolk. It's a long journey. I think I ought to leave at once."

"Today?"

"Yes, I'll get the ten-thirty for London. I shall have to go to London first, of course, and from there to Suffolk. You'll manage without me."

"Yes," I said. "Of course I shall."

She left the table hurriedly. She seemed very embarrassed, I thought. Jenner, the coachman, drove her in the jingle to the station.

I watched her go and I kept thinking of Nanny Tester. What had she said? "He goes away . . . and she's called away." But how could she foresee this? But that was what she had done.

I went upstairs to Nanny's apartment. She was standing by the window, her old-fashioned flannelette dressing gown wrapped about her.

"So she's gone," she said, "eh, my lady, she's gone. Didn't I tell you?"

"How did you know?"

"There's things I know, my lady. I've got a pair of eyes in my head that see far and they see for them I care for."

"So . . . you care for me."

"Did you doubt it? I cared for you the first minute I clapped eyes on you. I said: 'I'll watch over this one all the days of my life.'"

"Thank you," I said.

"It hurts me though to see the way you're treated. It hurts right in here." She struck her hand on where she supposed her heart to be. "He goes away . . . and she goes to join him. He's sent for her. They'll be together tonight . . ."

"Stop it! That's nonsense. It's absolutely untrue."

"Oh," she said. "I've seen it. I knew it was coming. She's the one he wanted. He took you for your money. That's it. And what for? So that they can go and dig up the dead. It's not right."

"Nanny," I said, "you're not yourself."

I looked at her wild eyes, her flushed cheeks. It was not without a certain relief that I saw that she was rambling.

"Let me help you to bed."

"To bed . . . why to bed? It's for me to put you to bed, my precious."

"Do you know who I am, Nanny?"

"Know you. Didn't I have you from three weeks after you were born?"

I said, "You're mistaking me for somebody else. I'm Judith, Lady Travers . . . Tybalt's wife."

"Oh yes, my lady. You're my lady all right. And a lot of good that's done you. I'd have liked to see you wife to some simple gentleman who didn't think more of digging up the dead than his own young wife."

I said: "Now I'm going to bring you a hot drink and you're going to sleep."

"You're good to me," she said.

I went down to the kitchen and told Ellen to prepare some hot milk. I would take it up to Nanny who was not very well.

"You'd think she'd be better now Mrs. Grey's gone," said Ellen. "Goodness, my lady, she does seem to hate Mrs. Grey."

I did not comment. When I took the milk up to Nanny she was half asleep.

Tabitha came back with Tybalt. On her way back she had had to go to London and as Tybalt was ready to return they had come back together.

I was uneasy. There were so many questions I wanted to ask; but it was so wonderful to have Tybalt back and he seemed delighted to be with me.

He was in a very happy and contented state. The financial problems had been straightened out. We should be leaving in March instead of February as he had hoped —but it would only mean delaying our start by two weeks.

"Now," he said, "we shall be very busy. We must prepare to leave in earnest."

He was right. Then there was nothing to think of but the expedition.

And in March we left for Egypt.

THE CURSE OF THE KINGS 164

V   The Chephro Palace

The Chephro Palace stood majestic, golden colored, aloof from the village. I was astounded that the great Hakin Pasha should have put so much magnificence at our disposal.

I was, by the time we arrived, completely under the spell of the strange, arid, and exotic land of the Pharaohs. The reality was no less wonderful than the pictures created by my imagination when I had nothing but dreams and a few pictures in the books I had read to guide me.

Several members of the working party had gone on ahead of us. They would be lodged about the site, and they had taken with them a good deal of the equipment which would be needed.

Hadrian, Evan, and Theodosia with Terence Gelding and Tabitha were sailing from Southampton with Tybalt and me, but as Tybalt had some business to settle in Cairo, he and I would spend a few days there before joining the party in the Chephro Palace.

The day before we left I went over to Rainbow Cottage. Dorcas and Alison said goodbye to me as though it was our last farewell. Sabina and Oliver had been invited to supper and I could not help knowing how much they wished that I had married Oliver and settled quietly into the life at the rectory which they had chosen for me.

I was rather glad when the evening was over, and the next day when we joined the S.S. *Stalwart* at Southampton my great adventure had begun.

It was a fascinating experience to be aboard ship and I couldn't help wishing that Tybalt and I were alone together. Evan and Theodosia, I daresay, felt the same for themselves; that left Hadrian, Terence, and Tabitha. Poor Theodosia was confined to her cabin for the first few days although the sea was not unduly rough considering the time of the year. Conversation was mainly about the expedition and as Theodosia was not present I couldn't help feeling the tyro because it was astonishing how much Tabitha knew.

The Bay, contrary to expectations, was fairly smooth and by the time we reached Gibraltar, Theodosia was ready to emerge. Evan was such a kind and thoughtful husband; he spent a great deal of time with Theodosia and I found myself wondering whether Tybalt would have made me his chief concern if I had suffered from the sea as my half sister did.

We had a pleasant day at the Rock and went for a trip up to the heights in little horse-drawn traps; we laughed at the antics of the apes and admired the magnificent scenery and the day was a happy one. Shortly after we arrived at Naples. As we were there for two days we took a trip as might have been expected to Pompeii. Excavations were still going on and more and more of that buried town was being revealed. As I walked arm in arm with Tybalt over those stones which until seventy-nine years after the birth of Christ had been streets I was caught up in the fascination of it all; and I said to Tybalt: "How lucky you are to have this profession which brings these treasures to the world."

He was delighted that I shared his enthusiasm. He pointed out to me the remains of houses and reconstructed in his mind the manner in which these people had lived under the shadow of Vesuvius before that fatal day when the great mountain had erupted. The town had been buried for centuries and it had only emerged just over a hundred years ago when archaeologists discovered it.

When we were back on the ship the discussion about the discoveries of that tragic city continued far into the night.

At Port Said we left the ship and traveled to Cairo—just the two of us—where Tybalt had business to attend to.

I had read a great deal about Egypt and as I had lain in my bed in Rainbow Cottage and at Keverall Court my imagination had transported me to this mysterious land. I should, therefore, have been prepared, yet none of my fancies could compare with the reality and the impact upon me was exhilarating, exciting beyond my dreams.

It was a golden land, dominated by a sun which could be merciless; one was immediately conscious of thousands of years of antiquity. When I saw a goatherd in his long white robes I could believe I was far back in the days of the Old Testament. The country held me spellbound; I knew that here anything could happen—the most wonderful things, the most fearful. It was both beautiful and ugly; it was stimulating, thrilling, and sinister.

We stayed at a small hotel which looked out onto the Nile. From my window I could see the riverbank and the gold colored Mokattam Hills; how different from the green of Cornwall, the misty dampness, the luxuriant vegetation. Here one was aware of the ever-present sun—relentlessly burning the land. If green was the color of England, yellow was that of Egypt. It was the ambience of antiquity which caught my imagination. The people in their white robes and sandaled feet; the smells of cooking food; the sight of disdainful camels picking their dainty ways. I listened in wonder when I first heard the muezzin from the top of his minaret calling the people to prayer; and I was amazed to see them stop where ever they were and pay homage to Allah. Tybalt took me into the *souks* which I found fascinating with him beside me but I think I should have felt them a little sinister had I been alone. Dark-eyed people watched us intently without staring, and one was constantly aware of their scrutiny. Through the narrow streets we wandered, and we looked into the darkened cave-like shops where bakers were making bread coated with seeds and where silversmiths worked over their braziers. There the waterseller demanded attention with the clatter of his brass cups and at the back of the dark openings men sat cross-legged weaving and stitching. In the air the heavy scent of perfumed oils mingled with that of the camel dung which was used as fuel.

I shall never forget that day—the jostling crowds of the noisy streets; the smells of mingling dung and perfume; the side glances from veiled dark eyes; the call to prayer and the response of the people.

"Allah is great, and Mohammed his prophet." How often I was to hear those words and they never failed to thrill me.

We paused by one of the shops which were like huts open to the street. At the back a man worked cutting and engraving stones and on a stall inside the hut was an array of rings and brooches.

"You must have a scarab ring," said Tybalt. "It'll bring you luck in Egypt."

There were several of them on a tray and Tybalt selected one.

"This is tourmaline," he said. "Look at the carved beetle. He was sacred to the ancient Egyptians."

The man had risen at the back from his work and came eagerly forward.

He bowed to me and to Tybalt. His eyes shone at the prospect of a sale and I listened to him and Tybalt as they bargained over the price, while several small children came round to watch. They could not take their eyes from Tybalt and me. I suppose we appeared very strange to them.

Tybalt took the ring and showed me the beetle. About it were hieroglyphs very delicately carved. Tybalt translated, "Allah be with you."

"There could not be greater good luck than that," he

said. "It is what every man should give to the one he loves best when she first comes to this land."

I slipped the ring on my finger. There were delighted cries of approval from the children. The ring was paid for and we went on our way with the blessings of the stonecutter ringing in our ears.

"We had to bargain," said Tybalt. "He would have been most disappointed in us if we had not." Then he looked at my ecstatic face and said: "You are happy today, Judith."

"I'm so happy," I said, "that I'm afraid."

He pressed my hand with the ring on it. "If you could have a wish what would it be?" he asked.

"That I could be as happy as this every day of my life."

"That's asking a lot of life."

"Why should it be? We are together, we have this great interest. I see no reason why we should not always be in this state of happiness. Aren't our lives what we make them?"

"There are certain outside factors, I believe."

"They shan't hurt us."

"Dear Judith, I do believe you are capable of arranging even that."

Back to our hotel and the warm scented night with the smells of Egypt and the great moon which made the night almost as light as day.

These were the happiest days of my life to that time because we were alone together in this exciting land. I wished that we could have stayed there together and not have had to join the others. An absurd wish because it was to join the party that we had come to Egypt.

The next day we went out to the Pyramids—that last remaining wonder of the ancient world; and to find myself face to face with the Sphinx was an experience which enthralled me completely. Mounted somewhat precariously on my camel, I felt exhilarated and I could see how much Tybalt enjoyed my excitement. One hundred thousand men had toiled for twenty years to achieve this wonder, Tybalt had told me; the stone had been quarried from the nearby Mokattam Hills and dragged across the desert. I felt, as everyone else must on witnessing this fantastic sight, speechless with wonder.

When we dismounted, I entered the Pyramid of Cheops and bending double followed Tybalt up the steep passage to the burial chamber where the Pharaoh's red granite sarcophagus was displayed.

Then over the sand perched high on our reluctant beasts of burden. I was in an exalted mood when we returned to our hotel.

We dined at a small table secluded from the rest of the diners by palms. I had piled my dark hair high on my head and wore a green velvet gown which I had had made by Sarah Sloper before I left home. I kept touching the pink tourmaline ring on my finger remembering that Tybalt had said that it was the gift of a lover that good fortune might preserve in a strange land the one he loved best.

Sitting opposite Tybalt I marveled afresh at the wonderful thing that had happened to me; and there flashed into my mind then the thought that even if my fortune had been a deciding factor in Tybalt's wishing to marry me, I didn't care. I would make him love me for myself alone. I remembered it was said of our late Prime Minister, Lord Beaconsfield, that he had married his Mary Anne for her money but at the end of their lives he would have married her for love. That was how it should be for us. But I was romantic and foolish enough to hope that it was not for my fortune that Tybalt had married me.

Tybalt leaned forward and took my hand with the scarab ring on it; he studied it intently. "What are you thinking, Judith?" he asked.

"Just of the wonder of everything."

"I can see that the Pyramids impressed you."

"I never thought to see them. So many things are happening that are fresh and exciting. You look suddenly sad, Tybalt. Are you?"

"Only because I was thinking that you won't go on being excited about everything. You'll become blasé. I shouldn't like that."

"I don't believe I ever would."

"Familiarity, you know, breeds contempt . . . or at least indifference. I feel since we have been together in Cairo that things which I have seen before seem fresh, more interesting, more wonderful. That's because I'm seeing them through your eyes."

It was indeed an enchanted night.

The *Kebab* served by the silent-footed men in their long white robes tasted delicious. I couldn't believe it was simply lamb on skewers which had been grilled over charcoal. I told Tybalt that the Tahenia sauce into which the meat was dipped and which I discovered later was made of sesame seeds, oil, white sauce, and a hint of garlic, tasted like nectar.

He replied prosaically that it was because I was hungry. "Hunger savors all dishes," he added.

But I thought it was because I was so happy.

Afterwards we ate *Esh es Seraya* which was a delicious mixture of honey, breadcrumbs, and cream. We drank rose water and grenadine with fruit and nuts in it, called *Khosaf*.

Yes, that was an evening never to be forgotten. After dinner we sat on the terrace and looked out on the Nile, while we drank Turkish coffee and nibbled Turkish delight.

The stars seemed to hang low in that indigo sky and before us flowed the Nile down which Cleopatra had once sailed in her royal barge. I wished that I could hold those moments and go on living them again and again.

Tybalt said: "You have a great capacity for happiness, Judith."

"Perhaps," I answered. "If so, I am fortunate. It means I can enjoy the happiness that comes my way to the full."

And I wondered then if just as I felt this intensity of pleasure I could feel sorrow with an equal fervor.

Perhaps that was a thought which Tybalt shared with me.

I would not brood on it though—not on this night of nights on the romantic banks of the Nile.

When we arrived at the Chephro Palace the rest of the party had already settled in and Tabitha had slipped into the role of housekeeper.

Hakim Pasha was one of the richest men in Egypt, Tybalt told me, and it was our great good fortune that he felt benign towards our cause.

"He could have hindered us in many ways," he said, "instead of which he has decided to be of immense help to us. Hence this palace which he has put at our disposal for just enough rent to preserve our dignity—a very important facet, I do assure you. You will meet him, I daresay, because when my father was here he was a constant visitor."

I stood in the entrance hall of the palace and gazed with wonder at the beautiful staircase in white marble. The floor was covered in mosaic tiles of the most beautifully blended colors, and the stained glass in the windows depicted the sea journey of the dead through hideous dangers until they came under the protection of the Sun God, Amen Ra.

Tybalt was beside me: "I'll tell you the story later. Look, here's Tabitha to welcome you."

"So you've come!" cried Tabitha. She was looking at Tybalt with shining eyes. "I thought you never would."

"It's a long journey from Cairo," said Tybalt.

"I visualized all sorts of disasters."

"Which is just what she should not do, don't you agree, Judith? But of course you do."

"Well, now you're here. I'll take you to your room. Then you can explore the rest of the palace and, I daresay, Tybalt will want to look at the site."

"You're right," said Tybalt.

"We'll have a meal then. Mustapha and Absalam are working in the kitchens so I am sure they will mingle a little English cooking with the Egyptian which might be more agreeable to our palates. But first to your room."

Tabitha led the way up that grand and imposing staircase and we went along a gallery, the walls of which were decorated with mosaic patterns similar to those in the floor of the hall. These were figures, always in profile,

usually of some Pharaohs giving gifts to a god. I had to
pause to examine those figures and the beautiful muted
colors of the tiles. On the ceiling was engraved the Sun
God, Amen Ra; his symbol was the hawk and the ram.
I remembered that Tybalt had told me that the gods of
Egypt were said not only to possess all the human virtues,
but in addition one from an animal. Amen Ra had two,
however, the hawk and the ram. Below him was his
son Osiris, God of the Underworld, who judged the dead
when they had made their journey along the river. Isis was
there—the great goddess beloved of Osiris, and their son
Horus . . .

"The figures are so beautifully done," I said.

"It would be an insult to the gods if they had not been,"
added Tybalt.

He slipped his arm through mine and we went into
the room which had been prepared for us. I stared at
the enormous bed standing on a platform. Mosquito nets
festooned over it from the ceiling like flimsy cobwebs.

"This is the bedroom used by the Pasha himself when
he is in residence," Tabitha explained.

"Should we use it?" asked Tybalt.

"You must. The palace is in full use and it is only
proper that our leader should have the state bedroom.
Your father used it, you remember, when he was here."

She showed us an antechamber in which we could
wash and generally make our toilet. There was a sunken
marble bath in the center of which was a statue and three
marble steps leading down to the bath; on the walls of
this chamber were mosaics depicting nude figures. One
side of the wall was composed of mirrors, and there was
a dressing table behind gold-colored brocade curtains; a
many-sided mirror reflected my image, and the frame of
the mirror was studded with chalcedony, rose quartz,
amethyst, and lapis lazuli. These stones were, I noticed,
in the decorations throughout the bed chamber.

I laughed. "It is very grand. We shall feel like royalty."

"The Pasha has given instructions to his servants that
any of our complaints will be met with dire punishment.
They are trembling in their shoes."

"Is he very autocratic?"

"He is the ruler of his lands and he regards his servants as slaves. He expects absolute obedience from them. We are his guests and if we are not treated with respect, that is tantamount to insulting him. He will not accept insults."

"What happens to offenders?"

"Their bodies are probably found in the Nile. Or they may be deprived of a hand or an ear."

I shivered.

"It's magnificent. It's beautiful," I cried. "But a little frightening. A little sinister."

"That's Egypt," said Tabitha laying her hand on my arm. "Now perform the necessary ablutions and come down to eat. Then I expect you'll want some sort of conference, eh Tybalt?"

"Well," said Tybalt when we were alone, "what do you really think of it?"

"I'm not sure," I replied. "I wish it was not quite so grand and this Pasha does sound rather diabolical."

"He's quite charming. He and my father became good friends. He's a power in these parts. You will meet him soon."

"Where does he live then since he has given us his palace?"

"My dear Judith, this is but *one* of his palaces. It may well be the most grand, but he would consider it quite ill-mannered not to give it up to us. You have to understand the etiquette. That's very important. Don't look doleful. You will in time. Now let's get cleaned up. I can't wait to hear what's been going on."

It had changed. That other love, his profession, was in the ascendancy.

The dining room with its heavy curtains was lighted by a chandelier containing about a hundred candles. It was dark now, for there was no twilight hour as at home. But there were others to greet us and add normality to this strange palace, for which I was glad. I laughed to myself thinking that the verdict of the servants at Giza House would be that it gave them the "creeps."

We sat at the big table under the chandelier—Hadrian, Evan, Theodosia, Terence Gelding, and others whom I had not previously met but who were all practiced archaeologists deeply interested in the task ahead. Tybalt sat at one end of the table, I at the extreme end; and on my right was Hadrian and Evan was on my left.

"Well, here you are at last, Judith," said Hadrian. "What do you think of this *kuftas?* Personally I prefer the roast beef of old England but don't let anyone know I said that. Old Osiris might not grant me admittance to heaven when my time comes."

"You are very irreverent, Hadrian; and I advise you to keep such thoughts to yourself. Who knows who might overhear?"

"There speaks our Judith," said Hadrian appealing to Evan. "She has just arrived and immediately is telling us what we should and should not do."

Evan smiled. "On this occasion she's right. You never know what's heard and misunderstood. These servants are no doubt listening and reporting to the Pasha and your jocularity would most definitely be misconstrued as irreverence."

"What have you been doing while you were waiting for Tybalt?" I asked.

"Going over the site, getting the workmen together, arranging for this and that. There's a great deal to do on an occasion like this. You wait until you go down there and see the hive of industry we've created. She'll be surprised, won't she, Evan?"

"It is a little different from Carter's Meadow."

"And we do face difficulties," said Hadrian. "You see, many of the diggers remember Sir Edward's death and believe that he died because he went where the gods did not wish him to."

"There is a certain amount of reluctance?"

"It's there, don't you think, Evan?"

Evan nodded gravely.

I looked along the table where Tybalt was deep in conversation with the men around him. Tabitha was sitting near him. I noticed with a pang of jealousy that occasionally she threw in a remark which was listened to with respect.

I felt I had lost Tybalt already.

After the meal Tybalt went out to look at the site and I was permitted to accompany the party. There was a fair amount of work going on in spite of the hour. The full moon and the clean air made it bright; it was easier to work at this hour than under the heat of the blazing sun.

The stark hills rising to the moonlit sky were menacing but rather beautiful. The parallel lines of pegs marking the search area, the little hut which had been set up, the wheelbarrows, the forks of the excavators, and the workmen were far from romantic.

Tybalt left me with Hadrian, who smiled at me cynically.

"Not quite what you expected?" he said.

"Exactly," I said.

"Of course, you're a veteran of Carter's Meadow."

"I suppose it is rather similar, although there they were merely looking for Bronze Age relics; and here it's the tombs of the dead."

"We could be on the verge of one of the really exciting discoveries in archaeology."

"How thrilling that will be when we find it."

"But we haven't done that yet, and you have to learn to be cautious in this game. As a matter of fact there are lots of things you have to learn."

"Such as?"

"Being a good little archaeological wife."

"And what does that mean?"

"Never complaining when your lord and master absents himself for hours at a stretch."

"I intend to share in his work."

Hadrian laughed. "Evan and I are in the profession but I can assure you we're not allowed to share in anything but the more menial tasks. And you think that you will be?"

"I'm Tybalt's wife."

"In our world, my dear Judith, there are archaeologists . . . wives and husbands are just by the way."

"Of course I know I'm nothing but an amateur . . . yet."

"But that is something you won't endure for long, eh? You'll soon be putting us all to shame—even the great Tybalt!"

"I shall certainly learn all I can and I hope I shall be able to take an intelligent interest . . ."

He laughed at me. "You'll do that. But in addition to an intelligent interest take equally intelligent heed. That's my sound advice."

"I don't really need your advice, Hadrian."

"Oh yes you do. Now! You're looking for Tybalt, I can see. He'll be hours yet. He might have waited until morning and devoted the first night in the Chephro Palace to his bride. Now had I been in his place . . ."

"You are *not* in his place, Hadrian."

"Alas! I was too slow. But mark my words, Tybalt's the man he is and so he'll remain. It's no use your trying to make him any different."

"Who said I wanted to make him any different?"

"You wait. And now let me take you back to the palace. You must be ready to sink into your bath of chalcedony."

"Is that what it is?"

"I expect so. Grand, don't you think? I wonder what Lady Bodrean would have thought of it. She wouldn't have approved of it for ex-companions even though it's turned out that you and she are connected—in a manner of speaking."

"I should love her to see me in my state apartments . . . especially if she had lesser ones."

"That shows a vengeful spirit, Cousin Judith. You *are* my cousin, you know."

"The thought had struck me. How are your affairs?"

"Affairs? Financial or romantic?"

"Well, both, since you raise the question."

"In dire straits, Judith. The former because that's their natural state and the latter because I didn't know in time that you are an heiress and missed the opportunity of a lifetime."

"Aren't you presuming too much? You don't think I would have allowed myself to be married for my money, do you?"

"Women who are married for their money don't know it at the time. You don't imagine the ambitious suitor comes along and going on his knees begs for the honor of sharing a girl's fortune, do you?"

"Certainly it would have to be done with more subtlety than that."

"Of course."

"Yet you imagine that you only had to beckon my fortune to have it in your pocket?"

"I'm only letting you into the secret now that it's too late. Come on, I'll get you back to the palace."

We did the journey back to the riverbank on mules where a boat was waiting to take us down the river to the short distance when we alighted on the opposite bank, almost at the gates of the palace.

When we arrived at the palace Theodosia came into the hall.

Evan was down at the site, she told us, and Hadrian remarked that he would have to go back. "You can depend upon it, it will be the early hours of the morning before we return. Tybalt's a hard taskmaster; he works like the devil himself and expects the same of his minions."

Hadrian went back and when I was alone with Theodosia she said: "Judith, come to my room with me and talk."

I followed her along the gallery. The room she and Evan shared was less grand than mine and Tybalt's, but it was large and dark, and the floor was covered by a Bokhara carpet. She shut the door and faced me.

"Oh, Judith," she said, "I don't like it here. I hated it from the moment we came. I want to go home."

"Why, what's wrong?" I asked.

"You can *feel* it. It's eerie. I don't like it. I can't tell Evan. It's his work, isn't it? Perhaps he wouldn't understand. But I feel uneasy . . . You don't of course. I wish they'd go home. Why can't they let the Pharaohs stay in their tombs? They couldn't have thought, could they,

when they went to all that trouble to bury them that
people were coming along and going where they shouldn't."

"But my dear Theodosia, the purpose of archaeology
is to uncover the secrets of the past."

"It's different finding weapons and Roman floors and
baths. It's this tampering with the dead that I don't like.
I never did like it. I dreamed last night that we found a
tomb and there was a sarcophagus just like the one that
time in Giza House. And someone rose out of it with
bandages unraveling . . ."

"I can't live that down, can I?"

"I cried out in my dream: 'Stop it, Judith.' And then
I looked and it wasn't you coming out of the thing."

"Who was it?"

"Myself. I thought it was a sort of warning."

"You're getting fanciful, Theodosia. I was the one
who was supposed to be that."

"But anyone could get fancies here. There's a sort of
shadow of the past everywhere. This palace is centuries
old. All the temples and tombs are hundreds and thousands
of years old. Oh, I'm glad you've come, Judith. It'll be
better now you're here. These people are so dedicated,
aren't they? I suppose *you* are a bit. But I feel I can
talk to you."

I said: "Are you worried about Evan?"

She nodded. "I often think what if what happened
to Sir Edward should happen to him."

I had no glib comfort to offer for that. Hadn't I wondered whether it could happen to Tybalt?

I said, "Of course we get anxious. It's because we love
our husbands and one gets foolish when one loves. If we
could only take a calm rational view . . . look in from
outside as it were . . . we should see how foolish all this
talk would be."

"Yes, Judith, I suppose so."

"Why don't you go to bed," I said. "You're not going
to sit up and wait for Evan, are you?"

"I suppose not. Goodness knows what time they'll come
in. Oh, it feels so much better since you arrived, Judith."

"So it should. Don't forget we're sisters—though only half ones."

"I'm glad of that," said Theodosia.

I smiled at her, said good night and left her.

I went along the gallery. How silent it was! The heavy velvet gold-fringed curtains shut me in and my feet sank deep into the thickly piled carpet. I stood still, suddenly tense because I had an instinctive feeling that I was not alone in the gallery. I looked round. There was no one there and yet I was conscious of eyes watching me.

I felt a tingling in my spine. I understood why Theodosia was afraid. She was more timid than I—though perhaps less imaginative.

There was the softest footfall behind me. Someone was undoubtedly there. I turned sharply.

"Absalam!" I cried. "Mustapha!"

They bowed. "My lady," they said simultaneously.

Their dark eyes were fixed on my face and I asked quickly, "Is there anything wrong?"

"Wrong?" They looked at each other. "Yes, my lady. But it is still not too late."

"Too late?" I said falteringly.

"You go home. You ask it. You are new bride. He cannot refuse his beloved."

I shook my head.

"You don't understand. This is Sir Tybalt's work . . . his life . . ."

"His life . . ." They looked at each other and shook their heads. "It was Sir Edward's life, and then his death."

"You must not be concerned," I said. "All will be well. When they have found what they seek they will go home."

"Then . . . too late, my lady," said Absalam, or was it Mustapha.

The other looked at me with deeply sorrowing eyes. "Not yet too late," he suggested hopefully.

"Good night," I said. "I shall retire to my room now."

They did not speak but continued to regard me in their mournful way.

I lay awake. The flickering light of candles showed the

ceiling on which had been painted pictures in softly muted colors. I could make out the now familiar outline of Amen Ra, the great Sun God, and he was receiving gifts from an elaborately gowned figure, presumably a Pharaoh. There was a border of hieroglyphs—strange signs full of meaning. I wondered whether while I was here I might try and learn something of the language. I had a notion that there would be many nights when I lay alone in this bed, many days when I did not see Tybalt.

I must be prepared for this. It was what I had expected in any case; but I did want Tybalt to understand that my greatest wish was to *share* his life.

It was two o'clock in the morning when he came in. I cried out in pleasure at the sight of him and sat up in bed.

He came to me and took my hands in his.

"Why, Judith, still awake?"

"Yes, I was too excited to sleep. I was wondering what you were doing out there on the site."

He laughed. "Nothing that would make you wildly excited at the moment. They've just been marking out the proposed areas and making general preparations."

"You are going on where Sir Edward left off?"

"I'll tell you about it sometime. Now you should be asleep." He kissed me lightly and went into our dressing room.

But I was not ready for sleep. Nor was Tybalt. We lay awake talking for an hour.

"Yes," he said during the course of the conversation, "we are exploring the same ground which my father did. You know what happened. He was convinced that there was an undisturbed tomb in the area. You know, of course, that the majority were rifled centuries ago."

"I should have thought they would have tried to keep the burial places secret."

"Up to a point they did, but there were so many workmen involved. Imagine hewing out the rock, making secret underground passages, then the chambers themselves. And think of all the transport that would be needed to bring the treasures into the tombs."

"The secret would leak out," I said, "and then the robbers came. It's odd that they were not deterred by the Curse."

"No doubt they were, but the fabulous riches found in the tombs might have seemed a worthwhile reward for damnation after death; and since they had been clever enough to find the hidden treasure no doubt they thought they could be equally shrewd in escaping the ill luck."

"Yet Sir Edward, who was merely working for posterity and to place his finds in some museum, is struck down whereas robbers who seek personal gain escape."

"In the first place my father's death had nothing to do with a curse. It was due to natural causes."

"Which no one seems certain about."

"Oh come, Judith, surely you're not becoming superstitious."

"I don't think I am unduly. But everyone must be a little, I suppose, when their loved ones are in danger."

"Danger. What nonsense is this? It's just a tale."

"Yet . . . he died."

He kissed my forehead. "Foolish Judith!" he said. "I'm surprised at you."

"It will teach you not to have too high an opinion of my sagacity where you are concerned. Wise men are fools in love—and you can be sure that applies to women."

We were silent for a while and then I said: "I have seen Mustapha and Absalam. They have said I should persuade you to go back home."

That made him laugh.

"It's such nonsense," he said. "It was a tale put about to frighten off robbers. But it didn't, you see. Almost every tomb that has been discovered has been tampered with. That's why it's the dream of every archaeologist to find a tomb which is just as it was when closed two thousand years ago or thereabouts. I want to be the first one to set foot in such a burial place. Imagine the joy of seeing a footprint in the dust which was made by the last person to leave the tomb, or a flower offering lying there, thrown down by a sorrowing mourner, before the door was closed, the mountainside filled in and the dead person left in peace for the centuries to come. Oh, Judith, you've no idea of the excitement this could give."

"We must try to see that your dream is realized."

"My darling, you speak as though I am a small boy who must have his treat."

"Well, there are many sides to people and even the greatest archaeologist in the world at times seems as a little boy to his doting wife."

"I'm so happy to have you here with me, Judith. You're going to be with me all the way. You're going to be the perfect wife."

"It's strange that you should say that. Did you know that Disraeli dedicated one of his books to Mary Anne, his wife. The dedication said 'To the Perfect Wife.' "

"No," he said, "I'm an ignoramus—apart from one subject."

"You're a specialist," I said, "and knowing so much about one thing you couldn't be expected to know others. He married her for her money but when they were old he would have married her for love."

"Then," said Tybalt lightly, "it must indeed have become a perfect union."

I thought: If that happened to me I should be content. Then he started to talk, telling me of customs, fascinating me with the exotic pictures he was able to create. He told me of what had been discovered in tombs which had been partially rifled centuries ago; and I asked why the ancient Egyptians had made such a fine art of the burial of the dead.

"It was because they believed that the life of the spirit went on after death. Osiris, the God of the Underworld and Judge of the Dead, was said to be the first ever to be embalmed and this embalming was performed by the God Anubis. Osiris had been murdered by his brother Set, who was the God of Darkness, but he rose from the dead and begot the God Horus. When a man died he came identified with Osiris but to escape destruction he had successfully to traverse the mythical river Tuat which was said to end where the sun rose in the kingdom of the Sun God, Amen Ra. This river was beset by dangers and no man could navigate it without the help of Osiris. The river was supposed to grow darker as the flimsy craft, in which the soul of the deceased traveled, progressed. He soon reached a chamber which was called Amentat, the Place of Twilight, and after he passed through that the horrors of the river increased. Great sea monsters rose to threaten him; the waters boiled and were so turbulent that the boat was in danger of sinking. Only those who had led good lives on earth and were valiant and strong could hope to survive—and only they with the help of Osiris. And if they were lucky enough to survive they at length came to the final chamber where the God Osiris judged them; those whom the god decided were worthy of making a journey to Amen Ra went on; those who were not, even though they had so far survived, were destroyed. For those who lived on, the tomb was their home. Their Ka, which is the spirit which cannot be destroyed, would pass back and forth into the world and back to the mummy lying in the tomb, and that is why it was considered necessary to make these burial chambers worthy of their illustrious inhabitants that they might not miss the jewels and treasures they had enjoyed during their sojourn on earth."

I said: "I can understand why they would not be very pleased with intruders."

"They?" he said. "You mean the long dead members of a past civilization?"

"There must be many people living today who believe in these gods."

" 'Allah is great and Mohammed his prophet.' You will hear that often enough."

"But there will be many who identify the old gods with Allah. Allah is all powerful as Horus, Isis, Osiris, and the rest. I think people like Mustapha and Absalam believe that Osiris will rise up and strike anyone who intrudes into his underworld."

"Superstition. My dear Judith, we are employing about a hundred men. Think what that means to these people. Some of them are very poor as you'll see. These excavations are a godsend to them."

"You take a practical view, Tybalt."

"You must too."

"I would of course, if you weren't involved."

I heard him laugh in the darkness. He said a strange thing then. "You love me too much, Judith. It's not wise."

Then I clung to him and we made love.

And at length I slept.

It was the time of Shem el Nessim, which I believe means the Smell of the Breeze and is to celebrate the first day of spring. At home it would be Easter time, I thought, and I pictured Dorcas and Alison with Miss Crewe decorating the church with daffodils and spring flowers—yellow most of them, the color, we used to say, of sunshine.

Sabina would be chattering away of church affairs and Oliver would be smiling tolerantly and my aunts would be thinking how much more satisfactorily things would have worked out if I had been the rector's wife instead of married to a man who had carried me off to share in an expedition in a foreign land.

The days since my arrival had disappointed me a little because I had seen so little of Tybalt. He spent every possible moment at the site. I had longed to accompany him but he explained that, although when there was work which I could do I should be allowed to participate, that time was not yet.

We took our meals in the great banqueting hall of the palace and many of us sat down at the long table. Tybalt was always at the head of it and with him would be the more senior members of the band. Hadrian and Evan were not very experienced, but Terence Gelding, who was several years older than Tybalt, was his right hand. He had been concerned in some of the successful excavations in England and Tybalt once told me that he had become well known in archaeological circles when he had discovered one of the finest Roman pavements in the country, and had also identified the period of some early Stone and Bronze Age relics. Tabitha had taken over the housekeeping with efficiency and it was clear she had been here before. This meant that Theodosia and I were together a good deal and we often took drives in the little horse-drawn traps called *arabiyas*. It was known that we were the wives of members of the archaeological party and for this reason we could more or less wander about at our will.

Sometimes we were driven away from the town and we saw the fellaheens working in the fields with oxen and buffalo. They looked dignified in spite of their none-too-clean long cotton robes and small skull caps. Often we saw them eating their meal which invariably consisted of unleavened bread and a kind of bean which I discovered was known as Fool.

We would go together in the *souk* and sometimes buy wares which were displayed there. Our presence always seemed to generate excitement because of a hoped-for sale, I supposed; but no one ever tried to force their wares on us.

There was one shop which interested us particularly because seated there was a young girl, wearing a yasmak, bent over a piece of leather on which she was embossing a design.

We paused and she stopped work to regard us intently out of enormous eyes made to look even larger than they were by the heavy application of khol.

She said in tolerable English: "You ladies like?"

I said that we liked her work very much and she invited us to watch her for a moment or two. I was astonished by the clever way she created a pattern.

"You would like?" she asked indicating a row of slippers, bags, and wallets into which the soft embossed leather had been made.

We tried on the slippers and studied the bags, and the outcome was that I bought a pair of oyster-colored slippers with a blue pattern and Theodosia a kind of dolly bag with a cord by which it was drawn up and shut. Her bag was in the same oyster color with a pale red pattern.

The girl was delighted with her sale, and as the transaction was completed she said: "You with English? They dig in the valley?"

I said yes, our husbands were archaeologists and we

had the good fortune to accompany them.

She nodded.

"I know, I know," she said excitedly.

After that we often stopped at her shop and now and then we bought something. We learned that her name was Yasmin, that her father and his before him worked in leather. Her two little brothers were learning to work on it too. She had a friend who dug for us. That was why she was so interested.

Whenever I passed the shop I always looked for her slight figure bent over her work or dealing with a customer. For me she was part of the now familiar life of the *souk*.

Neither of us ever went there alone, however. Although we felt perfectly at ease together, if, as we had done once or twice, we suddenly found ourselves alone, because one of us had paused to look at something or perhaps gone on ahead, an uneasiness would come over us and we would feel suddenly surrounded by an alien people. I knew that Theodosia felt this more intensely than I did. I had seen her when she thought she was lost and there was something near panic in her eyes. But that happened rarely and we usually managed to keep together even though the sights had become familiar to us. I imagined that the people had grown accustomed to seeing us. Although the children would stand and gaze up at us, the adults always passed us, aware of us, we knew, but keeping their eyes averted.

The blind beggars betrayed a certain eagerness as we approached. I couldn't tell why since they were blind. So we never failed to drop a coin into their begging bowls and always would come the grateful murmur: "Allah will reward you!"

Theodosia's attitude even changed and the feeling which the *souk* could arouse in her became like the delicious terror which children experience. She would cling to my arm, but at the same time she was enjoying the color and bustle of the markets as we passed men with brown faces and high cheekbones and the kind of noble profile which reminded me of the drawings I had seen on the walls of temples. The women were mostly veiled and all that was visible of their faces were the dark eyes made enormous by the khol they used. They were often clad in black from head to foot. When we went into the country we would see the women helping the men in the fields. In the early mornings or late afternoons we would take a trip in one of the boats up the Nile and see the women washing their clothes and chattering together. We often marveled at the way these women could carry a great jar of water on their heads without spilling a drop and walk so gracefully and in such a dignified manner as they did so.

It seemed that in a very short time the scene had become familiar to me. I was frustrated though, to be shut out from the main work.

Tybalt smiled at my continual demands to know if there was not *something* I could do.

"This is a very different operation from Carter's Meadow, you know, Judith."

"I do know that. But I long to have a part in it, even if it is only a small part."

"Later on," he promised. "In the meantime would you like to write some of my letters and keep some accounts? It will put you in the picture. You have to know so much, as well as working on the site."

I would be pleased to do this, I told him, but I did want to share in the active work as well.

"Dear Judith, you were always too impatient."

So I had to be content with that, but I was determined that it should be only temporarily.

Shem el Nessim was a public holiday and Tybalt was annoyed.

"Just because it's the first day of spring we have to stop work," he grumbled.

"How impatient you are!" I chided.

"My dear Judith, it's maddening. The cost of this is enormous and this is a sheer waste of a day. As my father always said, they never work as well after a holiday. They take a day or so to recover, so it is more than one day lost."

However, he was determined not to lose time and he

and the party were at the site as usual. That was why on
this Monday, which followed our Easter Sunday, Theodosia and I strolled down to the *souk*.

The shops were closed and the streets were different
without the sounds and smells and activities of the vendors.
There was a small mosque in one of the streets; the door
was always open and we had glanced in from the corners
of our eyes as we passed. It appeared to be a huge room
and we had often seen white-robed figures kneeling on
their prayer mats. But we had always averted our eyes
because we knew how easy it was to offend people by
what would seem prying or irreverence for their religion.

On this day many young people were making their way
to the mosque. They were dressed differently in their
best clothes and although the women kept to their black
some of the men wore bright colors.

We paused to watch the snake charmer who squatted
on the cobbles, his pipes in his mouth. We never failed to
marvel at the sight of the snake rising from the basket as
the music drew it out, fascinated it, soothed it, and sent
it back into its basket. On this day of Shem el Nessim
we noticed the soothsayer for the first time squatting on
his mat near the snake charmer.

As we passed he cried: "Allah be with you. Allah is
great and Mohammed his prophet."

I said to Theodosia: "He is asking to tell our fortunes."

"I love having my fortune told," said Theodosia.

"Well, then you shall. Come on. Let's see what the
future holds for us."

Two mats were set out on either side of the soothsayer.
He beckoned first to Theodosia and then to me. Rather
self-consciously we sat down on the mats. I was aware
of a pair of piercing hypnotic eyes fixed on my face.

"English ladies," said the soothsayer. "Come from
over the sea."

There was nothing very remarkable in his knowing
that, I thought, but Theodosia was pink with excitement.

"You come with many people. You come here to stay
. . . a week . . . a month . . . two months . . ."

I glanced at Theodosia. That was almost certain too.

"You will know, of course," I said, "that we are with the party who are excavating in the valley."

He darted a look at Theodosia and said, "You married lady," he said, "you have fine husband." Then to me: "You too, you married lady."

"We both have husbands. It is hardly likely that we should be here if we had not."

"From over seas you have come, back over seas you must go." He lowered his eyes. "I see much that is evil. You must go back . . . back across the seas."

"Which one of us?" I asked.

"You both must go. I see men and women weeping, I see a man lying still. His eyes are closed, there is a shadow over him. I see it is the angel of death."

Theodosia had turned pale. She started to rise.

"Sit," commanded the soothsayer.

I said: "Who is this man you see? Describe him."

"A man . . . perhaps he is a woman. There are men and women. They are underground . . . they feel their way . . . they disturb the earth and the resting places of the dead . . . and over them is the shadow. It shifts, but it never goes, it is always there. It is the angel of death. I see it clearly now. You are there . . . and you, lady. And now it is near you, and now it is over you, and it is waiting, waiting the command to take whomsoever it will be ordained to take."

Theodosia was trembling.

"Now it is clear," went on the soothsayer. "The sun is bright overhead. It is a white light up there but the angel of death is gone. You are on a big ship, you sail away. The angel has gone. He cannot live under the bright sun. There. I have seen two pictures. What may be is both of them. Allah is good. The choice is free."

"Thank you," I said, and I put coins into his bowl.

"Lady, you come again. I tell you more."

"Perhaps," I said. "Come, Theodosia."

He stretched out to take the bowl in which I had dropped the money. As his bare arm emerged from his robes I saw the sign on it. It was the head of a jackal. That was the sign of one of the gods I knew, but I could not remember which.

"The blessing of Allah fall on you," he muttered and sat back on his mat, his eyes closed.

"It would seem," I said to Theodosia, as we strolled back to the palace, "that there are many people who don't approve of our activities."

"He knew," she said. "He knew who we were."

"Of course he knew. It didn't need superhuman powers to tell that we were English. Nor to guess that we were with the party. We might even have been pointed out to him. Many people in the *souk* know us."

"But all that talk about the angel of death . . ."

"Fortunetellers' talk," I said, "to be taken with . . . no, not a grain of salt but a sip of *khosaf*."

"It worries me, Judith."

"I should never have allowed you to have your fortune told. You thought you were going to hear gypsy talk about a dark man and a journey across the water, a legacy and three children who will comfort your old age."

"I thought we might hear something interesting as he is an Egyptian. And instead . . ."

"Come in and I'll make some mint tea. Now that's a drink I do appreciate."

The fact was that I was a little uneasy. I didn't like this talk of the angel of death any more than Theodosia did.

As Tybalt was at the site with several of the party in spite of the fact that the workmen were not at their posts, and I did not know at what time he would return, I went to bed early and was asleep almost at once. It must have been an hour or so later when I awoke. I started up in terror because I saw a shadowy shape looming up beside my bed.

"It's all right, Judith."

"Tabitha!"

A candle which she must have brought in with her shone a faint light from the table on which she had laid it.

"Something's wrong," I cried and my thoughts still lost in vague dreams went to the soothsayer in the *souk* and the angel of death he had conjured up.

"It's Theodosia. She's had some ghastly nightmare. I was going up to my room when I heard her shouting. I wish you'd come in and comfort her. She seems quite distraught."

I leaped out of bed and put on the pair of embossed leather slippers I had bought from Yasmin and wrapped a dressing gown about me.

We went along to the room Theodosia shared with Evan. She was lying on her back staring up at the ceiling.

I went over and sat down beside the bed. Tabitha sat on the other side.

"What on earth happened, Theodosia?"

"I had an awful dream. The soothsayer was there and there was something in black robes like a great bird with a man's face. It was the angel of death and it had come for some of us."

"It was that old fortuneteller," I said to Tabitha. "We shouldn't have listened to him. He was just trying to frighten us."

"What did he say?" asked Tabitha.

"He talked a lot of nonsense about the angel of death hovering over us."

"Hovering over whom?"

"The whole party, I imagine, waiting to pounce on which ever one he fancied. Theodosia took it all too seriously."

"You shouldn't, Theodosia," said Tabitha. "They do it all the time. And I don't mind betting that he said Allah was giving you a choice."

"That's exactly what he did say."

"He's probably envious of someone who is working for us. This often happens. When we were here last there was a man who was uttering evil prophecies all the time. We discovered that his greatest enemy was earning more working on the site than he was himself. It was pure envy."

This seemed to comfort Theodosia. "I shall be glad,"

she said, "when they've found what they want and we can go home."

"These surroundings grow on you," prophesied Tabitha. "People often feel like that at first. I mean those who are not actually involved in the work."

She began to talk as she used to when I visited her at Giza House and so interesting was she that Theodosia was considerably calmed. She told us how last time she had been here she had seen the celebration of Maulid-el-Nabi which was the birthday of Mohammed.

"The stalls looked so lovely in the *souks*," she explained. "Most of them were decorated with dolls made of white sugar and wrapped in paper which looked like dresses. There were processions through the streets and people carried banners on which were inscribed verses from the Koran. The minarets were lit up at night and it was a wonderful sight. They looked like rings of light up in the sky. There were singers in the streets singing praises to Allah and tale tellers who were surrounded by people of all ages to whom they related stories which had been handed down through the ages."

She went on to describe these occasions and as she talked I noticed Theodosia's eyelids dropping. Poor Theodosia, she was exhausted by her nightmare!

"She's asleep," I whispered to Tabitha.

"Then let's go," she replied.

Outside the door she paused and looked at me. "Are you sleepy?" she asked.

"No," I told her.

"Come to my room for a chat."

I followed her. Her room was beautiful. There were shutters at the window, and she opened these wider to let in the warm night air. "I look down on a courtyard," she said. "It's quite beautiful. Cacti grow down there and there are bitter apple trees. They are one of the most useful plants in Egypt. The seeds are used to add flavor to all sorts of dishes and if the fruit is boiled the liquid which is produced makes goatskin watertight."

"You are very knowledgeable, Tabitha."

"Don't forget I've been here before, and if you're

vitally interested, you do pick up a great deal."

She turned from the window and lighted a few candles.

"They will probably attract insects," she said, "but we need a little light. Now tell me, Judith, does all this come up to expectations?"

"In many ways, yes."

"But not all?"

"Well, I thought I should probably have more work to do . . . helping . . ."

"It's a very skilled occupation. At the moment it is mainly workmen who are needed."

"And if they really did find a hitherto undiscovered tomb I suppose I should not be allowed near it."

"It would be such a find. Only the experts would be allowed to touch anything. But Tybalt was telling me how well you look after his papers and that you are a great help in many ways."

I felt suddenly resentful that Tybalt should discuss me with her, and then I was ashamed.

She seemed to sense my feelings for she said quickly: "Tybalt does confide in me now and then. It's because I'm such a friend of the family. You are of the family now and because of this I was saying to Tybalt that you should know the truth."

"The truth!" I cried.

"About me," she said.

"What should I know about you?" I asked.

"What only Tybalt and his father knew in their household. When I came to live with them and took the post of companion to Sir Edward's wife, we thought it best that I should be known as a widow. But that is not the case. I have a husband, Judith."

"But . . . where is he?"

"He is in a mental home."

"Oh . . . I see. I'm sorry."

"You will remember that I had a sudden call before we left."

"When you and Tybalt came back together."

"Yes, as I had to come back to London we met there and traveled down to Cornwall together. I had had a call because my husband had taken a sudden turn for the worse."

"He died?" I asked.

A hopeless expression came into her eyes which were large, brooding and very beautiful in the candlelight.

"He recovered," she said.

"It must be a great anxiety for you."

"A perpetual anxiety."

"You do not visit him often?"

"He does not know me. It is futile. It brings no pleasure to him and only great unhappiness to me. He is well cared for, in the best possible hands. It is all I can do."

"I'm sorry," I said.

She brightened. "Well, they say we all have our crosses to bear. Mine has been a heavy one. But there are compensations. Since I came into the Travers household I have been happier than I ever dreamed of being."

"I hope you will continue to be."

She smiled rather sadly. "I thought you ought to know the truth, Judith, now that you are a Travers."

"Thank you for telling me. Was it always so, from the time you married him? You cannot have been married so many years. You are very young."

"I am thirty," she said. "I was married at eighteen. It was a marriage arranged for me. I was without fortune. My people thought it was a great chance for me because my husband was wealthy compared with my family. Even at the time of our marriage he was a dipsomaniac, incurable they said. It grew steadily worse and when he became violent he was put away. I had met Sir Edward when he lectured on archaeology to amateurs and we became friendly. Then he offered me this post in his household as companion to his wife. It was a great help to me."

"How very tragic."

Her eyes were fixed on me. "But no life is all tragedy, is it? I've had days of happiness, weeks of it . . . ever since. But it is one of life's rules that nothing remains on the same level or at the same depth. Change is inevitable."

"I'm glad you told me."

"And I knew you would be sympathetic."

"You will stay with us?"

"As long as I am allowed to."

"Then that will be as long as you wish."

She came to me then and kissed me on the forehead. I was moved by the gesture; and as I drew away from her I saw the brooch at her throat. It was a scarab in lapis lazuli.

"I see you have a scarab brooch."

"Yes, it's supposed to be a protection against evil spirits. It was given to me by . . . a friend . . . when I first came to Egypt."

"Which was the last expedition, wasn't it, the fatal one?"

She nodded.

"It wasn't very lucky on that occasion," I said.

She did not answer but I saw her fingers were trembling as she touched the brooch.

"I suppose I should go to bed now," I said. "I wonder when they will come back from the site?"

"That's something of which you can't be sure. I'm glad I told you. I didn't think it was right that I should deceive you."

I went back to my room. Tybalt was not back.

I could not sleep. I lay in bed thinking of Tabitha. Memories from the past intruded into my mind. I remembered walking over to Giza House when I was a companion to Lady Bodrean and seeing Tabitha and Tybalt at the piano together. I thought of their arriving home together after she had been called away; and echoes from Nanny Tester's revelations kept coming back to me.

I wondered who had given her the scarab brooch. Was it Tybalt?

Then a horrible thought crept into my mind. Suppose Tabitha had been free, would Tybalt have married me?

A few days later Theodosia and I visited the Temple, taking a donkey-drawn carriage and rattling on our way over the sandy soil. Here had been the ancient city of Thebes, the center of a civilization which had crumbled away leaving only the great burial chambers of long dead Pharaohs to give an indication of the splendor of those days.

Although the Temple was open to the sky it was cooler within the shadows of those tall pillars than without. We examined with wonder the lavishly carved pillars each capped with buds and calyxes. It fascinated us both to study the carvings on the pillars and to recognize some of the Pharaohs depicted there with the gods to whom they were making sacrifices.

Wandering among the pillars we came face to face with a man. He was clearly European and I thought he was a tourist who had, like ourselves, come to inspect this renowned Temple.

It was natural on such an occasion that he should speak to us and he said, "Good morning." His eyes were a tawny color like so much of the stone we saw in Egypt and his skin was tanned to a pale brown. He wore a panama hat pulled down over his eyes as a shield against the sun.

We were pleased because he was English.

"What a fascinating spot," he said. "Do you live here?"

"No. We're with a party of archaeologists working on a site in the Valley. Are you visiting?"

"In a way. I'm a merchant and my business brings me here now and then. But I am very interested to hear that you are with the archaeology party."

"My husband is leading the expedition," I said proudly.

"Then you must be Lady Travers."

"I am. Do you know my husband?"

"I've heard of him, of course. He's very well known in his field."

"And you are interested in that field?"

"Very. My business is buying and selling *objets d'art.* I'm staying at the hotel not far from the Chephro Palace."

"It's comfortable, I hope."

"Very adequate," he replied. He lifted his hat. "We may meet again."

Then he left us and we continued our examination of the pillars.

In due course we returned to our *arabiya.* As we started

away we saw the man who had spoken to us getting into his.

"He seemed very pleasant," said Theodosia.

Next morning Theodosia did not feel well enough to get up; but by midday she was better. We sat on the terrace overlooking the Nile and talked desultorily.

After a while she said to me: "Judith, I think I may be going to have a baby."

I turned to her excitedly. "Why! that's wonderful news."

A frown puckered her brow. "That's what people always say. But they don't have to have the babies, do they?"

"Oh, it's uncomfortable for a while but think of the reward."

"Fancy having a baby . . . here."

"Well, you wouldn't, would you? You'd go home. Besides, if you're not sure, it must be months away."

"Sometimes I feel we shall be here forever."

"Oh, Theodosia, what an idea! It'll be a few months at the most."

"But suppose they don't find this . . . whatever it is they're looking for."

"Well, they'll have to go home. This is a very costly business. I'm sure that if they don't succeed in due course, they'll know they aren't going to and then we shall all leave."

"But suppose . . ."

"What a worrier you are. Of course it'll be all right. And it's wonderful news. You ought to be dancing for joy."

"Oh you're so capable, Judith." She began to laugh. "It's funny really. *I'm* Mamma's daughter and you know how *she* manages everyone. You'd think I'd be like her."

"She may manage everyone, but such people don't always know how to manage their own affairs."

"Mamma thought she did. And your mother was Lavinia, who was probably very meek. I ought to have been like you and you like me."

"Well, never mind about that now. You'll be all right."

"I'm frightened, Judith. It's since we've been here. I wish we could go home. I just long to see the rain. There's no green here and I want to be among normal men and women."

I laughed at her. "Yasmin would think the people in the *souk* were more normal than us, I do assure you. It's a simple matter of geography. You're just a bit homesick, Theodosia."

"How I wish Evan would lecture in the university and not do this sort of thing."

"No doubt he will when this is over. Now, Theodosia, you've got to stop worrying. This is the most marvelous news."

But she did continue to fret; and when it was affirmed that she was indeed pregnant, I could see that this caused her some concern.

$\mathscr{D}$ $\mathscr{D}$ $\mathscr{D}$

VI   Ramadan

It was the time of Ramadan—the months of fasting and prayer. I learned that this was the most important event in the Mohammadan world and that the date varied because of the lunar reckoning of the calendar so that it was eleven days earlier each year. Tybalt, who was always restive at such times because they interfered with the progress of the work, told me that in thirty-three years Ramadan passed through all the seasons of the year successively; but originally it must have taken place during a hot season as the word *ramada* in Arabic means "hot."

It began with the rising of the new moon; and until the waning of that moon no food must be eaten between dawn and sunset. Few people were exempt from the rule, but babies and invalids were allowed to be fed. In the palace we tried to fall in with the rules and ate a good meal before dawn and another after sunset fortifying ourselves with *herish,* a loaf made with honey nuts and shredded coconut which was delicious—although one quickly grew tired of it—and we drank quantities of the refreshing and sustaining mint tea.

The aspect of the place changed with Ramadan. A quietness settled on the narrow streets. There were three days' holiday although the fast went on for twenty-eight and those three days were dedicated to prayer. Five times a day twenty shots were fired. This was the call to prayer. I was always filled with awe to see men and women stop whatever they were doing, bow their heads, clasp their hands and pay homage to Allah.

Ramadan meant that I saw more of Tybalt.

"One must never offend them on a religious issue," he told me. "But it's galling. I need these workers desperately at the moment." He went through some papers with me and then he put an arm about me and said: "You've been so patient, Judith, and I know it isn't quite what you expected, is it?"

"I had such absurdly romantic ideas. I imagined myself discovering the entry to a tomb, unearthing wonderful gems, discovering sarcophagi."

"Poor Judith. I'm afraid it doesn't work out like that. Is it any compensation if I tell you that you have been of enormous help to me?"

"It's the greatest consolation."

"Listen, Judith, I'm going to take you to the site, tonight. I'm going to show you something rather special."

"Then you have made a discovery! It is what you came for!"

"It's not as easy as that. What I do think is that we may be on the trail of something important. Maybe not. We could work for months following what appears to be a clue and find it leads to nothing. But that's the luck of the game. Few know of this, but I'm going to take you into the secret. We'll go down after sunset. Ramadan moon is nearly full, so there'll be enough light; and the place will be deserted."

"Tybalt, it's so exciting!"

He kissed me lightly. "I love your enthusiasm. I wish that your father had had you thoroughly trained so that I could have had you with me at critical moments."

"Perhaps I can learn."

"You're going to get a grounding tonight. You'll see."

"I can't wait."

"Not a word to anyone. They would think I was being indiscreet or such an uxorious husband that I was carried away by my wish to please my wife."

I felt dizzy with happiness. When I was with him I wondered how I could ever have doubted his sincerity.

He pressed me to him and said: "We'll slip away this evening."

The moon was high in the sky when we left the palace. What a beautiful night it was! The stars looked solid in the indigo velvet and no slight breeze stirred the air; it was not exactly hot but delightfully warm—a relief after the torrid heat of the days. Up in the sky instead of blazing white light which was the sun was the glory of Ramadan moon.

I felt like a conspirator, and that my companion in stealth should be Tybalt was a great joy to me.

We took one of the boats down the river and then an *arabiya* took us to the site.

Tybalt led me past the mounds of earth over the brown hard soil to an opening in the side of the hill. He slipped his arms through mine and said, "Tread warily."

I said excitedly, "You discovered this then, Tybalt?"

"No," he answered, "this tunnel was discovered by the previous expedition. My father opened this up." He took a lantern which was hanging on the wall and lighted it. Then I could see the tunnel which was some eight feet in height. I followed him and at the end of the tunnel were a few steps.

"Imagine! These steps were cut centuries ago!" I said.

"Two thousand years before the birth of Christ to be exact. Imagine how my father felt when he discovered this tunnel and the steps. But come on and you will see."

"How thrilled he must have been! This must have been a miraculous discovery."

"It led, as so many miraculous discoveries have led

before, to a tomb which was rifled probably three thousand years ago."

"So your father was the first to come here after three thousand years."

"That may well be. But he found little that was new. Give me your hand, Judith. He came through here into this chamber. Look at the walls," said Tybalt holding the lantern high. "See those symbols? That is the sacred beetle—the scarab—and the man with a ram's head is Amen Ra, the great Sun God."

"I recognized him and I am wearing my beetle at the moment. The one you gave me. It will preserve me, won't it, in my hour of danger?"

He stopped still and looked at me. In the light from the lantern he seemed almost a stranger.

"I doubt it, Judith," he said. Then his expression lightened and he went on: "Perhaps *I* can do that. I daresay I would manage as well as a beetle."

I shivered.

"Are you cold?" he asked.

"Not exactly . . . but it is cool in here." I think I felt then as they say at home as though someone was walking over my grave.

Tybalt sensed this for he said: "It's so awe inspiring. We all feel that. The man who was buried here belonged to a world whose civilization had reached its zenith when in Britain men lived in caves and hunted for their food in the primeval forests."

"I feel as though I'm entering the underworld. Who was the man who was buried here . . . or was it a woman?"

"We couldn't discover. There was so little left. The mummy itself had been rifled. The robbers must have known that often valuable jewels were concealed beneath the wrappings. All that my father found here when he reached the burial chamber was the sarcophagus, the mummy, which had been disturbed, and the soul house, which the thieves thought was of no value."

"I haven't seen a soul house," I said.

"I hope I will be able to show you one one day. It's a small model of a house usually with colonnades in white stone. It is meant to be the dwelling house of the soul after death and it is left in the tomb, so that when the Ka returns to its home after its journeyings it has a comfortable place in which to live."

"It's fascinating," I said. "I seem to gather fresh information every day."

We had come to another flight of steps.

"We must be deep in the mountainside," I said.

"Look at this," said Tybalt. "It is the most elaborate chamber as yet and it is a sort of anteroom to the one in which the sarcophagus was found."

"How grand it all is!"

"Yet the person buried here was no Pharaoh. A man of some wealth possibly, but the entrance to this tomb shows us that he was not of the highest rank."

"And this is the tomb which was excavated by your father."

"Months of hard work, expectation, and excitement, and this is what he found. That someone had been here before. We had opened up the mountainside, found the exact spot which led to the underground tunnel and when we found it . . . Well, you can imagine our excitement, Judith. And then, just another empty tomb!"

"Then your father died."

"But he discovered something, Judith. I'm certain of it. That was why I came back. He wanted me to come back. I knew it. That was what he was trying to tell me. It could only mean one thing. He must have discovered that there was another tomb—the entrance to which is here somewhere."

"If it were, wouldn't you see it?"

"It could be cunningly concealed. We could find nothing here that led beyond this. But somewhere in this tomb, I felt sure, there was a vital clue. I may have found it. Look! You see this slight unevenness in the ground. There could be something behind this wall. We are going to work on it . . . keeping it as secret as we can. We may be wasting our time, but I don't think so."

"Do you think that because your father discovered this he was murdered?"

Tybalt shook his head. "That was a coincidence. It may have been the excitement which killed him. In any case, he died and because he had decided not to tell anyone, not even me, death caught up with him and there was no time."

"It seems strange that he should die at such a moment."

"Life is strange, Judith." He held the lantern and looked down at me. "How many of us know when our last moment has come."

I felt a sudden shiver of fear run down my spine.

I said: "What an eerie place this is."

"What do you expect of a tomb, Judith?"

"Even you look different here."

He put his free hand to my throat and touched it caressingly. "Different, Judith, how different?"

"Like someone I don't know everything about."

"But who does know everything about another person."

"Let's go," I said.

"You are cold." He was standing very close to me and I could feel his warm breath on my face. "What are you afraid of, Judith? Of the Curse of the Pharaohs, of the wrath of the gods, of *me* . . . ?"

"I'm not afraid," I lied. "I just want to be out in the air. It's oppressive in here."

"Judith . . ."

He stepped towards me. I couldn't understand myself. I sensed evil in this place. All my instincts were crying out for me to escape. Escape from what! This mystic aura of doom? From Tybalt!

I was about to speak but his hand was over my mouth. "Listen," he whispered.

Then I heard it distinctly in the silence of this place . . . a light footfall.

"Someone is in the tomb," whispered Tybalt.

Tybalt released me. He stood very still listening.

"Who is there?" he called. His voice sounded strange and hollow, eerie, unnatural.

There was no answer.

"Keep close to me," said Tybalt. We mounted the staircase to the chamber, Tybalt holding the lantern high above his head, cautiously going step by step resisting the impulse to hurry, which might have been dangerous I supposed.

I followed at his heels. We went into the tunnel.

There was no one there.

As we passed through the door and stepped over the heaps of brown earth, the warm night air enveloped me with relief and a pleasure that was almost bliss.

My legs felt numb; my skin was damp and I was trembling visibly.

There was no one in sight.

Tybalt turned to me.

"Poor Judith, you look as if you've had a fright."

"It was rather alarming."

"Someone was in there."

"Perhaps it was one of your fellow workers."

"Why didn't he answer when I called?"

"He might have thought you would have been displeased with him for prowling about there at night."

"Come on," he said, "we'll get the *arabiya,* and go back to the palace."

Everything was normal now—the Nile with its strange beauty and its odors, the palace, and Tybalt.

I could not understand what had come over me in the depth of that tomb. Perhaps it was the strangeness of the atmosphere, the knowledge that three thousand years or so before a dead man had been laid there; perhaps there was something in the powers of these gods which could even make me afraid of Tybalt.

Afraid of Tybalt! The husband who had chosen me as his wife! But had he not chosen me rather suddenly— in fact, so unexpectedly that the aunts, who loved me dearly, had been apprehensive for me? I was a rich woman. I had to remember that. And Tabitha, what of Tabitha? I had seen her and Tybalt together now and then. They always seemed to be in earnest conversation. He discussed his work with her more than he did with me. I still lacked her knowledge and experience in spite of all my efforts. Tabitha had a husband . . .

There was evil in that tomb and it had planted these

thoughts in my mind. Where was my usual common sense? Where was that trait in my character which had always looked for the challenge in life and been so ready to grasp it?

Idiot! I told myself. You're as foolish as Theodosia.

On the river side of the palace was a terrace and I liked to sit there watching the life of the Nile go by. I would find a spot in the shade—it was getting almost unbearably hot now—and idly watch. Very often one of the servants would bring me a glass of mint tea. I would sit there, sometimes alone, sometimes joined by some member of our party. I would watch the black clad women chattering together as they washed their clothes in the water; the river seemed to be the center of social life rather like the sales of work and the socials over which Dorcas and Alison used to preside in my youth. I would hear their excited voices and high-pitched laughter and wondered what they talked of. It was exciting when the *dahabiyehs* with their sails shaped like curved Oriental swords sailed by.

Ramadan moon had waned and now it was the time of the Little Bairam. Houses had been spring cleaned and I had seen rugs put on the flat roofs of the houses to dry in the sun. I had seen the slaughter of animals on those rooftops and I knew that this was part of a ritual, and that there would be feasting and salting of animals which were to be eaten throughout the year.

I was becoming immersed in the customs of Egypt and yet I could never grow used to its strangeness.

One late afternoon just as the palace was awaking after the siesta Hadrian came out and sat beside me.

"It seems ages since we've had one of our little chats," he said.

"Where have you been all the time?"

"Your husband is a hard taskmaster, Judith."

"It's necessary with slothful disciples like you."

"Who said I was slothful?"

"You must be or you wouldn't complain. You'd be all agog to get on as Tybalt is."

"He's the leader, my dear Judith. His will be the kudos when the great day comes."

"Nonsense. It will belong to you all. And when is the great day coming?"

"Ah, there's the rub. Who knows? This new venture may lead to nothing."

"The new venture?"

"Tybalt mentioned that he had told you or I should not have spoken of it."

"Oh yes, he showed me."

"Well, you know that we think we have a lead."

"Yes."

"Well, who shall say? And if we do find something tremendous, that is going to bring glory to the world of archaeology but little profit to us."

"Not still worried about money, Hadrian?"

"You can depend on my always being in that state."

"Then you are highly extravagant."

"I have certain vices."

"Couldn't you curb them?"

"I will try to, Judith."

"I'm glad of that. Hadrian, why did you become an archaeologist?"

"Because my uncle—your papa—ordained it."

"I don't believe you have any deep feeling for it."

"Oh, I'm interested. We can't all be fanatics, like some people I could name."

"Without the fanatics you wouldn't get very far."

"Did you know, by the way, that we are to have a visit from the Pasha?"

"No."

"He has sent word. A sort of edict. He will honor his palace with his presence."

"That will be interesting. I suppose I shall have to receive him . . . or perhaps Tabitha."

"You flatter yourselves. In this world women are of small importance. You will sit with hands folded and eyes lowered, and speak when you are spoken to—a rather difficult feat for our Judith."

"I am not an Arab woman and I shall certainly not behave like one."

"I didn't think you would somehow, but when you're in Rome you do as the Romans do . . . and I believe that is a rule for any place you might mention."

"When is the great man coming?"

"Very soon. I've no doubt you will be informed."

We talked for some time about the old days at Keverall Court.

"A closely knit community," he said. "Sabina and the parson, Theodosia and Evan, you and Tybalt. I am the odd man out."

"Why, you are one of the party and always will be."

"I'm one of the unlucky ones."

"Luck! That's not in our stars but in ourselves, so I've heard."

"I've heard it too and I'm sure both you and Shakespeare can't be wrong. Didn't I tell you I was one who never seized my opportunities."

"You could begin now."

He turned to me and his eyes were very serious.

"In certain circumstances I could." He leaned forward and patted my hand suddenly. "Good old Judith," he went on. "What a bully you were! Do you bully Tybalt? I'm sure you don't. Now I'm the sort of man who needs a bully in my life."

I was uneasy. Was this Hadrian's flippant way of telling me that in the past he had thought that he and I would be the ones to share our lives?

"You used to complain of me enough."

"It was a bitter sweet sort of complaint. Promise you won't stop bullying me, Judith."

"I'll be frank with you, as I always have been."

"That's what I want," he said.

From the minaret came the voice of the muezzin.

The women by the river stood up heads bowed; an old squatting beggar on the roadside tottered to his feet and stood in prayer.

We silently watched.

A subtle change had crept over the palace because the Pasha was coming. There was a growing tension in the kitchens where one heard excited voices; floors were washed with greater vigor than ever before; and brass was polished to look like gleaming gold. The servants lent to us by Hakim Pasha knew that the tolerant reign of the visitors was temporarily at an end.

Tybalt told me what we must expect.

"He is the governor of these parts, one might say. He owns most of the land. It is because he has lent us his palace that we are treated so well. He has made it easy for us to get our workmen, and they will know that to work well for us is to work well for the Pasha. So they dare do no other. He was of great assistance to my father. You will see that he comes like a great potentate."

"Shall we be able to entertain him in the manner to which he is accustomed?"

"We'll manage. After all we are entertaining him in his own palace and his servants will know what is expected. I remember when he came before it worked quite smoothly. That was about three weeks before my father's death."

"How fortunate that he is interested in archaeology."

"Oh there is no doubt of his interest. I remember my father's taking him on a tour of the site. He was completely fascinated by everything he saw. I expect I shall do the same."

"And what will my role be?"

"Just to behave naturally. He is a much traveled man and does not expect our customs to be the same as his. I think you will be amused by his visit. Tabitha will tell you about it. She will remember how he came here when my father was alive."

I asked Tabitha and she told me that they had been apprehensive but they need not have been for the Pasha had been goodness itself and as eager to please them as they to please him.

Tabitha and I had been to the *souk,* and as we were walking back to the palace, passing the hotel, we saw Hadrian and Terence Gelding sitting on the terrace there drinking with the man whom Theodosia and I had met in the Temple.

Hadrian hailed us and we joined them.

"This is Mr. Leopold Harding," said Hadrian. "Terence and I stopped here for some refreshment and as Mr. Harding knew who we were, he introduced himself."

"We have met already," I said.

"Indeed we have," replied Leopold Harding. "It was in the Temple when we were sightseeing."

"You two must be in need of refreshment," said Terence.

"I could do with the inevitable glass of mint tea," I replied.

Tabitha agreed that after our walk it would be welcome. We chatted while it was being brought.

Mr. Harding told us that he occasionally visited Egypt and he was very interested in the excavations because his business was involved with antiques. He bought and sold. "It's an interesting business," he assured us.

"It must be," replied Hadrian, "and you must be very knowledgeable."

"One has to be. It's so easy to get caught. The other day I was offered a small head—a flat carving in profile. At first it appeared to be of turquoise and lapis lazuli. It was so cleverly done that only an expert would have detected that it was not what it seemed."

"Are you interested in archaeology?" I asked.

"Only as an amateur, Lady Travers."

"That's all we are," I replied. "Don't you agree, Tabitha? I discovered that when I came out here."

"Mrs. Grey is more than that," said Terence.

"As for Judith," added Hadrian lightly, "she tries . . . she tries very hard."

Terence said gravely: "Both of these ladies do a great deal to help the party."

"You could say that we are amateurs with professional leanings," I added.

"Perhaps I'm in the same class," said Leopold Harding. "Handling objects—some of which are, most of the time wrongly, said to have come from the tombs of the Pharaohs—arouses an enormous interest. I wonder whether there is a chance of my being allowed to look round the excavations."

"There's nothing to stop your taking a drive along the Valley," Hadrian told him.

"All you would see," added Terence, "would be a few shacks containing tools, and men digging. A few heaps of rubble . . ."

"And Sir Tybalt has high hopes of discovering a hitherto undisturbed tomb, I believe."

"It's what all archaeologists who come here hope," replied Hadrian.

"Of course."

"It's going to be a long hard exercise," went on Hadrian. "I feel it in my bones that we are doomed to failure."

"Nonsense," retorted Terence sharply, and I added severely: "This is not a matter of bones but of hard work."

"They're a very reliable set of bones," insisted Hadrian. "And sheer hard work will not put a buried Pharaoh where there was none."

"I don't believe Tybalt could be mistaken," I said hotly.

"You are his doting wife," replied Hadrian.

I wanted to stop Hadrian's talking in this manner before a stranger so I said to change the subject: "Have you really dealt with articles which were discovered from tombs, Mr. Harding?"

"One can never really be sure," he answered. "You can imagine how legends attach to these things. The fact that an object may have been buried for the use of a Pharaoh three thousand years before Christ, gives it inestimable value. As a businessman I don't discourage rumors."

"So that's why you came to Egypt."

"I travel to many places, but Egypt is a particular treasure store. You must come along to my warehouse one day. It's very small, little more than a shed. I rent it when I'm here so that I can store my purchases until I can get them shipped to England."

"And how long shall you stay here?" I asked.

"I am never sure of my movements. I can be here today

and gone tomorrow. If I hear of a promising object in
Cairo or Alexandria I should be off to see it. It makes
life interesting, and, like you, I'm elated when a find comes
my way. I had a disappointment a few weeks ago. It was
a beautiful plaque which could have come straight from
the wall of a tomb—a painted scene showing a funeral
procession. The coffin was being carried on the shoulders
of four bearers, preceded and followed by servants carrying items of furniture—a bed, a stool, boxes and vessels,
the whole inlaid with silver and lapis. A beautiful piece,
but a copy of course. When I first saw it I was wild with
excitement. Alas, it had been made about thirty years
ago. It was beautiful but a fake."

"How disappointing for you!" I cried, and Hadrian
told them the story of my finding the bronze shield.

"And that," he finished, "is why she is where she is
today."

"It is clearly where she enjoys being," said Leopold
Harding. "You must do me the honor of visiting my little
store room. I haven't a great deal there but some of the
pieces are interesting."

We said we should enjoy that and with an *au revoir*
we left him sitting on the terrace of the hotel.

The Pasha had sent a message that he would dine with
us on his way to one of his palaces and he hoped, while
with us, to hear something of the progress which was
being made in this wonderful task to which he had given
his full support.

With Tabitha and Theodosia I watched his arrival from
an upper room of the palace. It was a magnificent sight.
He traveled in a carriage drawn by four beautiful white
horses in which he made slow progress preceded by a
train of camels, each of which had bells about its neck
so that they tinkled as they walked. Some of the camels
were laden with his luggage, polished boxes set with stones
and placed on cloths edged with deep gold fringe.

He dismounted at the gates of the palace where Tybalt,
with some of the senior members of the party, was there
to greet him. He was then taken into the inner courtyard

where he was seated on a special chair which had been brought for him. The back rest of this chair was inlaid with semiprecious stones and while it might have been a trifle uncomfortable it was decidedly grand.

Several of the servants were waiting with sweetmeats, large cakes made of wheat and flour and honey fried together, and glasses of tea. Three glasses must be drunk by each—the first very sweet, the second even more so, and the third with mint. All the glasses were filled to the brim and it was a breach of etiquette to spill any of the tea. I don't know what would have happened to any of the servants who did so. Fortunately on that occasion none did.

Tabitha told me what was taking place as of course we, as women, were not admitted to this ceremony.

But, out of respect for our European customs, we were allowed to sit at table and I was even accorded a place beside the great Pasha.

His fat hands were a-glitter with gems; and it was fortunate that the gem-studded chair was brought in for him, for it was wide and he was very plump. He was clearly delighted with his reception and rather pleased to see the women. He studied us intently, his eyes lingering on us as though he were assessing our worthiness in that field which for him would be the only one suitable for women. I think we all passed—Tabitha for her beauty, no doubt, which was undeniable, from any standards, Theodosia for her femininity, and myself? I certainly hadn't Tabitha's looks or Theodosia's fragile charm, but I did possess a vitality which neither of them had, and perhaps this appealed to the Pasha, for of the three he seemed most taken with me. I suppose I was more unlike an Eastern woman than any of them and the difference amused or interested him.

He spoke tolerable English, for as a high official he had often come into contact with our countrymen.

Dinner went on for several hours. The servants knew what should be offered and they were also aware of the enormity of our Pasha's appetite. Unfortunately we were expected to eat with him. *Kebab* was followed by *kuftas;*

and I believe they had never during our stay been served with such carefully prepared aromatic sauces. I noticed the expressions of fear on the faces of the silent-footed servants as they proffered the food to their master. He was served first, as the guest, and I, next to him, was appalled by the large quantities which he ate. Being a woman I was not expected to take such large portions. I was sorry for the men.

The Pasha led the conversation. He spoke glowingly of our country, our Queen, and the boon that the Suez Canal had brought to Egyptian trade.

"Think of this great achievement," he said. "A canal one hundred miles in length flowing through Lake Timsah and the great Bitter Lakes—from Port Said to Suez. What an undertaking. Moreover it has brought the British in force to Egypt." His eyes glinted slyly. "And what could be a greater pleasure to all concerned. And what has happened since we had the canal? People come here as never before. You British . . . what a flair for trade, eh! Your Thomas Cook with his steamers up the Nile. Chartering them from our Khedive for the purpose. What a clever man, eh! And what good for Egypt! Now he has a steamer to go between Aswan and the Second Cataract. Such good business for Egypt and we owe it to your country."

I said that Egypt had so much to offer the discerning visitors in the remains of an ancient civilization which was one of the wonders of the world.

"And who knows what else may be discovered!" he said, his eyes alight with joy. "Let us hope Allah smiles on your endeavors."

Tybalt said that he and the members of the party could never adequately express their gratitude for all the help he had given them.

"Oh, it is well that I help. It is right that I should place my house at your disposal." He turned to me. "My ancestors have amassed great wealth and there is a story in the family of how we began to build up our fortunes. Would you like to hear how we began?"

"I should very much like to know," I told him.

"It will shock you. It is said that long, long ago we were tomb robbers!"

I laughed.

"That is the story that has been handed down for hundreds of years. A thousand years ago my ancestors robbed the tombs here and so became rich men. Now we must expiate the sins of our fathers by giving all the help possible to those who would open tombs for posterity."

"I hope one day the whole world will be as grateful to you as we of this party are," said Tybalt.

"So I continue to placate the gods," said the Pasha. "And for my family sign I take the head of Anubis who embalmed the body of Osiris when his wicked brother Set murdered him. Osiris rose again and I honor his sacred embalmer, and he gives my house its sign."

Conversation then turned to the matter which I was sure was uppermost in the Pasha's mind—the expedition.

"The good Sir Edward suffered a great tragedy," he said. "This gives me much unhappiness. But you, Sir Tybalt, will, I know, find what you seek."

"It is good of you to show such sympathy. I cannot express my gratitude."

The Pasha patted Tybalt's hand.

"You believe that you will find what you come to seek, eh?"

"It is what I am working for," replied Tybalt.

"And you will do it, with the help of your genies." He laughed. It was an expression I had heard often since arriving in Egypt.

"I shall hope my genies will give me their assistance."

"And then you will leave us, and take away with you these beautiful ladies."

He smiled at me and it was my turn to be patted by the plump ringed fingers. He bent towards me. "Why I could wish that you do not succeed."

"We should have to depart in any case," said Tybalt with a laugh.

"Then I should be tempted to find some means of

keeping you here." The Pasha was waggish. "You think
I could do it, eh?" he asked me.

"Why yes," I replied, "with the help of your genies."

There was a brief silence at the table. I guessed I
had erred. However, the Pasha decided to be amused
and he laughed, which was the sign for everyone including the servants to join in.

Then he talked to me about my impressions of the
country and asked what I thought of the palace and if
all the servants had pleased me.

We had quite an animated conversation and it was
clear that although a few of my answers to the Pasha's
questions might have been somewhat unconventional I
had made a success.

There was some talk about the excavations in which
I did not join. The Pasha having eaten a tremendous meal
was nibbling a sweet rather like that which at home we
called Turkish Delight. Here it was stuffed with savory
nuts and was quite delicious, or would have been if one
had not eaten such a large meal.

The Pasha was to continue his journey to another of
his palaces by moonlight as it was too hot to travel by
day and before he left he would be taken to the site
by Tybalt on a rather ceremonious inspection.

While they were preparing to leave there was a heart-
rending scream from without and hurrying into the courtyard I saw one of the Pasha's servants writhing in agony.

I asked what had happened and heard that he had
been bitten by a scorpion. We had been warned to be
careful when near piles of stones for this was where
scorpions lurked and their stings were poisonous. I had
seen many a chameleon and lizard basking on the hot
stones and the geckos came inside the palace, but I had
not yet seen a scorpion.

The servant was surrounded by his fellows who were
attending to him, but I shall never forget the terror in his
face—whether for fear of the scorpion's sting or for
calling attention to himself during the Pasha's visit.

Pasha or not I was going to see that the man had
special attention. Before I had left England, Alison had

supplied me with many homemade remedies which were good she insisted for all the dangers I might encounter in a hot dry land.

There was one which was an antidote to wasps, horse-flies, and the occasional adder which we found in our Cornish countryside and although I doubted that our mild remedies would work very well on the poison of a scorpion I was determined to try.

So I brought my pot of ointment and as I applied it I noticed on the sufferer's arm that he had been branded with a sign I had noticed before. He immediately grew calmer, and I was sure that he thought there was some special healing power in that jar which I believed had at one time contained Dorcas's special mint jelly.

In any case the man was so sure that he would be cured by this foreign medicine that he seemed to be; and the dark eyes of his fellow servants regarded me with awe and wonder so that I felt like some Occidental witch doctor.

The Pasha, who had come to see me deal with his servant, nodded and smiled approvingly. He thanked me personally for what I had done.

Half an hour later they left and I watched their departure with Theodosia and Tabitha as I had their arrival. The Pasha walked to the boat which was waiting to take him upriver. The boatmen had decorated it with flags and flowers which they must have gathered, such as stork bill—a bright purple flower so called because when the petals fell and the center of the flower was exposed it had the appearance of a stork's bill—and the flame-colored flowers of the flamboyant tree. Many people had assembled to watch his progress and to call out their homage to him. It was clear that not only the servants of the palace but the fellaheen of the neighborhood lived in terror of the powerful Pasha.

Tabitha said: "It is exactly the same pattern as when he came here before. I think he was quite pleased with his reception and he has taken quite a fancy to you, Judith."

"He certainly smiled all the time," I replied, "but I

noticed that the servants seemed just as terrified when he was smiling as when he was not. It may well be the custom to appear especially benign when you are about to be most venomous. What do we do now? May we retire or are we expected to be here to pay homage when they return from the site."

"He'll not come back here," said Tabitha. "His entourage will set forth and meet him upriver. From there I believe he will go the short distance to his night's destination."

"Then I shall go to bed," I said. "Placating Pashas can be an exhausting experience."

It was not until early morning that Tybalt came in. I awoke at once.

He sat on a chair and stretched his legs out before him.

"You must be tired," I said.

"I suppose so, but quite wakeful."

"That enormous meal you consumed and all that *khoshaf* I should have thought would have had a soporific effect."

"I willed myself to remain alert. I had to make sure that all went as it should and no offense be given."

"I hope I was adequate."

"So much so that I thought he was going to make me an offer for you. I believe he thought you would be an admirable addition to his harem."

"And I suppose had the offer been high enough and you could have commanded a tidy sum to be dedicated to your pursuits in the archaeological field you would have readily agreed to exchange me?"

"But of course," he said.

I giggled.

"Actually," I said, "I didn't quite trust all that benignancy."

"He was very interested in what we were doing and made a thorough examination of the site."

"Did you show him the new discovery?"

"It was necessary to do so. There had to be some explanation as to why we were working from inside those subterranean passages. It's impossible to keep these matters entirely secret. He was most interested, of course, and asked to be informed as soon as anything is revealed."

"Do you think that will be soon, Tybalt?"

"I don't know. We have found an indication that there is something beyond the walls of one of the chambers. Because of the inevitability of robbers attempting to break into the tombs it has been known for one burial chamber to be hidden behind another—the theory being that the robbers having found one tomb would believe that was all to be discovered and fail to find the more important site behind it. And if this should prove the case, the one which was being thus protected would doubtless be of a very important person indeed. I am convinced that this was what my father was aware of." Tybalt frowned. "There was one rather disturbing incident during the tour. You remember when I took you there we heard a footstep?"

"Yes, I do." It came back to me clearly: the rising of goosepimples on my flesh, the terror which had over-taken me.

"It happened again," said Tybalt. "I was certain that some unauthorized person or persons were somewhere there."

"Wouldn't you have seen them?"

"They could have avoided us."

"They might have been hiding in the deep pit over which that rather fragile wooden bridge has been put. Did the Pasha hear it?"

"He said nothing, but I fancy he was alert."

"He might have thought it was a member of the party."

"It was a small group of us who went into the tomb. Myself, the Pasha, Terence, Evan with the two servants without whom the Pasha never seems to stir."

"A sort of bodyguard?" I suggested.

"I suppose so."

"He might have felt he needed some protection from the gods since the family fortunes were built on tomb robbing."

"That's no doubt a legend."

"What happened to the young man who was stung by the scorpion?"

"He seems to have made a miraculous recovery, thanks to you. You'll have a reputation as a sorceress if you're not careful."

"What a success I am! The Pasha contemplates offering me a place in his harem, and I am possessed of strange powers which I keep enclosed in Dorcas's mint jelly jar. I can see I'm a wild success. I hope I find the same favor in the sight of my true wedded lord."

"I can give you complete assurance on that point."

"So much so that I may one day be allowed to share in your work?"

"You do, Judith."

"Letters! Accounts! I mean the *real* work."

"I was afraid of this," he said. "I knew you always imagined yourself being in the thick of everything. It can't be, Judith. Not yet."

"I'm too much of an amateur?"

"This is delicate work. We have to go cautiously. It won't always be so. You're learning so much."

"What of Tabitha?"

"What of her?"

"You seem often to talk of your work to *her*."

There was an almost imperceptible silence. Then he said: "She worked a great deal with my father."

"So she is something more than an amateur?"

"She has had some experience."

"Which I lack?"

"But which you will have in time."

"Can I get it if I am not allowed to participate?"

"You will be in time. You must try to understand."

"I'm trying, Tybalt."

"Be patient, my dearest."

When he used that term of endearment, which was rarely, my happiness overcame my frustration. If I was indeed his dearest I was content to wait. It was logical. Of course I could not come into this vast and intricate field and expect to take my place beside him.

"In time I can promise myself then?"

He kissed me and echoed: "In time."

"How long shall we be here?" I asked briskly.

"Are you tired of it already?"

"Indeed not. It grows more fascinating every day. I was thinking of Theodosia. She longs to go home."

"She should never have come."

"You mean Evan should have left her at home."

"She is too timid for an expedition of this sort. In any case, if she likes to go home she can at any time."

"And Evan?"

"Evan has his job to do here."

"I suppose he's an indispensable member of the community."

"He is indeed. He's a good archaeologist really—though inclined to theorize rather than practice."

"And you do both?"

"Of course."

"I knew it. I admire you, Tybalt, every bit as much as Pasha Hakim admired me."

I slept, but I doubt whether Tybalt did. I suspect he lay awake enjoying daydreams of the glory he was going to find when he broke through into the tomb which would have been left undisturbed—until he came—for three thousand years.

In the early morning Theodosia and I went into the *souk*. The heat was becoming intense. Theodosia suffered from it very much and her desire to go home was becoming an obsession as were her fears of bearing a child.

I did all I could to comfort her. I pointed out that people here probably went out into the fields and had their babies and then continued working straightaway. I had heard such tales.

This consoled her, but I knew she would never be reconciled until we were making plans to go home.

She was torn between her desire to go home or to stay with Evan.

"Where would you go?" I asked. "To Keverall Court and your mother?"

She grimaced. "Well, at least there wouldn't be this frightful heat; and Sabina would be there."

Sabina was going to have a baby too. That would be a comfort for her, of course. Sabina's reactions were quite different from Theodosia's according to her letters, in which she rambled in the same manner as she talked. It seemed that she was delighted and so was Oliver; and Dorcas and Alison were being wonders. "They seem to know *everything* about babies—although why they should is a bit of a puzzle, except, of course, that they had you when you were little and it seems to me, my dear Judith, that you were a unique baby. There was never one so bright, intelligent, beautiful, good, naughty (although your naughtiness was something to cluck over), all this according to your aunts, of course, and I don't believe a word of it!"

How this brought back Sabina and I must confess that I too felt a twinge of nostalgia for those flower-decorated banks with the ragged robin and star-of-Bethlehem and bluebells giving patriotic color to the green background and here and there the mauve of wild orchids. So different of course from this hot and arid land. I missed Dorcas and Alison and I should have loved to call in at the old rectory and listen to Sabina's chatter.

I looked up at the sky, brilliantly blue through the narrow slips between two rows of houses; and the smells and sights of the market caught me and held me in that fascination which never failed.

We went past the shop where Yasmin usually sat, her head bent low over her work, but on that morning she was not there. In her place sat a young boy; he was bending over the leather working laboriously.

We paused.

"Where is Yasmin today?" I asked.

He looked up and his eyes were immediately furtive. He shook his head.

"She's not ill?" I cried.

But he could not understand me.

"I daresay," I said to Theodosia, "she is taking a day off."

We passed on.

I was sorry that the soothsayer was seated on the pavement.

He looked up as we passed.

"Allah be with you," he murmured.

He looked so hopeful that I couldn't pass, particularly when I saw that the bowl in which payment was placed was empty.

I paused and threw something into the bowl and immediately realized my mistake. He was no beggar. He was a proud man who was plying his profession. I had paid, so I must have my fortune told.

So once again we sat on the mats beside him.

He shook his head and said: "The shadow grows big, my ladies."

"Oh yes," I replied lightly, "you told us about that before."

"It flies overhead like a bat, a big black bat."

"Sounds rather unpleasant," I said. He did not understand me but this was to comfort Theodosia.

"And my lady has been blessed. My lady is fertile. Go back to the green land, lady. There you will be safe."

Oh dear, I thought. This is the worst thing we could have done.

Theodosia rose from the mat and the soothsayer leaned towards me. His fingers like brown claws gripped my wrist.

"You great lady. You say Go and they will listen. The big bat is near."

I was looking down at his arm and there on it I saw the brand again—the head of the Jackal. It was similar to that of the man who had been bitten by the scorpion.

I said to him: "You tell me nothing but of this big bat who is hovering around. Is there nothing else?"

"Allah would be good to you. He offers much. Great joy, many sons and daughters, a big fine mansion, but in your green land. Not here. It is for you to say. The bat is very close now. It can be too late . . . for you . . . and for this lady."

I put more money in the bowl and thanked him.

Theodosia was trembling. I slipped my arm through hers.

"It's a pity we listened to that nonsense," I said. "He says the same to everybody."

"To everybody?"

"Yes, Tabitha has been given the bat treatment."

"Well, she is one of us, you see. It's threatening us all."

"Oh come, Theodosia, you're not going to tell me you believe all this. It's the sort of thing that's handed out to everybody."

"Why should he want to frighten us away?"

"Because we're strangers here."

"But we're strangers who have our fortunes told and buy certains things in the *souk*. They all seem very happy to see us here."

"Oh yes, but he thinks we want to be frightened. It makes it all the more exciting."

"Well, *I* don't want to be frightened."

"There's no need for you to be, Theodosia. Remember that."

VII   The Feast of the Nile

Tybalt was getting excited. He was certain now that he was on the right track. Those working inside the old tomb had found indisputable evidence that there was another chamber behind the wall which they were now excavating.

We had now been several months in Egypt and it was time, he said, that we had something to show for our labors. This, he was sure, was what we had come for.

"It will be a bitter disappointment," he said, "if someone has already been there."

"But if it has been hidden behind this other tomb can they have been?"

"Not unless there is another entrance, which may well be the case. There'll be another hold-up, unfortunately, for the Feast of the Nile which must be imminent. The trouble with all these feasts is not only that they exist but that there is no definite date for them. This, of course, will depend on the state of the river."

"Why?"

"Well because it's a sort of placating ceremony. It dates back thousands of years to when the Egyptians worshiped the river. They believed it had to be soothed and pacified so that when the river rose it didn't overflow to such an extent that whole villages were carried away. This has happened frequently and still does. Hence the ceremony."

"Do they really think that if they perform this ceremony the river will stay within its bounds?"

"It's become a custom now, a reason for a holiday. But it was serious enough in the past. There really was a human sacrifice then. Now they throw a doll into the river—often an enormous life-sized beautifully dressed doll. This represents the virgin who used to be thrown into the river in the old days."

"Poor virgins! They did have a bad time. They were always being thrown to dragons or chained to rocks or something. It couldn't have been a lot of fun being a virgin in the old days."

"I've no doubt you'll enjoy the ceremony but it is going to hold up work which is the last thing I want at the moment."

"I can't wait, Tybalt, for you to take your step into that undisturbed tomb. It will be you, won't it? How happy I shall be for you! It'll be as you wanted it. You will see the footsteps in the dust of the last person to leave the tomb before it was sealed! What a thrill for you and you deserve it! Dear Tybalt."

He laughed at me in that tender indulgent way I knew so well.

I desperately wanted him to succeed.

We had a day's warning as to when the Feast of the Nile should take place. The waters were rising fast, which means that the rains in the center of Africa had been heavy that year; and it was possible to calculate the day when they would reach our neighborhood.

From early morning the banks of the river became densely populated. There were *arabiyas* everywhere; and some people had traveled in on camels, the bells on the necks of which tinkled gaily as had those on the necks of the Pasha's beasts. Disdainfully they walked down to the river as though they knew they were the most useful animals in Egypt. Their padded feet made it possible for them to walk with equal ease over the pavements and the sand; their wool made rugs and the hooded burnoose favored by so many Arabs, leather was made from their skin and the peculiar odor which seemed to permeate the place came from their dung which was used for fuel.

The great excitement on this day was: How would the river behave? If the floods were great the banks would be under water; if the rain had been moderate then there would be just the beautiful sight of the river's rising without the dangerous overflow.

But it was a holiday and they all loved a holiday. In the *souks* most of the shops were closed but there was the smell of cooking food. There was nutted Turkish Delight for sale, little flat cakes made of fried flour and honey, *herish* loaves and mutton or beef sizzling in a pan under a fire of camel dung and proffered on sticks so that the customer might dip them in the cauldron of steaming savory sauce. There were the lemonade sellers in their red striped gowns carrying their urn and glasses; there were stalls at which it was possible to buy glasses of mint tea. The beggars had come in from far and wide—blind beggars, legless and armless beggars, the most pitiful sight to take the joy out of a day of gaiety. They often raised their sightless eyes to heaven, their begging bowls before them, calling out for *baksheesh* and to Allah to bless those who did not pass the beggars by.

It was a colorful, bustling scene. Our party viewed the scene from the highest terrace of the palace; there we could see it without being part of it.

I sat beside Tybalt with Terence Gelding on the other side of him and Tabitha next to him; Evan was on my left with Theodosia.

Tybalt was saying that it looked as though the river was going to behave. It was to be hoped it would. If there was flooding it might mean that some of his workers would be commandeered to deal with disaster areas and that might mean delays.

Hadrian joined us. I thought he looked a little strained and wondered if he was finding the heat oppressive. Perhaps, I thought, there is a certain amount of tension. It has been so long and there is nothing decided yet. I knew how restive Tybalt was and that every day when he arose he was telling himself that this could be the day of great discovery, but every evening he came back to the palace disappointed.

The waters of the river looked red as they came swirling by, because they had swallowed some of the rich land as they passed through it. The people shuddered as they pointed out the redness of the water. The blood color! Was the river in a vengeful mood?

From the minaret rang out the voice of the muezzin: "Allah is great and Mohammed his prophet."

There was an immediate silence as men and women stood where they were, heads bent in prayer

We were silent on the terrace, and I wondered how many of those people were praying to Allah not to let the waters rise and flood the land. I believed then that although they prayed to Allah and his prophet Mohammed, many of them believed that the wrath of the gods must be placated and that when the symbol of a virgin was thrown into those seething waters the angry god who made the waters rise would be gratified and bid the river be calm and not wreak its vengeance on the poor people of the land.

We watched the procession wend its way to the river's edge. Banners were held aloft; there were inscriptions on them, whether from the Koran I did not know. Perhaps not, I thought, as this was a ceremony which had been handed down from the years before the birth of Mohammed.

In the midst of the procession was a carriage and in this sat the life-size doll which was to represent the virgin. At the river's edge, the doll would be taken from its place and thrown into the river.

I stared at the doll. It was exactly like a young girl— a *yasmak* hiding the lower part of the face. About the doll's wrists were silver bracelets and she was dressed in a magnificent white robe.

As the procession passed close to us for a few seconds I saw the doll clearly. I could not believe that it was not a real girl; and there was something familiar about her too.

She was lying back in her carriage seat, her eyes closed. The procession passed on.

"What a life-like doll," said Hadrian.

"Why did they make the doll with eyes shut?" asked Evan.

"I suppose," I put in, "because she knows of her coming ordeal. It's possible that if one was going to be thrown into the river one wouldn't want to see the crowd . . . all come to witness the spectacle."

"But it's a *doll*," protested Hadrian.

"It has to be as realistic as possible, I suppose," I said. "It reminds me of someone. I know. Little Yasmin, the girl who made my slippers."

"Of course," said Theodosia. "That's who I was trying to think of!"

"An acquaintance of yours?" asked Hadrian.

"A girl we buy things from in the *souk*. She's a sweet creature and speaks a little English."

"Of course," said Hadrian, "lots of people here look alike to us. As we must to them."

"You and Tybalt, for instance, don't look a bit alike and Evan is quite different from either of you and so is Terence and other people too."

"Don't be argumentative at the crucial moment. Look."

We watched. The doll was lifted high and thrown into the seething waters of the Nile.

We watched its being tossed about and finally sinking.

There was a long-drawn-out sigh. The angry god had accepted the virgin. Now we could expect the river to keep within its banks. There would be no flooding of the land.

Strangely enough, there was not.

Gifts arrived at the palace—a tribute from the Pasha

and an indication of his good will. For me there was an
ornament—I supposed it could be made into a brooch.
It was in the shape of a lotus flower in pearls and lapis
lazuli and very beautiful to look at. Both Theodosia and
Tabitha had received similar ornaments but mine was the
most elaborate.

Tybalt laughed when he saw them. "You are obviously
the favored one," he said. "That's the sacred flower of
Egypt and symbolizes the awakening of the soul."

"I must write a fulsome letter of appreciation," I replied.

Theodosia showed me hers, it was feldspar and chalcedony. "I wish he hadn't sent it," she said. "I fancy
there is something evil about it."

Poor Theodosia, she was having a miserable time. She
felt ill every morning, but it was the ever-growing home-
sickness that was most alarming. Evan must have been
most unhappy. He did tell me that when this expedition
was over he thought he would try to remain at home. He
thought the quiet university life would suit Theodosia. It
seemed that she was indeed getting into a state of melancholy when an unusual gift appeared evil to her.

As we took our walk to the *souk* she explained to me
that Mustapha had been horrified when he saw the ornament.

"Mustapha!" I said. "Oh dear, they are not going to
start that 'Go home, lady' talk again I hope."

"He was afraid to touch it. He said it means something
about your soul waking up as it can only do when you're
dead."

"What nonsense! The fact is that those two want to
go back to Giza House. So they're trying to frighten us
into persuading Tybalt to go home. Really they must
be half-witted to imagine we can do that."

"Tybalt would rather see us all dead as long as he
could go on looking for his tomb."

"That's an unfair, absurd, and ridiculous thing to say."

"Is it? He drives everyone hard. He hates all the festi-
vals and holidays. He just wants to go on and on . . .
he's like a man who's sold his soul to the devil."

"What nonsense are you talking!"

"Everybody is saying that there is nothing here. It's wasting money to stay. But Tybalt won't accept that. He's got to go on. Sir Edward died, didn't he? And before he died he knew that he had failed to find what he was looking for. Tybalt has failed too. But he won't admit it."

"I don't know where you get your information."

"If you weren't so besotted about him you would see it too."

"Listen! They're following a clue inside the tomb. There's a possibility that they are going to make the greatest discovery of all time."

"Oh, I want to go home." She turned her pale face towards me and so touched with pity for her was I, that I ceased to be angry because of her attack on Tybalt.

"It won't be long now," I said soothingly. "Then you and Evan can go back to the university. You will have a dear little baby and live in peace forever after. Try not to complain too much, Theodosia. It worries Evan. And you know you could go back to Keverall Court. Your mother would be pleased to have you."

She shivered. "It's the last thing I want. Imagine what it would be like! She would order everything. No, I escaped from Mamma when I married. I don't want to go back to that."

"Well, bear up. Stop brooding and seeing evil in everything. Enjoy the strangeness here; you must admit it's very exciting."

"I hated that river ceremony. I couldn't get it out of my mind that it was Yasmin they were throwing into the river."

"How could it have been? It was a doll."

"A life-size doll!"

"Of course. Why not? They wanted it to look as human as possible. We'll go and see her now and you can tell her how the doll reminded you of her."

We had reached the narrow streets, and wended our way through the crowds and there was the shop with the leather goods laid out on show. A man was seated in the chair usually occupied by Yasmin. We paused and he rose from his chair, seeing us as prospective customers.

I guessed that he was Yasmin's father.

"Allah be with you," he said.

"And with you," I replied. "We were looking for Yasmin."

I can only describe the look which passed across his face as terror.

"Please?" he said.

"Yasmin. She is your daughter?"

"No understand."

"We used to talk to her almost every day. We have not seen her lately."

He shook his head. He was trying to look puzzled but I felt sure that he understood every word we said.

"Where is she? Why is she not here any more?"

But he would only shake his head.

I took Theodosia's arm and we walked away. I was unaware of crowds, the chattering voices, the tray of unleavened bread, the sizzling meat, the colorful lemonade seller. I could only think of the doll which had been flung into the seething waters of the Nile and which had reminded us of Yasmin. And she had now disappeared.

When we returned to the palace it was to find that letters had come for us. This was always a great occasion. I took mine to the bedchamber so that I could be quite alone to read them.

First from Dorcas and Alison. How I loved their letters! They usually took weeks to write them and there was a little added each day so that it read like a diary. I could imagine the "letter to Judith" lying on the desk in the sitting room and whenever anything worth recording happened either Dorcas or Alison would take up her pen.

Such weather. There's going to be a good harvest this year. We're all hoping the rain keeps off. Jack Polgrey is hiring men from as far afield as Devon for he anticipates a bumper crop.

The apples are going well and so are the pears. It's to be hoped the wasps don't get at the plums. You know full well what they are!

Sabina looks very well. She's in and out a good deal and Dorcas is helping her make the layette—though it's months off yet. My word, I never saw such a cobble. And her knitting. Dorcas unravels what she does every day and then sets it right and I say why not let Dorcas do the whole thing except that Sabina likes to feel she's preparing for the baby.

Dorcas wrote:

It seems so long since we saw you. Do you know this is the first time in our lives that we've been separated like this. We're wondering when you're coming home. We do miss you.

Old Mr. Pegger died last week. A happy release for Mrs. Pegger, I think. He has been a hard husband and father although we mustn't speak ill of the dead. They had a fine funeral and Matthew's the new sexton. He dug his own father's grave and some think that's not right. They should have got someone else to do it.

Oliver is thinking of getting a curate. There's so much work, and of course in Father's day he had Oliver. He never seems to stop and it's a pleasure to see him holding the parish together.

And so on; the harvest had come in and was up to expectation. Jack Polgrey, who was an extravagant man compared with his cheeseparing father, had given a harvest dance afterwards and there had been fiddlers in the big barn. They had made corn dollies to hang in the kitchen and keep till next year to ensure as good a harvest.

The letter brought it all back clearly to me and I felt the desire to be there sweeping over me. After all it was home, and I felt so far away.

There was a letter from Sabina—one of her inconsequential scrawls, mostly about the help the aunts were giving her and how she was looking forward to the baby and wasn't it odd that Theodosia should be in the same condition . . . not odd really but natural and what about me? Surely I wasn't going to be left out. I was to tell her as soon as I was sure because the aunts were very wistful and wished I would come home and be pregnant and give them a chance of having a new baby in the family for although they were angels and treated her as though she was their niece there would never be anyone who could take the place of their Judith.

I was reading this when there was a knock on the door. Tabitha came in. She was holding a letter in her hand.

She looked at me as though she were scarcely aware of me.

"Tybalt . . ." she began.

"He's at the dig, of course."

"I thought perhaps . . ."

"Is anything wrong, Tabitha?"

She did not answer.

I jumped up and went to her. I noticed that her hands were trembling.

"Is it bad news?"

"Bad . . . I don't know whether one would call it that. Good perhaps."

"Do you want to talk?"

"I was hoping Tybalt . . ."

"You could go down to the site if it's all that important."

She looked at me. "Judith," she said, "it has happened . . . at last."

"What has happened?"

"He's dead."

"Who? . . . Oh, is it your husband? Come and sit down. You've had a shock."

I led her to a chair.

She said: "This is a letter from the home where they kept him. He was very ill before we came here. You remember I went to see him. Now . . . he's dead."

"I suppose," I said, "it's what they call 'a happy release.'"

"He could never have recovered. Oh, Judith, you don't know what this means. At last . . . I'm free."

I said gently: "I can understand it. Let me get you something. Perhaps a little brandy?"

"No, thank you."

"Then I'll send for some mint tea."

She did not answer and I rang the bell.

Mustapha appeared. I asked him to bring the tea, and in a very short time it came. We sat there sipping the refreshing beverage and she told me of the long and weary years when she had been a wife and no wife. "It is more than ten years ago that he had to be put away, Judith," she said. "And now . . ." Her beautiful eyes were luminous. "Now," she added, "I'm free."

She was longing to talk to Tybalt. He was the one whom she wanted to tell. There was no opportunity for that when they came in, for Tybalt and the others had stayed late at the site and dinner was ready when they arrived, and immediately the meal was over Tybalt wanted to go back to the site. I watched Tabitha. She wanted to break the news to him when they were alone.

She was waiting for him when he came home that night. It was past midnight. I watched him come in but he did not come up to our room at once. I guessed Tabitha had waylaid him.

I waited. An hour passed and still he did not come.

I asked myself why it should take so long for her to tell him what had happened. Insidious little thoughts like niggling worms—and as obnoxious—crept in and out of my mind. I kept thinking of Nanny Tester's ominous words. She had been rambling in her mind but they *had* come back together on that occasion. I remembered seeing them at the piano. They had looked like lovers then, I had thought. No, that was my imagination. If Tybalt had been in love with Tabitha why had he married me? Because Tabitha was not free?

And now she *was* free.

The letter from the aunts had brought them back vividly to my mind. I seemed to see Alison standing there: "You speak without thinking, Judith. That way a lot of harm can be done. When you're going to burst out with something, it's a good idea to stop and count ten."

I could count ten now but that would not help. I had to watch my tongue. I must not say anything I would regret. I wondered how Tybalt would react to a jealous wife.

Why should he be with her so long? Were they cele-
brating her freedom?

A wild rage rose within me. He had married me because he had known that I was Sir Ralph's daughter.
Had he? How could he have known? He had married
me because he knew that I would inherit money. Had
he known? He had married me because Tabitha was not
free. *That* he knew.

I had proved nothing, yet why were these thoughts in
my mind? Because his proposal had been so sudden? Because I had always known that there was some special
relationship between him and Tabitha? Because he was
dedicated to his profession and this expedition in particular, and he had needed money to finance it?

I loved Tybalt absolutely. My life had no meaning
without him. I was unsure of him; I suspected he loved
another woman who until now had been tied by a cruel
marriage. And now she was free.

There was a step outside the door. Tybalt was coming
in. I closed my eyes because I could not trust myself to
speak. I was afraid that I might give voice to all the
suspicions which crowded into my mind. I was afraid
that if I confronted him with my doubts and fears I might
find them confirmed.

I lay still, feigning sleep.

He sat down in a chair and remained deep in thought.
I knew he was thinking: Tabitha is free.

It must have been an hour that he sat there. And I
still pretended to be asleep.

Why does everything seem different with the rising of
the sun? Here it was a white blazing light in the sky which
one could not look at. At home it was benign and if it
could not be relied on to show itself every day it was
all the more appreciated when it did. But it only had to
appear, and fears which had seemed overpowering by
night began to evaporate.

How foolish I was! Tybalt loved me. He had made
that clear. But at the same time it was possible for him
to have affection for others and this he undoubtedly had

for Tabitha. She had been a member of his household before I had, a friend of the family, so naturally her affairs would be of deep concern to him. Nanny Tester was feeble-minded. That was obvious. She had taken an unreasoning dislike to Tabitha, and I had built up these suspicions on that.

I could see it all clearly in daylight.

I laughed at myself. I was as bad as Theodosia.

I began to realize that I had felt uneasy ever since the Feast of the Nile. If I could see Yasmin and talk to her as we used to I would feel differently. I did not like mystery.

Theodosia was not feeling well and Tabitha offered to walk with me into the *souk*.

Naturally we talked about her news.

"It seems wrong to feel this relief, but I can't help it," she said. "It was no life for him in any case, Judith. He was unaware of who he was for the greater part of the time."

"I don't think you should blame yourself for being relieved," I assured her.

"One does nevertheless. One wonders if there was anything one could have done."

"What could you have done?"

"I don't know. But I was only happy when I could forget his existence, and that seems wrong."

I glanced at her. But she did look different—younger— and there was a shine about her beauty which made it more obvious.

We passed the shop where Yasmin used to sit. The old man was in her place. He looked up and saw me. I knew that he was about to murmur the usual "Allah be with you!" but he changed his mind. He appeared to be intent on his work.

We went on. As we passed the soothsayer he spoke to us.

Tabitha sat down on the mat beside him.

"A great burden has been lifted," he said. "You are happy as not for a long time."

He looked up at me and touched the mat on the other side of him.

"You are loved," he said to Tabitha. "You should go away, far away to the land of the rain. You should go, and live in great joy, for you are loved and the burden has dropped from your shoulders."

Tabitha's color had deepened.

I thought: He means Tybalt. Tybalt loves her and she loves Tybalt and she is free . . . though he is no longer so. Why didn't they wait a while? He should not have hurried into marriage for the sake of . . .

The soothsayer's eyes were on me. "Go back, lady," he said, "the bat hovers over you. He hovers like the great hawk, lady. He is there waiting."

"Thank you," I said. "My future is always the same. One of these days I hope I shall have a batless one."

He did not understand; and we put our money in the bowl and walked away.

"Of course," said Tabitha, "he is just the same as the gypsies at home. They give the fortune they think will make the most impression."

"Well, I am no longer impressed by these premonitions of gloom. And they quite upset Theodosia."

"These people have a different outlook from us, you know. They rather like the fatalistic approach. They like to visualize danger which is avoided by wisdom. That is what he is giving you."

"It's most inhospitable. He's always telling me to go home. I do wonder why when I have been quite a good customer. He'd miss that, wouldn't he, if I took this death talk seriously."

"I admit that's a bit odd."

"At least he was right about the burden dropping from your shoulders. I believe that information about us is passed on to him and he uses it in his prognostications."

"That would not surprise me," said Tabitha.

Evan came to me while I was sitting on the terrace late that afternoon. I always enjoyed sitting there and watching the sun set. It fascinated me how it would be there one moment and then gone and the darkness would descend almost immediately. It would make me remember nostalgically the long twilight of home when it grew darker gradually and the evening came almost reluctantly.

Evan said: "I'm glad I found you alone, Judith. I wanted to talk to you about Theodosia."

"How is she today?" I asked.

"She's very depressed."

"Do you think she ought to go home?"

"I'd hate for her to and yet I begin to think it might be for the best."

"She wouldn't want to leave you. Couldn't you go with her?"

"I doubt whether Tybalt would be prepared to release me."

"Oh . . . I see."

"I suppose if it were imperative he would but . . . it's hardly that. The climate doesn't agree with Theodosia and now that she is going to have a child . . ."

"I know, but we shall have left here before that happens."

"Undoubtedly, but she doesn't seem to get any better . . . worse in fact. There is something about the place that has a strange effect on her."

"Would she perhaps then go home and wait for you to come back?"

"I don't think she would want to go back to our university quarters. She could go to her mother, but you know how things are there. Lady Bodrean never really approved of our marriage. I think Theodosia wouldn't be very happy at Keverall."

"Perhaps she could go and stay at Rainbow Cottage. The aunts would love to coddle her. Or to Sabina at the rectory."

"That's an idea; but I know she doesn't want to leave me . . . nor do I want her to."

"You could ask her anyway."

"I will," he said, and he seemed a little more cheerful.

The next day I was in the courtyard when a voice whispered: "Lady."

I looked round and at first could see no one and then a figure slowly emerged from a bush in the corner of the courtyard. It was a young Arab whom I could not remember having seen before.

"Lady," he said, "you have magic in jar."

He held out his hand, which was bleeding slightly.

"Why certainly, I'll dress it," I said. "But the first thing is to clean it. Come inside."

I took him into a little room which Tabitha used a good deal and which opened onto the courtyard. Here she arranged flowers when we could get them. She had put a spirit lamp there so that it was possible to boil water. I took some from a jar which was kept on a bench and boiled it in a pan. I told the young man to sit down and went up to my room to get Dorcas's ointment.

He watched me as I bathed the wound, which was very slight; and while I was drying it he whispered: "Lady, I come because I want talk with you."

I looked intently into his bright dark eyes; I could see that he was frightened.

"What do you want to say?"

"I want to speak of Yasmin. You very kind to Yasmin."

"Where is she?"

"She is gone. I pray to Allah to bless her soul."

"You mean she is dead?"

He nodded and a look of infinite sorrow passed over his face.

"How did she die? Why?"

"She was taken away."

"By whom?"

He was struggling to understand me and to convey his meaning. It was difficult for him.

"I loved Yasmin," he said.

"You work on the site?" I said. "You work for Sir Tybalt Travers?"

He nodded.

"Very good master with very good lady. Very secret."

I said: "You can trust me to keep your secret. What is your name."

"Hussein."

"Well, Hussein, tell me what you know of Yasmin's disappearance and you can rely on me to say nothing if it is advisable not to."

"Lady we love. But her father say No. She is for the old man who keeps many goats and sells much leather."

"I see."

"But love is too strong, Lady, and we meet. Oh, this I dare not say. We have offended the Pharaohs."

"O come, Hussein, the dead Pharaohs wouldn't be offended by two lovers. I daresay they had a few love affairs in their time."

"Where can we meet? There is no place. But I work. I am trusted workman. I work inside the old tomb. I am one of Sir Travers's best workmen. I knew when there will be workings and when there will not; and when there are not we meet there, in the tomb."

"You are bold, Hussein. Few people would wish to meet in such a place."

"It is the only place and love is strong, Lady. Nowhere else could we be safe and if her father know he would marry her at once to the man of many goats."

"I understand, but where is Yasmin?"

"It is the night the great Pasha comes. We are to meet. Together we go to the tomb. But Sir Travers says to me, 'Hussein, you are to take a message to Ali Moussa.' He is a man who makes tools they use. 'And you are to bring back what I ask. I will give you paper.' So I must obey and then I cannot go to the tomb. Yasmin went alone . . . and it was the night of the Pasha's coming. I never saw her again."

"But you talk of her as though she is dead."

"She is dead. She was thrown into the river on the day of the feast."

I drew a deep breath. "I feared it," I said. "But Hussein . . . why?"

He lifted his eyes to my face. "Please tell me, Lady. You are wise. Why is Yasmin thrown to the crocodiles?"

"Crocodiles!" I cried.

He bowed his head. "Sacred crocodiles. I have seen sacred crocodiles with jewels in their ears and bracelets of precious stones on their paws." He looked over his shoulder as though he feared he would be struck dead.

"Who could have done this?" I cried. "Who could have thrown Yasmin into the river."

"Big men, Lady. Big strong men of power. She has offended in some way. It is because she is in the tomb, the sacred tomb. It is the Curse of the Pharaohs."

"But Hussein, the Pharaohs couldn't have done this. Someone else has done it and there must be a reason."

"I see not Yasmin since the day I am sent to Ali Moussa; but I think she goes to the tomb, alone."

"She is a brave girl."

"For love one is brave, Lady."

"You think she was discovered there by someone?"

"I do not know."

"And when she was thrown into the river she gave no sign of life. She was like a life-size doll."

"Perhaps she is dead already, Lady. Perhaps she is drugged. I do not know. All I know is that she is dead."

"But why do this? If anyone wanted to kill her why go to this elaborate method of disposing of her?"

"Lady, you see pictures on these walls. You have seen the prisoners the Pharaohs bring in from their wars. Have you seen, Lady?"

"I have wondered who the people were. I have seen men tied upside down to the prows of ships on these pictures; and others without a hand or an arm or leg."

"You have seen, Lady, what happens to those who offend the Pharaoh. They are given to the crocodile. Sometimes they take an arm, a leg . . . and the captive lives on. It shows him and others what happens to him who offends. Sometimes they are thrown to crocodiles. You understand?"

"I can't understand how Yasmin could have offended."

"She went into the tomb, the forbidden place, Lady."

"And what about the rest of us?"

He shivered.

"Hussein," I said, "are you sure the figure that was thrown into the river was Yasmin?"

"Does the lover not know his beloved?"

I said: "I knew her but slightly but I thought I recognized her."

"It was Yasmin, Lady. And I was in the tomb, though not on the night she disappeared."

"You are afraid that they will take you, too?"

He nodded.

"I don't think so, Hussein. They would surely have done so by now. I think somebody was there on the night she went there alone and whoever that was killed her. You should say nothing to anyone of your relationship with her."

"No, I do not. It was our secret. It is for this reason we choose such a place for our love."

"You must be clever, Hussein. Do not speak of Yasmin! Do not show your sorrow."

He nodded, his dark eyes on my face. I was touched and a little afraid by the obvious faith he had in me.

"This," he pointed to his hand, "nothing. I come to see wise lady."

I wanted to protest at such a description but I could see that the only way I could comfort him was by allowing him to believe it fitted.

"I am glad you came to me," I said. "Come again if you learn anything."

He nodded.

"I knew you wise lady," he said. "You have magic in jar."

I could scarcely wait to see Tybalt alone. I wanted to tell him what the boy had told me and ask what could be done about it.

But how difficult it was to see my husband alone! I chafed against the delay. It was late afternoon when I saw him come into the palace. He looked dejected. He went straight up to our room and I hurried after him. He was sitting in a chair, staring at the tips of his boots.

"Tybalt," I cried. "I have something to tell you."

He looked up rather vaguely as though he scarcely heard what I said.

I burst out: "Yasmin is dead."

"Yasmin?" he repeated.

"Oh, of course, you won't know her. She's a girl who made leather slippers in the *souk*. She was thrown into the river at the Feast of the Nile."

"Oh?" he said.

"This was murder," I said.

He looked at me in a puzzled way and I realized that he was not giving me his attention.

I cried out angrily: "A girl has died . . . has been killed and you don't seem to care. This Yasmin was in the tomb that night when the Pasha came and . . ."

"What?" he said. I thought in exasperation: One only has to mention the tomb and he is all attention! That she had trespassed there was of more importance to him than that she had met her death.

I said: "One of your workmen has been to see me. He is terrified so please don't be hard on him. They had a meeting place in the tomb and the girl has died."

"A meeting place in the tomb! They wouldn't dare."

"I am sure he was not lying, but the point is the girl is dead. She was thrown into the river on the day of the Feast."

Tybalt said: "They throw a doll into the river nowadays."

"This time they threw in Yasmin. I thought I recognized her. So did Theodosia. And now we know. Tybalt, what are you going to do about it?"

"My dear Judith, you are getting excited about something which is no concern of yours."

"You mean to say we look on calmly while someone is murdered!"

"This is just a tale someone has told you. Who was it?"

"He was one of the workmen. I don't want you to be hard on him. He has suffered enough. He loved Yasmin and now he has lost her."

"I think you have been the victim of a hoax, Judith.

Some of these people love a drama. The storyteller in the *souk* always tells stories which are supposed to be true of lovers who die for love and they make up the stories themselves."

"I'm sure he wasn't making this up. What can we do about it?"

"Precisely nothing . . . even if it's true."

"You mean we stand by and countenance murder!"

He looked at me warily. "We are not these people's judges. The first thing one has to learn is not to interfere. Some of their customs seem strange to us . . . even barbaric . . . but we come here as archaeologists and consider ourselves lucky that we are allowed to do so. One of the cardinal laws is No interference."

"In the ordinary way yes . . . but this . . ."

"It sounds absurd to me. Even in the old days when a girl was thrown into the river as part of the ceremony it had to be a virgin. It seems to me that your Yasmin was not likely to be that since she had been meeting her lover in such an extraordinary place."

"It was someone who wanted to get rid of her."

"There are many ways of disposing of bodies other than such an elaborately public one."

"I think it was a warning."

He passed his hand wearily over his forehead.

"Tybalt, I don't think you are really paying attention."

He looked at me steadily and said: "We have completed the excavation on which our hopes rested. And it has led us to a chamber which is a blind alley. It goes no farther. It must have been put there to trick robbers. Well, *we* have been thoroughly tricked."

"Tybalt!"

"Yes, all our work of the last months has led to this. You may say that our efforts and all the money we have put into this have been wasted."

I wanted to comfort him; I wanted to put my arms about him and rock him as though he were a disappointed child. It was then that I realized that we were not really as close as the passion we shared had led me to believe.

He was aloof; there was nothing I could say which

would not seem banal. I realized in that moment that this work was more important to him than anything else on earth.

"So," I said coolly, practically, for my emotions were held completely in check, "this is the end."

"This is the ultimate failure," he said.

To say I was sorry seemed foolish. So I just sat silent.

He shrugged his shoulders and that terrible silence continued.

I knew that he had completely forgotten Yasmin, indeed that he had scarcely given her a thought. I knew that he was scarcely aware of me.

There was nothing in his mind but Failure.

_&_ _&_ _&_

VIII   Tragedy on the Bridge

All next day everyone was talking about going home. It had been one of the most expensive expeditions ever made and it had led to nothing—a blind alley in an already depleted tomb!

Tybalt had made a great mistake. He had been deluded by his father's words before his death. It all came back to that. Because his father had died mysteriously—and it *was* mysteriously whatever anyone said about it—Tybalt had believed he was on the verge of a great discovery. So had others. And now they had learned through bitter disillusion, the destruction of hope, and the squandering of a great deal of money that they had been deluded.

Theodosia was unfeignedly delighted. The thought of going home was a tonic to her.

"Of course I'm sorry for Tybalt," she said. "It's a great disappointment to him. But after all it'll be wonderful to be home."

Hadrian said: "Well, so it's all off. We shall soon be home and our great adventure at an end. Has it cured you,

Judith? You were so crazy to come out here, weren't you? And it wasn't quite what it seemed. Oh, I know our Judith. You saw yourself leading us all on to victory. Playing the Mother Superior to the party and finally breaking your way through and discovering the undisturbed tomb of a mighty Pharaoh. And this is the reality."

"I have found it fascinating."

"And you haven't minded being an archaeological widow? Do you think I haven't seen you gnashing your teeth! Who wants to take second place to a lot of dead bones?"

"I soon became reconciled to my position and although it has ended like this, a fact which we must all deplore, I can truthfully say it has been a wonderful experience."

"Thus spake the good and loyal wife."

"I knew this was what to expect," I said, "and I have always understood that Tybalt would have to be working most of the time."

He came closer to me and said: "I shouldn't have neglected you like that, Judith. And all for nothing!"

I turned on him angrily. "A loyal supporter of your leader, I see," I said.

He grinned at me. "You and I were always good friends, weren't we?"

"Until this moment," I snapped.

That turned the grin into a laugh. Then he was serious suddenly. "Don't you believe that. We always were and always will be. If ever you needed me . . ."

"*Needed* you!"

"Yes, my dear cousin. Even the most self-sufficient of us need others at times."

"Are you hinting something?"

He shrugged his shoulders and gave me that crooked smile which I had always found rather endearing. It was there in his serious moments when he was pretending to be lighthearted over something which affected him deeply.

I thought then: He *knows* something. He is warning me. What about? Tybalt!

I said sharply: "You had better explain yourself."

He seemed then to decide that he had gone too far.

"There's nothing to explain."

"But you implied . . ."

"I'm just being my nonsensical self once again."

But he had succeeded in planting seeds of uneasiness in my mind.

A few days later there was great excitement throughout the palace. Tybalt was jubilant. He had been following a false clue for months but he had picked up another trail.

He talked to me excitedly about it.

"I have this notion that we have been working in the wrong place. There's something behind the wall which we have yet to probe."

"What if it's another blind alley?"

"I don't think there could be two."

"Why not?"

"Oh for Heaven's sake, Judith, why should there be?"

"I don't know, but there was this one."

"I've got to try it," he said. "I won't give up until I've tried it."

"And that means that we shall stay here for how long?"

"Who can say? But we're going to try."

The effect on everyone was startling.

People like Terence Gelding and the senior members of the party were delighted. So was Tabitha. Poor Theodosia! She was so disappointed. So was Evan I believed, but solely on Theodosia's account. He was so kind and tender to her—a husband first, I thought, archaeologist second.

And I knew that in my secret thoughts I was making comparisons.

Theodosia was melancholy. Her hopes of going home were dashed.

Tabitha said: "She's upsetting Evan. Tybalt is quite concerned. He says Evan is not concentrating on his work because he is continually worrying about his wife."

I felt resentful. Why should Tybalt talk to Tabitha about Evan? I suspected he talked to her about a great deal.

I had come upon them more than once in earnest conversation. I remembered that scene with Hadrian and
wondered whether others had noticed these things as I
did.

Tabitha was always energetic in smoothing the way
for Tybalt. It was she who had the idea that since Theodosia was fretting about a prolonged stay she ought to
take more interest in what was going on. She thought it
would be a good idea to make up a little party and go for
a tour of inspection. Theodosia should be a member of
it. Leopold Harding, who called now and then at the
palace and never lost an opportunity of talking to any
of us when we met by chance, had asked if he might
have an opportunity some time of being taken on a tour
of the dig.

"Let Theodosia see for herself how interesting it is,"
said Tabitha. "I'm sure that would help her overcome
her nervous fears."

Tabitha spoke to Tybalt who gave his permission and
then she arranged the party. To my surprise Theodosia
agreed to join it. She genuinely wished not to worry Evan
and was determined to put on a bold face in spite of her
fears.

Leopold Harding was very interested in what was
happening at the site. Hadrian told me that he had met
him once or twice and he always asked how things were
going. He had been very sympathetic when we had believed the expedition had failed and had told Hadrian
how pleased he was that hopes had been revived.

"He is longing to have a real look round," said Hadrian,
"and has asked me if there is a hope of his joining this
tour. He was delighted when Tybalt gave his permission.
He invited me to go along to that storehouse of his.
Would you like to come?"

I said I would so Hadrian and I went together.

It was a small shop on the edge of the *souk,* heavily
pad-locked, and I gathered that some of the pieces he
had there were very valuable.

The small space inside was full of the most fascinating

things. Leopold Harding glowed with enthusiasm as he pointed out various objects.

"Look at this folding stool. It's carved with inter-laced foliage. You see the lions' heads on the upper terminals and the claws on the lower ends. I found it here but it might well be Scandinavian. But one never knows what one is going to pick up where. This could be twelfth century."

Hadrian had picked up a plaque. "Why look at this. I could swear this was genuine." I saw the profiled figures —a Pharaoh presenting gifts to Horus.

"A lovely piece," said Leopold Harding, "and it would fool most people. Wouldn't you think it had been plucked from the walls of a tomb? Not so. It is old—though not old enough. Three hundred years, I'd say. You can imagine how excited I was when that came into my hands."

Hadrian allowed Leopold Harding to take it from him very reluctantly, I thought.

"Look at this," went on Mr. Harding, picking up a box. "It's for jewels. See the ivory inlay and the small check-ered panels on the lid. This is one of my most valuable pieces."

We admired the box and went from one object to another. He told us about the difficulties of getting the goods shipped to England and how glad he was when he was able to acquire jewelry or small pieces which he could carry himself.

He showed us some collar-necklets and earrings of lapis and turquoise cut and set in the Egyptian manner. I was fascinated by them. There was one statue which intrigued me. It was of the god Horus with his hawk-like face and at the feet of the god was a small and beautifully carved figure of a Pharaoh. Over this small figure the hawk-god towered protectively. It seemed to take on life; it was some five feet in height but as I looked, as though hypnotized, it appeared to grow to enormous proportions. I could not take my eyes from it. There was about it a quality which made me want to escape from it and yet held me there.

When I felt a touch on my shoulder I started. It was

Leopold Harding and he was smiling at me.

"Fine, is it not?" he said. "A wonderful copy."

"What was the original?" I asked.

"That I never saw, but it was clearly meant to decorate some long dead Pharaoh's tomb. The sort of image which was put there to ward off tomb robbers." He turned to Hadrian. "But you would know more of that than I."

"I doubt it," said Hadrian. "I have never seen the inside of an undisturbed tomb."

"That image is certainly a little chilling, don't you agree? Now I want your opinion of this alabaster ornament. The Sphinx, no less. It's rather good. Quite valuable too. It's very cleverly carved."

We agreed and went on to examine the other interesting articles he had assembled, but I kept thinking of the stone Horus and whenever I turned to look at it, I imagined those hawk's eyes were on me menacingly.

It was certainly an interesting experience and when we left we told Leopold Harding so and thanked him warmly.

"One good turn deserves another," he said lightly. "Don't forget you are taking me on a tour of the site."

The party consisted of Terence Gelding, who was in charge, with Hadrian and Evan to assist him, Leopold Harding, the interested guest, Tabitha, Theodosia, and myself.

We went to the site in the evening when the workmen were not there.

I could never enter those subterranean passages without a thrill of excitement so I guessed how Theodosia would be feeling. She was now noticeably pregnant and leaned on Evan's arm; but I was surprised how reconciled she was and she seemed almost prepared to enjoy the adventure.

This was an excellent plan and it didn't seem too much to hope that this might induce Theodosia to cast aside her terrors and begin to be what Tabitha called "a good archaeologist's wife."

Terence had one lantern and Hadrian the other—

Terence leading and Hadrian taking up the rear.

Theodosia clung to her husband's arm and gingerly picked her steps.

It was cold, of course, after the heat outside but we had been warned by Terence to bring light coats or wraps.

Terence lifted his lantern high and pointed out wall pictures of the gods and the Pharaohs. I recognized the Ram-headed Amen Ra, Horus the Hawk or was that Amen Ra too, for he was both Hawk and Ram? There was Anubis the Jackal, which reminded me of the mark on the arm of the man whose wound I had dressed and also I had seen it on the soothsayer's skin.

Terence was saying: "This was not the tomb of a very important man. These wall paintings have not been executed with the care that we have seen in some of the palaces—our own palace for one. It was evidently the last resting place of some minor potentate, a man of wealth, though, because even a secondary tomb must have cost a great deal. It could even be that several people were buried here."

"And made a sort of syndicate to pay for it?" asked Leopold Harding.

"Wouldn't they have been dead?" asked Theodosia and we were all delighted to hear her express interest.

"No," said Terence. "Long before their deaths, work was started on the tomb. In the case of a Pharaoh his went on for years and only stopped at the time of his death."

"When they were ready to use it," added Hadrian. "So the longer they lived the better the tomb, which seems hardly fair on the young. To be deprived of life and a fine tomb all at one stroke."

We proceeded carefully along the narrow passageway, Terence leading. Then the passage opened into a chamber. "This is not the burial chamber," said Terence. "That would be farther on. This pit you see here might have contained something which was removed when the tomb was robbed. It's hard to say. This wooden structure of a bridge was put up by us to be used when we needed to cross the pit to get into the passage just beyond. But first look at the engraving on this wall."

He held the lantern high and Theodosia, I believe in an endeavor to show Evan that she was unafraid, started to cross that wooden structure which did service as a bridge.

We were all horrified by what happened next. The bridge crumpled; Theodosia was thrown up into the air before she fell, taking part of the bridge with her down into the pit.

There was a terrifying silence which seemed to go on and on but which could only have lasted half a second.

Then I heard Hadrian cry: "Good God." I saw Evan. He was scrambling down into the pit; it was not easy to get down for it was a drop of some twelve feet.

Terence took charge. "Harding, go and get a stretcher somewhere. Get a doctor someone. Take this lantern." He thrust it into my hands. "I'll get down there." And then he was scrambling down and kneeling with Evan beside the prostrate form of Theodosia.

It was like a nightmare: the gloom of the tomb, the silence all about us, the limp unconscious Theodosia, the stricken Evan.

Everything seemed to take such a long time. Of course there were difficulties. We did improvise a stretcher but bringing Theodosia out of the pit on it was no easy matter; nor was conveying the stretcher along those passages. Terence proved himself a leader on that night and Tabitha was beside him, cool and authoritative. I did all I could to comfort Evan. He kept saying: "It's my fault. I should never have let her come here."

When we finally got Theodosia back to the palace we put her to bed. Her child was born that night—dead—a five months' girl. But it was Theodosia who gave us such cause for anxiety.

She remained unconscious and Tabitha, who had some experience of nursing, stayed with her while I sat with Evan in an adjoining room trying in vain to comfort him.

I kept saying: "It'll be all right. You've lost the child but you'll have another."

"If she comes through this," said Evan, "I shall never bring her away from home again. She was terrified. You know how frightened she was. She *sensed* disaster. It's my fault."

I said: "Nonsense. It's not your fault. Of course she came with you. You're her husband."

"She wanted to go back, and I kept her here. She was trying hard to adjust herself. Oh God, why didn't I go home."

"You couldn't," I assured him. "Your work was here."

"I did speak to Tybalt. But it was impossible to release me without a lot of trouble. He would have had to find a replacement."

Tabitha had come to the door. Evan was on his feet. She beckoned us to come in.

I looked at Theodosia's pallid face on the pillows; it was clammy with sweat and I would scarcely have recognized her.

A terrible desolation came to me. She was my sister and I knew she was going to die.

Evan knelt by the bed, the tears running down his face. Theodosia opened her eyes.

"Evan," she said.

"My love," he answered, "my dear, dear love."

"It's all right, Evan. I . . . I'm not afraid . . ."

She was aware of me.

"Judith."

"I'm here, Theodosia."

"My . . . sister."

"Yes," I said.

"It's right over me now, Judith . . . the big black bat . . ."

"Oh Theodosia . . ."

"I'm not afraid though. Evan, I'm not . . ."

I heard Evan whisper: "Oh God."

And Tabitha's hand was on my shoulder.

"It's all over, Judith," she whispered.

I stood up.

I could not believe it. Yesterday she had been well. Only two days ago we had been in the *souk* together.

And now Theodosia was dead.

The effect of Theodosia's death was dynamic.

Had not Sir Edward died? And now another death. This was the Curse of the Pharaohs!

Mustapha and Absalam watched me with great pleading eyes. "Go home, Lady," said those eyes. "Go home before the Curse strikes again."

Tybalt was distressed. "This has upset Tabitha," he said. "She can't forget that she suggested the expedition. I tell her that she did it to help Theodosia, but that doesn't comfort her."

I had rarely seen him so affected. For Tabitha!

What was happening to me? I was growing resentful and suspicious. Now, I was telling myself, he is more concerned with the effect this is going to have on Tabitha than on Evan, whose wife Theodosia was, and on myself who was her sister.

"I have set up an enquiry immediately," he told me. "We have to find out how such an accident could have happened. The bridge was used frequently and had been strong enough to hold men and a certain amount of heavy equipment. Why should it have broken when a young woman attempted to cross it? There has to be a logical explanation. If we don't find one, those ridiculous rumors will start up again."

There was, however, nothing he could do to prevent that—particularly when it was proved impossible to discover how the bridge had broken.

The Curse had made the bridge fall apart, was the verdict of many. It was the work of the angry gods.

But why should the victim be Theodosia, who had done nothing to offend? It was her first visit to the tomb; she had wanted to go home. If the gods were angry why should they haven chosen to wreak their vengeance on her?

Some of the workmen would not go into the tomb, a fact which held up operations considerably.

I was chiefly concerned with Evan who was beside himself with grief.

He could not concentrate when one spoke to him. His eyes would fill with tears; sometimes he would talk of

Theodosia and his happiness with her and the hopes they had shared for the future of their child. It was painful; it was more than that. It was unendurable, and I spoke to Tybalt about it.

I said: "Evan will have to go home. He can't stay here."

"We need him here," said Tybalt.

"Not in his present state surely."

"He's pretty useless of course."

I said sharply: "He has just lost a wife and child."

"I know that. I thought perhaps it would be good for him to immerse himself in work."

I laughed shortly. "I'm going to make a suggestion," I said, "which will horrify you. Everything here reminds him of what he has lost. He must go home at once."

"What will he do there? He will only mourn for his wife. Work will help him to overcome his grief."

"Do you realize, Tybalt, how much Evan loved his wife?"

"He was devoted to her, I know."

"I daresay you would find it difficult to understand Evan's feelings for Theodosia."

He looked at me oddly.

"Yes," I continued sharply, "I know you would. But *I* understand them. At the moment he is dazed by his grief. We have to help him, Tybalt. He has lost what is most dear to him, more dear than anything you can understand. Work cannot save him. Nothing can save him. I think he must go away from here. Here there are too many memories."

"Are there not at home?"

"Different memories. Here he keeps thinking of her as she was here . . . all her fears. She always wanted to go home. He is reproaching himself. He's on the verge of a breakdown. If you could have seen his face when they brought her out of the pit . . . and then at her bedside when she was dying . . ."

My voice broke; and he patted my shoulder. I looked at him and thought angrily: He is calculating who can be put in Evan's place if Evan is too distraught to continue.

I went on: "This is not a matter of archaeology. This

is a matter of human decency, human kindness. I have to look after Evan . . . if others won't."

"Well, naturally we want to do what is best . . ."

"Yes, I know, the work must go on. No matter what happens, that is important. I know that. But Evan is of no use to you in his present state. I am going to write to my aunts and tell them what has happened. I shall ask them if Evan can go to Rainbow Cottage and there they will nurse him and make him want to live again."

Tybalt did not answer and I turned from him and said: "I shall now go and write to my aunts. No matter what you say I shall ask them to take in Evan."

Tybalt looked at me in astonishment but he said nothing.

I sat down and wrote:

Dear Aunts, I want you to take Evan and look after him. You will have heard about this fearful accident. Poor Evan is distracted. You know how much he loved Theodosia. I can't believe it. We grew close, particularly out here. She was my sister and we were as sisters. And Evan loved her . . .

I had not been able to cry until that moment. Now the tears started to fall down my cheeks onto the paper, smudging the ink. My aunts would weep when they saw it. It was something to weep about.

Poor sad little Theodosia who was frightened of life! All the time she had feared death; and yet when she faced it her last words had been: "I am not afraid."

If only she had never set foot on that bridge. But then it would have been someone else. Tybalt! My heart missed a beat. What if it had been Tybalt. Since we had come to Egypt my idyllic dreams had become tinged with doubt, fears, even suspicions. I was remembering too frequently how people had reacted to the announcement of our intended marriage. Some—including Dorcas and Alison—had suspected Tybalt's motives. It was true that I had become an heiress.

I had always felt that Tybalt withheld some part of himself. I had revealed myself entirely to him, I was sure. He knew of my sudden impulses, my enthusiasms, my faults, my virtues. I had never been able to conceal my feelings for him; but although we were now husband and wife in some respects he was a stranger to me. Did he lack human warmth, and that need for others which makes us all so vulnerable and perhaps lovable? How much did he depend on me? How much did he need me?

Why was I tormented by these doubts—I, who had always believed wholeheartedly in my ability to mold the pattern of my life? Why was I failing now when I had everything I had always longed for? The answer was: Because I did not altogether know this man to whom I had given myself completely. I suspected his feelings towards me and the motives which had led him to marry me. I believed that his work came before anything in his estimation, before me. Before Tabitha?

I had said it. I was jealous. I was unsure of his relationship with Tabitha and his reasons for marrying me. I had built up a nightmare and it was shaping into reality.

I picked up my pen and went on writing resolutely:

I think he needs special care and you could give him that. Will you take him in and care for him and teach him to live again? Sabina and Oliver will help you. Somehow I think that the calm peacefulness of Rainbow Cottage and you two with your philosophy of life can help him. Dearest Alison and dearest Dorcas, will you try?

I knew them too well not to expect an immediate response.

It came.

Evan did not protest; he expressed no surprise. He seemed like a man in a dream . . . or a nightmare.

And so he left us and went to Rainbow Cottage.

Ever since the death of Theodosia, Leopold Harding seemed to have attached himself to our party. He was often seen at the site; he would talk to workers and Hadrian invited him to dine with us. He would ask all sorts of questions and expressed his enormous fascination in the work.

He asked Tybalt if he might look round now and then, and Tybalt gave permission. He asked intelligent questions. He had evidently read up on the subject or cross-examined Hadrian. He and Hadrian were constantly together and we all saw him quite often.

Tybalt's depression had vanished. He felt now that he was on a new trail, success was imminent. He was sure that beyond the wall of the old tomb was the way into another. It had been cunningly concealed but he would find it.

The aunts wrote to me often.

We did hope you would be home before this. It seems that you have been away a very long time. Evan talks a little about it now. He is certainly better than he was on his arrival.

Sabina is very happy. Her baby will be born in a very short time. We are all very excited about it. We never mention it to Evan though. It might make him brood and be sad.

Lady Bodrean is having a memorial set up to Theodosia in the church. There was a service for her. People are talking as they did when Sir Edward died. Oh dear, I do wish you would come home.

Lady Bodrean asked us up to Keverall Court for tea. She mentioned you. She said it was odd how you, her companion, had now become a woman of considerable wealth. She was referring to the fact that you have all now that Theodosia is dead.

My heart began to beat fast. It was amazing but I had not thought of that clause in Sir Ralph's will until now. I had twice as much money as I had before and Keverall Court would be mine on the death of Lady Bodrean.

Money had no concern for me except that now and then I wished I had not inherited a fortune. Then I could have been assured that I had been married for myself.

The aunts were right. Now I was a very rich woman.

She seemed more concerned about your having that money than her daughter's death. I marvel that you were able to stay with her so long. She is not a very agreeable woman. It was very brave of you, dear. Oh, how I wish you would write and say you were coming home.

How their letters brought back the peace of the countryside, the cottage in the quiet cul-de-sac a stone's throw from the old rectory.

Tybalt had said that we must behave as though the tragedy had not taken place. It was the best way to quell the rumors. When we went out though, people looked at us furtively. They thought we were mad to brave the Curse of the Pharaohs. How much warning did we want? How many more deaths must there be?

Tabitha said to me: "You don't go into the *souk* much now."

"I don't want to. Theodosia and I went so often together."

"They will probably notice that you don't go."

"Does it matter?"

"I think you should behave as normally as possible."

"I don't care to go alone."

"I'll come with you sometime."

The next day she suggested we go.

As we walked we spoke, as we always seemed to, of Theodosia.

"Don't brood, Judith," said Tabitha. "I have to stop myself doing that. Remember, I was the one who suggested the tour. If I hadn't . . . she would be here today."

"Someone else would have died. The bridge was ready to collapse. And how were you to know?"

She shook her head dismally. "All the same I can't forget it was my idea."

"Why should the bridge have broken!" I cried. "You don't think someone . . ."

"Oh no, Judith!"

"Who could possibly have done such a thing?"

"It was an accident. How could it have been anything else?"

A silence fell between us. I thought: Suppose it were not an accident. Suppose someone wanted to kill Theodosia. Who would gain from her death? I was the one who had become twice as rich.

I said: "She was my half sister. I loved her. I bullied her, I know, but I loved her just the same. And now . . ."

Tabitha pressed my arm. "Don't, Judith. There's nothing to be done. It's over. We must do our best to put it behind us."

We were in the open market square. There was noise and color everywhere. The flame swallower was about to perform and a crowd of excited children hopped round him; the snake charmer was sitting half asleep, his snakes in their baskets. A juggler was trying to attract a crowd. We went across the square and into that now familiar maze of streets, past the leather shop where Yasmin sat no more, past the meat on sticks and the cauldron of hot sauce . . . and there was the soothsayer.

He eyed us slyly.

"Allah be with you."

I wanted to move on but Tabitha hesitated. He knew, of course, of Theodosia's death.

"The little lady," he said, "she heed not my warning."

Tears pricked my lids. I could imagine Theodosia so clearly sitting on the mat beside him, her eyes wide with terror.

"I see it," he said. "It hovered. It hovers still." His eyes were fixed on me.

"I do not wish to hear," I said almost petulantly.

He turned from me to Tabitha.

"A burden has dropped from you," he said. "There is happiness now. The obstacle will go and there is the reward if you are wise enough to take it."

I was about to put money into his bowl but he shook his head.

"No. Not this day. I do not want *baksheesh*. I take only

payment for service. I say, Lady, take care."

We walked away. I was shivering.

"He was right . . . about Theodosia."

"He is bound to be right sometimes."

"He is warning me now."

"But he always warned you."

"You are the lucky one. You, it seems, are going to get your reward when you have removed the obstacle. Or is it already removed?"

"They talk," said Tabitha. "It's a kind of patter. But we must not let them see that we are disturbed. That would be the very way to increase the rumors."

But I was disturbed . . . deeply disturbed.

How I missed Theodosia! I suffered a certain remorse because when she had been alive I had never let her know how much it meant to me to have been her sister. I would sit and brood on the terrace where we had often sat together and remember our conversations. Tabitha was no substitute for her; I was unsure of Tabitha.

I was constantly aware of that friendship between her and Tybalt. Once when Tybalt had come back from the site, I was on the terrace and he joined me there. He began to talk earnestly about the work and I listened avidly. But Tabitha joined us. She remembered so much from the previous expedition and she and Tybalt discussed this at length, so that I was shut out. I became apprehensive and resentful.

I was being unfair. Previously I would have believed nothing but good of Tybalt. He meant everything to me, but I was unsure of him. I had begun to see Tybalt as a man who could be utterly ruthless in the interests of his work. And would that ruthlessness be only for his work?

Tybalt was becoming a stranger to me.

As I sat on the terrace one day Leopold Harding joined me. He had almost become a member of the party. His enormous interest appealed to Tybalt who was always ready to help amateurs. He now even dined occasionally at the palace and he would come to the site and watch the men at work.

He sat down beside me and heaved a sigh.

"What a sight," he said. "There's always so much to see on the river. Imagine what it must have been like three thousand years ago!"

"The royal barges," I said. "All those wonderful decorations of people doing strange things . . . like carrying stones to build the Pyramids or offering libations to the gods."

"Why are the figures always in profile?"

"Because they had such handsome ones, I suppose."

"Is your husband happy with his progress?"

"Each morning he is full of hope. 'This will be the day' he feels sure. But so far it has not been, of course."

"It was so sad about Mrs. Callum."

I nodded.

"So young, just beginning life you might say and then that terrible accident. The people at the hotel talk of it constantly."

"I know they do. They talk of it everywhere."

"They believe it is the Curse of the Kings."

"That's absurd." I was talking as Tybalt would have talked. He was so anxious that these rumors should not be encouraged. "If it were a curse—which is absurd anyway—why let it descend on Theodosia, who was the most inoffensive member of the party."

"She was a member of the party though."

"Hardly that. She was the wife of one of them, that's all."

"But there is a lot of talk. The general opinion seems to be that this expedition, like the previous one, is unlucky . . . and it's unlucky because the gods or the old Pharaohs are angry."

"Well, of course, there will be this talk."

"I had a letter from England. Theodosia's death was given some prominence in the newspapers. 'Another death,' it said, and the Curse was mentioned."

"Another! I see they are referring to Sir Edward's death. People love this sort of mystery. They believe it because they want to."

"I daresay you are right," he said. "I have to go soon.

I have sent most of my purchases to England now and very little remains to be done. But it has all been so fascinating. Do you think your husband objects to my prowling round the site?"

"He would say so if he did. He is pleased when people show interest. As long as they don't get in the way."

"I shall be very careful to avoid doing that. I realize how very knowledgeable you are."

"When one is with professionals one realizes how little one really does know. Before I married I read a great deal and Evan Callum was at one time our tutor . . . that was for Hadrian, Theodosia, and me. You know the relationship, of course."

"Well, I did hear. You and Mrs. Callum were half sisters, I believe."

"Yes, and Hadrian a cousin."

"All childhood friends. You must feel Mrs. Callum's loss sorely."

"I do. And I know Hadrian does."

"I gather he is very fond of you both . . . in particular you."

"Oh Hadrian and I were always good friends."

"So you studied archaeology in your youth."

"It was all very amateurish, but I was always particularly interested in the tombs."

"A fascinating subject."

"The idea of embalming the bodies is so macabre and clever. No people do it as they did. They perfected the art. I remember reading about it in my rectory bedroom— I was brought up in the rectory—and sitting up in bed shivering."

"Imagining yourself incarcerated in a tomb?"

"Of course. They didn't do much after the year 500 A.D. I wonder why? A gruesome process, removing the organs and filling the shell of the body with cassia, myrrh, and other sweet-smelling herbs. Then they used to soak it in some sort of soda for about three months before wrapping it in fine linen and smearing it with a sticky substance."

"It was certainly thrilling to see the inside of a tomb

on that fatal night . . . until the accident. What do you think happened about the bridge?"

"It must have been faulty."

"Do you think someone tampered with it?"

"Who should . . . and for what purpose?"

"To kill someone?"

"Theodosia! Why? What had she done?"

"Perhaps to kill a member of the party?"

"It certainly might have been any one of us."

"Exactly. So it seems as though it didn't matter which one . . . as long as it was someone."

"You mean that someone just wanted one of us to die as a sort of warning?"

"It could, of course, have been an accident merely—if it had been anyone else. Mrs. Callum's condition helped to make it a fatal one perhaps. You would be far more aware of these things than I. I consider it a great privilege to be allowed these little peeps at what is going on. I shall never forget this visit to Egypt."

"I don't think anyone who is here will ever forget this expedition. It was the same with the previous one when Sir Edward died. That finished it because he was the leader and they could scarcely have gone on without him."

"What did he discover?"

"Precisely nothing. But Tybalt believes that he would have, had he gone on. Tybalt was going on where he left off."

"Well, it's been a great privilege. I have to get back to the hotel so I must leave you. I've enjoyed our talk."

I watched him walk away and then I went into the palace, for the sun was beginning to get hot. I remembered then that I had left Dorcas's pot of ointment in the little room which led off from the courtyard. As I came into it, I heard voices and paused.

Tabitha was speaking. "Oh yes, it's a great relief to be free. If only it happened before. And now, Tybalt, it's too late . . . too late . . ."

I stood absolutely still. There was a singing in my ears; the courtyard seemed to recede and I felt faint.

Too late! I knew too well what that meant.

I had suspected for some time. Perhaps I had always suspected; but now I knew.

I turned and ran to my room.

I lay on the bed. Tybalt had gone back to the site. I was glad. I did not want to see him—not yet—not until I had decided what I must do.

I remembered so many incidents. The manner in which he had looked at her when she sat at the piano; the warning words of Nanny Tester; the time when she had gone up to see her husband and Tybalt had discovered that he must be away at the same time. And she was beautiful and poised and experienced. Compared with her I was plain and clumsy; and I was not patient as she was. I was angry and passionate because he cared more for his work than for me.

She understood perfectly. She was the one he loved, the one whom he would have married had he been free.

But even so, why should he marry me? Why should he not wait for her?

His proposal had been sudden. I had been completely taken by surprise. He had asked me because he knew that I had inherited money from Sir Ralph. It was all becoming very clear, too clear for comfort.

And here she was close to him. I wondered how often when I believed him to be working on the site he was with Tabitha. I pictured them together; I seemed to delight in torturing myself. I couldn't bear these imaginings and yet I could not stop myself from creating them.

I felt young and inexperienced. I did not know what I could do.

Of whom could I ask advice? I could not confide in Theodosia now. As if I ever could have! What would she have known of my problem—she with her innocence and her inexperience of life and her doting Evan who had loved her faithfully and would have done so to the end of her days. Dorcas and Alison knew nothing of relationships like this; and they would nod their heads and say "I told you so. We never liked him. We felt something was *wrong*." That would not do. Sabina? I could hear her voice coming to me over space. "Of course Tybalt is wonderful. There is no one like him. You ought to be glad he married you. But of course you don't know enough and Tabitha does and she is beautiful. And she was always in the house, really like his wife, only she had that husband and he couldn't marry her because of him. At least you are Tybalt's wife and Lady Travers, aren't you? So I suppose that ought to be enough. After all he's not like the other people, is he . . . ?"

How foolish to let my mind run on with these imaginary conversations. But I could not stop myself. In whom could I confide?

I wanted to talk to someone. I wanted to say: What can I do?

I thought of Hadrian. We were fond of each other in a cousinly way, although he had hinted at stronger feelings. We had protected each other when we were children —I protecting him more than he did me, because I seemed to be able to do it better than he could, and he, being the boy, was more often blamed. Dear, uncomplicated Hadrian!

Yet I could not tell him of my fears, because I could not bear to discuss Tybalt. It was bad enough that I, in my private thoughts, could build up such a monstrous fabrication. He had asked me to marry him suddenly; I was an heiress and now Theodosia's death had made me a very rich woman. Theodosia's death! Oh no, I would not accept such absurdly wicked thoughts. Anyone might have stepped onto the bridge. Yet it *had* been Theodosia and her death had made Tybalt's wife a very rich woman. Tybalt needed money for his work. Was this why he had married a rich wife? If Tabitha had been free . . . But her release had come too late. "Too late . . ." I could hear her voice with that note of sadness in it, that deep and bitter regret.

I stood between them. If I were not here Tybalt and Tabitha could marry, and who would inherit a rich wife's fortune but her widower!

My imaginings were becoming fantastic.

I don't know whether I imagined it but from that time I
began to feel that I was often followed. I was nervous.
I was afraid to be by myself in a lonely part of the palace;
footsteps began to sound stealthy, and in the silence I
would find myself looking over my shoulder furtively.
This was unlike me. I had been the one to laugh at the
stories of the big black bat. I had teased Theodosia but
now it seemed that I had inherited her fears as well as
her money.

Yet I had an irresistible urge to come face to face
with my fears. I wanted to know because at the back
of my mind was the thought: It is Tybalt. He wants to
be rid of me. And on the heels of that thought was another: That's a lie. He cares more for his profession than
for you, which is natural since he loves another woman.
But he would never harm you. You know that.

But I was not sure which side of the question was the
true one and because it was imperative to my peace of
mind, to my future happiness to find out, I could not

resist the temptation to frighten myself.

It was in this mood that alone I took an *arabiya* to the Temple. I left my driver and told him to wait for me.

As I entered the Temple I was aware of the stillness all about me. I was the only person, it seemed, who had come here today. I stood among the tall pillars and remembered the day when Theodosia and I had come here together.

I tried to give my entire attention to the carvings which depicted the history of Egypt. I was not really concentrating though; I kept listening for the sound of footsteps, for the sudden swish of robes. I don't know what it was but I had a strange sensation that I was not here alone and that something evil was close to me.

I studied the elaborate carving on the pillar. There was King Seti with his son who was to become Ramses the Great. And on another carving was Queen Hatshepsut.

I was sure someone was close to me, watching me. I fancied I heard the sound of deep breathing. He had only to stretch out a hand and catch me.

I felt my heart thundering. I must get out of this maze of pillars; I would get right out into the open. With all speed I must make my way to my *arabiya* and tell my driver to take me back to the palace.

Thank God the *arabiya* and the driver would be waiting. If I did not return they would know that I was missing. But would they?

The pillars of the ancient ruined Temple were close together like trees in a forest. Someone could be standing behind one of them, close to me, yet I would not see him if he were using one as a shield. At any moment murderous hands could seize me. I could be buried here in the sand. And the driver of my *arabiya*? A little money exchanging hands. Not a word to be said about the lady he had brought out to the Temple. It would be very simple. If a girl could disappear from a shop in the *souk* and be thrown into the Nile in place of a doll, surely I could be disposed of. But I was the wife of the leader of the expedition. There would have to be some explanation of my disappearance. But if that leader was content to accept some explanation which could be fabricated . . . He had been ready enough to accept the fact that Yasmin had been murdered and regard it as of little importance. But this would be his wife. A wife of whom he wished to rid himself?

That was the thought which had been in my mind, and here in this sinister and ancient Temple I could come face to face with my real fears. Perhaps I could also come face to face with a murderer.

Yes. Someone *was* close. A shadow had fallen across my vision, a tall shadow. Someone was stalking me. The pillars protected him from my view, but suddenly he would catch me; his hands would be about my throat and I would look up into his face. Tybalt's face? No. That was going too far, that was being absurdly wild. It was someone who was trying to stage another accident. Someone who wanted us to go from here. Someone who had tampered with the bridge, who had killed Theodosia and now it would be so much more effective to kill the wife of the leader.

I stood very still, trying to calm myself. I was being dramatic, stupid, letting my imagination run away with me. Hadn't Dorcas and Alison said I used to do that and that I would have to stop it.

There was one thing of which I was certain. I was afraid.

I started to run; I touched the pillars as I passed.

I emerged from the shadow of the pillars into the open. The sun hit me like a blow. It sent little chinks of brilliant white light through the weave of my chip straw hat.

I had almost fallen into the arms of Leopold Harding, who was coming towards me.

"Why, Lady Travers, what's wrong?"

"Oh . . . nothing. I didn't see you."

"I saw you come rushing out of the Temple. I was just about to go in."

"Oh . . ." I said, "I'm glad you came . . ." I was thinking: Perhaps *he*, that anonymous murderer, heard your *arabiya* arrive, perhaps that was why he allowed me to escape. I added quickly: "It's worth a second visit."

"A wonderful old place. Are you sure you are all right?"

"I think I was a little overcome by the heat."

"You shouldn't rush about, you know. Would you like to take a walk round with me?"

"Thank you, but I think I'll go back to the palace. My *arabiya* is waiting for me."

"I shall not allow you to go back alone," he said.

I was glad of his company. It helped to dispel my absurd fears. He talked about practical matters such as how he had succeeded in making his arrangements for the despatching of his goods.

"It has been a very successful trip," he said. "It is not always so. Of course one buys a lot of stuff which we call 'run-of-the-mill.' One makes a small profit and this makes these transactions worth while. But occasionally there are the real finds."

"Have you any this time?"

"I think so . . . yes, I think so. But one is never sure, and however fine the piece one has to find the buyer for it. That's business. Here is the palace. Are you all right, Lady Travers?"

"Perfectly, thank you. It was the heat, I think."

"Very trying and exhausting. I'm glad I was there."

"Thank you for your kindness."

"It was a pleasure."

I went to my room and lay on my bed. The fear still hung over me.

Had I been right? Was it a premonition which had set my skin pricking and the goosepimples rising? Had I really been in danger? Was, as the soothsayer would have said, the big black bat hovering over me? Or was I imagining this, because I had discovered that my husband loved another woman and wanted to be rid of me?

I must have been there for ten minutes when there was a knock on my door. I sat up hurriedly while the door opened slowly, stealthily. A pair of dark eyes were watching me.

"Lady would like mint tea? Lady very tired."

Mustapha was regarding me pityingly.

I thanked him. He stood for a few moments and then he bowed and left me.

The intense heat of the day was over. I put on my shady straw hat and went out. People were rising from their beds where they had slept behind shutters which kept out the sun. The market square was getting noisy. I heard the weird music of the snake-charmer's pipes. I saw the snake beginning to rise from its basket for the benefit of the little crowd who had assembled to watch.

I paused by the storyteller, cross-legged on his mat, his dark hypnotic eyes dreamy. The faces of his listeners were rapt and attentive; but as I approached they seemed aware of me. In my cotton blouse, my linen skirt, and my big straw hat I was alien. The storyteller even paused in his narrative.

He said in English for my benefit: "And where she had died there grew a fair tree and its flowers were the color of her blood."

I dropped some coins into the bowl as an expression of my appreciation.

"Allah be with you," he murmured; and the people drew back for me to pass.

I went on into the *souk*. The soothsayer saw me and dropped his eyes to stare down at the mat on which he sat.

On through the narrow streets I went, past the open shops with their now familiar smells; and I was aware of eyes that watched me, furtively almost. I belonged to those who had twice felt the wrath of the dead. I was one of the damned.

I went back to the palace.

During the last few days I had neglected the paper work I did for Tybalt. I did not want him to know that anything was wrong so I decided that everything must be in order as it had been in the past.

There were papers in his bureau which he had left for me to put away. They were notes of the day's progress—each dated; and I had filed them in a sort of briefcase in perfect order so that he could refer to them and find what he wanted without a moment's delay. He had told me that this particular case, which was of very fine sealskin, had belonged to his father. It was lined with a black corded silk.

I had noticed some time before that the stitching of the lining had come apart and I had made up my mind that at some time I should mend it. I decided that I would do it now.

I took out needle and thread, emptied the case of its papers and set to work, but as I thrust my hand inside the lining I realized that there was something there.

At first I thought it was a sort of packing but as it was crumpled I drew it out and to my surprise saw that it was a sheet of paper with writing on it. It was creased and as I smoothed it out, certain words caught my eye. It was part of a letter and it was signed Ralph.

. . . an expensive project even for you. Yes, I'll subscribe. I wish I could come with you. I would but for this heart of mine. You wouldn't want an invalid on your hands, and the climate would just about finish me. Come round tomorrow. I want to talk to you about that plan of ours. It's something I've set my heart on. Your son and my daughter. He's getting so like you that I could sometimes believe it is you sitting there talking about what you're going to do. Now I'm leaving a tidy sum to your cause on condition that your son marries my daughter. Those are the terms. No marriage no money. I've set my heart on this. I've had the lawyers work on it so that on the day my daughter marries your son the money goes to your cause. Tell the boy what depends on it. A daughter of mine and a son of yours! My dear fellow, your brains and my vitality! What a combination we'll have for the grandchildren. See you tomorrow. Ralph B.

I stared at the letter. The words seemed to dance a mad dance like the dervishes in the market place.

"A daughter of mine and a son of yours." He had meant Theodosia at the time. Tybalt knew the terms of the will. And, of course, when Sir Ralph had become so taken with me and Theodosia had wished to marry Evan, he had offered me as the bride. It was for this reason that he had sent for Tybalt. He would have explained to him. "Judith is my daughter. The will stands if you take her." And Sir Ralph who had loved me had known that I wanted Tybalt. He had given Tybalt to me even though Tybalt had had to be bribed to take me.

It was all becoming clear, heartbreakingly clear.

Theodosia had married for love. Poor Theodosia who had enjoyed married bliss so briefly! And I had married Tybalt and the settlement had been made.

And now that the money was safe in the coffers of the "Profession," Tabitha was free.

Tabitha had always been a strange woman, full of secrets. And Tybalt, what did I know of Tybalt?

I had loved him for years. Yes, as a symbol. I had loved him from the moment I saw him in my foolish, impetuous way. I loved him no less now. But I had had to learn that he was ruthless where his profession was concerned. And where his marriage was concerned too?

What had come over me?

I went to the window and opened the shutters. I could look out beyond the terrace to the river. White-robed men; black-robed women; a train of camels coming into the town; a shepherd leading three sheep, carrying a crook, looking like a picture I had seen in Dorcas's Bible. The river dazzling in the bright sunshine; up in the sky a white blazing light on which none dared gaze; the hot air filling the room.

Then from the minaret the muezzin's cry. The sudden cessation of movement and noise as though everyone and everything down there had been turned to stone.

It is this place, I thought. This land of mystery. Here anything could happen. And I longed then for the green fields of home, the golden gorse, the soft caressing south-west wind; the gentle rain. I wanted to throw myself into the arms of Dorcas and Alison and ask for comfort.

I felt alone here, unprotected; and an ominous shadow was creeping closer.

I was passionate in my emotion. Hadn't Dorcas always said I was too impulsive? "You jump to conclusions." I could hear Alison's voice. "You imagine some dramatic situation and then try to make everything fit it. You should stop that."

Alison was right.

"Look at it squarely," Alison again. "Look it right in the face. See the worst as it really is, not as you're trying to make it and then see what is best to do."

Well, I am jealous, I said. I love Tybalt with a mad possessiveness. I want him all to myself. I do not want to share him even with his profession. I have tried to be proficient in that profession. Ever since I was a child and loved him I have been interested. But I am an amateur and I can't expect to be taken into the confidence of these people who are at the head of their profession. I am jealous because he is at the site more than with me.

That was logical and reasonable. But I was forgetting something.

I had heard Tabitha's voice: "It's too late, Tybalt, too late."

And I had read Sir Ralph's letter to Sir Edward. A bribe to marry his daughter. A quarter of a million pounds for the cause if he did so.

The money had been passed over. It was safe in the hands of people who would use it to further the cause. And now Tabitha was free. I had served my purpose.

Oh no. I was being ridiculous. Many people married for money; loving one woman they married another.

But they did not murder.

There. I had faced it. Could I really suspect Tybalt and Tabitha of such a criminal deed? Of course I could not. Tabitha had been so kind to me. I remembered how sorry she had been because I had had to work for the disagreeable Lady Bodrean; she had lent me books; she had helped me improve my knowledge. How could I suspect her? And Tybalt? I thought of our marriage, our love, our passion. He could not have feigned that, could he? True, he had never been so eager, so fervent, so completely in love as I and I had accepted that as a difference in our natures.

But was it so?

What did I know of Tabitha? What did I know of Tybalt?

And here I was, with evil thoughts chasing themselves round and round in my head. I had inherited Theodosia's fear. I knew how she had felt when she had listened to the soothsayer. I understood the terror that had gripped her.

We had come to a strange land. A land of mystery, of strange beliefs, where the gods seemed to live on wreaking their vengeance, offering their rewards. That which would have seemed ridiculous at home was plausible here.

Theodosia's premonitions of disaster had proved to have substance. What of mine?

I could not stay in my room. I would go and sit on the balcony.

On the way down I met Tabitha, going up to her room.

"Oh hello, Judith," she said, "where have you been? I was looking for you."

"I took a little walk in the market and then came back. It was so hot."

"I must just have missed you. I was out there too. What do you think the soothsayer told me this time: 'You will have your bridegroom,' he said. 'It will not be long now.' So you see I'm fortunate."

"No black bat for you then?"

"No, a husband no less."

"Should I congratulate you . . . both. Who is the bridegroom to be?"

Tabitha laughed; she lowered her eyes; then she said: "It is a little premature to say. No one has asked me. Perhaps that's to come."

She was smiling secretly as she passed on upstairs.

I had begun to shiver as I had in the Temple. I went out into the hot air but I felt cold and could not stop the shivering.

I did not tell Tybalt about the letter. I hid it in a little box of embossed leather which I had bought from Yasmin some time before. I had mended the case and filed the letters in order.

Leopold Harding came to say goodbye. He said he had already stayed longer than he intended to. "Meeting you all and talking to you made it so fascinating. Even now I find it hard to tear myself away."

Tybalt told him that he must visit us in England.

"I shall take you up on that," was the reply.

There was to be a conference which would be held at the hotel. I gathered that the funds which had been set aside for this expedition were getting low and it had to be decided whether work could be continued.

Tybalt was anxious. He was afraid it would be voted to discontinue, something which he could not accept.

"To stop now at this stage would be the utmost folly," he said. "It was what happened to my father. There has been a fatal accident but that could have happened anywhere. It's these absurd rumors."

He went off with Terence, Hadrian, and other members of the party to the hotel. The palace seemed very quiet without them.

It was during the morning that one of the servants came to tell me that a worker from the site had come to see me. He had hurt himself and wanted me to dress his wound with my now famous salve.

When I went down to the courtyard I found the young man whose wound I had dressed before and whom I knew as Yasmin's lover.

"Lady," he said, and held out his hand. It was grazed and bleeding a little. I told him to come in and I would boil some water and wash it before anointing it with my salve and bandaging it.

I knew that the hand was not badly hurt, and had perhaps been grazed purposely. He had something of importance to tell me.

"Yasmin will never come back," he said. "Yasmin is dead. Yasmin was thrown into the river."

"Yes, I know that now."

"But, Lady, you do not know why."

"Tell me."

"Yasmin was found in the tomb. I was not with her that day, or I would be dead. Because she was found

where she should not be she was taken away and killed.
I know because I have confession from the man who did
it. He dared do nothing else. It was the order. And then
there came another order. There must be an accident.
There must be a warning because it is important to some
. . . that you go away."

"I see," I said. "And who gave these orders?"

The boy began to tremble visibly. He looked over his
shoulder.

"You may tell me," I said. "Your secret would be safe
with me."

"I dare not tell," he said. "It would be death."

"Who should know you told?"

"His servants are everywhere."

"Everywhere. Not here."

"Yes, Lady, here, in this house. You see their mark. . . ."

"The Jackal?"

"It is the sign of Anubis—the first embalmer."

I said: "The Pasha?"

The boy looked so frightened that I knew I was right.

"So," I said, "he gave orders that Yasmin should be
killed; and then that one of us should have an accident
which could be fatal on the bridge. One of his servants
could easily have tampered with the bridge. But why
should he?"

"He want you away, Lady. He want you leave it all.
He fears . . ."

But he would not go on.

"So Yasmin died," I said, "and my sister died."

"Your sister, Lady. She your sister?"

I nodded.

He was horrified. I think more by the fact that he
had betrayed this information to me than by the death
of Theodosia, and that she should turn out to be my
sister might mean that I would want to take a personal
vengeance.

He said suddenly: "Yasmin, she wait for me in a secret
place . . ."

"A secret place?" I said quickly.

"Inside the tomb. There is small opening not far from

the bridge. We have not worked in that small opening so I thought that is our spot. That was where she would have been waiting for me. That was where we lay together."

I tied the bandage and he said: "I tell you, Lady, because you good, good to me, good to Yasmin. And there are orders that there should be more accidents, that all may know the Curse is alive, and the kings are angry with those who defile their resting places."

I said: "Thank you for telling me."

"You will tell the Sir. But not tell that I told. But you will tell him and go away, and then you will be safe."

I said: "I will tell him."

"He will go then for fear it should be you who will die next, for you are his beloved."

I felt sick with horror. I wanted to be alone to think.

I wished Tybalt were here so that I could tell him what I had discovered. He should have listened to me, I told myself angrily. When Yasmin disappeared he had not appeared to be interested. But her disappearance concerned us all.

The Pasha! He wanted us out of the way. Why? I thought of his sitting at the table, eating, paying compliments, assessing our feminine attributes. He had lent us his palace. Why, if he did not want to help us? To have us under his eyes; that was why. His servants waited on us and reported everything we did. It was becoming very clear.

And little Yasmin, what had she done to deserve death? She had been found in the tomb waiting for her lover. In the little alcove, which I had not noticed but which Yasmin's lover had described.

I remembered suddenly that the soothsayer had the brand of the Jackal on his arm. So he too was the servant of the Pasha. Was it his task to predict death and disaster, to drive us away?

I must talk to Tybalt. I must tell him what I had heard. But he was at the conference. I would have to wait for his return.

The palace had become really sinister. How did we

know who was watching us, listening to every word we uttered? Silent-footed servants following us, reporting on everything we did!

All the servants were the Pasha's servants. They would all have their duties. There were only two we had brought with us: Mustapha and Absalam.

And what of them?

I must find out. I went to my room and rang the bell. Mustapha came and I asked him to bring me mint tea.

I stood beside him as he laid it on the table. I said: "There is an insect. Oh dear! It's gone up your arm." Before he could move I drew up his loose sleeve. It would be on the forearm where I had seen the others.

My little ruse had told me what I wanted to know. On Mustapha's forearm was the brand of the Jackal.

I said calmly: "I don't see it now. The insects here are a pest, and their stings can be so poisonous. People are always coming for my ointment. However, it's gone."

Mustapha's suspicions had not been aroused, I was sure.

He thanked me and left me with my tea.

I sat there sipping it and thinking that if Mustapha was the Pasha's man so must Absalam be.

Then my thoughts went to Sir Edward. He had died in the palace. He had eaten food prepared by Mustapha or Absalam or both and he had died.

If he had a doctor to attend him that doctor could have been the Pasha's man.

Tybalt was in danger as his father had been. We were all in danger.

Sir Edward had discovered something in the tomb and that had necessitated his immediate death. So far it seemed that Tybalt had not found what his father had, as no attempt had been made on his life. But if Tybalt were to make that discovery . . . .

I began to shiver. I must see him. I must make him listen, for I was sure that what I had learned was of the utmost importance.

$\mathcal{T}$ $\mathcal{T}$ $\mathcal{T}$

X   Within the Tomb

How quiet the palace seemed. How long would the conference go on? There was no one about. I might have tried to find Tabitha, but I had no desire to confide in her for I no longer trusted her. I no longer knew whom to trust.

I went to my favorite seat on the terrace and as I sat there I saw someone coming up the steps towards me. To my surprise it was Leopold Harding.

"I thought you had gone," I said.

"No, there was a slight hitch. Business, you know. I have just come from the hotel. I have a message from your husband."

I stood up. "He wants me to go there?"

"No. He wants you to meet him at the site."

"Now?"

"Yes, now. At once. He has gone on."

"Then the conference is over."

"I don't know, but he asked me to give you this message as I had a few hours to spare before leaving."

"Did he say where at the site?"

"He told me exactly. I said I would take you there."

"But where was it?"

"It's better if I show you."

I picked up my hat which was on the seat beside me and without which I never went out.

I said: "I'm ready. I'll come now."

He was already leading the way out to the river. We took one of the boats and went to the site.

The Valley looked grim under the glare of the late afternoon sun. In spite of the windlessness there always seemed to be a fine dust in the air.

The place seemed deserted because the men were not working today. I had understood from Tybalt that they were awaiting the outcome of the conference.

We came to the opening in the hillside which was the way into the tomb, but to my surprise Leopold led me past that.

"But surely," I began.

"No," he said. "I am quite sure. I was here yesterday and your husband was showing me something. It is here . . ."

He led me into what looked like a natural cave but which could well have been hollowed out. To my amazement there was a hole in the side of this cave.

He said: "Let me help you through here."

"Are you sure?" I began. "I have never been here before."

"No. Your husband has just discovered that it is here."

"But what is this hole?"

"You will see. Give me your hand."

I stepped through and was surprised to find myself at the top of a flight of steps.

"If you will let me help you, we will descend these stairs."

"Is Tybalt here then?"

"You will see. There are lanterns here. I will light them and then we can have one each."

"It seems strange," I said, "that you, who are a stranger here . . ."

He smiled. "Well, Lady Travers, I have explored a little. Your husband has been very kind to me."

"They knew of this place then. Is it connected with the tomb?"

"Oh yes, but I don't think it was considered worth exploring until now." He handed me a lantern and I could see steps which had been cut out of the earth. They turned and there facing us was a door. It was half open.

"There," said Leopold Harding as we went through. "This is the spot. I'll go ahead, shall I?"

Tybalt had never mentioned this place to me. It must be a new discovery. But then lately I had been aloof. I was not able to prevent myself being so; for while I could not bring myself to talk of my suspicions, at the same time I could not behave as though they did not exist.

We were in a small chamber not more than eight feet in height. I saw that there was an opening ahead and I went towards this. I looked up and saw three or four steps.

I mounted these and called: "Tybalt, I'm here."

I was in another chamber; this one was larger than the other. It was very cold.

The first shadow of alarm touched me. "Tybalt," I called. My voice sounded rather shrill.

I said: "There is nobody here?"

I looked over my shoulder. I was alone.

I said: "Mr. Harding, I think there's been a mistake. Tybalt isn't here."

There was no answer. I started down the steps. I went back to the smaller chamber. Leopold Harding was not there either.

I went back to the opening. It was completely dark because the door was shut.

I called: "Mr. Harding. Where are you?"

There was no reply.

I went to the door. I could see no handle, no bolt . . . nothing with which to open it. I pushed it. I tried to pull it. But it remained fast shut.

"Where are you? Mr. Harding, where are you?"

No answer. Only the hollow sound of my own voice.

I knew then what it meant to have one's flesh creep. It was as though thousands of ants were crawling over me. I knew that my hair had risen on my scalp. The awful realization had come to me. I was alone and only Mr. Harding knew I was here.

Why? Who was he? Why should he do this? My imagination was running wild again. It was so senseless. He had stepped outside for a moment. He would come back. Why should a tourist, an acquaintance merely, shut me in a tomb?

I tried to be calm. I lifted the lantern and looked about me . . . at the steps cut out of the earth, at the earth walls of the little chamber. Tybalt must be here. He would come out in a moment.

Then I remembered my suspicions of Tybalt. Could it be that he had had me brought here to . . . to rid himself of me. But why did he send Leopold Harding to bring me here? Who *was* Leopold Harding? Why did Tybalt not bring me himself? Because he did not wish to be seen coming here with me? When I did not return . . .

Oh, this was folly. This was madness.

To be shut in a tomb alone could drive one mad.

I set down the lantern and banged my fists on the door. It did not give. How was it shut? How had it opened? All Leopold Harding had appeared to do was to push it and we stepped inside. It was as easy as that. And now it was fast shut and I was on the wrong side of it.

He must be hiding to tease me. What a foolish trick. I remembered myself suddenly rising from the sarcophagus in Giza House. I could almost hear Theodosia's shrieks.

"Oh, God, let somebody come. Don't let me be alone in this place."

Tybalt must be here somewhere. It was better to look, to assure myself before I allowed this creeping terror to take a grip on me.

I picked up the lantern and walked resolutely towards the steps. I descended them and was in the larger chamber. I must explore this. There might be a way out here.

Tybalt might be somewhere beyond, waiting for Leopold to bring me to him.

I held my lantern high and examined the walls of the chamber; there was no decoration on them, but I saw that there was an opening. I went through this and was in a corridor.

"Tybalt," I called. "Are you there, Tybalt?"

No answer.

I lifted my lantern. I saw that these walls had been decorated. Rows of vultures were depicted there, their wings stretched as though they hovered. Now I had reached yet another chamber. I examined it with care. There seemed to be no outlet from this one. I had come to the end of my exploration; and there was no one here.

I felt my legs trembling and I sank down onto the floor. Now I knew a fear that I had never known before. I had been brought here for some purpose. All the warnings I had received, all the premonitions, they had some meaning. I should have heeded them.

But why should Leopold Harding wish to trick me? Why had he lied to me? I remembered coming out of the Temple and running straight into that man. He had been the one who had stalked me there. He had meant to kill me. Oh, but this was a better idea!

Had Tybalt ordered him to do this, and who was he that he must take his orders from Tybalt?

I was sure something moved overhead. Something was looking down at me. I held up the lantern.

On the ceiling had been carved a great bat with enormous wings. Its eyes were some sort of obsidian and the light of the lantern catching them had made them seem alive.

I fancied I could hear the soothsayer's voice: "The bat is hovering, waiting to descend."

I stared up at it, hideous, malevolent; and I said to myself: "What is to become of me? What does it mean? Why have I been brought here?"

I was cold. Or was it fear that made me shiver so violently that I could not keep still? My teeth chattered . . . an unearthly sound.

I could not bring myself to stand up and go back. I was fascinated by that hideous bat on the ceiling of the chamber.

Now I could make out drawings on the walls. There was a Pharaoh offering a sacrifice to one of the gods. Was it Hathor the Goddess of Love? It must be because there she was again and her face was that of a cow, and I knew the cow was her emblem.

I was so cold. I must move. I stood up unsteadily. I examined the walls. There might be a way out of this place. There *must* be a way out. Now I could see the drawings of the walls more clearly. There were pictures of ships and men tied upside down on their prows. Prisoners I remembered. And with them were men without one or more limbs. And there was the crocodile who had maimed them, sly, ugly, with a necklace about his neck and earrings hanging from his ears.

Where was I? At the entrance to a tomb? Then if I was at the entrance it must lead on. Somewhere ahead perhaps was a burial chamber and in it the stone sarcophagus and inside the sarcophagus the mummy.

One can grow accustomed to anything, even fear. Fear was creeping up on me and yet I felt calmer than I had at the first realization that I was alone in this gruesome place.

I walked a few paces. If there was a way out of this chamber . . . but to what would it lead . . . only to a long dead mummy. What I needed was a way out into the open, the fresh air.

I thought: There is little air in here. I shall use what there is in a short time. I shall die; and I shall lie here forever until some archaeologist decides to explore this place just in case it leads to a great discovery; and his discovery will be my dead body.

"Nonsense," I said as I had said so many times to Theodosia, "there must be something I can do."

The very thought inspired me with courage. I would not sit here quietly and wait for death. I would find the way out if it was to be found.

I picked up the lantern. I examined the walls again.

I now saw some significance in the wall drawings. This was meant to depict the progress of a soul along the river Tuat. There was the boat on a sea from which rose hideous sea monsters, snakes with double heads, waves which enveloped the vessel; but above was the God Osiris, God of the Underworld and Judge of the Dead. This meant that he was giving his protection to the traveler in the boat and he would conduct him through the turbulent seas of the Tuat to the Kingdom of Amen Ra.

There was an opening in the wall. My heart leaped with hope. Then I saw that it was merely an alcove, similar in size to that one in which Yasmin and her lover had lain together.

As I examined it my foot touched something. I was startled and immediately thought of some of the horrible creatures I had seen rising from the river Tuat. I stooped and looked down. What I saw was not a hideous serpent but a gleaming object.

A matchbox! A small, gold box. What a strange thing to find in such a place. It was no antique piece. It belonged to this century. I turned it over in my hand and I saw the name engraved on it: *E. Travers.*

Sir Edward's matchbox! Then he had been here!

I felt dizzy with this discovery. My incarceration was already having its effect. I could not think clearly. Sir Edward had been here at some time. What if it was the night when he had died? Had he died because he had been here? But he had gone back to the palace. He had told no one what he had seen, but Tybalt knew he had found something, something which excited him. Then he had eaten something which had been prepared for him. Who prepared his food? Mustapha and Absalam—those two who were branded with the Jackal, servants of the Pasha.

Sir Edward had been murdered. I was certain of that. And he had been murdered because he had been here. It would have been at the orders of the Pasha, who had ordained that he should die just as he had commanded that Yasmin be killed and thrown into the river and that there should be an accident at the bridge which would show that the Curse was in force.

The Pasha wanted to drive us away; he wanted our expedition to end in failure. Why? Because there was something which he did not want us to discover. If the Pasha's interest in archaeology really existed, why should he be ready to kill rather than allow discoveries to be made.

Because *he* wished to make them?

In my present state of fear and panic memories of the past seemed clearer than they normally were. I recalled vividly the Pasha's plump face, his shaking jowls, his lips greasy from the food he was eating. He had looked sly as he murmured: "There is a legend that my family founded its fortune on robbing tombs."

Could it possibly be that he continued to build up his fortune in this illegal way?

If that was so he would not be very friendly towards archaeologists who might expose him. Was that why he offered his palace, why his servants waited on us, why they had orders to frighten us away?

I knew that that was the answer.

But it did not answer the pressing question: Why was it necessary to bring me here?

I thought, Leopold Harding is another of his servants. In the papers they will be reading: Wife of archaeologist disappears. Lady Travers, wife of Sir Tybalt, left the palace where the party of archaeologists are lodged and has not been seen for two days . . . three days . . . a week . . . a month. She can only be presumed dead. How was she spirited away? This is another instance of the Curse of the Kings. It will be remembered that a few months ago the wife of one of the archaeologists suffered a fatal accident.

I could see Dorcas reading that. Alison with her. I could see their blank, miserable faces. They would be truly heartbroken.

It must not be. I must find a way out of it.

I clutched Sir Edward's golden matchbox as though it were a talisman.

Darkness! Was the lantern growing dim? What should I do when the oil ran out? Should I be dead by then?

How long could one survive in an atmosphere such as this?

My feet were numb. With fear or cold I could not know. Above me the eyes of the great bat glittered . . . waiting . . . waiting to descend.

"Oh God," I prayed, "help me. Show me what to do. Let Tybalt come and find me. Let it be that he wants me to live, not to die."

Then I thought, when we are in need of help why do we always tell God what to do? If it is His will I will come out of this place alive—and only then.

I think I was a little delirious. I thought I heard footsteps. But it was only the beating of my own heart which was like hammer strokes in my ears.

I talked aloud. "Oh, Tybalt, miss me. Search for me. You will find me if you do. You will find that door. Why should there be such a door? Something will lead you to me. If you want to find me . . . desperately . . . you must. But do you want to find me? Was it by your order? No . . . I don't believe that. I won't believe that!"

I could see the old church now with the tower and the gravestones tottering over some of them. "You can't read what's on them." That sounded like Alison's voice. "I think that they should be removed . . . but you can't disturb the dead . . ."

"You can't disturb the dead. You can't disturb the dead." It was as though a thousand voices were chanting that. And there was the boat all round me and the sea was boiling like the water in the big black saucepan that used to be on the kitchen fire at the rectory when Dorcas or Alison was making Irish stew or boiling the Christmas puddings.

This was delirium. I was aware of it, but I welcomed it. It took me away from this dark and fearsome place. It took me back to the schoolroom where I teased the others; it took me to the graveyard where old Pegger was digging a grave.

"And who's that for, Mr. Pegger?"

"It be for you, Miss Judith. You was always a meddler and now look where it 'as brought you . . . to the grave . . . to the tomb . . ."

There were the echoing voices again. "To the tomb," and I was back in this cold place of death and terror.

"Oh God, help me. Let Tybalt find me. Let him love me. Let it have been a mistake. . . ."

"There's a wedding at the church," said Dorcas. "You must come with us, Judith. Here is a handful of rice. Be careful how you throw it."

And there they were coming down the aisle, married by the Reverend James Osmond. Tybalt and Tabitha . . .

"No!" I cried; and I was back again in the tomb.

My limbs were stiff. I tried to get up. I would try to get out.

As I stood I kicked something. It was the matchbox which I had dropped. I stopped to pick it up; as I did so the wall seemed to move.

I'm imagining something, I told myself. I'm delirious. In a moment I shall be opening the door of my bedroom at the rectory.

The door did open. I fell against it. I was in a dark passage, facing another door.

Some impulse made me bang on this door.

The small hope which had come to me brought back with it panic because I realized full well what was happening to me then in a flash of clarity. I was trapped. I had been led here and the purpose could only be to kill me. I was losing my strength. The lantern would not remain alight forever. And I could not get out.

I kicked the door. I tried to open it. But it did not move.

I sank down beside it. But at least the door which led to the chamber was open and might that let in more air?

I stumbled along the passage. It was short and came to an abrupt end. It was nothing that I had discovered; only another blind alley. I went back and kicked at the door in fury. And then I sank down and covered my face with my hands.

There was nothing I could do . . . nothing but wait for death.

I lost consciousness. I was sitting in the half open doorway and in the chamber beyond the great bat was waiting.

How long? I wondered.

The light of the lantern was growing fainter. It would go out at any moment.

When the darkness came what should I do?

I would be frightened perhaps because then I should not be able to see anything at all, not even the eyes of the bat in the ceiling.

In sudden panic I rose again. I stumbled to that door. I cried: "Help me. Help me. God, Allah, Osiris . . . anyone . . . help me."

I was half sobbing, half laughing and I kicked and kicked with all the strength of which I was capable.

And then . . . the miracle happened. There was an answer.

Knock, knock, on the other side of that blessed door. With all my strength I knocked back.

There was the answering knock. Now I could hear noises beyond that wall. Someone knew I was here. Someone was coming to me.

I sank back. While I could hear that blessed noise I knew they were coming. It increased. The door trembled. I sat back watching it, the tears falling down my cheeks, the babble of words on my lips.

"Tybalt is coming. He has found me. I shall be free . . ."

I was happy. Had I ever known such exaltation? Only when one is about to lose it does one realize how sweet life is.

The lantern was flickering. Never mind. They are coming. The door is moving.

Soon now.

Then I was no longer alone. I was caught up.

"Judith . . ."

It was Tybalt, as I had known it would be. He was

holding me in his arms and I thought: I did not die of fear, but I shall die of bliss.

"My love," he said. "Judith, my love."

"It's all right, Tybalt," I said, comforting him. "It's all right . . . now . . ."

XI The Great Discovery

During the days that followed I lived in a kind of daze.

There were times when I was not sure where I was and then Tybalt would be beside me, always Tybalt, holding me in his arms, reassuring me.

I had suffered a severe shock; and I was constantly told that everything was all right. All I had to do was remember that. And Tybalt was with me. He had come to me and rescued me; and that was all I must think of as yet.

"It is enough," I said.

I would lie still clinging to his hand; but when I dozed I would often awaken shouting that the black bat was in the ceiling and that his eyes were glittering. I would find myself crying: "Help. Help. God . . . Allah . . . Tybalt . . . help me."

It had been a terrible ordeal. There could be few who had been buried in one of the tombs of the Pharaohs and come out alive.

Who had done this to me? That was what I wanted to know. Where was Leopold Harding? And why had he taken me down into that underground vault and left me there?

Tybalt said: "We shall know in time. He has disappeared. But we shall find him."

"Why did he do it, Tybalt? Why? He said he was taking me to you. He said you had asked for me to come."

"I don't know. It is a mystery to us all. We are trying to find him. But he has disappeared. All you need think about now is that you are safe and I shall never allow you to be lost again."

"Oh, Tybalt," I said, "that makes me happy."

Tabitha was by my bed.

"I want to tell you something, Judith," she said. "You've been talking a great deal. We were shocked to know what was in your mind, how you could have believed such things possible. Tybalt knows I'm talking to you. We think it best so that you should understand right away. You thought that Tybalt and I were lovers. My dear Judith, how could you? I love Tybalt, yes . . . I always have . . . as I would love a son if I had one. I came to the household, as you know, when my husband was put into a home. Sir Edward's wife was alive then, but ill. Oh, I know it was wrong but Sir Edward and I loved each other. Nanny Tester knew it and spied on us. She was devoted to Sir Edward's wife and she hated me. She hated Sir Edward too. When Lady Travers died she blamed me. She all but suggested that I had murdered her. Sir Edward and I were lovers. As you know I accompanied him on some of his expeditions. We would have married had I been free. But I was not . . . until it was too late . . ."

"I understand now," I said.

"My dearest Judith. You were always so in love with Tybalt. He realizes how lucky he is. You never did things by halves as your aunts used to say. So you had to love Tybalt with that fierce possessiveness. Such determination as yours had to have its effect. Even Tybalt was vulnerable. He confided to me long before he asked you that he

wanted to marry you . . . that was when you were Lady
Bodrean's companion . . . and I must admit you didn't
fit into the role very comfortably. There was nothing
meek about you, which is a quality one always associates
with companions."

"I can see," I said, "that my wild and foolish imagination built up the situation."

"It was not a real one. It did not exist outside your
imagination, remember that. I've something else to tell
you too. Terence Gelding has asked me to marry him."

"And you've accepted?"

"Not yet. But I think I shall."

"You'll be happy, Tabitha. At last."

"And you will be happy too. I never saw Tybalt work
so hard or so fervently as when they were pulling down
that door which separated him from you, not even when
he believed himself to be on the verge of the biggest discovery of his career. No, I have never before seen that
purpose, that desperate need . . ."

I laughed. "I do believe I must be of greater importance
to him than a Pharaoh's undisturbed tomb after all."

"I am sure of it," said Tabitha.

Tybalt was by my bed.

"As soon as the doctor has seen you we are going
home. I have asked Dr. Gunwen to come out and make
sure that you are fit to travel."

"You have sent for Dr. Gunwen! And we are going
home. Then is the expedition over?"

"Yes, it's over for me."

"My poor Tybalt."

"Poor. When you are here, alive and well."

Then he held me against him.

"At least," I said, "I found happiness that I never
dreamed possible."

He did not answer but the way in which he held me
told me that he shared my joy.

"Where is Hadrian?" I said. "Why doesn't Hadrian
come to see me?"

"Do you want to see Hadrian?" asked Tybalt.

"But of course. He is all right, isn't he?"

"Yes," he said, "I'll send him to you."

I saw the change in Hadrian at once. I had never seen him so sober before.

"Oh, Hadrian!"

"Judith." He took my hands, kissed me on both cheeks. "That! To happen to you. It must have been frightful."

"It was."

"The swine!" he said. "The utter swine. Better to have put a bullet through your head than that. Judith, you'll forget it in time."

"I wonder whether one ever does forget such an experience."

"You will."

"Why did he do it, Hadrian?"

"God knows. He must be a madman."

"He seemed sane, an ordinary merchant who was excited to come across an expedition like ours because in a way it was a link with his business. What could have been his motive?"

"That we shall have to find out. Thank God, the conference ended when it did, about the time you and Harding entered that place. They had agreed that there was to be an extension of a few more weeks and when we came back to the palace, Tybalt wanted to tell you this. One of the servants had overheard Harding telling you that Tybalt wanted him to take you to him on the site and that you had gone off with him. Tybalt was alarmed. I think he had been more uneasy than he has let us know about a lot of things. We went to the site. We searched for you. We thought it was hopeless but Tybalt wouldn't give up. He kept going over and over the same ground. And finally we heard the knocking."

"What *could* have been his motive? I believe he tried to kill me in the Temple one day."

"But how could your death possibly profit him?"

"It's so mysterious."

"There was Theodosia. Do you think that was Leopold Harding?"

"No, that was the Pasha and his servants."

"The Pasha!"

"One of the workmen . . . Yasmin's lover . . . warned me. Yasmin was discovered in the tomb and they killed her. She was there on the day the Pasha came to us. You remember the Feast of the Nile."

"Good God, Judith. We're in a maze of intrigue."

"Theodosia's death could have been anyone's death. She was the unfortunate one. The bridge had been tampered with because the Pasha wanted a victim. It didn't matter which."

"But the Pasha has helped us."

"He wants us out of this place. It may well be that he will attempt to kill another of us."

Tybalt came in and sitting on my bed regarded me anxiously.

"You've been tiring Judith," he accused Hadrian.

I reveled in his concern but insisted that I was not tired and that we had been talking of Leopold Harding and the Pasha and once again looking for a reason why this attempt had been made on my life.

Tybalt said: "In the first place Harding must have known something about the layout of the ground."

"He had been there on several occasions," I reminded him.

"He knew too much. He must have acquired the knowledge from somewhere."

"It is certain," I said, "that Leopold Harding was not what he seemed. Tybalt, I wonder if that boy, Yasmin's lover, knows anything. It was he who told me that the Pasha wanted to drive us away."

"We'll send for him," said Tybalt.

"On some pretext," I warned. "No one must know that he is suspected of helping us. How can we be sure who is watching us."

The boy stood before us. We had decided that I should be the one who questioned him because I had won his confidence.

"Tell me what you know of Leopold Harding," I said.

The manner in which he looked over his shoulder assured me that he knew something.

"He comes at times to Egypt, Lady."

"He has been here often then? What else?"

"He is friend of the Pasha. Pasha give him beautiful things."

"What beautiful things?"

"All beautiful things. Jewels, stones, furniture . . . all kinds. Leopold Harding goes away and comes back to the Pasha."

"He is a servant of the Pasha then?"

The boy nodded.

"Thank you," I said. "You have served me well."

"You very good lady," he said. "You good to Yasmin. You were shut in the tomb." His big dark eyes filled with horror.

"But I came out," I said.

"You very great wise lady. You and the great Sir will go back to the land of the rain. There you will live in peace and joy."

"Thank you," I said. "You have done me good service."

Dr. Gunwen arrived. He sat by my bed and talked to me. I asked how Dorcas and Alison were and he said: "Making preparations for your return."

I laughed.

"Yes, I'm going to prescribe an immediate return. I've spoken to your husband. I want you to be back there . . . a nice long rest in the country you know well. Help the rector's wife with the bazaar and jam-making sessions."

"It sounds wonderful," I said.

"Yes, get away from these foreign parts for a bit. I think then I shall be able to pronounce an immediate cure. There's nothing wrong with you, you know. Only that sort of incarceration can have a devastating effect. I think you're strong minded enough to suffer fewer ill effects than most."

"Thanks," I said. "I'll live up to that."

"Tybalt," I said, "we're going home."

"Yes," he answered. "Doctor's orders."

"Well, the expedition was over, wasn't it?"

"It's over," he said.

I lay against him and thought of green fields. It would be autumn now and the trees would be turning golden brown. The apple tree in Rainbow Cottage would be laden with russets and the pears would be ready for gathering. Dorcas and Alison would be fussing about the size of the plums.

I felt an inexpressible longing for home. I would turn Giza House into the home I wanted it to be. Darkness should be banished. I never wanted darkness again. I would have bright colors everywhere.

I said: "It will be wonderful to be home with you."

Now that I was well and we were making our preparations I learned more of what had happened.

Mustapha and Absalam had disappeared. Had they heard my explanations of how I suspected the Pasha? There was more than that. There was great excitement because in that narrow passage, which I had stumbled into and which they had entered when they broke the wall of the alcove in which Yasmin had been discovered, there was evidence that there was something beyond, and that the passage was not a blind alley after all.

It was the greatest discovery of the expedition and it was clear that Sir Edward had been aware of this on the night that he died.

Tabitha told me that Terence was taking over the leadership because Tybalt had decided to come home with me.

I said: "No. I can't allow it."

I stormed into our bedroom where he was putting some papers together.

"Tybalt," I said, "you're staying."

"Staying?" He wrinkled his brow.

"Here."

"I thought we were going home."

"Did you know that they are probably on the verge of one of the greatest discoveries in archaeology?"

"As a budding archaeologist you must learn never to count your chickens before they are hatched."

"Archaeology is all counting chickens before they're hatched. How could you go on with this continual work if you didn't believe it was going to be successful? That passage leads somewhere. You know it. It leads into a tomb. A very important one, because if it wasn't important why would they have gone to all the trouble with the subterfuge of blind alleys all over the place?"

"As usual, Judith, you are exaggerating. There were three blind alleys."

"What does it matter? Three is a great many. It must be a wonderful tomb. You know it. Confess."

"I think that maybe they are on the verge of a great discovery."

"Which was the purpose of this expedition."

"Why yes."

"The expedition which you had been planning ever since your father died."

He nodded.

"And he died because he got too close. He was there in that place where I was."

"And because you were there we have been led to this."

"Then it wasn't in vain."

"My God, I'd rather never have found the way."

"Oh, Tybalt, I believe that. But you're going to stay now."

"Dr. Gunwen wishes you to go back as soon as possible."

"I won't go."

"But you must."

"I won't go alone and you are not coming with me."

"I'm getting ready to leave now."

"I will *not* have it," I said. "I will *not* let you go now. You are going on. It's *your* expedition. When finally you reach that tomb when you see the dust there undisturbed for three thousand years . . . and perhaps the footprint of the last person to leave . . . *You* are going to be the first. Do you think I would allow Terence Gelding to have that honor?"

"No," he said firmly. "We are going back."

But I was determined that it should not be so.

That was a battle of wills. I was exultant. It seemed so incongruous. I was standing out against his giving up that which I thought he would rather sacrifice anything for than miss.

I thought: I am loved . . . even as I love.

I simply refused to go. I wanted to stay. I could not possibly be happy if we left at this stage. I made Dr. Gunwen agree with me and I finally won the day.

It is well known what happened. That was *not* the discovery of the century.

Tybalt's expedition found the tomb a few days before the Pasha's men working from a different part of the hillside reached the burial chamber.

What treasures there would have been! It was clearly the burial place of a great King.

The Pasha had been working towards it for some time; he knew that there was a way in through the chambers in which I had spent those terrifying hours; that was why when Sir Edward discovered it he had died. He knew too that the alcove in which Yasmin had been discovered was a way in to the corridor and it may have been that he thought she had discovered something. Her death was a warning to any of his workpeople who might have thought of exploring the subterranean passages.

Alas, for Tybalt's great ambition. There was the sarcophagus, the mummy of the Pharaoh but robbers—perhaps the Pasha's ancestors—had rifled the tomb two thousand years before; and all that was left was a soul house in stone which they had not thought worth taking.

We heard that the Pasha had left for Alexandria. He did not come to bid us farewell. He would know through his servants that we had unraveled the mystery of Sir Edward's death and that of Theodosia.

We came back to England.

There was great rejoicing at Rainbow Cottage. I had asked that the aunts should not be told of my adventures because as I said to Tybalt, we shall go off to other places together and they would fret all the time and say "I told you so"—which is what I could not endure.

A few days after we had arrived home there was a paragraph in the press about an Englishman, a successful dealer in antiquities—mainly Egyptian—who had been found drowned in the Nile. His name was Leopold Harding. Whether his death was due to foul play was not certain. Head injuries had been discovered but these could have been caused by his striking his head against the boat when it was overturned. As a dealer in rare objects his clients had been mainly private collectors.

It was clear that he had been one of the Pasha's servants, just as those who had tampered with the bridge, the soothsayer, and Mustapha and Absalam had been. Harding disposed of priceless objects which the Pasha may have taken from tombs in the past, for naturally it would take him years to dispose of articles of this nature. Many would have to be broken up and if there were jewels decorating them, these would have to be sold separately, and these transactions would be carried out under the cover of legitimate business.

The Pasha had clearly been hoping to make the discovery of a lifetime. Sir Edward had found the same trail, so he had died through Mustapha and Absalam. Then Tybalt had arrived to take up where his father had left off and Theodosia had died as a warning. As we remained, Leopold Harding had been ordered to kill me. He had failed. The Pasha did not like failures; moreover he was no doubt afraid that Harding, over whom he would have less control than he had over his Egyptian servants, might betray the fact that he had been commanded to kill me. So Leopold Harding had been murdered as Yasmin had.

The adventure was behind me. Leopold Harding had attempted to take my life and had instead taken away my fears. Because of what he had done to me I had greater understanding than I had ever had before.

And Tybalt too. He will never of course be the man

to show his feelings; and when perhaps he is most moved he is most reticent.

But for Leopold Harding and the Egyptian expedition, I might have gone on for years doubting Tybalt's love for me for he could never have expressed in words what he did when he came to get me and when he was ready to give up his life's ambition when he believed it—erroneously it turned out—to be within his reach.

"My poor Tybalt," I said, "I did want you to make the great discovery."

"I made a greater one."

"I know. Before you thought you wanted more than anything in the world to find the greatest treasure ever known to the world."

"But I did that," he said. "I discovered what you meant to me."

So how could I but be grateful to all that had gone before? And how could I not rejoice when I looked forward to the richness of the life we would lead together?